MORE
POINT REYES
SHERIFF'S CALLS

SUSANNA SOLOMON

Lucky Bat Books

A Lucky Bat Book

More Point Reyes Sheriff's Calls
Copyright © 2016 by Susanna Solomon

All rights reserved.

Cover Design by Brandon Swann

Summary: The author's second short story collection based in Point Reyes, Northern California. The author conceived these fictitious characters by reading 'Sheriff's Calls' published in the *Point Reyes Light.*

Fiction: Short Stories by single author and Fiction: General

See more titles by Susanna Solomon at
http://susannasolomon.com

Published by Lucky Bat Books

http://LuckyBatBooks.com
10 9 8 7 6 5 4 3 2 1
ISBN-10:1-943588-33-3
ISBN-13:978-1-943588-33-6

Also available in digital formats.

For Owen and Miela

Acknowledgements

"Use your imagination, goddamnit," my writing teacher and mentor Jim Frey yelled at me one summer afternoon while we shopped for groceries for one of his workshops where I was again an abject failure. As far as advice goes, that wasn't half bad. Thanks, Jim.

Thanks also to Tess Elliott, editor of the Point Reyes Light, who saw something early on about the stories I wrote about the community we share. Thanks also to Lieutenant Doug Pittman, Marin County Sheriff's Office, who doesn't mind at all that I take liberties with his district.

Thanks to Cyn Cady and the Tuesday Night Writers who taught me to write short in order to avoid the dreaded and much too loud "time's up" horn at Peri's Bar.

Thanks to Charselle Hooper of West End Wednesdays, a poetry reading event, who always welcomes me and my stories with a laugh and a hug.

Thanks to Patricia V. Davis who asked if I could write a few more short stories and started me on the path to publication. I will always be grateful.

Much appreciation to Sher Gamard of Redwood Writers for her afternoons of literary readings and great food, a combination no one can resist. Mildred sends a kiss.

Thanks and hugs to my writing critique group who have been wonderful beyond compare; John King, Jim Beach, Pat Morin, Robert Evans and Christie Nelson.

Thanks particularly to Stacey Spain of Lucky Bat Books, who has been nothing but enthusiastic and supportive and also loves dogs. Thanks to editor Deke Castleman for infinite patience and dedication to the proper use of commas.

Thanks and big hugs to family and friends, writers and colleagues, clients and loved ones who have seen this dream growing for longer than I care to say. Love to all of you. Mildred will make you all cupcakes once she finds her muffin pan.

A particular thanks to the people of Point Reyes and West Marin, who call the cops for reasons that befuddle me; a bag of carrots in the road, more people running around naked than I can count, drivers who can't stay in their lane, and people who are sure that the sound of breaking branches in the woods is nothing other than Bigfoot himself. For without the reality-challenged people of West Marin, I wouldn't have any imagination at all.

With much love and appreciation,
Susanna Solomon, Inverness, Ca, June 2016.

Contents

From the Sheriff's Calls section of the Point Reyes Light
December 12, 2012

TOMALES: At 6:50 p.m. a driver saw a person on the ground in a red jacket, with a dog, off Chileno Valley Road. Deputies found just the dog.

The Picnic

"But what about the guy?" Mildred pulled on her husband's arm. "Fred—he's missing."

Fred wasn't feeling well. Unaccustomed to hard liquor, he'd had two margaritas the night before at the Station House, and combined with his wife's cooking, things were uneasy in his belly. He moaned a little.

"You okay?" Mildred tightened her eyes and examined him. He'd done nothing all day, and got up, at, well, eleven. "I don't care if it is New Year's Day." She ran her hands through her hair. Frizzy as hell. She'd changed shampoo and everything damn. She missed Doris, who was on vacation in Florida, visiting her mother.

"Me? Uh, I'm fine," Fred mumbled. But things weren't fine, not in the least. It was winter, there was no baseball, there was no rain, and he'd been grumpy all morning. His wife's cheerful voice wasn't helping, not at all.

"So, Fred, where'd the guy in red go?" Mildred came around him and plopped down in her favorite overstuffed chair. Some of the horsehair was peeking out from a seam, but she didn't mind. The chair and her hair—well, they were about the same. As for Fred, he was looking a little off. His pants were unbuttoned and he hadn't shaved. He was losing it fast. Over the years they'd been married, she couldn't remember when he'd had it, whatever it was.

1

"At least they saved the dog," Fred said, perking up. Three trips to the bathroom, maybe he was done. He'd have to pick next time, margaritas or Mildred's cooking—heck, he'd go hungry. That was an easy choice. He sat back down on his recliner, satisfied.

"Who cares about a dog?" Mildred sat up. "There's a man missing. I just know it. Coming out to Point Reyes for an afternoon, and no one cares about him at all." She paced the small kitchen, looked outside at the King tides lapping the shore on Tomales Bay. "Shall we go to the beach? I'll pack a lunch."

Fred examined the remote in his hands. He'd just started feeling better, and he was tired. If he could hold her off long enough, maybe he'd dig into his Negra Modelo stash. Nothing like the hair of the dog. "Lunch?" he croaked. "No, don't bother with me, I'll stay here, get a load off."

"A load of what off? All you do is sleep!" Mildred bustled around the kitchen, folding hand towels and wiping her counters down. That is, as much as she could. There were piles of notes everywhere, her to-do lists, and she wasn't going to mess them up. Without them, where would she start? With last week's chores? Last year's? There was no telling. She stacked them carefully, slipping paper clips around bunches of ten.

"Mildred, please don't fuss. Go on to the beach, if you like, honey. I'll help you with the basket."

"And touch my dishes? I should think not," Mildred snapped. "Peanut butter or liverwurst? Which would you like today?"

"Oh brother," Fred sighed. "Neither. No. Not hungry, not at all. No thanks," he mumbled, feeling bad for her. She was happy when she fussed, but he wasn't happy when she fussed over him. He had his slippers, he'd changed into sweats. He slipped one hand into the pocket of his recliner and touched his ice-cold beer.

"I don't know why you don't like liverwurst; it's good for you." Mildred dug into the refrigerator for peanut butter. It was hard, inside the jar. It would take a chisel to get it out. As for bread, uh, that was frozen, all the slices packed together in a ball. "I can't do it, Fred. I can't do anything," she sobbed, dropping into her chair next to him. Getting old sucked.

"Dear." Fred raised himself, patting her arm. "It's okay. You want me to make sandwiches? How many would you like?"

"I don't know. Everyone forgets about me." She cried into her handkerchief. "I can't seem to do anything anymore. Oh Fred, don't leave me. Don't ever leave me."

Fred, surprised with the turn of events, turned to his lovely, fragile, little wife. "Now, what brought this on, dear?" He was concerned, sore belly or not; without her, he would be lost. "Did I do something to offend you?" Half the time he didn't know why, half the time he didn't even say anything—she just went off, either sobbing or making a lot of noise. At least this time she wasn't yelling. He smiled.

"You're laughing at me." She blew her nose, hard into her hanky. "You don't want to go anywhere with me anymore. It's just the beach, Fred, just the goddamn beach." She narrowed her eyes.

"But there's no beach today," he replied. "King tides."

"Then we'll go somewhere else. Come on."

"But dear," Fred mumbled.

"But nothing, unless you want me to get upset again? You haven't been very attentive lately. You want to leave me alone? Like that guy with the dog, abandon him when the sheriff came by?"

"They shouldn't have taken the dog." Fred tried to stay up with her. It was hard to know just where she was going these days.

"They were a pair, you know, that guy and his dog. The guy in the red jacket. The guy who abandoned his dog."

"He can get him at the pound," Fred suggested, "or call the sheriff, or something. He can get his dog back," Fred repeated, punching in the numbers on his remote, trying to save the rest of New Year's Day.

"My dear husband, so, if there's a spate of trouble, a disturbance, you'll abandon me, to save your soul, just dump me on the side of the road like that guy with the dog?"

"Which beach did you say you wanted to go to, dear?" Fred asked, standing up.

"Limantour. It's my favorite. And sweetheart, while you're up, can you make me lunch? Not too much jelly, if you please."

From the Sheriffs' Calls Section of the Point Reyes Light, Jan 3, 2013

MUIR BEACH: At 11:44 a.m. a car drove into a ditch, landing precariously on the edge of a ravine.

Victor

"Victor! What are you doing?" Stella asked, grabbing onto the handle above the passenger's side door inside Victor's father's 2010 Lexus RX 350.

Victor, crestfallen, looked out the window. Just in front of the car there was nothing, no ground, no guard rail, just air. The rear wheels were on the pavement, but he didn't know where his front wheels were. He looked out the driver's-side window and felt the car move. He froze. "Shit," he said, his mouth dry.

He went to zip his pants but that made the car wobble. Stella was the one who had suggested that perhaps he had wanted a little fun. She said, they did it in the movies, didn't they? But now it didn't seemed like such a good idea. He killed the engine. They were halfway down the hill on the way to the beach. He could see the Pacific, sparkling out there, so peaceful and closer by, a ravine just in front of the car.

"Jesus Christ!" Stella screamed. "You lunatic! We're going to die!" She kissed her ring, the one her mother had given her for being such a good girl on her sixteenth birthday. "Oh God, oh God, oh, God. Victor, do something!"

"I'll figure it out," Victor cried. As if he had any idea. It was like, a hundred-foot drop down there. "Shit, shit, shit." He was usually a good kid, and aside from the fact that he hated chemistry and his dad lived with Brad - his boyfriend - out in Bolinas, Victor didn't think his life was so different from anyone else's. He liked girls; he was particularly relieved about that, but this one, not so much. "Stella, shut the hell up."

"Screw you, asshole!" The car wobbled.

"Don't move!!!" Victor shouted.

Stella froze, thought she was going to wet her pants.

"Yoo hoo!" A woman's voice broke into Victor's reverie. He turned his head ever so slowly to see a middle-aged woman, thin and sleek and a runner, from what he could tell. He covered his lap with his hands, and smiled weakly.

"Could you call the cops, ma'am?" he croaked, trying not to move.

"What I don't understand, guys, is that maybe you were thinking you could fly? I mean the beach is just down there, couldn't you have just, you know, used the road?" she asked, her head at an angle. Her breath came out in rasps, as if she didn't have any air. "I'm getting a head start on the Dipsea," she said with a smile. She stretched her legs. "And you?"

"Ma'am, please? Just dial nine-one-one?"

"You want a hand?" she asked, going for the door handle. "I'm Katie, Katie Palmer. I just moved over the hill."

"Ma'am, no! Please! Don't!" Victor called out through the closed window as she reached for the door.

"Touchy, touchy. I'm not going to steal anything, if that's what you're thinking." She checked her watch.

"I don't care what time it is! Jesus. What are you doing? The cops! Call the cops!"

"If it hadn't been for you two idiots, I could have beat my best time of three hours, forty-five minutes, thirty seconds."

"Ma'am, please!" Victor asked. "Listen," it was like talking to Stella, "Quit jumping around. If you're cold, I can give you my jacket – after you call the cops. Please! Do something, don't just stand there."

"That's what my husband used to say, and now, look, he's dead."

"MA'AM. We're going to be dead too if you don't call the COPS!"

"Oh, you want to get out?" Katie said, opening the door and pulling on Victor's arm. The car shifted.

"Dear God!" Stella said, grabbing the handle of her door.

Victor went flying. He thought he was going to tumble down the hill and the car would roll over and kill him, but instead he fell on the hard gravel on the side of the road. The car wobbled, slipped, and wobbled some more, but held. He stood up quickly, assembled himself, amazed he was okay and the car still there. Stella was inside, her face white.

He wanted to grab it, hold the car with everything he had, protect Stella, protect the gal he hardly knew, protect his reputation, protect his dad's car. As he reached the trunk, Katie leaned on the back bumper to re-tie her shoes.

"Jesus, don't!" he yelled. Katie's hand was six inches from the fender when the car creaked, teetered, and slid away. Victor ran around to the passenger side, swept over bushes and rocks, trying not to stumble as the car crackled underbrush and crept forward. He went for the door, yanked it open with one hand, and grabbed Stella with the other. She fell out onto him as the Lexus continued on its onward journey, picking up speed, until it came to rest against a rock, halfway down the hill, billowing dust marking the way.

Behind him, Victor heard a truck pull up. He turned and saw Cheda's yellow tow truck, amazed it was already there. Did Tiny have a sixth sense or something? Stella was crying in his arms. "You okay?" he asked. "I thought .... I was a goner," she choked. He helped her back up the hill to the road and turned to Katie. "You call the tow truck?" he asked. She laughed. "I saw her wobble all over the road a mile up, and I called Cheda's. I know what you kids were doing," she said with a snort.

Victor smiled almost, but not quite, showing grateful tears. Stella held him tighter. He smelled her sweat, felt her heart pound through his thin Aerosmith T-shirt. Her legs were wobbly. She leaned closer.

"Next time let's take your dad's Porsche," she whispered in his ear. "I bet we could have fun in that car."

"Oh God," he murmured, and watched Tiny release the cable from the tow truck. He always liked this part, but the warm girl beside him, he liked her a whole lot better. His heart was banging around, making him sweat, making him hot all over, making him ...."Yes," he said, and held her tight.

Susanna Solomon

From the Point Reyes Light, December 12, 2013

WOODACRE: At 4:17 p.m. a woman called from under her bed to say that someone was in her house.

Crackers

"All I know is ..." Lulu Garcia stuttered into the phone, "... it's big. And it's coming this way."

Lulu kept her head low under the bed, trying to keep her long brown hair from catching in the metal springs above. If she wasn't careful, she'd be eaten by the thing while her stupid hair was caught in the springs. She dropped her face down onto some dust bunnies and held her breath.

There it was again—scritch, scratch, slide—coming down the hall, right toward her door. She knew she was a scaredy cat—her friends had teased her about it ever since the Bigfoot event —but this time she hadn't even smoked a doobie, not even a little one, and this time the creep was already in her house.

She slid down toward the corner of the wall and listened. Bump, scrape, thump, and then chewing. Chewing? Oh God, no.

Lulu wished she wasn't alone. Mom was out shopping. Holiday shopping! At a time like this? Oh God. Had she closed the bedroom door all the way? Uh, no. The stranger, the thing, the bad thing, was pushing it open.

Lulu squinted under the bed, trying to convince herself that she could handle anything. Without a weapon? The baseball bat Mom kept in the garage for protection, was, well, in the goddamn garage. Who was she fooling? The damn bed skirt kept falling in her eyes. She lifted it slowly, one eye open, the other closed.

The door opened all the way. Lulu would protect her virtue, if she had any virtue, and protect her good name, if she had one—if that stupid Jason Bean at high school hadn't been telling all the boys about her and what she'd, good God, done with him. That wasn't Jason, was it, out in the hall?

Crawling forward for a better look, Lulu pulled up the bed skirt, eyes wide open, so she could yell at him. She looked for his black hi-tops. Instead of the sound of a squeak or slide on her Mom's cork floor, Lulu heard nails and snuffling. Snuffling? The door wasn't moving anymore and whatever it was had headed down the hall, away from her. She'd called the sheriff, but they were taking their sweet time. Now was her only chance to act.

Keeping an eye on the door and listening for any sound, she slid out and, ignoring the dust bunnies that clung to her velour top and blue jeans, grabbed the closest weapon she could find—her mom's table lamp. She yanked it out of the wall, held it over her head, and stood silently behind the open door.

She peered around it, expecting blood. Had Mom come home? Had the thief strangled her? Lulu looked down and saw evidence, bits and pieces of whatever the creature had been after. She saw a tan speck, and picked it up. A cracker. Triscuits. The thief liked Triscuits?

Lulu heard the roll of tires on gravel outside. Could it be the UPS delivery she was expecting? Or another thief? She marched down the hall, lamp over her head, following the evidence. She was going to get the culprit before he could get her.

She came around the last door in the hall, the one to the living room, and there, besides the dark brown Naugahyde sofa, was her dog, clawing and barking at something near the sofa.

Lulu raised the lamp, expecting to find the culprit behind the couch. "Way to go, Tara! Good girl!"

"What's going on here?" demanded a man's voice not more than a few feet away.

Tara barked louder.

Lulu squeezed her eyes shut, then swung the lamp toward the sound. She opened her eyes when the lamp hit something soft.

"Oof," the man said and fell.

Tara was on him in a sec, growling and baring her teeth.

Lulu put the lamp down. Mom would be proud she'd nailed the intruder her own self.

"Oh, for God's sake," the man said, scrambling to his feet. "You knocked the wind out of me, honey."

Lulu bristled at the word 'honey'.

The man brushed off his tan pants and shirt. Lulu squinted. He had something bright and shiny on his chest. A medallion? She hadn't been wearing her glasses in an attempt to strengthen her eyes, but now she wasn't sure that was such a good idea.

"It's a badge, ma'am," he said. "I'm Deputy Bernard. You called. What did you have to go and hit me for?"

"Sorry, officer," Lulu said. "Somebody, or something, was after me."

Lulu pulled herself up to her full height of 5'-3". "We had an intruder, sir," she said.

"I see," Deputy Bernard said. "Where'd he go?" He stared around the house, at the trail of cracker bits down the hallway, at the teeth and claw marks on the bottom edge of the sofa. He bent down, extracted a beaten-up crackly bag of Triscuits. "This your intruder?"

"I'm not that stupid," she said, and clocked him again.

From the Sheriff's Calls Section of the Point Reyes Light
February 7, 2013

SAN GERONIMO VALLEY: At 7:39 a.m. someone reported that a man did donuts in the parking lot at the golf course at night. Deputies attempted to contact the man, who was busy meditating, and left a note requesting that he call "after his chakras were aligned".

Doing Donuts

Monroe thought that he'd been particularly clever this time. Those silly deputies—what did they know? It was just that there was this patch of ice, in the front parking lot at the San Geronimo Valley Golf Course, and how could he avoid having fun with that?

He peered out the window of his girlfriend's house. Making sure the sheriffs were long gone, he untangled himself from the horrible meditation pose. Hell, he didn't meditate, and he didn't know shit about chakras, but his girlfriend Betsy did, and as soon as she woke up, he was going to tell her how clever he'd been. He wrapped a brown dog blanket around his shoulders and went to put the kettle on for tea.

On the way to the kitchen, he saw a glass pipe—his favorite—on the coffee table and had to have just the right buzz to start his day. Having the sheriff around had been a bit of a bummer.

After working his way through stuffing the pipe for the second time, he heard footsteps through the blur. It was Betsy, bless her heart, in a T-shirt and panties, her short teased hair sticking out every which way. Sexy little thing.

"I heard a car? Was that you?" she asked, wrapping herself in a silk robe, the one Monroe had given her for her 25th birthday.

He loved showering her with gifts.

"You got candles and shit all over, Monroe. And where's my zazen stool?"

"I was using it," Monroe said through a puff of smoke.

"Jesus. Can't you ever stop? It's only eight in the morning."

"They'll come back," Monroe said.

"Who?"

"You know, them."

"You're smoking too much dope again," Betsy said, grinding her coffee.

"It wasn't my fault. I didn't say anything."

"To whom didn't you say anything to? What did you say, Monroe?"

Monroe twisted around in his seat, looking for a lit match. Sooner or later he would feel it through his sweat pants. He knew he hadn't put a lit match in his pocket, or had he? "The sheriffs, the friggin' sheriffs. They stopped by."

"You asshole, why didn't you tell me?"

"Betsy, you are just the cutest thing when you're angry." He tried to put his arms around her but she slipped away. His leg felt a little warm, was it her or the match? He looked on the carpet. Nope, not there.

"What did you tell them?"

"Me?"

"No, the poodle from next door, Jesus, earth to Monroe, what did they say?"

"Goddamn deputies got my nerves all shot, so I had to have some way to calm down, darlin'," he said, offering her a puff.

"Monroe, what we are doing here is ... secret. I told you and I told you. Don't you listen? Listen now," she said, straightening up the magazines that were all over the floor. "What if they come back and take a whiff, what are you going to say then?"

"Medicinal marijuana," he said, feeling clever.

"Not this much! Shit! That is for personal use, Monroe."

"For mine? Yes, I thought so, you are so right," he said, and dug into his pocket for his pouch.

Betsy looked out the front door, up and down the road and didn't see anything. She couldn't trust Monroe to take point, he'd babble all the way to San Quentin. He'd been so cute in his plaid shirt and soul patch months ago at Starbucks, but the appeal, was, as her girlfriends tried to tell her, somewhat fleeting. Fleeting? Hell, that bus had left long ago.

"When I invited you to come work, I didn't plan on living with a pothead. You were supposed to work, trimming, not smoking the product. What are you going to say when they come back, then, something that closely approximates the truth?"

"That I love and adore my little bird," Monroe answered, feeling a little like he was flying. The new stuff was smooth. "Uh, no ... not that, but it sounds real good, doesn't it?"

"We can't have them here. Cops and pot don't mix. It's like milk and whiskey."

"Gee, I've never tried that." Monroe put down his pipe. He supposed he'd had enough. It was just that it went down so easy.

Betsy opened the door to the back room. The lights were bright in there, as they should be. Wafts of sweet air met her senses. Fans hummed silently. She turned away and closed the door behind her. "So what made the cops come to the door, Monroe?"

Truth was an elusive quality to him, but Betsy was a bit of a probing type, so he thought it best to just fess up. "I was spinning donuts in the golf-course parking lot last night. There was just this perfect patch of ice, and I—I loved it, Betsy," he said. "Reminded me of when I was in high school back East, when we had snow."

"Oh Christ, you big dope."

"I didn't do anything else, and I didn't say anything, either, except," Monroe said, hurt. Twenty years old, twenty years wiser, and she was making him feel like he was six. "I told him I was aligning my chakras and he went away. Cool, hunh?"

"Let's go for a walk."

"Is this like in the *Sopranos*, when I don't get to come back?" Monroe asked.

"Am I armed?" Betsy asked.

"Uh, no," Monroe answered, "unless you're carrying a shiv."

"Bring the zazen stool."

"But it's your favorite," Monroe said. "You going to kill me with the zazen stool?"

"You watch too many movies, sweetheart." Sweetheart, hell, it would take a while for the cops to come to the house, and a while to get a search warrant and they wouldn't have a reason, would they, unless Monroe talked.

"It's now yours. Come on," Betsy said. "You want another spliff?"

Monroe couldn't believe she was being so nice, but there was a niggling doubt in his mind, somewhere in his mind, and like lots of times, he always did better just ignoring that little voice. She shared a puff with him as they walked out the door, and another on the way, and a part of him still felt warm, and had she been that sexy, but no, it was the match, finally going out on his skin, but he didn't want her to think he was that dumb so he left it there, kind of burning him, and she was leading him to a nice spot of shade under a big pine tree, almost on the golf course and he'd always liked the outdoors, and she gave him the rest of the spliff, and another one and made him sit on the zazen stool.

"Monroe," she said. "You know what? I think you're wonderful. And your chakras, they feeling a little funny? Thought so. I'll be back when they're aligned." She leaned down and gave him a big kiss. "Then we'll have some fun. That okay with you?"

From the Sheriff's Calls Section of the Point Reyes Light, February 7, 2013

SAN GERONIMO VALLEY: At 7:39 a.m. someone reported that a man did donuts in the parking lot at the golf course at night. Deputies attempted to contact the man, who was busy meditating, and left a note requesting that he call "after his chakras were aligned."

Aligning Chakras

"You did what, Bernard?" Walter peered around his ficus plant. The plant had become quite wild, but Walter hadn't the heart to trim it.

Bernard blinked, not knowing whether he should sit or stand. Either way he couldn't see his boss very well. "Boss, you know the guy was busy."

"Bernard." Walter paused, knowing that pauses made all his officers nervous.

"Did he hurt anything, Walter? I mean, he was only in the parking lot."

"If he went on the greens, Bernard, I promise..."

"There were no tracks, I checked. Of course I heard the noise from Drake." And that he had, for sure, unexpectedly he had been driving slowly down the 60-mph section with his windows down two inches just like his beagle Molly liked. He'd been at the job two years, and some of the yahoos he'd met over that time pleased him no end. He'd watched the guy for a while, just out there, spinning doughnuts on the frost, then he'd lit him up. The car had slid and stopped at an island. "Didn't you ever spin doughnuts in high school, boss?"

Walter chewed on a pencil. Of course he had, but should he indicate to Bernard that foolishness was to be tolerated? "It's not that part I'm worried about. It's what you did after," he said, trying not to laugh. Out here in West Marin, Walter had seen them all, old people clutching for their next breath, tenants and landlords in dispute, Unit B attendees having a tough day, and of course, all those cows in the road. "I don't care what kind of perpetrator you talk to, but you're the law, the one authority in these parts, and you...you..." he sputtered.

"He was adjusting his chakras, boss," Bernard said.

"Bullshit, Bernard. He was trespassing on private property and disturbing the peace. In addition," Walter puffed up behind his plant, "you let him take advantage. You let him win, Bernard."

Bernard, confused now, pulled on a lock of what was left of his hair. A meditator himself, he knew that taking care of your center was vital. That's what they taught him at Spirit Rock. He had another class with Sylvia Borstein tonight—this time he'd stay awake.

"Bernard!" Walter shouted.

Bernard stood up straight, looked his boss right in the eye. "Yes, sir."

"Go back there, make this perpetrator know you're in charge. Chakras, indeed. You're the law, for God's sake—behave like it."

Bernard, crestfallen, left his boss' office feeling like a disgrace. Spinning doughnuts wasn't a crime, not really, not even a misdemeanor. Out by the back door, he looked across at the Giacomini Wetlands. This would be a good time for a cigarette, if he smoked, and a good time for a toke, if he smoked weed, but he'd gone cold turkey five years ago and wasn't going back.

The rear door slammed open. It was Linda, the fresh-faced newest deputy on the force, though he had her by only three month's seniority. If she started in on him, he thought he'd scream. Instead, she leaned back against the building wall, rested her hand on her sidearm, and leaned back. "Nice day, eh, Bernard?"

"Hmmm," Bernard answered, not wanting to talk.

"Crazy town, this, eh? First it's these lost tourists, then all the hippies in Bolinas, all the new-age loonies and the cows." Linda laughed. "I swear, I can't make this stuff up."

"I don't feel like talking, Officer Kettleman," Bernard said.

"We've all been there," Linda said. She wanted to press her hand on his arm to reassure him, but she was an officer, and the proper decorum was required. "Remember, our boss talks to plants."

They both laughed.

"Regardless, I have to go back. To redeem myself, I guess. I hope the guy's still there." Bernard scratched at his bald spot.

"With all the fruits and nuts out there, he probably is."

"Then he's an idiot," Bernard answered. He was about to say something clever but his words were drowned out by Walter's voice coming over the loudspeaker.

"Another tourist has been going too fast and has gone off the road. Taylor Park."

Bernard, relieved, grabbed his keys.

"Not you, Bernard," Walter said.

"How can he know everything?" Bernard asked.

"He's aligned his chakras," Linda said with a laugh.

From the Sheriff's Calls Section of the Point Reyes Light, February 7, 2013

SAN GERONIMO VALLEY: At 7:39 a.m. someone reported that a man did donuts in the parking lot at the golf course at night. Deputies attempted to contact the man, who was busy meditating, and left a note requesting that he call "after his chakras were aligned."

Whiskey and Milk

Bernard was surprised to see the guy still there, waiting, at the main entrance to the golf course, sitting under a tree in the shade. He was nodding off.

Shit, did Bernard have to use his Narcan to bring the guy back? He'd heard that addicts can react quite violently and he was alone. Should he call for backup? He'd never given it before.

But when he pulled up in his cruiser, the guy lifted his head, opened his eyes and waved. "Want some, Officer?" He held out a spliff.

Bernard started to laugh, and then corrected himself. "Your name, sir?"

"Morgan," Monroe said. It was close, it seemed familiar, and so it would work, wouldn't it? Betsy would be proud he was being so clever. What did he care? He didn't have I.D. on him.

"Is it Morgan, or Mr. Morgan?" Bernard asked, pulling out his steno notebook and favorite pen. "You look familiar."

"Like potatoes and toast, jam and coffee, whiskey and milk," Monroe said. He didn't care what he said, he wasn't doing anything wrong. Smoking dope, even in broad daylight, in public, in the middle of San Geronimo Valley, wasn't a crime. If it was, the whole community would be in jail.

"You were here, spinning doughnuts on the asphalt, early this morning, Morgan?"

"Gee, Officer, I don't have a car, and there isn't any ice. It's a sunny day —See? The sky is blue and everything. Is it illegal, then, spinning doughnuts? They didn't say anything like that on the Internet. Did I do something wrong?" Monroe stood up, unsteady on his feet. "Go ahead, cuff me. Life's not worth living anymore, anyway."

"Now, wait a moment," Bernard said, confused. Walt had asked him to check out the guy, but he was a jellyfish. If he put Morgan in cuffs, the guy would melt. "Never mind all that," he said, pulling over a log and resting his foot on it. He set his notebook on his thigh. "Just tell me, you admit to spinning doughnuts?"

"I wasn't yelling or whooping it up or nothing like that. And the radio was off," Monroe said. "It was dark. No one was around."

Bernard hesitated. He wanted to complain, tell this perp that his boss was on his case, make it go away, and make the whole goddamn thing go away. He wondered whether going into police work had been the right choice for him. "Okay, Morgan," Bernard sighed. "This is a warning—unless you want a ticket?"

"A ticket to ride? Can you do that for me?"

"Had a few joints today, Mr. Morgan?"

"My girlfriend? She loves me. She really does," Morgan said proudly. "She gave me her favorite zazen stool."

"I see."

"She lives around here. Oh, hell, I wasn't supposed to say that. Up the hill, this long and windy road and there's no houses for the longest time. You'll never find it."

"I'm not interested in her, I'm interested in you," Bernard said. "Full name and address, please," he said, feeling a little better. Following orders, doing the correct procedures, made him feel like he had some control over his raggedy little world. "Morgan Truesdale," Monroe said, standing up. "Fifty-One-fifty Terrace View Drive, Fairfax."

Bernard wrote this down. The 5150 seemed odd.

"ID?"

Was this a trick? Did the cop want to find Betsy and her stash? How much could he say? "Sorry, Officer. But I lost my wallet in the woods when I was out hiking the other day. Haven't had a chance to go to the DMV."

Bernard gave up. "Next time, don't rev your car, not here, and no messing around. This is private property."

"It wasn't my car," Monroe said, as if saying this would remove all the weight from his shoulders.

"If I see you again, in a car, Mr. Morgan—"

"Mr. Truesdale," Monroe lied.

"—I'll have to take you in."

"Of course."

"You have a good attitude, we appreciate that."

"I should say." After all the energy he expended, Monroe wobbled over to his stool. "Mr. —uh, Mr. Bernard, it's been a pleasure." Monroe stuck his hand out for the officer to shake.

But Bernard wasn't looking at him. He was looking along the road, at a car that just shot by at about 80 miles an hour. "Another time, sir," he said and hopped into his cruiser and drove away in pursuit.

Monroe, chastened, relieved, and just plain worn out, collapsed on his stool. He'd done everything little Betsy had asked for. He'd been a good boy and now he was ready for a reward. He imagined kissing her and pulling her close. He grabbed his stool, started walking up the long driveway past the golf course to her house, his cell phone tucked under his ear. "Betsy, Betsy, hello," he jabbered into the phone. "Are you there, Betsy?"

But Betsy, back at the grow house, had no desire to talk to Monroe. She put down her binoculars. She had to get rid of him and quick, and hadn't yet decided what she would do. A knife, a cleaver, a handsaw, and a gun lay on the table in front of her. Now what? She thought long and hard, and decided to do the right thing, the easy thing, and just take him for one long, last ride.

From the Sheriffs' Calls Section of the Point Reyes Light, February 14, 2013

BOLINAS: At 7:57 p.m. a man reported there was a woman he did not know in his bed. The woman told deputies that another woman had given her permission to be there.

Marjorie May

"Well, she wasn't his wife, that's for sure, Officer. We all know that," Marjorie May Wentworth said.

Linda Kettleman pulled out her steno notebook and licked her pencil. "Your name, ma'am?"

"Barbara Lee Benton said it was okay," Marjorie May said, sticking out her hip.

"I don't know any Barbara Lee Benton," Matt McKinney complained, pulling out his new snowfield jacket from L.L. Bean. "My bed is not a revolving door for wayward women," he snorted.

"I am not a wayward woman," Marjorie May snapped. "I was on the road, I called Barbie, and she said, 'Go on now, Marjorie May, take a load off, crash at Matt's house, he's out of town.'"

"The door was unlocked?" Linda asked, doing her best trying not to laugh. She would love having someone in her bed, someone aside from her dog Maisie, someone as good looking at Matt. She stopped herself— even though it had been way too long, she had to behave. "Do you want to press charges, Mr. McKinney? She was breaking and entering."

"The door was unlocked, Officer," Marjorie May said, incensed. "And open. I'd been up half the night, driving here from Salt Lake City, and with Barbie's place locked and all, and she hadn't left a key, what's a girl to do, Officer?" she asked, tugging at the front of her low-cut blouse. So what if she exposed her twins a little bit—it wasn't like she was ashamed or anything. Caused stares, this blouse, but did nothing for Matt at all. What was the matter with him?

"Miss," Linda sighed. "Your last name please?"

"Wentworth," Marjorie bowed. "Glad to meet you, Officer, Mr. Matt." Gold, Barbie would say, you struck gold, dear, don't let this one get away. She flashed her just-whitened teeth. "Didn't mean to startle you, Mr. Matt." Unless he was gay. He didn't look gay.

"Well now," Linda said. "Mr. McKinney, you called, I came, what now?"

Matt McKinney reviewed his options. Marjorie had long black hair, one eye was a smidge bigger than the other, she was cute, and if he closed his eyes he could imagine touching her treasures. "No charges, Officer. Thank you," he said, trying to figure out how to entice Marjorie back into the sack. He'd been surprised, that's all, unaccustomed to finding girls he didn't know in his bed. But James Bond did it, didn't he, and he didn't mind. Matt stood up straight. "Thank you, Officer, we're done here," he said, shaking the officer's hand and watching her descend the stairs.

Marjorie May threw her pink sweatshirt over her shoulders, grabbed her purse, and followed.

"Wait, Marjorie May," Matt said, words tumbling out in a hurry. He could make a great day happen, right here, right now. "Would you like to hang around?"

Marjorie May stopped, looked at him, her hand on his rickety metal railing. Her hair blew in the evening breeze and Matt caught his breath. How could he have been so stupid as to call the cops?

"How foolish of me, Marjorie May." Heart pounding now, palms sweaty, his nervous system all akimbo, it had been four long days since Ellen Lipsak had been in his bed, and Ellen was not nearly as cute. "Want some coffee?" he croaked.

She just stared.

"Beer? Gin? A mojito? I make a great mojito."

"Something stronger," Marjorie May requested.

"Adderall?" he said, guessing widely, the first thing that popped into his mind, even though he didn't have any. He had felt her heat, her soft skin, her hot breath in his face. "You know ... umm, didn't mean, whatever. I screwed up."

"I did too," Marjorie May huffed, shouldering her purse and descending the stairs.

"Marjorie May, please don't leave," Matt stuttered, following her, leaving the front door open and inadvertently letting out his two cats. He caught her by the hand and gave her a deep kiss.

"That's not at all what I had in mind," Marjorie May said and hit him with her purse.

From the Sheriffs' Calls Section of the Point Reyes Light February 14, 2013

WOODACRE: At 2:24 a.m. three women in a silver minivan reported that they had been lost for over an hour, and blamed their navigation system.

Violet

"It's not my fault your stupid navigation system thinks we're on Mars." Pamela Brockman tapped on the car's computer screen and pressed all the buttons. "Damn."

"But Woodacre's not that big, Pam," Violet said from the back seat. "Matt says it's just an itty bitty town."

"If it's such a small town, then how come we're lost?" Teresa Comstock shoved the car into park. She'd bashed the rear bumper into a tree, and hoped that her mother, who had let her use her new car, wouldn't get mad. It was her own fault, anyway. She should never have bought such a big van. That and the doobie she'd just smoked weren't helping in the least.

"I told you we shouldn't have tried to make it to Matt's party," Pam scolded, watching trees go by in a rush. She would have left Violet at home, but Dad had insisted. "Be a good girl and take your sister out, Pam," he'd said. "She never goes anywhere." If he only knew.

"Maybe we should call the cops," Violet said, nervously fingering her gold necklace, the one Mom had given her last week for her sixteenth birthday. Her scoop-neck top kept slipping down; she didn't like that one bit. It was a top Pam had insisted she wear. She tongued her braces; that last adjustment still hurt.

"Matt's house has got to be here somewhere," Teresa said, picking up speed and flying down a hill.

Soon they were back on Railroad Avenue in front of the big rock. Violet burst into tears.

"Matt said it was easy, piece of cake, and here we are at the damn fire station again. You suck as a navigator, Pam," Teresa said. "What kind of wacky town is this? I can't even get any cell reception." She threw her cell phone into the console and slammed it shut. "I don't care how late it is, I'm going to find that dumb party." She checked her scrawled directions on a scrap of napkin. It would have been okay if she hadn't put a wet glass on it. Hillside or Hilldale? All the damn streets were too narrow and went every which way. "Help me out here, Pam. Make yourself useful."

Violet looked out the window at the red light over the entrance to the fire station. "They take care of babies at fire stations in the middle of the night. Why not three lost girls? Let's wake them up."

"Not on your life," answered Teresa, who gunned the engine and turned around. "Let's try again Pam," she said. "Read it to me again."

Pam turned the soggy napkin right side up and squinted. "Matt said something about the street being named after a tree—but I can't see the street signs. Flip on your brights."

"They're already on." Teresa peered through the windshield. "Why can't towns like this, you know, put up street signs you can read?"

"They do in Berkeley," Pam piped up. "I don't get lost there."

"But we're not in Berkeley, Pam," Teresa said, taking a particularly hard turn. The road narrowed to dirt. "Damn. And I can't see shit. Get out and guide us so I can turn around."

"But it's dark as hell out there," Pam said.

"You want me to go off the side of the road?"

"It's not my fault you went up this way."

"Let's go somewhere different, that's what you said, Pam. Now look where we are. Can you see anything?"

"Trees," Pam said.

"I don't feel like going to a party anymore, I'm tired and cold and we're lost," Violet sniffed, reaching for her handkerchief. She kept one stuffed under the cuff of her sweater, just like Mom had taught her. But this one was a little wet. Gross. She threw it on the floor.

"Now you've gone and upset my little sister," Pam said.

"Little sister? She's only two years younger than you are."

"So?" Pam said. "Light years difference in my book."

"Light years? Light saber? Shit. You're both useless." Teresa backed around the hillside carefully, wishing she hadn't smoked that doobie. What would Mom say if something even worse than a bumper scratch happened to her car out here? A broken axle, an accident, a breakdown? She would kill her, for sure.

"It's okay, honey, we'll find it," Pamela said, wishing she'd left Violet at home.

"I need to get out of the car," Violet said suddenly, hand on the door latch.

"You sick or something, honey?" Pam asked.

"Me, not yet," Violet said. "But you never know."

"You want to get out here?" Both Teresa and Pam asked simultaneously. Outside it was dark, not dark like city dark, but dark like deep country, black, foreboding and not a soul in sight.

"But isn't there a Seven-Eleven or gas station around? There's always a gas station somewhere," Violet said.

"Out here, there's a lot of nothing, darling," Teresa replied. She felt proud she'd brought the car back down a steep road and was on the flats again. Problem was, she wasn't sure which way to go.

"Stay in the car," Pamela said once Teresa had pulled over. "Let me think."

Violet sniffed, but obeyed. Girls. Company. Someone to talk to. She'd been lonely, but this— this didn't cure it at all. This was torture. Her first night out in a month, and she'd thought she was going to find a guy to talk to, or something. She'd been so happy when they invited her. Maybe Mom had been right. 'Stay home, honey, go to church, that's the only way to find a husband,' she'd said. Except Pam thought Mom was wrong. Phooey on both of them.

Teresa kept the van on the flats, then pulled up in front of the dark post office with one light on over the door, stalled, and killed the engine. The gas tank was near empty and she had no idea if they had enough to get back over the hill. "Well, girls, happy now?" She searched for service on her iPhone.

"I didn't want to come in the first place," Violet said.

"Next time stay home," Teresa snapped.

"You don't have to be so mean to my sister, Teresa," Pam said.

"I hate you guys." Violet dropped her face in her hands. She'd had enough. She slid open the back door and stepped into darkness. Out here, she heard crickets and frogs and the sounds of the night. Her sister's borrowed three-inch heels crunched gravel as she looked up at the stars. There were so many of them. Maybe God was up there, looking out for them. Maybe ... nothing. She was heading back to the car when she heard the sound of wheels coming up behind her and turned into full headlights. "Oh, thank God," she said, clasping her hands. "I knew someone was up there."

"Post office is closed this time of night," a man said out of his rolled-down window. "Come back in the morning."

"You a mailman?" Violet asked, confused. The car looked more like a truck.

"No, I'm a local," he answered, dimming his lights. "What seems to be the problem? You girls lost?"

"Pam?" Teresa whispered from inside the car. "Do we know him?" She eyed the truck driver. She'd seen his picture somewhere. On the pole outside the Palace Market? Was he in a band? A post office most-wanted poster?

"Good to meet you," Violet said, taking the guy's hand.

"Violet. Wait a sec," Pam said to her sister.

"You girls look tired," the truck driver said. "I'm Robert. Kind of late, don't you think? Need something? Drink? Cup of tea? Doobie? Directions?"

"You know someone named Matt?" Violet asked.

From inside the car, Pam could see Robert close in on her sister. She climbed out of the car, sidled up to her. "Sorry to bother you, Robert. We know where we're going."

"You do?" Robert asked. "Which way to Drake then? Right or left?"

"Don't worry about us," Pam said. She put her hand on Violet's shoulder.

"But why now? Robert can help." Violet stood her ground.

"She's right. I know Matt," Robert said. "Matt Cavanaugh."

"He was about to tell us which way to go, Pam. Like I said, God was listening. I prayed," Violet said.

Pam sniffed. The football player? Fat chance. She remembered. It was at the post office where she'd seen that soul patch, that brown disheveled hair.

"Get in the car."

"But why?" Violet asked.

"Because we don't know him, Violet."

"But you do now," Robert said, putting out his hand.

"The cops should be here any minute," Teresa said.

"Cops? Here? In Woodacre?" He laughed.

"Get in the van, Violet," Pam said. "Now."

"But he was about to help us," Violet said.

"Stuff it," Teresa said, shoving her into the van and climbing in behind her.

"But the back door's still open," Violet answered, confused. "Isn't that dangerous?"

"Don't you read the papers, honey?" Teresa asked, gunning it and grateful they were still on the flats.

"Of course I do," Violet answered, but she was lying. She only glanced at the headlines before checking out the entertainment pages.

"He's a bad guy, honey," Pamela said.

"Oh," Violet answered, grateful. She felt scared, alive, and loved, and held in comfort. "Anyone want to come to my dad's place for pancakes? I make the best pancakes," she asked, feeling shy.

"Oh honey, I thought you'd never ask," Teresa said, pulling out onto Drake. If they had any luck they'd be in Fairfax in fifteen minutes, just in time for tea.

From the Sheriff's Calls section of the Point Reyes Light
March 28, 2013

CHILENO VALLEY: At 6:17 p.m. a woman reported that her boyfriend's other girlfriend had threatened to damage her car if she did not leave the man's house.

Girlfriends

"Who are you, the boss of me?" Lulu Garcia spat.

"Louie's my boyfriend too."

"Since when?" LaChandra asked. She touched her hair, still perfect, but her love life, not so much. "Get your stuff and get lost, sister."

"Oh, come on." Lulu paced in front of the little green house. Louie was here, and she loved Louie. "Hey big boy, come here!"

Louie, no fool, stayed in the kitchen. He was making up a batch of margaritas and if he could give one to each of them, he wouldn't have a thing to worry about. He heard something fall.

"LaChandra?" He bounded into the living room and saw broken floor lamps. And his mother's best china. She would not be amused. "Honey, where are you?"

"Louie?"

He ran toward the sound of her voice and stopped mid-stride. Was she hiding behind a door with an axe? "LaChandra?"

"Louie," Lulu called through the open living room window. "She's threatening to hurt my dad's car!" She stood in front of a 45-year-old Kharman Ghia. "Do something! Don't just stand there!"

Louie saw LaChandra holding a baseball bat and marching towards the vintage cherry-red convertible.

"Honey," Louie pleaded with the taller, older girl. "Just wait a minute. I know you're upset, but, way, no. There is just so much wrong with this. Wait a sec. You mad at me, that I understand, but Lulu, she doesn't know much. She doesn't mean diddly-squat to me."

Lulu bristled. "Hey."

Louie waved her off.

LaChandra looked at her, back at the car, back at him, a soft smile across her lips. "Then why did you sleep with her, you asshole?"

"Sleeping with Louie didn't mean anything to me either," Lulu babbled, but it did, and it had and she didn't like to lie. But still. Shit.

"That's what they always say," LaChandra said.

"So what?" Lulu asked. First time in her twenty-two years anybody had made a big deal of that.

"Please, I can explain everything," Louie murmured. "Darling." LaChandra raised the bat higher over her head. Maybe that hadn't been the right thing to say. "Want a margarita?" He had no idea how to deal with girls. God had granted him a special compensation and he used it. Wisely, maybe not so much, but use it he did. This morning they'd both been in bed with him and everyone had been getting along great. Until Lulu had said something stupid.

LaChandra smashed the windshield.

"Now, now, we'll have none of that," Louie said, the fog in his brain from this morning's doobie not helping his thought processes at all. "LaChandra, what about that margarita? You don't like margaritas? Want something else? Mojito? Adderall? Xanax?"

"Shit and double shit!" Lulu screamed. "What the fuck am I going to tell my Dad about his car?" Bravely and with maybe a singular lack of sense, she slipped behind LaChandra. "Hit me, and not the car, asshole."

LaChandra spun around. "Get the fuck out of the way, you stupid little shit."

"Hey. Don't call me names," Lulu said, jumping around staying just out of range. "It was your idea to make it a threesome, LaChandra. You want him, take him. Hey, Louie." He didn't move. "She wants to marry you." His face blanched.

"Now, wait just a sec ...." Louie felt a noose tightening around his neck. "LaChandra. Baby, sweetheart. Lulu. Girls, please." He held up his hands. "Peace." That had no effect. "Love? Understanding?" They gave him funny looks, stepped closer to each other. "Knock it off!"

Shit, that worked. They froze.

"Louie! Now!" Lulu screamed. She sprang onto LaChandra's back. "Grab the fucking bat!"

LaChandra, tangled in the other woman's arms and legs, staggered around trying to keep her balance. "Let go, you lunatic! Let go of my goddamn hair."

Lulu twisted tighter. "Drop the bat."

Louie stepped out of the way. He could get hurt. He held the pitcher of margaritas in one hand and three plastic glasses in the other. "Girls! Great action! Save some for the bedroom!"

Lulu dug her nails into LaChandra's scalp.

LaChandra turned and twisted, stumbled and fell.

Despite his best intentions, the action was helping Wendell's special compensation more than he thought possible. He came a little closer.

"Lulu," he called gently. "LaChandra. I love you both."

They sat up, looked at him blankly. "What did you say?" Lulu asked. She released her hands from LaChandra's hair.

Louie came closer. "My sweethearts." He took LaChandra's face into his big hands and kissed her, hard.

"Oh, Louie," LaChandra sighed.

"Share and share alike, you said, Louie," Lulu said, puckering up.

"Sorry about your car, darling." Louie put out his hand, brought Lulu close to his chest. "Come here. Come here, sweet." He kissed her ears, her face, her wet cheeks, snuggling closer. "Don't worry. My brother works in a body shop. He can fix everything."

"Not my broken heart," Lulu sniffed.

"That's his specialty," Louie cooed.

"Oh Louie." She buried her face in his shirt. "What about her?"

"Oh, I love her too," Louie said, opening up his other arm. "LaChandra, meet Lulu, light of my life. Lulu, meet Miss Fire and Ice. Now girls, what about those margaritas?"

From the Sheriff's Calls Section of the Point Reyes Light, May 23, 2013

SAN GERONIMO: At 10:42 a.m. a middle-aged man in a straw hat and sweater was holding a cardboard box and mumbling to himself.

The Doozy

"So, what do you have in the box?" Deputy Linda Kettleman asked. She'd been making the rounds in San Geronimo Valley, covering for Bernard who was out of town for his cousin's wedding. The Valley was new to her, but the people, not so much. Same mayhem and confusion as in Point Reyes. "Sir?"

"I don't have to show you anything," the man huffed, shoving the box under his other arm. "First Amendment rights, search and seizure—or is it the Fourth?" Calvin had forgotten everything from high-school civics class.

"Well, actually, I don't care what's in the box, but you are acting rather strangely," Linda said, and added, "Sir."

"Everyone talks to themselves these days. Haven't you noticed? Jabbering into those little ear bugs. So you can't see mine. Big deal," Calvin said proudly, showing her his ears. "This new thing—surgically implanted." His mind felt clever; but his stomach hurt. He'd had a few too many raw onions in his salad earlier and his belly felt like it was full of rocks. "Don't you have other work to do? I haven't done anything wrong. Thank you very much, officer. And no, you can't see what's in the box."

Linda sighed. She was just about to put away her steno notebook when she heard a scratch. A scratch like cat claws on a post? But there were no cats around and it was too close to be a squirrel.

"Sir?" she asked, gesturing to the box. "Bet you don't have a snake in there."

Calvin shook his head. "No snake, ma'am. Guess again." She was way off.

"Where do you live, sir? Your name, please? And don't give me the names of movie stars. I've heard them all."

"Jackie Pearson," Calvin said, trying to see how clever she was. He didn't have the girth for Jackie Gleason, but he did have his big buggy eyes.

Linda studied the man. Plaid trousers like Rodney Dangerfield in *Caddyshack*, short tufted hair, long in the back, old mullet, perhaps, small teeth, big ears, and a straw hat. She was thinking of giving him a ticket for outlandish clothing, but Walter didn't care for what she thought was her fine and acute sense of humor. "Sir, the box? What's in it?"

"I gotta get going," he said, feeling movement from the box.

Linda heard some more scratching. "If you have an animal in there, Jackie, it would be best to have some air holes. It's kind of warm out and hotter in the box."

"I would've gone home long ago if you hadn't detained me," Calvin spat. "See you later, officer."

"Sir." Her voice was strident. "I must see what's inside. Animal cruelty."

"No, you mustn't, you can't, you shan't. The answer is no, no, no." Calvin ran with the box, behind the fence, along the back road, over his neighbor's low fence, and into the woods. Once he was far enough away from prying eyes, he slipped open the lid of his old paper box. A pair of brown eyes stared at him, with warmth, Calvin thought. He slipped a finger inside and touched the baby raccoon.

A second later, he pulled back. Blood was pouring from his finger. He stood up, wanting to kick at the box, break the box, show that critter exactly who was the boss. He held his finger to his lips. Damn thing wouldn't stop bleeding. He raised his shoe. His mother's voice came into his mind. "Calvin, no reason to hurt little critters. They're just trying to make their way in the world. Patience, my boy." So Calvin, being a good boy, carefully lifted the top of the box and let the critter go.

That night he brought out kitty kibble and a bowl of water. By morning the food was gone. The next day, he brought out more and by morning of the fourth day, he sat in the woods, his back against a tree, and his bandaged finger on his lap, and the little critter came near.

"Mom would be proud," Calvin said and reached for it again.

By the time the sheriff's call came into the station, Calvin had been bit three more times. They said he had to have rabies shots, and they would hurt. Calvin wasn't ready. He would never be ready.

"Stay still, please, sir," the paramedics said as Calvin twitched and moaned.

"But it was only an itty bitty critter," he wailed.

"That's what they all say," the paramedics added, depressing the plunger on the syringe. Nearby Linda filled out a report. This one was going to be a doozy.

*From the Sheriff's Calls section of the Point Reyes Light,
June 20, 2013*

MUIR WOODS: At 1:4 p.m. a resident had a question about shooting trespassers.

Gone

"So, then, it's okay if I shoot a trespasser?" Mary Ann Forster asked, clutching the phone. "Really?"

Officer Linda Kettleman eased into her chair at the public safety building. She'd bought an extra-long cord for the receiver and liked that she could reach for it anywhere. But now she was too close to Walter's plants and was tangled up in his beloved ficus. "Would you please repeat the question, ma'am?"

The word "shoot" had gotten her attention.

Mary Ann Forster smoothed the apron on her favorite rose-colored dress. She'd been alone for six months since Harold had died, and wasn't quite sure about the best way to defend herself. She'd had a terrier, who yapped so much it drove her crazy, so she got rid of him. Then she'd thought about a Great Dane but he would have been bigger than she was. Then she'd considered a goose, but they were messy. So she'd settled on a gun. "Just a small one, Officer, you know, like those pocket pistols on the TV show '*Sons of Guns*'?"

Linda had untangled herself from the ficus and was sitting down at her own desk, staring at a stack of incident reports. It was summer, and people were crazy, but this year, there seemed to be more than ever. "You in any danger, ma'am?" she asked, pushing the adoption papers aside on her desk and reaching for an incident report. It was just too much for a tiny little town. Someday she'd get out, but for what, less crime? There was nowhere else with less crime.

"I'll come and show you, Officer," Mary Ann Forster suggested.

"Show me your gun? You have a permit for that, ma'am?" Dispatch crackled over the intercom; thankfully, this time, it wasn't for her. She'd been out on a date—and had a headache. That'd teach her.

"I got it over the Internet," Mary Ann giggled. "But it works just fine. I blasted the shit out of some robin in the back yard yesterday." She paused. "So it's okay to shoot if someone tries to break in?"

"It depends," Linda answered, somewhat alarmed. There were lots and lots of people who visited West Marin. "Perhaps you should come in for a seminar on gun safety?" She looked at Walter.

He rolled his eyes.

"Oh, I know how to use the safety. It's on, I think. Hang on, I'm looking." There was a pause.

"What a cute little firearm," Linda heard the woman mumble, "and it fits perfectly into my fifteen-hundred-dollar Prada purse."

"Ma'am, one has to exercise restraint. Today robins. Tomorrow, what? Deer? Miss, your name please?" Linda asked.

"They're all out there, I know it," Mary Ann clucked her tongue. "And I'm not going on any facethingy—they spy on you, you know."

Linda sighed. "Well, I guess, but it can be..."

"And no frigging smart meter either," Mary Ann huffed.

"I should think not," Linda answered, hoping to get on this woman's good side—enough to get her name and address and check for a gun permit.

"Haven't had a license in years. So, I don't drive. Big deal." Mary Ann's voice rose. At 74, she couldn't care less. She pulled out the gun-cleaning instructions and oil ... was it time again?

"As to your question, ma'am," Linda went on. "You just can't shoot a trespasser when you want. What if it turns out to be, say, a gardener? You can't just ..."

"Don't have a gardener. I'm all alone in the woods," Mary Ann sniffed, looking at the green world outside. Goddamn pine trees were pressing up against the glass again.

"Visitors? People who are lost? Cleaning ladies? All people aren't bad guys, ma'am."

Mary Ann let out a snort. "Me? I have no need for all that shit. Officer, I just wanted to know ... if someone breaks in ..." Mary Ann eyed her front door with the police lock, the bars on the windows. "No, nobody comes in here. So ..." she ruminated, "so, if I'm out walking, and if someone attacks me, can I shoot? How 'bout a bear? How 'bout a bartender who makes me the wrong drink?"

As the lady's voice rose, Linda gestured to Walter. "Trace the call." She paused. "You go to bars, ma'am?"

"Only in my dreams....Hey! Stop that! Stop...Wait!"

Linda heard a shot.

"You all right, ma'am?"

There was silence at the other end of the line.

"Ma'am?"

"I took care of it," Mary Ann said.

"Took care of what?" Linda asked.

"Forget it. I don't need police protection. Hell, once you have a gun, you can do just about anything you want. He's gone."

"Gone, as in taken off?" Linda sat up in her chair and waved to Walter to get a move on. "Gone to someone else's house, then?"

"Gone that way? No, I don't think so. I think this guy's dead and gone."

**From the Sheriff's Calls Section of the Point Reyes Light
June 20, 2013**

DILLON BEACH: At 12:34 a.m. a picnic table appeared to be on fire.

The Date

"It's not my fault the friggin' picnic table is on fire!" Jason Hurley yelled, shielding the flickering light from his eyes. It looked kind of cool, flames licking the old dry redwood. Dramatic as hell.

"Of all the stupid things to do, Jason," Lizzie Johnson accused. "You started it, you end it. I'm taking a walk."

Jason ignored her and downed his beer. He hadn't been thinking about the fire at all, he'd been thinking about Josie, texting her in Mexico, trying to write the perfect message to get her to move back to California, and maybe, not paying that much attention and pouring a little too much lighter fluid on the barbecue. Big deal. It was just a picnic table. She'd said yes. Oh my God, oh my God, Josie'd said yes.

"If you don't put it out, the cops will come," Lizzie said in her bossy-pants voice. It had been a dark, clear night, once. Now smoke from the fire curled up and around them, obscuring the beautiful stars. She liked order, and this night had been anything but.

"How the hell am I supposed to put it out?" Jason asked, seriously perturbed. If Lizzie would just disappear, he could daydream about Josie again, perhaps send her another message.

"You've got to do something, Jason," Lizzie said. "You could still save it. It's licking at the benches too, now." The world was full of idiots. Why did she have to go out with this one?

"Not having a bucket, perhaps I should use beer?" Jason suggested, and giggled.

"Guess you could, if you really wanted to," Lizzie said. "Longboard or Bud Light?"

"Perhaps it would be best to move the lighter fluid," Sue, Lizzie's best friend suggested.

On the ground, the bottle dribbled out more fluid, and the fire licked at the ends of the picnic table and snaked down the legs, following the stream of fluid.

Even though Sue had had four beers, one more than her limit, and was a bit confused, she scrounged around to find something on the empty beach to move the lighter fluid, and found only a folding chair. She lifted it up. It was wood; it would burn too. Oh dear.

"How stupid can you be, you idiots!" Lizzie cried, marching up to Sue and grabbing the folding chair. She edged close to the fire and, with the chair, pulled away the lighter-fluid container.

Jason, in a bit of a panic that maybe now with the flames so high the cops would come, closed the lid on the container and threw it down the beach.

The kids watched the flames settle on the picnic table, as the wood crackled and burned and finally went out. It helped that the evening was chilly. The fog was settling on the beach.

"Man, that was cool," Jason said.

"So, it was you, then, who poured lighter fluid on the table?" Lizzie asked.

Ignoring her, Jason pulled a lighter out of his pants pocket and a cigarette from his shirt pocket.

"No, no more flames—no fire of any kind," Sue said, her eyes alight and full of energy. This night had been better than staying home and watching TV any old day. Feeling bold, she grabbed the lighter out of his hand.

"And who are you—the president?" Jason sneered. He hadn't invited Sue; his brother James hadn't invited Sue. "Chill out." He reached for the matches in his backpack, lit the cigarette, and took a long drag. "What's it to you?"

"A soft answer turneth away wrath; but grievous words stir up anger, Proverbs 15:1," Jason recited, walking around the picnic table. "See? I'm not so bad; I've been to church and everything." Yeah right, and if he could persuade Mom to let him stay at home Sundays that would be a godsend. He laughed at his little joke.

"Jason," Sue suggested. "Maybe it's time you went home?" She was tired, it was almost the Fourth of July, and she'd promised her mother she'd be home before one. At this rate she'd never make the fifteen minute drive to Tomales in time.

"Not I said the little red hen," intoned Jason. "If you don't like Proverbs, I can do nursery rhymes. Anyone aside from me know any?"

James, Lizzie and Sue stood together, watching Jason. He was practically running around the half burnt picnic table, half-stumbling now.

"Maybe we should call his mother?" Lizzie asked.

"For what? Tell my mother his son set fire to a picnic table, is wild-ass drunk and has completely lost it at Dillon Beach?" James asked.

"But I came here, I feel responsible," Lizzie said.

"Then you can have him," Sue said. "C'mon James." She took his hand and walked away.

Lizzie watched them leave, turned to watch Jason collapse by the picnic table. He was curled up, his eyes closed, his hands over his heart, in the fetal position. The embers from the fire hit him on his face, and he looked cherubic, if Lizzie squinted hard enough and ignored the scattered and empty beer cans by his feet. She left him there, turned and walked up, back to the car. Screw Jason, screw his mother, and screw the summer. It was the worst date of her life and July of her sixteenth year had barely begun.

From the Sheriff's Calls Section of the Point Reyes Light June 27, 2013

STINSON BEACH: At 1.01 p.m. a youth turned down some music and agreed to behave.

Broken Hearts

It had been three weeks since Jason set the picnic table on fire at Dillon Beach. He'd been lucky then, but he wasn't so lucky now. He and James had been sitting on the beach, shooting the shit, sipping beers, when the old biddy down the beach had come their way and made him turn down his iPhone. He hadn't been doing anything wrong, just listening to Nine Inch Nails. Now there was no music, no singing, and no fun. Even the sound of the waves wasn't soothing to his sore and bruised heart.

After being so happy that Josie was coming back, he'd texted her for her flight info, and she informed him that no, she'd changed her mind. She'd mumbled and changed the subject and been cagey. That was when he knew she had some stupid boyfriend down there, and when he asked her, point blank like, she didn't deny it. So there, point, match, set, he lost his whole frigging life in one goddamn afternoon.

Jason took another sip of his beer. Not yet old enough to drink legally, he handed the bottle back to his brother, who tucked it in a hole in the sand. Jason scowled and dug out his cell phone.

"How 'bout those girls we invited to Dillon Beach?" James asked. "They were cute."

Jason grunted.

"I'm sure they already forgot how loaded you were."

"Lizzie left me alone on the beach all night."

"So? You were ranting and raving, reciting Proverbs."

48

"Big deal. They're poetry. You love basketball. We have to be different in some way, James."

James shrugged.

"Shit, it was cold as hell out there at four in the morning. Didn't even leave me a blanket."

"You think we should've brought you home, Jason? I can't exactly carry you."

"Well, you can carry Sue. So the two of you could've got me home. I bet you had a grand old time – all three of you, actually, having fun on my behalf."

"Sue's pretty enough, but she wanted to go home early. And that Lizzie, she's not that into me ...."

Jason looked up, brightened.

"Or you either," James said.

"Back to the drawing board, eh?" James suggested. There must be some girls they could call.

"Kind of a dismal summer, isn't it?" James grumbled.

"You're only seventeen. Don't worry about it," James said. "There are a lot of fish ...."

"Don't you start. Don't say anything. Josie was beautiful, clever and smart."

"And took your heart away and stomped that sucker flat, Jason."

"I know." Jason thought a moment. "But ... you know ...."

"Don't give me that. Mom didn't like her either."

"Sure, but that made her more appealing," Jason said, also thinking of the way she looked in the moonlight while she stood naked by the window in his bedroom.

James whistled. "Would you take a look at that."

Jason looked at his toes. James was always teasing him. He would have none of it.

"They're two of them, right here. One's a blonde. They're coming this way."

"Jesus, James, cut the crap. Don't do this to me."
Jason gathered his shoes and shirt and turned. Then he saw them. "They're looking right at me," he said, his voice a whisper.

"Then you better pay attention, buddy boy," James said, smoothing back his hair. "Look sharp, look appealing, and wipe that gloom off your face."

Jason tried, oh God, he tried, but the idea of that Josie with some other guy made him crazy.

"Good afternoon girls," James said. "Nice day, isn't it?" He did his best to sound cool, disinterested, but shit, he was lying. These girls were knockouts.

A blond and a brunette, wearing straw hats and bikinis, were silhouetted by bright sunlight. Jason wished he could see their faces.

"Say hello, Jason," James said. "My brother's not too bad, once you get to know him."

The girls stopped, hesitated, drew near.

"What do you think, April?" one of them said.

Jason's heart skipped a beat. This was not a girl with dulcet tones, this was a deep voice. He poked his brother in the hip.

James, noting his brother was being a pain, stood up, and extended his hand.

Jason grabbed his brother's ankle.

"Let me introduce myself. I'm James, and this is my brother Jason," James said.

Jason looked more carefully at the girls' legs. Thicker—and hairier—than usual.

"James!" Jason shouted.

"Oh, ignore my brother, please," James said, "he's got a broken heart."

"Oh good," said a deep voice from under the hat. "Me and April, we're great at broken hearts."

From the Sheriff's Calls Section of the Point Reyes Light
June 27, 2013

INVERNESS PARK: At 11:49 p.m. a woman heard someone cough and then turn a doorknob. It was her husband.

Lights

"You didn't have to call the cops, I'm here too, Mildred," Fred said, gathering the pages of the *Point Reyes Light* and leaving it neat on her bedside table, just the way she liked.

"Still," she said, looking out the window at her neighbor. "People have been outside, lurking."

"Well, it wasn't me, honey. I'm here, right next to you," Fred said, trying to get her to stay out of his hair. Since he'd retired, years ago now, she'd been following him around, into his business. Was it too late to go to the Western? Probably. He sighed. "I'm your husband, dear."

"So?" she sniffed. She was in bed. "I've been trying to get *Brideshead Revisited* on the stupid iPad and it's broken." She kept stabbing her finger on the screen. "Sure scared me, Fred. And with your hearing, these days, being next to nothing, you wouldn't even know if a mouse was knocking on our door." She slapped the iPad with the palm of her hand.

"Don't do that, honey, I'll fix it."

"You didn't hear it. You didn't hear anything, as usual."

"That's not the point. Give it over," he asked. "Unless you want to break it again?"

"It could have been anyone," she sniffed. "A burglar. Out here we do have burglars." She tossed the iPad at him.

It landed on his belly, hard. "Doggone it, sweetheart, I'm still flesh and blood."

"That's for sure," she said. "Find that delicious Jeremy Irons, I want to dream about him again."

Fred scowled as he fiddled with the iPad. Mildred was, well, still so Mildred-like, but now, instead of thinking their neighbor Mrs. Flanagan was about to break in, she'd decided he was the culprit. Maybe it was time to get some peace and quiet and both of them should go live with Janet who lived in Palo Alto.

He frowned.

That would never work, Mildred would never put up with being so far from the water, and Fred wouldn't be able to walk to the Western.

He stood up, walked out to the deck and looked out into the dark night. Not being able to see anything, he could imagine Tomales Bay shimmering in the morning light; the fog perched along the top of Inverness Ridge. He could no more leave West Marin than he could leave his delicate, precious, little wife. He walked back to her bedside. "I fixed the iPad for you. Don't bang on it; it's delicate, like me."

Mildred snorted.

"Look. If you are scared, call my name, but don't call the cops, honey. It's embarrassing."

"For you or for me?" Mildred spat. "Just think. I'm one-third your size. I don't have a weapon —"she thought a moment. "Not with me, anyway."

Good thing that Fred had dropped all her guns in the well.

"I'm all alone," she whispered.

"You are not. You have me."

"There's no one in the world who loves me. You're a big brute, Fred, and could hurt me at any time."

"Never have. Never will."

"Nevertheless. I get scared. What if a bear broke in? What then?"

"We don't have bears in West Marin, honey. They left years ago."

"Forget bears, then. Mountain lions—elk, deer, coyotes, foxes, squirrels, raccoons. Burglars, Fred. Human burglars."

"Oh dear. Sweetheart," Fred said, not knowing where to begin. "There are so few burglaries out here."

"They're in Marshall! They're all in Marshall! What if they come here, Fred? I read about them in the *Light*. Robbing banks in broad daylight. What's to stop them from coming out here in the middle of the night, and robbing little old ladies?"

Fred knew that most facts, including that, yes, they were still married, and living together, eluded Mildred these days. And it was true about Marshall. He decided to take a different road. "Quite the game, then, that last one. Giants went down swinging. That Sergio Romo ..."

"You know I've never cared about baseball, Fred. You see the lights, out there?" She peered out the bedroom window.

Fred came up beside her, placed his arm around her thin waist. "Across the water, my love. A car driving along Route One."

"They're heading this way," Mildred said. "They could be anywhere," she said, shivering.

"Sweetie pie. The car is heading north to Marshall. Remember, I'm here. I'll be here to protect you, always." Shit, if he made such promises he'd never get to the Western. "I'll protect you from cougars, and raccoons, and foxes, and coyotes, and skunks, dear. I'm your go-to man," he murmured, leaning over to kiss her ear.

"Not when you smell like skunk. Ooof! Get offa me, you big lunk. You and all those wild animals. You love 'em so much, you go sleep with them," she declared and pushed him out the door.

From the Sheriff's Calls Section of the Point Reyes Light
June 27, 2013

INVERNESS: At 10:18 a.m. a woman said she was having problems with her boyfriend.

Trouble

"Problems? What kind of problems?" Linda asked, putting down her bear claw. "Walter —what kind of call is that?"

Walter, tucked behind his enormous ficus, was going through the latest sheriff's calls, preparing to send them to the *Light.* They were the same as a big city which used to surprise him, but not anymore. People just seemed to be angry and unhappy. As for him, the summer was turning out to be a good one, lots of fog and less tourists because of it. "What did you say, deputy?"

"Who do they think we are? A counseling service? Problems with her boyfriend?" Linda set down the phone. "Money problems? Bedroom problems? Someone's not listening? Come on. We need something serious."

"Count your blessings it's a slow week. Check it out, deputy. But make it snappy. I need you here." The stack of paper on his desk was a big one; it was going to take all day. If he just hadn't put it off all week ....

Linda headed out. It was a nice day—uncharacteristically clear—for so early in the day. Problems with a boyfriend indeed. Problems were why she didn't even have a boyfriend.

The place was tucked way back inside the woods, up an impossibly steep one lane road. Linda was wondering how she was going to turn the cruiser around when the front door of the 1930s shack opened and a woman came out.

"Oh, I'm so glad you came, deputy—it's Harvey. I know, it seems so trivial, but it isn't to me. He just seems so weird. Arguing with me, Harvey would never argue with me. Come on in."

Tightening up her equipment belt, Linda walked up the path, overgrown with daisies. Problems indeed; this woman was going to have serious problems if she didn't make some defensive space around her house. A fire in these parts would head up the hill like the Mt. Vision fire of 1995.

"I'm Sarah May Caruso," the woman said, putting out her hand.

Linda stepped forward. Sarah May—unlike most West Marin residents—had perfectly coiffed hair and well-made-up eyes. She was wearing a loose pink-satin chiffon dress, which billowed out behind her while she walked. She looked more Park Avenue than Inverness.

"Harvey? What are you doing?" Sarah May demanded. "I said no artichoke leaves down the sink. Harvey?" He was staring out the window into a meadow beyond.

"Deer," he mumbled. "I love deer. I'll get my gun."

"See, officer?" Sarah May asked. "He doesn't listen. That's why I called. Harvey?"

"Don't bother me," Harvey groaned. "The damn fork is stuck and the tines keep poking my fingers. That asshole John Foote put it in months ago. He knew he wasn't supposed to have a disposal with a septic system. Now it's gone and stuck."

He pulled out his hand. "Got any soap? My hands are all chapped and shit."

Sarah May clucked her tongue.

Harvey splattered his hand with dishwashing liquid and plunged it back in.

"John said, 'Harvey, you want me to call the County on an illegal install or do you want your disposal?' So I shut up." He swore. "John moved away last week. Now, who am I supposed to call, Sarah May? Both my hand and the fork are stuck now."

"Is this why you called, Miss Caruso?" Linda asked.

"He doesn't do what I ask, officer," Sarah May complained.

"I was doing the dishes just like she asked," Harvey said, grunting, finally pulling his hand out, "and the fork got stuck. I was trying." He turned, his face full of a thick beard.

"He just makes such a mess," Sarah May went on. "It's not like we don't talk about things, you know, work stuff out, but we keep having these arguments. He's a difficult man to get along with, my Harvey."

Linda brightened. That "my Harvey" had a nice ring to it.

"I don't have any idea why you called the cops, dear," Harvey said and left the kitchen in a huff. Standing at a small back door, he put his hand on the door jamb. "I get along with everyone, usually." Then he was out the door.

"Ma'am," Linda turned to Sarah May. "You can't just call the cops when you're having an argument." The idea, however, made her smile. If she had to respond to every argument in West Marin, she'd never have to work in the office at all.

"You don't understand." Sarah May stroked her hair, fiddled with the oversized buttons on her jacket. "He's a good man, but he has his own mind sometimes. Watches too much football. Starts to fix things, then breaks them. When I want to argue, he stays silent and walks away. Other times he argues with me for hours. Lives in his own dream world. Doesn't listen for shit."

Sounds like every man Linda had ever known. "And?" she asked. The change in Sarah May's voice caught her attention.

"There he goes again, marching around the back yard like a hero in a western, officer. Hiding behind trees, strolling around, waving his hands in the air, singing at the top of his voice, dancing around. He's a lost man, officer."

"And that's a problem?" Linda asked, wondering if she could get home in time for Mom's bridge club. She was tired of always losing: she'd been studying up.

"He's retired?" Linda asked, a moment later. "Keeps to himself? Has quirks? Doesn't listen? Stays out of your business?"

"Oh, I wish," Sarah May said, reaching out to the officer. "He's a nut."

Not surprising, living out here, with you. "And what are the police supposed to do about it?"

"Shoot him. Shoot him and put him out of his misery," Sarah May said. "I'd do it myself, but then I'd get in too much trouble."

From the Sheriff's Calls Section of the Point Reyes Light, October 3, 2013

FOREST KNOLLS: At 2:12 a.m. someone heard howling and screaming at the rear end of a trailer park, surmising it was an injured animal or Bigfoot.

Bigfoot

Lulu Garcia giggled in the dark. She hadn't been able to sleep, at least not well, not since that slimeball Jeff Morse had moved out. Now, with the place nearly empty, and the noises from the back yard getting louder and louder, she stopped laughing in a hurry.

Bigfoot? Here? Rubbing her eyes, she peered into the computer again. There, in front of her, the *Light's* website, and Sheriff's Calls, bright as day, and the first call. Bigfoot. Right in her own backyard.

Lulu moved her cat Fluffy Toes from off the keyboard. Fluffy liked to doze on the 6, and fill up the screen with numbers, but Lulu had cleaned those up at least twice, and there it was, still. Bigfoot.

She thought of calling her mother in Stinson Beach, but Mom had found a new boyfriend —a new guy from the City named LeVaundre — and Lulu, she just knew, Mom would not like to be disturbed. Disappointed, she turned down the volume on her computer and listened to the noises outside. Crackles, still, then silence. Had she locked all the windows and doors? Yes? No? She couldn't remember.

Lulu was sharing the trailer with her friend LaChandra. At least she had someone with her, while Mom was not helping in the least. Lulu stamped her feet under the small desk made out of plywood and 2 x 4s.

What if the big lunk came in? What then? Weren't they eight feet tall and hairy, and could rip doors off their hinges? Lulu would call Jeff Morse, her last boyfriend, but she'd dumped him when he'd called her "difficult." Now she wished he was here.

She heard a branch break. In back? By the trash cans? The trailer was just too damn small. She couldn't hide under the desk — and that gosh darn LaChandra was sprawled across the double bed, and every single closet, drawer and cubby, was full of her clothes. That left … what? Lulu tried to think through the fog of smoke that curled off a joint she held between her two fingers. That left, she gulped, the bathroom.

"LaChandra?" she whispered.

LaChandra let out a moan, turned over, and went back to sleep.

Some more branches broke outside. Oh shit. Maybe Lulu shouldn't have been watching horror movies like Chained in Texas, or My Boyfriend Jack's a Zombie But I Still Love Him, and smoking a doobie before she'd crashed on the makeshift sofa. She wished she had LaChandra's ability to sleep.

Something big was walking around outside. Lulu sat up. Had someone knocked on the walls of the trailer? She couldn't be sure. She ran into the bathroom, locked the door with a hook and eye. Fat lot of good that would do with Bigfoot on the loose. It was tight in there and without any windows, hard to breathe. Maybe Bigfoot would charge in and eat LaChandra first. Then go on back to the woods, satiated. Oh my God! Lulu felt guilty at the thought, but not guilty enough to come out of the bathroom and make herself Bigfoot's first meal. Good God, no.

She crouched down on the toilet and waited. At least she had on her T-shirt and underwear. That would be the last thing anyone would find. Sweet Jesus. Hearing more scratching and crackling of leaves and twigs, Lulu started to cry. "Make it quick, please, oh please," she said, her sobs growing louder as she heard pounding on the door.

The door to the trailer? The door to the bathroom? He was coming closer and closer. Lulu heard the rattle of the hook and eye. She grabbed a shampoo bottle and bottle of hair spray. She could squirt him in the eye with hair spray, and with her tools in each hand she faced the door, wide-eyed, hopped up, ready for her maker.

"Lulu! Open the goddamn door!"

It was Bigfoot, trying to get in, right outside the door. Bigfoot knew her name? How did he know her name?

"Oh my God," Lulu screamed.

"I need to pee, you dingbat! Get out of the bathroom!" LaChandra shouted, and in between the din of Lulu's pounding heart and the rush of blood in her ears she saw someone's coral rose nails creep between the door jamb and the door, and Lulu knew, just knew, that Bigfoot did not paint his nails. At least not coral rose.

***From the Sheriff's Calls Section of the Point Reyes Light,
October 3, 2013***

WOODACRE: At 8:37 p.m. a man reported that someone
kept calling with death threats. When deputies called him
back, he asked them over for tea and cookies.

Tea and Cookies

"Boss?" Linda asked, putting down her old, stale
bear claw from the morning. She was going on a double
shift and the half-dead pastry tasted like the cardboard
box she'd opened from littleme.com she'd opened this
morning. That had been the best part of her day: inside
were clothes for Hannah Bea's baby, who would soon be
her own. Ever since that bright light, her day had gone to
hell. And now this. "Boss, I mean, really, death threats?"

"Just go. And don't bother me. I have a migraine,"
Walter said. And with a shot of Miracle Gro on his now
enormous ficus, he was out the door.

Bernard, another deputy, was home sick, and that
left Linda to work his shift as well as her own. The money
was good, but she'd feel like hell tomorrow. And what
was she going to do with these impossibly long hours
once she got the baby? Mom wasn't strong enough.

"Hell's bells," Linda muttered, and picked up the
call on hold. "Death threats, sir? What kind, again?"

"It's my neighbor, Officer. She's crazy. First she
came onto my property, and bent and cut branches—a
full fifty feet into my yard ..." The caller took a huge
breath. "So I built a fence. Now, she's piling up leaves
and branches along the fence line, piling it all higher and
higher, and it's going over the top of the fence, and it's a
fire hazard, ma'am."

The line went quiet. "Sir?" Linda asked, wondering
what kind of pizza she could order. She knew every menu
in town.

"Now, this." The caller held a long pause and Linda jumped in.

"And what is this, sir?"

"She promised to kill my dog if I don't get rid of her," the man said in a strained, high tone.

"Jeesus," Linda mumbled. People in West Marin were a little close to the edge on a good day. "Sir, you think she's serious, I mean, about your dog?"

"She came over with a gun! So, you see why I'm worried. What am I going to do?"

Well, that was different. "I'll be over in a few minutes, sir," Linda said. "Your name, please? And address?"

"Kurt. Kurt Cousins. I'm just down past the Green Bridge. I'm down Levee Road."

It was pretty dark by the time Linda made the final turn down Sir Francis Drake Blvd., where there were no lights, but that was no problem for most of the cars that sped more than 60 in the 45-mph zone. She pulled up onto a gravel drive and opening the door to the cruiser heard the honking of geese and ducks and the squawk of birds as she got out.

"I'm the bird man, Officer," a voice spoke out of the darkness.

She flipped on the floodlights on the top of the cruiser. "I thought that was a lot of birds for a house near the wetlands," she said to the short, bearded, gray-haired man. "I've heard of you."

"You think this is a lot? I used to have over a hundred. We lost the emu about a year ago."

"Ah, I see," Linda said. And right on the creek too. What would SPAWN* say?

"Anyway, there's the fence," Kurt said, holding a large flashlight and pointing at an eight-foot-tall fence behind the pampas grass. "Hush, Molly." A beagle had been barking. She stopped, nudged up to Linda, and wagged her tail.

Linda drew closer to the fence, holding her two-foot-long flashlight up at an angle, like she'd been taught. It was dark back there, under the branches, where she couldn't see the birds as much as smell and hear them. They were making a racket.

"Sir, uh, Kurt, this is the problem?" she asked.

"Ma'am, you have no idea. My neighbor, she never leaves me alone. She has a megaphone that she used to tell me to be quiet the day I had guests in the backyard. We were only having a barbecue. When bird buyers come by, she sprays water over the fence, blasts an airhorn, and scares the hell out of the birds. And with all that fluttering and beating of wings— well, you wouldn't want to buy an agitated bird either, would you, deputy?"

Linda wouldn't get a bird under any circumstances, but she wasn't going to say any of that.

She pushed her way through branches and bushes and took a closer look at the fence.

"The hardest part is," Kurt said, "Molly's a good dog, ma'am. But you know, she's still a dog. She doesn't like to be sprayed by a hose over the fence. She doesn't like to be yelled at. Molly's my only one, since, you know," he suppressed a sniffle, "since we lost Patches."

They were whispering by the fence.

"Sir, why are you being so quiet?" Linda asked.

"It's my property, but it's not. It's war. Now she wants to kill my dog." He petted Molly. "Mrs. Brainerd, she shoved this in my mailbox." Kurt dug into his pockets, pulled out a ragged piece of paper. "I've been handling this on my own all right. Until now. I hate calling the cops."

"Is that recent, then?" Linda pulled out her steno notebook and pencil.

"All the goddamn environmentalists are trying to sue me for a little bird-poop runoff. As if in nature, there's no bird poop anyway? Seems cruel to me. Birds need a sanctuary where they can heal. See the swan with the broken leg? Petunia's done well here. I should be able to release her in another month or two."

"May I see the document, sir?" Linda held her flashlight up and read: "Say goodbye to Molly, Kurt."

"Dear God," Linda said. "And written in thick red ink, too."

"Looks like blood to me," Kurt said. "One of my ducks went missing last week."

Linda wondered whether it was time to call for backup. She heard a crackling in the trees above the fence. Too loud to be a squirrel. She ran her flashlight across the ground, sniffed for skunk. No normal critters would make any noise when people were around. Was it the sick coyote they'd seen around town?

Branches broke overhead. She lifted her flashlight. "Hello?" she called out, her hand on her sidearm.

"Yoo-hoo!" called a voice from the other side of the fence. "You guys need something? What are you doing over there? Hello? Hello? It's Mrs. Brainerd from next door. Kurt?"

Kurt shrugged his shoulders, touched the officer's arm. "See?" he whispered.

"Kurt? I swear you're making me lose my mind. You want a snack? What are you doing? Lurking in the bushes again?"

Kurt didn't reply.

In a minute the fence, the bushes, the trees, the lawn, all exploded in a fountain of light. Huge lights, hidden in the tree, shot down, illuminating everything.

"Mrs. Brainerd? I'm from the Sheriff's Department," Linda said, holstering her flashlight and shielding her eyes. "What's going on here?"

The lights went out, all of them, plunging Linda and Kurt into darkness. She couldn't see anything. Couldn't even feel the presence of him in the dark. She reached for her mag light, but it was gone from her belt. "Kurt?" she shouted. "Mrs. Brainerd?" All she could hear was the squawking of birds. "Kurt?" Linda asked again. Ever since Ardys and the cats, she'd carried an extra flashlight, a little one, tucked into her bra. She grabbed it, flipped it on.

There, by the fence, on the ground, was Kurt, out cold. Molly beside him, standing watch. Over him, at the top of the fence, branches moved again. Linda scanned the trees.

She checked on Kurt, still breathing, thank heavens, and reached for her radio.

"No need, ma'am," a woman's voice spoke right next to her ear. "Of course, we have a pass-through. Good fences make good neighbors, or haven't you heard of Robert Frost?"

"Ma'am, you can't just go round knocking people on the head," Linda said, reaching for her handcuffs.

"He didn't want my tea and cookies, ma'am," Mrs. Brainerd said and disappeared into the trees.

*SPAWN: Salmon Protection and Watershed Network.

From the Sheriff's Calls Section of the Point Reyes Light, January 12, 2014

POINT REYES STATION: At 4:58 a.m. deputies checked to see that a downtown transient named Jorge was okay despite the cold, wet weather. The man insisted that he was fine, they wrote.

Jorge

"Fine?" Jorge Hansen asked the officer. "You assume I'm fine?"

Deputy Linda Kettleman rocked back on her heels. It was early in the morning, pitch dark out, and downtown Point Reyes seemed a little creepy. So did the perpetrator. "People were worried, sir. They called me, I came out. One of the officers said you didn't want assistance, Jorge. That your name, right? You don't want any help? Is that right?"

"Is what part right?" Jorge stood in the pale light from the Palace Market. He was standing under the overhang, next to the carts. "That doesn't make any sense," Jorge grumbled. "It's freezing out here."

Linda agreed. Even with her regulation coat hat and gloves, she still shivered in her thin wool pants and shirt. The glint off her badge caught Jorge in the eye.

"Do you mind?" He crossed one hand over his eyes and squinted. He was holding all he owned in the world – at least that's what he was going to tell her – sleeping bag, cotton blanket, metal coffee cup, empty cans for heating food and matches. He nodded his head when the officer stepped into shadow and the glint from her badge disappeared. "Thank you." He extended a hand.

Somewhat of a germaphobe, Linda didn't want to shake his hefty hand with broken fingernails and ground-in dirt. But good community relations meant she needed to, she had to. "Your hand is warm, sir," she added, thinking how much she wanted to wash. "So, what else can we do for you?"

"Hot shower." Jorge thought fast. "Steak dinner, for two," he grinned. "New clothes, a backpack, a home, a warm fire, a homemade afghan, and, of course, a dog." He wouldn't show her little Patsy and ruin his spiel. "I've always loved dogs. Beagles especially."

"Sir." Linda pulled up to her full height of 5'5". "We had a call. We sent out a deputy. He said you were fine." She sighed. These late nights were killing her and she had to care for Bernadette during the day. "I'm not sure what we can do for you, not at this hour. You in pain?"

Jorge checked his symptoms. Legs fine, breathing fine, and no flu he could speak of. "Just cold, ma'am." He wrapped his arms around his chest. "If I was one of those – you know, drug addled nincompoops, you could take me to the hospital. You think I should take drugs so I can eat, ma'am?" He reached for Linda's arm.

She recoiled.

"Don't like our kind much, do you, sister?"

"I have a stale bear claw in the cruiser, and a blanket. Will that suffice, Jorge?"

"Over a house ... a ...."

"Don't you start."

"Yes. Of course, yes." Jorge gazed inside the Market's big windows. All the food. Going to waste? Maybe.

"But you can't stay here," Linda repeated, handing him her dog blanket and pastry.

"So, where am I supposed to sleep?"

"Over the hill they have shelters, sir. And counseling. Job training. Free dining rooms." Her compatriots in San Rafael – who complained incessantly about the transients on B Street – wouldn't be too happy to have another lost soul.

"And how am I supposed to get over the hill at 5 a.m.?" Jorge wrapped the blanket tighter around his shoulders. Wool. Warm. "Nice," he offered. "Thank you."

"Just don't let me see you here at daybreak. The market doesn't need any trouble."

"Hey, I have shelter here. Should I try the restrooms? Ever slept in an outhouse?"

"Locked at night, Jorge." Her cell phone buzzed. Problems with Bernadette? Colic, again? "I have to go. I've helped you the best I can. Enjoy the bear claw. In the morning find someplace else to live."

She turned, slowly, keeping an eye on him. Maybe he would stay, maybe not, but he kept still, blanket around his shoulders, chewing on his bear claw, watching her with his calm brown eyes.

She shivered. She'd been there, once upon a time. Begging. Sleeping rough. Not taking care of herself. She made an illegal U-turn and headed back to the station. Hesitated at the stop sign. In a few minutes the hay trucks would arrive, charging their bulk around the corners. They were late today.

Hell. She'd made her way up and out of the streets. Jorge could do the same. She pulled down her visor, examined her tired face in the mirror. Those old days were etched on her face. More lines than she needed. Jeesus, she was only 34.

She headed back to Jorge. She'd take him to the station, give him coffee, let him sit in a jail cell, let him get warm, for Chrissakes. How could she leave him out there all night, in this brutal cold? Dad had always said she had a cruel streak, and with most things he'd said, he was mostly right. She sped back to the market, jumped out and headed into the vestibule. This time she'd redeem herself, be generous, and be a good girl.

But there was nothing left in front of the market, no dust, no bear claw crumbs, only the lingering scent of someone needing a shower. She headed through the alley toward the outhouses. Surely Jorge would be there, tucked under the overhang, shivering in her blanket, homeless, and starving.

Half-way through the alley, she did not hear the soft footstep behind her, and with surprise she turned, a moment too late, and went down in a pile on the pavement.

"Works every time, doesn't it, Patsy." Jorge smiled, gathered his beagle in his arms and headed to Linda's cruiser. "Sorry about the clunk on your head, ma'am," he giggled and reached for her keys. Tonight, at least, Patsy would have a warm place to sleep, and in the cruiser, with the heat on, he could listen to the chatter over the radio and lull himself to sleep.

**From the Sheriff's Calls Section of the Point Reyes Light
January 23, 2014**

FOREST KNOLLS: At 2:03 p.m. someone heard a man screaming, "Doris!" for an hour in a vacant lot.

A Date with Brando

"Well, he certainly wasn't calling my name," Doris said, folding foil in Mrs. Rhinehart's thin bluish hair. "Anyway," she said, "I don't live in Forest Knolls."

"Well, you could have been driving through," Mildred snorted. They were alone in the beauty salon, except for half-dead Beatrice, sitting in the corner, muttering to herself.

"So, what do you think? What's he like, Doris?"

"And who might that be, Mrs. R.?" Doris had mentioned—only mentioned to Beatrice—that she'd been on one date, one lousy date, with Max from Cheda's next door, and now everyone knew. She shouldn't have even tried to have a life.

"Oh, you know, him." Mildred went on. She loved it when Doris messed with her hair. "Ah," she moaned. "Is he at all like Joshua? I know you girls like your ex-husbands, Doris, but do you think you're settling for less?"

Oh brother. One lousy date, one lousy marriage, and everyone knew her business. Doris swore under her breath. She was going to have to play it even tighter. But give up dating? Her one date in two years? She changed the subject. "And how do you like the color, Mrs. R.?" she asked gingerly. Jesus. Her hair was almost cerulean blue. The color of the sky. Could she rinse it out? Now?

"Are you sure that guy in Forest Knolls wasn't calling your name? Like Stella in *A Streetcar Named Desire*? Stel-la! Isn't that right? Maybe your boyfriend looks like Marlon Brando." Mildred took a breath. "And in West Marin too."

"Ma'am, quit wiggling, please. I have sharp scissors in my hand."

"I went out with Brando once. What a dream," tiny Beatrice piped up. She jumped out of her seat. "He came to West Marin, Mildred? Where? Oh, I've got to see him." She fussed with the Light, flipping through the pages. "Do you think Art Rogers took a photo of Brando?"

"Rogers takes photos of babies and farmers, Mrs. Fishman," Doris said. "Anyway, Brando is dead, isn't he? Didn't he die quite a few years back?"

"How can you be so cruel, Doris?" Beatrice fell into one of the chairs. "I loved him, Doris. And to think that he was here, in Forest Knolls. Mrs. Willis told me!" She got up and peered out onto the street.

"Beatrice. Sit down. You're bothering my concentration," Mildred said. "How's it going, Doris? You finished yet?"

"Just one final rinse, Mrs. R.," Doris replied. "Would you mind stepping over here?" She gestured to a wash basin.

Beatrice, one gnarly hand on the window frame, was focused on something out on the street. It was a limo, parked in front of Toby's. "It's him."

"Who?" Mildred turned suddenly, knocking the spray nozzle out of Doris' hands. Water flew onto the mirror, the counter, and the floor.

"Mrs. R., Mrs. Fishman. Please. Sit down and be quiet. Only ten in the morning, ladies, please," Doris said.

"Whoever it is, he's handsome as hell," Mildred said. Both ladies were at the window, peering out, Mildred with a head full of foil and blue tint on the cotton near her ears, and Beatrice's head decorated with curlers.

"He can't see us like this!" they both said in unison and hurried to hide in the back of the shop.

Doris turned to look. Whoever it was, he was coming this way. Toward the salon? Toward Dan's next door? The ladies were right—he did look a little like Brando. She smoothed back her hair, threw off her apron, came to the front door, made it jingle.

The man stopped, mid-stride in the middle of the street. "Doris!" he called. "Doris?"

Brando or not, Doris didn't know him but it didn't matter. What a gorgeous man.

"Go talk to him! Bring him inside! Give him a do!" Beatrice cried from the back of the shop.

"Ladies, please, some decorum," Doris answered. But still. He was calling her name. She stepped out onto the sidewalk.

"Doris!" the man cried again.

My turn, it's my turn, finally, Doris thought. My prayers have been answered. I've been rescued from a lifetime of the blue-rinse set by a guy who looks like Brando. And in a limo, too! She moved farther out onto the street.

Two police cars screeched to a halt in front of the shop, lights flashing, sirens blaring.

Linda Kettleman was emerging from the cruiser, a few steps away from Doris, who was now in the middle of the road. The man stepping forward, calling her name.

"Doris, stop!" Officer Kettleman cried.

Doris, puzzled, shifted her gaze from the man to the cop and back to the man again.

"Go get him, Doris!" the ladies at the salon were outside now, cheering her on. "You go, girl."

"Bernard, quick," Officer Kettleman called.

The cop from the other car hurried up to the man who looked like Brando. "Mr. Henderson, sir."

The man stopped, blinked, saw the two uniforms in front of him. "Doris?" he asked in a small voice.

"If you wish," Linda said, and escorted him to Bernard's cruiser. She walked back to Doris who standing in the middle of street, gasping for breath. "He's on his way to Unit B," she said.

"So sorry, Doris!" Mildred yelled from the front door of the shop. "Guess it wasn't really Brando."

"I really did go out with Brando, once," Beatrice said. "Even if you don't believe me. I have a picture to prove it. Want to see?"

"How can I resist," Doris said, following them back into the salon. It was going to be a long week.

From the Sheriff's Calls Section of the Point Reyes Light
February 13, 2014

TOMALES: At 11:19 a.m. a woman reported that doctors had injected the top of her head with pure surgical acid or LSD. She asked to be airlifted to Stanford Hospital, but agreed to ask her neighbor to drive her.

Calling Sugar

"Have you ever heard about that—surgical acid?" Thomas asked Justin. They were sitting out in front of the bakery in Tomales trying to decide whether they should head down to Dillon Beach. Thomas took a bite out of his sticky bun, looked over at his friend.

Justin thumbed his finger on the wheel of his father's Audi. "More fruits and nuts than ever, Thomas. They don't have crazy people like this in Cambridge."

Justin was home on spring break. The open hills of Western Marin County pleased him no end—such a change from Cambridge where he shared a suite with an Indian kid from Karachi, and two Asians from Shanghai. Snow, cold, ice, slush, and sleet. He was glad to be in Tomales, on familiar ground.

"Its lysergic acid—you know, Thomas, LSD. It was started at Harvard, in the early 60s." Justin flicked hair back from his forehead.

Thomas sighed. His best friend had moved away and thought he knew everything. With his snooty ways and 'know it all' attitude. Maybe it had been a stupid idea to come to the beach. The once beautiful day had turned into clouds—a mackerel sky, he called it. No rain, just bright light. "So, Justin, what are the girls like out there?"

Justin smiled. He smoothed his fingers over the pages of the *Light*. "I think my mom might know who this is," he said, peering closer to the paper." She knows some old hippies who never moved on."

"But this woman is crazy, Justin. Just plain nuts." Thomas tapped his fingers on his iPhone. "Send me her picture."

"The girl in Cambridge?" Justin answered, thinking about the sophomore he'd met at Starbucks on Church St. Blond, curves, and brains. Weren't too many of that type in West Marin. He grinned. "Or the crazy woman from here?"

Thomas laughed. "What I don't understand is, this woman's friend. She agreed to drive the lunatic to Stanford. Whatever for? Couldn't she just put down her cup of coffee, and say, hey, Franny, Eunice, come on, snap out of it?"

Justin grumbled. He was taking psychology 101. "They don't recommend telling people who are crazy that they're really crazy. Just go along with it, they say."

"You think so?" Thomas finished off his sticky bun. He would order another but they'd sold out. Again. "So, really, if I was off my rocker, you'd drive me to Stanford? Tell the guys at the ER that doctors had injected the top of my head with LSD?"

"I wouldn't do that," Justin said.

"I didn't think so. So how empathetic are you, anyway?" Thomas asked. Ever since Justin had left him on the beach, alone, with the cops, he'd had his, well, doubts about him. "Told you you were a heartless ass."

"Thomas." Justin let out smoke from an electronic cigarette. He thought they made him look cool.

A thundering noise came up the road. And another and another. All Thomas could see were motorcycles. They all pulled in front of the bakery, down the side roads, their engines purring in soft contentment. You're too late for sticky buns, he silently cheered.

"Thomas," Justin repeated. "First, you're not crazy."

"Oh boy, here it comes." Thomas, feeling bitter, was waiting for the normal lecture from Justin on how to get his shit together. He was working on it, wasn't he? Two classes at College of Marin, he got his license back, and his girlfriend was, well, gone. "Go ahead, asshole, tell me again what to do. What to do with my life—since you've done such a good job on yours."

"Going away to college is a different experience than going to a JC. Thomas, if you had just tried in high school."

"Just 'cause your dad is on the Ballet Board—that's right, isn't it? He works for Twitter. You're rolling in money, that didn't hurt either." Thomas' parents were struggling, they always had, two teachers in elementary school, four kids. He hadn't helped matters by getting all those speeding tickets either.

"You didn't have to keep driving off the road," Justin said, watching one of the motorcycle riders take off his helmet. Holly crap, this one was a girl. A blond.

"It was you who kept pushing me to go faster, Justin."

"Well, well, well," the blond motorcyclist had been eyeing Justin. She came over, flipped her long blond hair from one shoulder to the other. "Ever been on a Harley?" She set one leather bound heel on the Audi's front right tire. "Are you boys going to pay attention to a pretty girl—or are you, you know, one of those?" She batted her eyes.

"Sugar! Get over here," bellowed one of the motorcycle guys. "Leave the boys alone."

Sugar heaved a sigh, turned away from Justin and Thomas but not before she pulled out a card and let it flutter onto Justin's lap.

He looked at it, at her, but she was lost in a fog of exhaust and rumbling engines and sped down Route One.

"See? Just what I told you," Thomas said. "You're just a lucky kind of guy. You lead a charmed life."

Justin beamed.

"So, I should tell you that didn't just happen, that some blond bombshell in a motorcycle gang didn't just give you her card?"

Justin fanned himself with her card. "She could've just as easily given it to you."

"No. She didn't. Your fantasies come true, Justin. I just live in the reality of life. Junior College. Marin County. Work and school. What else is new?"

"And if I told you that your dreams do come true, if you dream them, if you just set goals, if you just get it together, Thomas." Justin examined Sugar's card, wrote her phone number in ink on his palm. He lost things, usually; he wasn't going to lose this.

"If I have fantasies about Harvard, then, it'll come true, Justin?"

"Didn't hurt me," Justin said, puffing himself up again.

"Like that poor lady whose head is full of LSD. Her fantasy, it's a little odd, wouldn't you say? Her fantasy is coming true, then, she's going to the hospital?"

"Stanford, she's going to Stanford, Thomas. Dream and dream big. Get there any way you can. Worked for me. Now," he paused, "are we going to the beach or not? Otherwise, I'm calling Sugar."

From the Sheriff's Calls Section of the Point Reyes Light
February 20, 2014

SAN GERONIMO: At 11:12 p.m. a passerby asked deputies to check on a barefoot woman in a red dress walking down the highway.

Monsters in the Living Room

"Do you think that was Mrs. Willis, Fred?" Mildred asked.

Fred had been dreaming. He'd been riding a horse bareback through downtown Point Reyes Station. He woke with a start. "What is it this time, dear?"

Mildred tightened the buttons on her bed jacket. "It's that Mrs. Willis. She's crazy, walking down the road, in a red dress, barefoot. Why can't she stay home like normal people, Fred?"

"Normal people sleep at this hour. If you keep me up, I'll go to the guestroom. I need my beauty rest."

"You? Beauty rest? Ha!" Mildred caught her breath. "Hey, Fred, should I put cucumbers on my eyes again? Beth Cristensens at Doris's says it works great." No sound from his side of the bed.

"Fred?" she asked again. "You listening?"

Fred moaned, turned over, tried to go back to sleep.

"That Mrs. Willis scared the hell out of our Alice," Mildred stated. "Six months ago, she called the cops on her and everything."

Fred tucked his head under the covers. Maybe he wouldn't hear her. Maybe he wouldn't be able to breathe. "Sleep, honey?" he ventured.

"Why would she be out there barefoot, I mean, in the middle of Drake? That old bag usually wears pedal pushers—with pink puffballs on the toes, I bet. But a red dress? I don't know what the world's coming to." She thrummed her fingers on the bedside table. "Fred? You listening?"

"Not today, not tomorrow, not any day."

But Mildred was on a tear. "Fred." She turned to him, lifted the covers off of him. "Fred! I'm talking to you!"

He sat up in a hurry. Without his glasses she was a blur, but a blur he knew well. "What's the matter?"

"Listen to me! This is important! When I was mean to Mrs. Willis, I called her names at the Station House. Now—I'm sure I caused this, I made her lose her mind." She spun through the bedroom like a terrier. "I made her go crazy."

"The only person you're making crazy is me. Now, get back into bed. Better yet, get into bed in the guest room."

"My, oh my, it's Mister Cranky-Pants. It was the onions, wasn't it? The onions in the salad. I told you not to eat them."

Fred moaned. "Sweetheart." She never listened. She wasn't going to start now. "Go downstairs, have a glass of milk."

"It's dark down there."

"You've lived here for forty years; you know the way."

"With monsters in the living room? Rats in the kitchen? Deer on the couch, watching me? Their little tails flicking flies? Never."

"Mildred, you sound like Mrs. Willis."

"What? How could you?" She turned on him, sudden tears coursing down her cheeks. "I've fed you thousands of meals. Thousands ...."

"Meals I could barely eat," mumbled Fred.

"What did you say?"

"Nothing, dear." Just 'cause he couldn't hear her didn't mean anything about how well she could hear him. She could hear him opening a beer from a block away. "I'm going next door to the guest bedroom. See you in the morning." He held onto the doorknob. "Goodnight, darling," he said and slipped out. The floorboards creaked under his heavy footfall.

Oh Heavenly peace. He hesitated. Silence behind him. Silence beyond. Golden.

He tucked into the guest bed. Cold, scratchy, flannel sheets covered with little pills. He'd warm up if he stayed really still. He curled up into a ball as if he could, as if he were still a boy. Tried to catch that dream about a horse. He could feel the reins, hear the sigh of the horse pulling up in front of Cheda's, the warmth breath in the cool morning air. Although this breath was no horse. This breath smelled of onions, and from what he could remember, horses never ate onions.

"Sweetheart," Mildred planted a kiss on his warm cheek. "Sweetheart, I'm lonely. It's cold without you."

"Then come on in," Fred sighed, pulling up the covers. It was a single bed, he took over the whole thing, but there was room, wasn't there, for his little wife?

She slipped in, unaided, tucked under his shoulders, and whispered in his ear. "In the morning, can you take me to town, so I can buy a red dress, darling?"

"You want shoes too?" Fred asked.

"Of course. Pedal pushers, pink ones, with fluff balls on the toes. You think they have them at Cabaline?"

From the Sheriff's Calls Section of the Point Reyes Light, March 20, 2014

INVERNESS: At 9:49 p.m. a vehicle drove into a telephone pole, but kept on driving.

The Telephone Pole

"I wouldn't be so stupid as to drive through a telephone pole. Didn't they see it?" Lulu was sitting at the Fairfax Roastery with her best friend Sasha, sharing a double decaf caf cappuccino.

"Maybe they were loaded, or maybe they were thinking about their boyfriend," Sasha suggested. "Or maybe someone cut them off or maybe they thought they were lost." She giggled.

"You're kidding, right?" Lulu replied.

"Lulu." Sasha stirred their coffee with a wooden stick.

"But seriously, Sasha. The drivers? Out there? They're crazy? They drive while talking on their cell phones! They put on makeup at red lights! Or shave! All kinds of stuff." Lulu noticed a man at the adjacent table. He looked like one of them. "My dad said to keep an eye out, and I do, I do."

"For you or for them?" Sasha asked.

"For everybody!" Lulu cried. She peered out the window at the late afternoon traffic, everyone heading home, everyone heading to the Valley, everyone heading to Nothing-To-Do.

"You want to go to the movies, we can go all the way to Sausalito," Lulu said. "Then I could get more driving practice."

"We could stay local," Sasha said. "Then I could be home in time for dinner."

Lulu couldn't remember the last time anyone had made her dinner. She usually scrounged around the refrigerator and settled on hot dogs and beans, or mostly beans and popcorn. Mom had left years ago, and Dad, well, she saw him twice a month if she was lucky and he was sober. He was probably looped again and passed out behind the Woodacre Market. "Hey Sasha, we could see a Marvel movie. I mean, if you could, which character would you want to be?"

"In the movies? Peter Pan!" Sasha exclaimed.

"But that's ages ago," Lulu replied. "Think of something this century, Sasha. Quit living in the past."

Sasha couldn't recall. As far as she knew, she loved the old days. She wore 70s clothes with lots of fringe, and bell-bottoms and wedge sandals and spent hours trying to make her hair look like Farrah Fawcett's.

"Let's blow this joint," Sasha said suddenly. A man had come in who was staring at her. Wearing old clothes was her thing, but for some horny old toads, it made them want to pick her up.

"But I'm not done with our cappuccino," Lulu complained.

"Put it down, just put it down." The creepy guy was preparing to sit down beside them, unpacking his computer, his cell phone, looking at Lulu, pulling out his wallet. And smiling.

The girls took the back door. "Ever driven Bolinas Road?" Sasha said. "We can hike up to the lakes."

"You want me to go? Hiking?" Lulu asked. "Just last week there was a mountain lion sighting," She grabbed Sasha's arm. "I don't like wildlife."

"You'll be okay," Sasha said.

"If you say so," Lulu said, but she didn't feel okay.

"It's so narrow," Lulu said, grasping the wheel with both hands and peering through the windshield.

"There's lots of room," Sasha said until Lulu swerved when she crossed the yellow line on a turn.

"Stay in your lane," Sasha ordered.

"But I can't."

"Yes, you can," Sasha said.

Lulu drove slowly, unconvinced.

"A little higher. Here, now turn left onto Sky Oaks Road."

Lulu turned onto a narrow one lane road, with a huge drop off on the left and a cliff on the right. She slowed to ten miles an hour. "This is worse! We're going to go over!" She stopped the car.

"Lulu, don't be silly," Sasha replied. "Another car could be coming along."

"Where do they pass? Oh my God."

"Just keep going, Lulu. Sometimes when you're scared, it's not really that big of a deal. Just keep going and it will pass."

By the time they got to a level spot, Lulu's T-shirt was damp.

"Five minutes from here. It's easy now," Sasha said. "You ever been up here before?"

"Here? Why would I?" Lulu asked, looking at a dirt parking lot, other cars and endless hills.

"Just take a walk with me, Lulu, you'll like what you see," Sasha said. She loved the lakes for their pristine beauty, their silence, the water. The birds. "Look."

As they walked up a dirt road, Lulu thought Sasha had lost her mind. They were going to the end of nowhere. But when they came to the top of the hill, she could see a dam and the wide spread of the lake, hills rising around them, and Mt. Tam, towering in the distance.

"See?" Sasha said. "It's my favorite place."

"I've never seen it. And so close too. When I was a kid, my father never took me anywhere."

"So, now you can," Sasha said. "You can drive me up here anytime."

"And how are we going to get back down?"

"Carefully," Sasha said. "Leave it to me."

"You're going to drive?" Lulu asked.

"Me? Hell no. Driving scares the hell out of me. I could run into a telephone pole or something, Lulu."

Susanna Solomon

From the Sheriff's Calls Section of the Point Reyes Light, March 26, 2014

BOLINAS: At 6:33 pm the gardener of a Terrace Avenue house reported that someone had broken in, leaving water in the bathtub and the television on.

A Thousand Little Lies

"So? I needed a bath, Officer." Norman Hubert pulled himself up to his full height of 6'-1". He read her badge.

The police lady, Officer L. Kettleman, frowned. "Sir, this isn't your house. You can't just come on in and use someone else's tub."

"Nora said it would be okay." Norman threaded his belt through his blue jeans. That tub had been nice; first bath he'd had in weeks.

"And Nora is?" L. Kettleman pulled out her pencil and steno notebook.

"My cousin," Norman said proudly. "She's a beaut."

"Ah, I see. And this house is hers?"

"Oh, I wish. And she wishes too. She would love it. You see, she's housing challenged like me. She would love a tub, but she said, 'You go on ahead, Norman and be first. I'll be back in a little while.'"

"Then she's a housekeeper?" Linda asked, licking her pencil.

"Well, she would be right proud if she was, but no, even though she's probably good at cleaning houses, she doesn't move very well, on account of the polio. You remember polio? You're probably too young, perhaps. Lucky for you."

"So, you're saying Nora has nothing to do with this house?"

Norman buttoned up his shirt. "It's tough out there, ma'am, for both of us."

85

"This is private property, Norman."

"So? What's the problem? The house is clean, the owners are away, what would they care about a needy person using perfectly good equipment that was going to waste? I'll wash the tub when I'm finished, Officer, I am a tidy kind of guy."

"Not today, not tomorrow, and not yesterday."

"Ah, c'mon."

"If you please, your license, Norman."

Norman buttoned the new cranberry-red shirt he'd found outside the thrift store in town. He looked good in it: it set off his white hair.

"Sir. License?"

Norman grinned, pulled out his empty wallet. "I haven't driven in years." He picked up his dirty shoes and jacket. "I bet you bathe regular-like, have a nightcap, sleep nice and cozy." He gestured outside to a drizzling rain. "Do you blame me for wanting the same?"

"There are shelters, Norman, San Rafael. You can bathe there."

"There are crazy people there—dirty crazy people—and besides," Norman eased into his worn-out tan Birkenstocks, "no tubs. Last name's Snively, if you still want to know."

"Thank you, Mr. Snively. You'll have to come with me." She stood tall and proud. "No funny business. No running. No talking."

Norman eyed the white sheriff's car with the badge on the door, the hard plastic seat in back, the barred windows. No way was he getting in.

He took off, charged across the street into an oak forest, poison oak be damned. He ran into prickly bushes, through great swaths of blackberries, and deep into the woods. He heard the cop call him for the longest time, her regulation boots pounding sand, gravel and dirt, her voice an irritant to his calm and gentle spirit. And then she was gone.

When it was completely quiet Norman made his way to a deer trail, back onto the dirt road, and onto Terrace Avenue again.

He was just filling the tub for the second time and was reaching for bubble bath when he heard someone out front. A salesman, probably. They'd go away. Norman poured three capfuls of Lemon Delight bath balm into the tub, turned on the TV, admired the bubbles, and climbed in. If they were going to chase him all around hell and gone, he'd return to the scene of the crime. No harm in that. The cops never came back.

Over the noise from a talk show, he didn't hear a key in the lock, the click of the doorknob, or the sound of feet coming into the master bedroom.

He'd forgotten to lock the bathroom door. He buried himself under the suds, just a bit of his white hair in the foam, and held his nose.

The bathroom door opened with a swish.

"Honey, turn off the TV, please," a voice said, an authoritarian voice, a voice with dignity and power.

Norman kept still.

A hand slipped into the tub.

Norman hoped it would not come too near.

"Nice," the voice said.

Norman heard clothes drop. And without making a sound, he pulled his legs over to one side.

It was a woman, by the feel of her slippery skin.

"Hello," she said, easing in. "I thought you'd never come, Albert."

Norman stayed still.

"How sweet of you to run a tub for me, darling. Now, come here."

This time, Norman did as he was told.

From the Sheriff's Calls Section of the Point Reyes Light
April 14, 2014

SAN GERONIMO VALLEY: At 3:03 p.m. someone reported that a naked man and woman were running around a neighbor's property.

Let's Dance

"Oooh, ooh, ooh, Fred, do you think it was Mrs. Willis who called that in?" Mildred peered out the kitchen window. "Nothing that exciting ever happens around here."

And for that Fred was thankful. "Have a sit down, take a load off."

"Not with my bridge party tomorrow." She hustled around the room. "You think I should go out there and take care of things, Fred?"

"Honey, the only people you need to worry about are me and Alice."

"She's in San Geronimo Valley staying with that Beth-Ann. You got the car keys?"

Fred had hidden them in the freezer. She kept on wanting to drive in the middle of the night, so he had to find the places she wouldn't look. But she was getting wise to him. She'd checked all his shoes and was at work in the veggie drawer. "Yes, dear. I'm ready when you are."

"Hey Fred, how about you and I run around naked?"

"Dear. No." Fred climbed out of his recliner, carefully this time, stared at his wife's dancing ox-blood Oxfords. "Take a breath. Keep your clothes on."

"Oh, to feel spring air on my ...., Fred, it's been years."

"What has?"

She dropped a five-pound bag of flour on the counter. "Yes, Fred, I was one of those. Skinny dippers."

"Everybody skinny dips at Bass Lake. Despite what they say, the water is quite clear. You can see everything ..." Oh, how he wished he were seventeen again. He'd had Elizabeth Lopez completely convinced he couldn't see anything through the brackish water, but he could and he did.

"Not just Bass Lake." Mildred giggled.

"Where? With whom?"

"A lady never tells tales out of school."

"After fifty years you can't tell me your deepest darkest secret?"

"Who says it's my deepest darkest secret? You seen the molasses?"

"You mean, you still have secrets you're keeping from me?" he asked, feeling shaken. Had she found another man and been unfaithful—did they do the nasty in this house, in his bed? "Running around naked is not an appropriate exercise for adults, dear."

"What do you know?" Mildred spun through the kitchen. "Now, help me find my recipe book. Make yourself useful."

"You've got me all in knots. Mildred, you're eighty. What are you keeping from me?"

"But I did. The bagman at the Palace Market, he was the first; I never did get his name. Then the postman. He comes over when you're sleeping or watching baseball. The Bronson boys, twins, cute as hell, thirty-six years old and they adore older women. Three times I met Bart at Divide Meadow. A little bit of a walk, but you can step into the bushes quite easily. You remember that time I had poison oak on my particulars?"

Fred had gone white. His beloved? Prancing around the park in her birthday suit? Coming on to half the men in Point Reyes Station? Would he be the laughing stock of the whole community? He threw down his paper, slung himself up from the recliner. "You have no shame."

"Oh Fred." Mildred tightened the straps on her apron and laughed. "My dear darling Fred, of course I didn't do any of those things," she giggled. "Sweetheart, I'm as faithful as the sun, I rise and shine every day. I would never do anything to hurt you dear; I was just fooling."

"It's nothing to laugh about," Fred said, his hand on the front door jamb. "We took vows."

"Of course we did, honey, a thousand years ago. You were there, remember?"

"Of course I was there, Mildred, don't be silly." He pulled up the waist of his pants to just above the middle of his belly. They slipped down otherwise—maybe it was time for suspenders? Nah, he'd look like an old fart.

"Isn't it okay to dream?" She reached up on her tippy toes to kiss him on his ear.

He stepped forward. "I dream too, you know."

"About other women? How dare you?" She pulled back one hand to slap him.

He caught her arm. "Not so fast, sister."

"Okay. Have it your way." She bent down, untied her Oxfords, her back creaking. Unsteady, she grabbed the counter for balance.

"Need some help, my love?" Fred asked, giving her a hand.

"My dress is just one zipper, Fred. Everything comes off real easy. Come and join me outside—and make it snappy, pretty soon it's going to be too cold to dance."

Susanna Solomon

From the Sheriff's Calls Section of the Point Reyes Light, May 15, 2014

CHILENO VALLEY: At 6:25 p.m. a man reported that his brother, who is in a wheelchair, hit him in the head with the bristles of a broom.

Twenty-Two-Twenty-Seven

"Let me read that to you again, Fred," Mildred said, fixing her hair and looking in the drop-down mirror in the visor.

"Who said what?" Fred jammed the car into second. Ever since he'd sold his Buick—with air-glide ride—over a year ago, he'd had to drive their VW and the transmission was sticky. They were heading to see an artist in Inverness Park and he didn't like the narrow roads at all.

"The guy was in a wheelchair, Fred." Mildred thought they both were going to be in wheelchairs before the day was up if he couldn't get the car up a short, steep driveway. "And the guy hit him with a broom."

"What was that street number again?" Fred asked, grinding the gears.

"Twenty-two-twenty-seven." Mildred tapped her finger on the GPS Janet had given her for her birthday. "This thing says we're in Contra Costa County."

"The East Bay?" Fred slammed on the brakes, dropped into a pothole and gunned it. Dirt flew out from under the tires.

"Woops. No. Marin County," Mildred giggled. "Point Reyes Station."

"But we're in Inverness Park."

The road was narrow, dirt and overgrown. Fred got to out to check. The driveway ahead turned into two ruts. Cowpaths, indeed. He walked back to the car and leaned in the window. "Now what, smartie-pants?"

92

"I was just reading something in the *Light*. You don't have to get so upset. It was just another of those Sheriff's Calls."

"Get out." One more minute with Mildred and he thought he would knock her silly. He tightened his hands into fists. Oh God, how could he think about being so cruel?

"Of the car? Why?" She batted her eyes. Her long eyelashes had always been her best feature, but now they were kind of straggly. They didn't seem to work on Fred.

"Twenty-two-twenty-seven?"

"We're not going there today. Or anywhere. We're trapped, unless," he rested his hands on the window, "my sweetness, you can direct me out?"

"And put down my knitting?"

"I told you not to knit in the car. Those needles are dangerous. They don't let you fly with knitting needles."

"No reason to be fresh. I'm in a car, not a seven-forty-seven."

Fred slapped his head with his hand. If he insisted on her help, she'd put them further into the bushes.

"Hey there!" someone yelled.

Fred was relieved when he saw an ATV approaching, throwing up dirt.

"Howdy," a man said, tipping his fedora. "You're blocking the road. I'm late for church."

"At three in the afternoon?" Fred asked.

"Vespers."

"Vespers is early out here." Fred scratched his head. "We're stuck. Can you help?"

The guy in the fedora was cute, Mildred thought, with that chin dimple she liked so much on Robert Mitchum. She wondered if the guy knew him.

"What are you guys doing all the way up here?"

"Twenty-two-twenty-seven," Mildred said brightly. Fred was always telling her she kept forgetting things, but she remembered that.

"Way down the bottom of the hill," the guy said. "I'm Wendell. Wendell Butler."

"Have we met before, Mr. Butler?" Mildred asked, pressing her hands on her curls.

"Fred," Fred said, taking Mr. Butler's too-warm hand. "Do you mind helping us?"

"Should I ask your wife to get out?" Wendell asked, peering through the window at a woman in a flowered hat.

"Do you value your life?" Fred asked.

Together Fred and Wendell pushed the VW beyond the pothole. Wendell gestured for Fred to take the seat of his ATV while he got in the car. Wendell drove the VW into the bushes, backed it into some trees, all the time Mildred saying, "Oh me, oh my," and covering her eyes, until Wendell got the car turned all the way around.

"Fred," he asked, "can you make down from here?"

Fred ran his hands along the handlebars of the ATV, caressed the light, the wide seat. "Could I drive this, please?" He'd always dreamed about riding a motorcycle until Mildred had put a stop to it, years ago. Now was his last big chance.

"Are you sure?"

"Wendell," Fred sighed. "I've been driving for more than sixty years. You reckon I can handle a wussy single-cylinder engine with four fat tires?"

"Just go slow, then, please," Wendell said, "and follow me. Let me start it for you."

With a whoop, the ATV came alive under Fred's seat and he felt like he was twenty again; an engine thrumming under his loins and Mildred was, well, with another guy and life was great.

Mildred was very careful not to look Wendell in the eye. "You know how to drive a stick shift, sonny? My husband's always grinding the gears. Old Darlene here, she can't take it."

"Smooth as rain," Wendell said, easing the car into gear and jerking down the rutted dirt road.

"How well do you do with wheelchairs, Wendell?"

"I wouldn't know. My Grandma lives in Louisiana."

"I just turned eighty," Mildred said. "But I feel twenty." She adjusted her Peter Pan collar. "They say, sooner or later, I'll be in a wheelchair."

"That's too bad, ma'am," Wendell answered, negotiating a tight turn and hoping the old man, behind him, wouldn't run into him with his own ATV.

"Oh—there's twenty-two-twenty-seven," Mildred chirped as a bright yellow mailbox flew by.

Wendell pulled the car to a stop 50 feet from the main road in Inverness Park. "Can you get there from here?"

"I'll ask him." Mildred marched back to find Fred on the ATV, his face flushed.

"What a ride, what a ride," he mumbled, letting the engine rumble underneath him.

"May I drive?" Mildred asked.

"What? No. Never. You can drive a wheelchair."

"But I'm ambulatory."

"So?" Fred said.

"Fred, the keys. Please," Wendell asked, feeling proud he'd helped someone this week. Now he could tell his mother he wasn't the selfish jerk she always said he was.

Fred hesitated. He was hearing the rumble from the ATV. He was Paul Newman, cruising the back roads of America on his Harley. He climbed off the ATV, sadly.

"Thank you for your kindness, Wendell, and thanks for the ride." He walked back to the VW where Mildred was already inside, the *Light* in her hands.

"When and if I'm ever in a wheelchair, Fred, I'm going to carry a broom. That's the only way you'll ever listen. I've been calling your name for over an hour and you haven't been listening. Shall we go to twenty-two-twenty-seven, now that we know where it is?"

But Fred didn't answer. Back in the VW, he slid the clutch into first, carefully and slowly moved out onto Sir Francis Drake Boulevard and turned right. He thought he remembered where he'd stored his old videos. Paul Newman had always been one of his favorites. "Shall we watch Paul Newman again, dear?"

"With eyes like his, I can't resist," Mildred said. "If you make popcorn, I'll promise to never hit you with a broom when I'm in a wheelchair."

"Well, that's a relief," Fred said, speeding up to twenty-five.

From the Sheriff's Calls Section of the Point Reyes Light,
May 29, 2014

STINSON BEACH: At 2:45 p.m. a man said his marijuana business partner had taken twenty-seven of their plants without his consent.

Twenty-Seven Plants

"So, who would even do that?" Lulu Garcia asked her friend Sasha. They were sitting in front of Toby's, in the sun, after going swimming in the creek. The heat felt good on Lulu's shoulders which were still damp from her hair.

"You mean steal plants? Or call the cops?" Sasha asked.

Lulu was wearing Capri pants, Birkenstock sandals with socks, a T-shirt that said "I Write For Food"—Sasha guessed it was Lulu's dads—and a straw hat with a droopy red flower. Sasha had talked to Lulu about her clothes once, but Lulu hadn't explained properly.

"Were they twenty-seven plants out of like, fifty, or a thousand?" Lulu asked.

"Does it matter, Lulu?"

"Well, yeah, it matters. If it was just a few plants then the partner took almost all of them. That would be devastating. But if, like, there were, you know, a thousand plants, then maybe it wouldn't matter so much?"

"Why call the cops, then?"

"Well, yeah ... but," Lulu said. She knew about grows, because that was what her Mom did. Mom was a big grower. Crew of five, usually. Any loss was a terrible thing. But if the partner in this grow called the cops, would someone call the cops about Mom? Lulu had been a trimmer, one summer, until her hands hurt and bugs got into her eyes.

"Would you call the cops if someone stole your dope?" Lulu asked.

"I don't carry more than a little bag. Not enough to go to jail," Sasha said.

She seemed distracted, eyes focused on a boy on the table over. Lulu checked him out, muscular under his tight-fitting T-shirt. Nice.

"They'll arrest me if I carry any more," Sasha said. "I bet the plants were for medicinal uses. That's why they called the cops."

"My mom says ..." Lulu said.

"Someone robbed your Mom?" Sasha blurted out.

"Why do you ask?" Lulu said, taking out her gum. Bubblicious, spearmint or cinnamon, all gums lost their flavor after an hour. She carefully squished it into a ball and stuck it on the underside of the table where there were so many. Gross. She choked. She'd touched them.

"What's the matter? Catch your finger on a splinter?" Sasha asked.

"No, no, of course not," Lulu answered, looking furtively around the picnic tables.

Sasha waved to the boy.

"Sasha, you don't even know him," Lulu said. She only went out with boys she knew and there weren't very many boys who liked her in town. Even up in Forest Knolls, pickings were kind of slim.

"What I don't understand," Sasha said, tracing letters in the picnic table with her pinky. "If I were the one growing pot ..." she stuffed the rest of the cookie in her mouth.

Did she know? Lulu decided to keep quiet, very quiet. Mom always said silence was best, even at home, especially at home.

"I wouldn't call the cops," Sasha said, finally finishing her cookie. "I mean, really, unless it was legal— you know— grown for patients. Then it's different."

Lulu didn't know different. All she knew was Mom's obsession, meeting people at all hours, her care with the mother plants, the misters, and all those hot lights.

The guy rolled a cigarette and gathered what he'd spilled and put it in a pouch.

"Do you think he's smoking pot?" Sasha asked. "Do you think he wants to share?"

"Doesn't smell like it. But you go ahead, and ask."

Lulu, disgusted, stood and stretched. All she knew was that Sasha was kind of loony. Chasing boys, smoking tobacco or God knows what else in front of Toby's, not knowing enough to be silent. "See you later, Sasha," she said, and walked down the street.

"Wait! Lulu! Don't just leave me like that!" Sasha called, running up beside her. "Did I say something to offend you?"

"You have boys to chase, Sasha. I have stuff to do."

"No big deal," Sasha said. "I kinda know him. He lives in Stinson."

"That's where they said the pot was stolen," Lulu said, wondering how she was going to get home. She'd forgotten to meet Mom at the market again.

"Yeah," Sasha said, slipping her arm through Lulu's and sidling up to her. "A lot of pot farms are there—even your Mom's."

Lulu stopped, looked at her friend, her supposed friend.

"Its old news in this town," Sasha said, "but I wasn't the one."

"The one? The one who what? Did you steal the plants? Called the cops? Keep your voice down." She pulled her friend into the Building Supply parking lot by the piles of fencing. "Who told you about my Mom?"

"I had to, Lulu. I had no choice." Sasha sniffed back tears.

Real tears, Lulu thought.

"My Mom's desperate. We haven't been able to make rent for months. What else was I supposed to do?"

Susanna Solomon

From the Sheriff's Calls Section of the Point Reyes Light, November 26, 2014

BOLINAS: At 12:34 p.m. someone reported that a construction sign at the entrance to town read, "BEACHES CLOSED, ZOMBIES AHEAD." (Deputies noted that the sign was coming down.)

Zombies Ahead

"I don't think that's a very good idea," Beatrice said as Doris fluffed her smock. "You never can tell about Bolinas—visitors need all the warning they can get."

"It's a joke, Mrs. Fisher," Doris said, pulling a comb through the elderly woman's very fine, very white hair.

"It's not a joke. They're making all kinds of movies about zombies and vampires and the walking dead," Beatrice replied, standing up and throwing off her smock. "Pay attention, Doris. One of these days a zombie could be coming after you."

Doris sighed. Wednesday before Thanksgiving. She had a long schedule and Mrs. Fisher wasn't helping in the least.

Beatrice sat. She'd seen the movie posters, she'd seen those ads. "If they're not real, Doris, then why are they so popular? People aren't afraid of stuff that's not real, usually."

"Lots of people are afraid all the time," Mildred said. She'd been sitting under a dryer and her head was pleasantly baked along with Beatrice's mind. "I'm afraid of heights, Doc Martin's afraid of dogs. And Hortense, she's afraid of everything. She's been in bed for a week."

"She's staying away from the zombies," Beatrice said, satisfied.

"Anyone in to see her? She's getting on, that Hortense. Not good to be a shut-in. You think she's all right, Mrs. Rhinehart?" Doris asked.

101

Mildred snorted. "Anyone seeing wild-ass colors in her bed would also see zombies." She touched her hair. "Doris, come and get this junk out of my hair."

"Mrs. Rhinehart, Mrs. Fisher, give me a minute, please," Doris said, going out of the shop and enjoying the beautiful warm day. Outside was grand, and fresh and full of flowers, while inside was, well, different. She turned around and went back in. "Mrs. Fisher, let me tend to Mrs. Rhinehart a moment."

"Did you see that?" Mildred peered out the window of the salon. "People in costumes and it's not even Halloween."

"They were zombies," Beatrice said. "I told you so."

"No ma'am," Doris said. "It's our officer, Linda Kettleman. She always dresses in costume."

The ladies giggled, went back to their chairs. Beatrice picked up her knitting.

"Just a trim, Officer?" Doris asked. "Take a seat."

"What's the reason for the quiet, ladies?" Linda asked. "Usually, it's as noisy in here as the Station House on a busy night."

Beatrice held her hand over her mouth. If she mentioned zombies again, they might take her to Unit B. They'd taken her cousin Julian there last week and he'd only been talking about ghosts— "Maybe it was the yelling that did it," she said suddenly.

"Yelling?" Linda asked, adjusting her gun belt and standing up. "Who was yelling?"

"No one, really," Beatrice chirped up. "We were talking about," she lowered her voice, "zombies."

"Officer Kettleman, Mrs. Fisher has lost her mind," trilled Mildred who, noticing that no one was paying attention, buried her nose in a copy of Vogue.

"Oh, you mean that sign in Bolinas, Mrs. Fisher?" Linda asked.

"Need highlights today?" Doris held out her comb. The law was something she took comfort in, the law came first, but today, the law was slowing her down. Her planned close at two p.m. was rapidly approaching. The sooner she got started, the better.

"Mrs. Fisher is a sane as my own mother," Linda said, lying. Her mother had been nutty as a piece of pecan pie since last Christmas, though her private life was no one's business but her own.

"Mrs. Fisher believes in zombies," Mildred said.

"Mrs. Rhinehart, Mrs. Fisher, enough," Dories said, accidentally poking herself in the hand with her scissors.

"I only wish I'd written all those books about zombies," Linda said, staring out the window. Point Reyes had its own source of lunatics, but zombies, never. "I'd be rich and I could move to the country."

"But you already live in the country," Mildred snapped. "Point Reyes Station is an itty bitty town."

"But it's not Bolinas," Linda said. "Less people there."

"But more zombies," Beatrice said, clapping her hands.

"Exactly," Linda said, looking in the mirror at her new haircut. "Sounds like it was time I got down there, don't you think?"

**From the Sheriff's Calls Section of the Point Reyes Light
May 29, 2014**

POINT REYES STATION: At 9:21 p.m. illegal revelry was reported.

Calling Me Home

"And what might that be, Beth-Ann?" Alice asked. The girls were watching TV at Alice's grandmother's house on the Mesa and there was nothing on. It was quiet. Grandma and Grandpa had gone to bed hours ago.

"Revelry? Sounds like a party to me," Beth-Ann giggled. "Where did you say it was, again?"

"Not too far. On the Mesa, somewhere," Alice replied, throwing down the remote. At least at Mom's, there was HBO and Showtime. At Grandma's, only thirty channels and half of them were in Spanish.

"I know a boy with a car, you know Jason, he'll drive us," Beth-Ann said.

"He's got a mole on his cheek," Alice said.

"It makes him look cute. Toss me my cell phone— or better yet, press five and say hello. He'll be curious."

"Jason's twenty-five."

"So?" Beth-Ann twirled a strand of hair around her finger while she took the phone from Alice.

"Way too old for you," Alice said. "Don't."

"I matured early." Beth-Ann put the phone down. "At least that's what my mom says. He's not answering. I'll text him."

"What are you going to do when you're twenty, date guys in their forties, and when you're thirty, date older guys—like in their eighties?" Alice asked, but it was serious, this stuff. Beth-Ann was always pushing her age.

"Okay, no go. He's not answering. How 'bout we go to the Western?"

"I can't. My grandpa, he'd kill me," Alice answered. She stood up, scattering popcorn kernels off her sweater. "We're kids, Beth-Ann. No one will let us in there anytime. Besides, I don't have any money."

"I don't need cash," Beth-Ann answered. "I have my iPhone."

Alice walked around the crooked glassed-in porch. If she dropped a tennis ball, it would roll into a corner, under the couch. She bet a whole bunch of stuff had gone in there over the years.

"We're wasting time," Beth-Ann said suddenly. "There's not only revelry, there's illegal revelry. Do you think there's music, dancing, a DJ, boys? Couldn't we just try and find it?"

Alice threw on a sweater, opened the front door to a pitch-black Point Reyes night. Branches swung in the breeze and twigs clattered to the ground. "I'm not wandering around Point Reyes at this hour to try to find a party."

"Wuss." Beth-Ann stood next to Alice. She was holding a foot-long mag flashlight. "I have one for you too." She handed Alice a pocket flashlight. "The Mesa's not that big. No one would party downtown. All we have to do is walk around and listen."

Alice stood silent outside the front door. She heard crackling in the woods off Mesa Road, the swish of an owl across a field. Something fluttered near her ears. She ducked.

"Bats," Beth-Ann said. "They won't hurt you."

"I know that," Alice said. Still, they were creepy. They headed down Mesa Road. A few lights burned from distant houses, but they were far away and through more trees.

Alice's tennis shoes crunched gravel.

"Can you hear the party yet, Alice?"

Alice couldn't hear anything. Just her heart about to burst in her ears.

"No one gives a party like Jason's brother Chris. His place is on Cypress. This way. There's a shortcut."

Alice followed Beth-Ann's voice. Her feet were no longer on asphalt, but on a dirt path. She turned to look back at Grandma's house. The light was distant and growing dim.

"Hurry up!" Beth-Ann shouted as Alice made her way slowly. Her flashlight illuminated only a foot or two past her toes. Beth-Ann, with the bigger light, trotted on ahead.

"Beth-Ann!" Alice cried. "Wait up!" She watched her friend's light bounce, drift, and then disappear into the woods. "Beth-Ann?" Alice held her flashlight in front of her, the narrow beam fading into a yellowish spot. "Beth-Ann?" Alice whispered. "You there?"

Her flashlight went out.

Alice fumbled with it and slammed it against her palm. The light came back on. She was standing on a slightly worn path, in a clearing. All around the trail was a carpet of dead oak leaves. She remembered what Grandpa said. When lost, turn around. Stay safe.

Alice pivoted 180 degrees. Her feet were lined up with the trail. She stepped from the clearing back into the woods. The path led through a copse of cypress trees and meandered a little bit. Up ahead, the lights of home. She could do this.

"Beth-Ann?" Alice cried in the darkness. No answer. She kept her head down and looked at the ground. Two paths diverged. Which way had she come? One led to the darker woods, the other a path to a house, perhaps. Wasn't that Grandma's porch light?

Alice stepped forward, moving slowly. Five feet later, her flashlight dimmed and went out again. She unscrewed the back of the flashlight. A gasket, a spare light bulb, and the batteries scattered to the ground. She dropped down on all fours, patted the earth and leaves around her and found the gasket. But the spare bulb? The batteries? She picked up twigs, ends of branches, hopeful each time turning them over in her hands and placing them back down on the side of the path. Darkness enveloped her. Crouching on the ground with the remnants of the dead flashlight somewhere at her feet Alice felt like crying. A little bit. But she knew better. Crying never fixed anything. She rose, thinking hard. Which way? Which way? She put out her hands. Tree. Not the path. Put out her hands again. Another tree. And the area in between? The path? She wasn't sure.

She heard the hoo hoo of an owl in the branches above, wished she had their eyesight. Wondering about mountain lions, she knew she couldn't stand still.

Her eyes slowly adjusted to the darkness. One solitary light, one faint yellow light. A house? Perhaps. Not a street light—her town didn't have any. She peered through the trees. Whatever lay in front was civilization. Home. Safety.

Putting her hands out cautiously and moving her feet slowly, she realized at this rate, she'd get to the house by midnight. No. Best to walk as fast as she could.

Keep an eye on the light, she told herself. Her bare legs brushed against thorny bushes. She couldn't go around or she'd lose the light. Alice scraped her way through. Her leg hit something hard. Looking down, seeing nothing, she felt a branch. Yes, there it was, knee high, crossing her path. She struggled to get over it, holding onto the trunks of adjacent trees until her legs were clear. And there, still, the light, calling her home.

Something howled. It was a creepy sound, but Alice relaxed. She'd heard coyotes all her life. She stepped forward, feeling confident, and brushed up against something else. A log? She extended a hand. Met with a growl, the flash of green eyes, pupil-less. A hurt coyote? Alice stepped back, around, tried to locate the light. Walked into a couple of trees. Where had the light gone? The coyote continued to growl. Branches pulled at her sweater, the ground under her feet fell away. "Beth-Ann!" she shouted. "Beth-Ann! Where are you?"

Light exploded in her eyes. She jumped back, tried not to fall. "Beth-Ann?"

"What are you doing out here in the dark?" a man's voice answered.

"There's a hurt coyote, just back there. My flashlight went out."

"Where is it?" the man asked.

"If you take the light out of my eyes I can show you," Alice replied. "You're blinding me."

"Oh, sorry," the man answered. "I heard crackling in the forest." He put his flashlight under his chin lighting his face from below. "Don't worry, it's me."

"You look like a ghoul. Who's me?" Alice asked. She pulled up a branch to defend herself.

"It's Jason. Beth-Ann's friend," he said, holding the flashlight at arm's length and illuminating his face properly. "You must be Alice."

"What are you doing out here?"

"Finding you. Now follow me."

"Look, I don't want to go to any party anymore," she said. "I want to go home."

"That's where we're heading," Jason said, slowly and carefully taking them back to the clearing.

Alice felt vulnerable. She didn't know this Jason at all. What if he was a bad guy? What should she do if he attacked? Run? Where? She tightened her grip on her branch. "You seen Beth-Ann? If she's missing we'll have to call the cops. It's impossible to see anything out here."

"I got the call and missed it." Jason's light bounced a little away from her, turned and settled on Alice's hands. "Don't worry, she's fine. She got spooked and went back to your grandma's house. Called me. She was worried about you."

Alice kept her hand on her branch.

"Here we are."

They came through the last branch of a gnarled cypress tree. A lit porch lay ahead, with two, no, three figures on it. One large, one small, one running toward them.

"Alice! Oh Alice! We were so worried about you!" Beth-Ann shouted, running up and hugging her.

By the time Alice stepped up on the porch, she was expecting a lecture from Grandma and Grandpa. Instead, they stood tense, Grandma in her flannel lacy nightgown, Grandpa in his plaid pajamas and flannel robe. Both of them held flashlights and wore glasses.

"Scare the hell out of me, child," Grandma said, putting her arm through Alice's. "Come on in, and thank you, Jason."

At the doorway, Alice felt herself stopped short.

"What were you thinking, my dear, going off in the woods in the dark?"

Alice opened her mouth, took a look at Beth-Ann who was staring at the porch floor.

"I heard something cry out in pain and went looking it," Alice said. "There's a hurt coyote out there."

"That's my girl, my animal lover," Grandpa said. "But next time—tell us first, okay?"

"Anyone want biscuits?" Grandma said, leading them into the kitchen. She glanced at Alice, at Beth-Ann. "And whose idea was it, then?" She scraped blackened blobs onto a plate.

Alice looked at Beth-Ann, at Jason's mole.

"It's okay, girls," Grandma said. "Better to eat a biscuit than get eaten by a mountain lion. Now, Jason, Alice, show me that hurt coyote. I think he may have had a little too much revelry for one night."

From the Sheriff's Calls Section of the Point Reyes Light, July 4, 2014

INVERNESS: At 8:08 p.m. someone saw a white man in a red shirt driving a blue Saab while holding a pitcher of beer in his hands.

Independence Day

"It's not the Fourth of July, Fred, so why would anyone dress up in the old red, white, and blue?" Mildred asked. She was busy cleaning up the kitchen—Hattie, oh bless her heart, her little Hattie was coming over today.

Fred snuffled awake. He'd been dozing—his favorite pastime since he'd retired from Western Pacific a decade ago. "What's that you said?"

Mildred sipped her tea. It was late, but she'd finally made the perfect cup. "In the paper—there was a white man in a red shirt driving a blue car," she giggled, "or was it a blue man in a white shirt in a red car?"

"Blue man? I saw them on TV, but I didn't think they were real." Fred had been daydreaming about Sophia Loren; what a woman. Mildred, she wasn't, how could he say it nicely, not quite the same. Years ago, he'd taken the wrong turn with Mildred or her with him. Half the time he was not only on a different track, but in a different time zone.

"Fred, she'll be here within the hour. I told you last week and again today while you were brushing your teeth. And you still don't remember?" She fussed with her rolling pin. Cookies or pie? She couldn't remember which one was Hattie's favorite. "Maybe you don't want to see her? How could you not want to see our little girl?"

"Hattie's always been the difficult one. The other kids have always been much more sensible."

"But I miss her the most. What's her favorite? Coconut, chocolate, strawberries, banana cream?" Mildred didn't have any of the ingredients but that didn't matter. She still had time to send Fred to the store. She paced through the tiny kitchen and looked out the window at her neighbor, the nosy Mrs. Willis who was on her hands and knees in the garden. Chasing snails again?

"Any kind will do, I'm sure, sweetheart. It's the thought that counts." Fred wasn't quite comfortable with his little fib, but if it made his wife happy, it was worth a go. She was an agitated little hen.

Mildred pulled the kitchen curtains shut. That doggone Mrs. Willis had noticed her. "Fred," she spun on her heels. "Do you think Hattie will like my new hairdo? Doris did it special."

Fred watched her pat her thin, wispy, mostly blue hair. "She'll love you no matter how you look."

"How could you be so mean?" She marched into the bathroom prepared for war. Grabbed a lipstick, a bright red one. That doggone Fred wouldn't know beauty if it bit him. She began to feel better. Maybe a little more rouge? A darker pencil on her thin brows? More lipstick? Hattie had always loved makeup. That Fred. He didn't know anything. She charged back into the living room. "This messy house will never do. Hop out of your recliner and help me tidy up. She can't see us like this."

"I don't hop, dear, you know that." His corner of the living room was tidy. As for clean, he wasn't so sure. But at least his five years of *Sunsets* were boxed up and in the garage, his *Field and Stream*, *Garden and Gun*, and *Fishing Forever* in stacks by his feet.

"Honey, Hattie doesn't care. Take a load off. She knows us. Remember?"

"She hasn't been here for ten years, Fred. Things change. You know that."

Fred didn't think anything changed. Mildred was the same, bless her little heart. She'd missed her mouth with her lipstick, again. He was the same, mostly, too, except for his belly, which had kind of grown over the years. But still. Not seeing Hattie for ten years bothered him a bit. She only lived in Palo Alto, for goodness sake. "She'll be as glad to see us as we are."

But Mildred wasn't listening. She was thinking color. Blue scarf over her white hair? She checked the hallway mirror. No, better yet, white scarf over her blue hair. Doris did love her dyes. Maybe not blue enough? Maybe she should go in again.

She circled the living room. Something was not right. "I thought so." The afghan she'd made when Hattie had been a baby was stretched over Fred's ample form and full of holes and stains. "Hattie will think I don't take proper care of you." She snatched it off and marched into the back bedroom to hide it.

Fred suddenly felt cold. He sat up gingerly, hoping not to break the recliner again. His bare toes twitched. It wasn't a cold day, just a little chilly with the fog coming in over Inverness Ridge. Now that his wife was gone, he took a long sip of the Negra Modelo he had in the side pocket of his recliner. Hattie, indeed. She knew how they lived. Big deal. He strolled over to the mantel to look at her picture from grade school.

She'd been eight. Hazel eyes, twinkling little nose, inquisitive eye, and holding their cat Morgan a little too tightly. Typical Hattie. Always wanting to see how things tick. And next to that photo, Peter. The frame was dusty, as was the table holding all the kids' photos from when they used to go to Chicken Ranch Beach and try to dig holes to China. It seemed like last week. That was the last time when he could remember everything.

He paced the small cabin, feeling like a stranger, or even an intruder, he wasn't sure. There were sweaters in the sink—not sitting in water, but stacked and folded by color and size. He peered into the oven. Eight empty Straus milk bottles were set in rows of four, along with full bottles and a slab of butter. Feeling a touch of trepidation, he jerked the icebox open. Bowls of cookie batter were splattered with something green. Why hadn't he noticed? Why hadn't he helped her? He was in the middle of carefully pulling the sweaters out of the sink when he heard her behind him, tapping the floor with her cane.

"And what do you think you're doing, buster?" she asked, hands on her hips and her delicate feet set wide. "My kitchen, my property. God says. I saw you..."

"But, but...," Fred sputtered, holding the sweaters.

"Put them back."

He held his hands over the sink. "Here?" he croaked.

"Where else do you expect me to put clothes? Honestly, what were you thinking? I had everything just perfect—and now, now," she snuffled back tears. "You've gone and messed everything up." Crying, she headed to her straight back chair and dug into her knitting basket on the floor.

"Wait, honey, but —," he pleaded.

"But nothing. Sit. In your recliner. TV and sports, that's your job. Kitchen and the rest of the house, my job. Keep yourself to yourself and we'll get along fine. So everything comes back to me, doesn't it?"

Fred set the sweaters back gingerly. "But sweetheart."

"But sweetheart nothing," she snorted.

Dear God, where had she been washing their dishes?

Fred backed out of the living room, out the front door, turned and climbed the steep stairs up to Dream Farm Road to see their neighbor. Jake was a young doctor; maybe he knew things. As for Fred, he could no longer drive at night—things jumped out at him and he didn't know whether they were real or not—and, as for the phone, he couldn't remember where Mildred had hidden it.

He was opening up his neighbor's front gate when he heard wheels crackle gravel behind him. They were nice wheels—Pirellis, and a nice car, blue with white trim. A woman in a red dress looked out, a woman who did not look like Sophia Loren at all. A woman with a twinkly nose.

"The roads up here are worse than I thought," she said.

"Hattie?" He squinted. She sounded like Hattie whose voice was usually distorted over the phone from whatever she was. She traveled a lot. "You've driven this road a thousand times, sweetheart," he called out, eager to see her, eager to fold her in his arms.

"Your daughter said I could find you here. My GPS got all screwed up. You're missing street signs, the roads go all over the place and they're dirt. Mr. Rhinehart? Mr. Rhinehart?"

But Fred was not listening. He was stuck on the word "friend". "Where's my Hattie? She in the back and I can't see her?" He peered into the car.

"She sends you her regrets," the woman said. "But she asked me to bring this." She climbed out of the car, pulled out an enormous red, blue and white bouquet and held it out for him.

"Tell her we don't want it," he said and turned his back, and, holding onto the banister, too dizzy to descend the stairs, kept thinking. Oh God, oh God, what am I going to tell Mildred?

Overheard in front of Toby's, July 20, 2014

POINT REYES STATION: "Goats are cuter than bulldozers, any old day."

Goats

"They said that?" Fred asked, raking dry grass into a pile. The firemen had requested that homeowners clear 30 feet of brush from all sides of their houses, and Fred had tried. Boy had he tried. But the hillside had a bit of a slope to it and Mildred kept coming at him with suggestions and ideas. This one involved goats.

He struggled to stand upright. "I mean how do you handle them?" He wiped sweat from his forehead. He didn't want animals, for Chrissakes. "And what about your roses, my dear?" he ventured. With her, he had to ask about everything. He stepped around a pile of brush. He would be making progress, if there hadn't been any wind, but now grass stalks and all kinds of detritus were taking off along with his hat. That he grabbed. "Well?"

"I didn't read it in the *Light*, Fred, if that's what you asked," Mildred replied. "I do read other things, you know." Fred hadn't done much, just move some grass and weeds around. "It's my bridge party, this Friday, Fred. Looks like a tornado came along out here. Do something."

Fred smirked. Of course she'd say that. She was sitting under an umbrella, on their one and only patio chair, nursing an iced tea, and he was the one, out in the sun, sweating bullets. "Mildred, can you come help me?" He knew better. She was making one of her faces. She waved her cane at him, buried her nose in the paper, and snorted.

Goats? Maybe not such a bad idea. A whole passel of them, eating their way through the poison oak, the blackberry bushes, the four-foot-tall grass? She wouldn't mind goats? He'd call Doc at Building Supply. It would be fun to hear those little bells, see those cute faces, munching everything in sight, munching what, beer cans? His hidden stash? Never.

Mildred was snoozing in her lawn chair. He hesitated to wake her, remembered. She was always waking him up when she had some cockamamie idea. Fair was fair. Before he decided what to say, he sat down with a groan on the picnic-table bench, managed to find the only splinter, and rose with a howl.

"What is the matter with you?" Mildred clutched her newspaper to her chest. "You scared the hell out of me."

"So did the splinter," Fred answered, rubbing his backside. He sat down, more carefully this time. He said, keeping his voice even and calm which made her quiet too. Oh how he loved her, loved her more when she was still.

"No, no goats, they're horrible animals. All that poop," he said.

"Don't you want all your troubles to go away, Fred?"

"Of course, dear," he sputtered. If she only meant her indigestible cooking he'd be set. "But I've got stuff out there, stuff I need to save."

"Like what?"

"What the hell," Fred huffed, tired of her complaints. "Why don't we get a bulldozer and clear out the whole goddamn thing?"

"That'll take the house down," Mildred replied, horrified. "It wasn't built right, and the living room slopes like hell, but its home —at least to me," she sniffed. "You can move out, if that's what you want. Forget the bulldozers, forget the goats. If you're going to be like that, go. Leave an old lady to fend for herself, then."

"I love our little house," Fred said. "I built it, remember?"

"How can I ever forget? Every time I bake a cake, the layers come out all crooked." She slammed her newspaper down on the table. "Be practical, Fred. Clear all that junk from the yard. The wind's died."

"But dear."

"But dear, nothing, Fred. Get the goats or hustle."

Fred sighed. He'd never be able to do it all himself. He'd call Doc at Building Supply. But later tonight, while she was asleep, he'd sneak out to the yard in his pajamas, robe and mag flashlight, and remove his beers. That is, if he could remember where, exactly, he had put them.

From the Sheriff's Calls Section of the Point Reyes Light, November 6, 2014

BOLINAS: At 8:56 a.m. the bar reported that two men, one with a frying pan, were verbally harassing customers.

Flynn

"It wasn't me, Officer," LeVaundre Flynn said, smoothing down the stray hairs on his mustache as the cop entered the bar and customers scattered. "I was just here, watching these guys, minding my own business, and wow. This time of day, you have to be so careful."

"So what are you doing holding a frying pan, mister?" Linda asked, and stood in the tough-guy position, legs apart, and hands on her equipment belt. She leaned back a little, making them think she wanted to be in charge. As if. She'd been up half the night with Bernadette, who was six months old and teething.

"Flynn," LeVaundre answered. "LeVaundre Flynn. Those two guys were drunk, you see, ma'am, and a fry pan, that could be dangerous, and I asked them to hand it over. No worries." He placed the pan on the counter. "You know a gal named Nell?"

Deputy Linda Kettleman tapped her chin with her pencil and pulled out her steno notebook. Two drunks, one man with a frying pan, eight in the morning at Smiley's. When did the bar open, six? And already a fight. She wished somebody would close the place down.

She knew the two drunken white guys, Roger and Paul Millner, two useless brothers who'd taken a left turn off of Highway One in the '60s, headed to Bolinas, and never looked back. They stared at her with a blank look and started for the door. But this black guy? He stood his ground, looked her right in the eye.

"I live in the City, Officer. Mission District. Want to see my license?" LeVaundre was used to cops. He always wanted to stay one step ahead of them, give them what they needed before they asked. If he kept up his good behavior, he'd break his own record and stay out of jail a whole year. He straightened his shoulders. All was good, except he was alone in a bar with a cop, and a heavy cast-iron frying pan stood between them. "You think someone was cooking eggs?"

Linda walked around the bar, feeling officious. Didn't anyone ever go to sleep in this town? "Mr. Flynn. There's been a complaint. Now that no one is here, you can tell me what happened. Let's start with the basics. Where are you staying?"

LeVaundre would say Nell's place but he couldn't remember where it was. Besides, he'd been stoned then too, and the details were, well, a little fuzzy. "Nell's," he said and rocked back on his heels. "It's up the hill." He gestured wildly, a little too wildly and the next thing he knew he was sitting in the back of the police car. "How can I help you, ma'am?" he asked politely. Holy shit. All he wanted to do was get laid and now he was going to jail?

"Mr. Flynn." Linda ran his license. He was on probation. But there was no crime coming to Bolinas that she knew of. This time she'd been fast enough to check him for weapons before folding him into the car. Walt would be proud. "And you got here, when?"

"Last night," he said, not wanting to lie. Otherwise she'd ask, you really got up at 6 a.m. and drove here from the City in the dark? "I stayed in the campground."

"Olema?" she asked, making a note.

"Yes," he answered, though it hadn't been there at all, it had been here, on the beach. By the naked-lady sculpture. Where the hell was Olema? "Camping stuff in my car."

"I see."

He watched her punch something into her computer.

"You've been in Bolinas before?" she asked. "How'd you find it? The locals hid the sign years ago. Their little joke." She tried to place him. Where'd she seen that face before?

He just stared back at her, his eyes blank.

She adjusted her rear view mirror, couldn't see enough, turned around and studied him.

"Mr. Flynn. Start from the beginning. The altercation was last night? This morning?"

"Early, it was early. Today, at breakfast," LeVaundre answered. "Hence the frying pan," he said, feeling clever.

"Who was fighting over what?"

"Two guys, fighting about potatoes."

"Potatoes? Why?" The longer she worked in West Marin the less she understood.

Hell, it wasn't potatoes; one of them had shorted him on some weed. LeVaundre wasn't dumb enough to carry his own into Marin County—there was plenty enough to go round in Bolinas, enough for everyone. Twice over.

The back doors of the police car had no handles and the seat was hard plastic. He yearned to get out, walk the beach, watch the seagulls, and find Nell. But first, a restroom; God's little sense of humor was working overtime.

Linda saw him squirm. "I have no grounds to arrest you, Mr. Flynn, unless you give me cause. Was anyone hurt? Anyone swing that pan?"

"When I entered the bar, Officer, someone was, indeed. He was holding the frying pan over his shoulder. You could see he was not having his best day. I asked him to hand it over, and I almost dropped it on my foot it was so heavy. Then someone screamed."

"That so." She tapped the computer screen.

"I guess it was that thin guy making all the noise. Anyway, there was another man, a white man, leaning against the bar. He seemed to know the bartender. Why? What would make him so frightened? I was wondering about that ..." he trailed off, though he knew full well why. Armed black man, drug deal gone south, bar, morning. Drunks. He hadn't had much except one very powerful spliff. "But the other guys, they'd been drinking whiskey, seemed like they'd been doing that for a while." He put his hands in his lap and waited quietly.

"I know those other — ." Linda stopped short, feeling a lurch. Someone was knocking on the rear fender. She turned around to check.

It was the two drunks, the Millner brothers, tapping and swinging and kicking at the tires, starting at the back and coming up to the driver's window. They leaned in.

Shit! LeVaundre thought. They could say anything. He tried to wave them off.

"LeVand! My man! Going to the clinker? At this hour? Hello, Officer." The brothers sauntered off, almost tripping over a sleeping dog in the street.

"Mr. Millner!" The cop shot out of her car, leaving her keys in it.

LeVaundre kept an eye on those keys. He could split like right now, no one would ever know—but. But.

"Millner!"

The Millners stopped.

LeVaundre leaned toward the front of the car. Easy, easy! The keys were just swinging there. Right next to her rifle. He slipped his hand over the top of the bench seat.

There was only so much of this he could take. Soon, he would bust out. Soon, he would have to. Two drunken guys, one meaty—but female—officer. He reviewed his options. His rap sheet was as long as his leg, but nothing big on it, nothing to bring him back to jail, not yet anyway. Had he broken probation? He went through the list; firearms, yes, two feet away; fleeing the country, yes, crossing into Marin; contraband, uh, yes, nothing he was going to show her. If he tucked his stash under her driver's seat, she'd find it. He stuffed it farther down his pants.

"Flynn!" She turned, eyed him, leaned into the car, and grabbed the keys. "You want to go to the station, like right now?"

"No, ma'am."

"The Millner boys have spent a lot of time in jail. I see by your rap sheet you've been a guest of the state too. Enjoy it much?" She'd have been there too, if Dad hadn't bailed her out. Funny though, in that one night, she'd fallen in love with the procedure, rules, uniforms. The law. And the weapons.

"Yes, that's true, ma'am, but I've changed."

"I've never heard that one before." She laughed.

"Beautiful little town," he said. The bag was deep in his front pocket. Might as well enjoy his last few minutes of freedom. He watched the Millner brothers drift back into the bar. If he hadn't been such a dufus, he could have joined them.

"But in this case."

"Yes, ma'am?"

"There's nothing I can hold you with. Today." Maybe, with her little act of kindness, he'd turn his life around too.

"And?" he looked at her eagerly through the rear-view mirror, his hands folded in prayer.

"You know how this usually turns out?"

"Only too well, ma'am."

She expected him to get belligerent, but he looked at her with soft, sweet, brown eyes. Her baby's eyes. She'd waited months for the agency to release her sweet girl. If she could finish up here, maybe she could ask Walt for the day off. Take Bernadette to the beach, pretend she got another felon off the streets. But first, she had to be a cop.

"What the hell were you thinking, Mr. Flynn, brandishing a frying pan? Don't you know people call the cops for less?" She drummed her fingers on the wheel. "From now on, Mr. Flynn," she opened his door. "Stay out of Bolinas."

"Yes, ma'am."

"And next time you're doing drug deals ..."

LeVaundre blanched.

"... Don't bring a frying pan."

"You got it," he said and ambled away, trying his best not to run.

Behind him, Linda stood, stretched, and watched him go. Walt had been bugging her to be more vigilant and she had, hadn't she? As she watched the sun rise over Bolinas Lagoon and giggling children come to the beach to play, her computer screen, in the car, came back to life. Line by line, slowly at first, a black face filled the screen, a black face with familiar sweet brown eyes. Wanted, the crawl across the bottom of the photo said, alleged car break-in at Stinson. Yellow 458 Ferrari Spider. That car filled the screen. Less than an hour ago. Be careful.

By the time Linda got back to her cruiser, the computer had gone dark again and there was another call, this one from Olema; a deer was injured by the side of the road.

Not wanting to let the animal suffer, she made a U-turn, took off up Route One, her equipment belt on the seat beside her and her rifle loaded and ready to go. She passed a yellow car heading to the beach. "Nice," she said and shot up the hill.

From the Sheriff's Calls Section of the Point Reyes Light November 13, 2014

NICASIO: At 5:54 p.m. a woman reported that a man she lives with had assaulted her; deputies dismissed it as an argument between "non-dating sexual partners".

Partners

"What's that you said, Mildred?" Beatrice asked scooching over in her chair at Doris's place and adjusting her hearing aid. She had heard the word "sex" which always brightened her day, but the words "non-dating" bothered her.

"It's these goddamn kids, up to no good." Mildred sniffed. "In my day, people asked first."

"Asked about what?" Doris piped up.

"For a date," Mildred replied. "The man put on a jacket and tie and asked for a date. He —Fred, my Fred— asked my dad first."

"The world has gone to hell in a basket," Hortense said. "Sex without dating. What's it for, then?"

"Damned if I know," Mildred replied. "All the restaurants are going to go out of business —no reason to take a girl out at all. Just take her home, then wham, bam, not even a thank you ma'am."

"But they move in together, Mrs. Rhinehart," Doris said. "Cozy, I'll say." As if she knew anymore. She hadn't had a man in her house for months, and that was Doc's helper, fixing her toilet.

The beauty salon was quiet a moment. Beatrice, nearing 100, tried to remember what sex was. The word kept making her feel bright and free and no more than 80, but she couldn't remember if it was a new exercise or a fad.

Mildred snorted. "But why get married then? Why buy the cow if you can get the milk for free?"

"You talking about livestock, girls?" Beatrice chirped.

"No," both Hortense and Mildred said.

Beatrice frowned. She had missed the bus, again? Doris froze. Hortense agreeing with Mildred? They usually argued like old hens.

"Did you hear the rest of it, Hortense that the guy was wailing on her?" Mildred asked.

"The guy was crying?" Beatrice sat up. "In my day, men didn't cry."

"That's not what she meant," Beatrice and Hortense said.

Doris adjusted her mirror. No telling what these ladies would do if they got agitated. Only last week, Hortense had threatened to throw her solution at Mrs. Rhinehart.

"If the guy is hitting her, why would she give him sex?" Hortense asked. "That doesn't make sense to me. My Harold—he'd never hurt a fly."

"Your Harold was a wuss, Hortense."

"He was a gentleman, Mrs. Rhinehart. Not like your Fred."

"My Fred?" Mildred rose on her tippy toes. "You dare insult my Fred? At least he's alive, you old bat."

"You didn't have to remind me." Hortense blurted out, face covered in tears. It didn't matter what happened these days, tears came unbidden and unbound. "You just wish you got some, you old hag."

"Ladies, please." Doris put down her scissors and her comb. The two slender-as-beans customers were circling each other in her tiny shop.

"A parade!" squealed Beatrice. "How I love a parade!"

"It's not a parade, you tri-colored myna bird," Mildred said. "It's a fight. Keep yourself to yourself and no one will get hurt." She slipped her hand inside her purse.

"You think she's armed?" Hortense whispered to Doris. "I heard she's been having a love affair with firearms."

"Mrs. Rhinehart, you all right, ma'am?" Doris asked. "Would you like a glass of water? Tea? Whiskey?"

"Got my own." Mildred pulled her flask out of her purse. She took a long sip, noticed the other ladies' white faces and wide eyes. "What's the matter, you want some?"

"Time to close, girls," Doris said.

Mildred squinted into the mirror. Something was definitely wrong. "Not on your life, Doris. You can't send me out into the world like this."

"But you look so sexy, Mrs. Rhinehart," Beatrice giggled. "Maybe you'll get picked up by that stud-muffin Kelly who works at Cheda's."

"He's not even twenty, Mrs. Fisher. Get a grip."

"Bet he wails real good," trilled Beatrice.

"Did you forget your Xanax, Beatrice?" Hortense asked.

"I don't have to take drugs—I'm no pill-popper," Beatrice said. "The nerve." She stood up, gathered her purse and things. "Next time, Doris, make sure they're not here when I have an appointment." And without another word, she marched out of the shop.

Mildred and Hortense looked at each other and laughed. Doris moved her solution out of reach.

"So who do you think is going to win the World Cup this year?" Hortense asked.

"I hate baseball," Mildred said. "Hand me the *Light*, Doris. I want to read what else it says. What do you think we'll see next? Naked men wandering through downtown?"

Doris didn't want to say she'd seen that just last week. She pulled out her hand mirror, handed it to Mrs. R., and pivoted her chair. "You like it?"

"Seems like yesterday, my sweetheart was courting me, Mrs. Rhinehart," Hortense said. "He was lovely. He brought me flowers."

"And what came next?" Mildred asked.

"I'm not telling." Hortense giggled into her hand.

"No surprise there," Mildred snickered. "I remember. You didn't show up in town for a week."

Susanna Solomon

From the Sheriff's Calls Section of the Point Reyes Light
December 12, 2014

INVERNESS PARK: At 10:59 p.m. a call came in on a rainy night from an empty Sunnyside house.

Ellen Lipsak

"So, who do you think made that call?" Thomas asked. He was sitting on a bench just inside Toby's Feed Barn looking through the *Light*. It was raining slightly. He pulled his sweatshirt tighter and jabbed his finger at the newspaper.

"I wasn't in Inverness Park. I was at home, studying," Justin said.

"Studying?" Thomas took a long sip of his coffee, a taste that had taken him years to like. "During vacation?"

"You wouldn't believe the amount of homework I have to do. Enough to make you weep. Two novels a week for English One-Oh-One. How am I supposed to do that when I'm at school, attending classes and chasing girls?" Justin pulled out a dog-eared copy of *Madame Bovary*. "This story's too goddamn long."

"What's it about?" Thomas couldn't remember when he'd read a novel all the way through. Tenth grade. Maybe.

"Adultery," Justin said.

"Adultery! How could that be boring?"

"They take so long to explain everything. So, why not, love? Why not short sentences, like, "So, you want to, you know?""

"Let's rewrite it, like it's a text," Thomas suggested.

"Like C U 2 nite?" Justin laughed. "The whole Harvard curriculum in text, four pages for your B.A., six for your masters. Ten for a PhD."

"Wouldn't that be crazy?" Thomas asked. "Maybe they'd let me attend too."

131

A blonde, about sixteen, came in out of the drizzle and headed for the coffee bar. She was wearing pink high-heel boots, skin-tight blue jeans and a sexy smile. Justin whistled. "A week 'til Christmas and look what Santa just brought." He stood up.

"Whoa, college boy. My turn." Thomas slapped Justin's shoulder, and walked right over to the girl.

"Miss?" Thomas said, startling the blonde who was digging into an enormous purse. "Let me take care of this for you." He jammed his hand in his pocket, pulled it out, scattering coins across the hay-covered concrete floor.

"Butterfingers!" Justin laughed.

"Thanks." The blonde leaned over, making Justin swoon.

Thomas scrabbled for change and, with his hands full of coins, got in line at the coffee bar. "What'll it be?"

"Oh, a fat-free iced caramel macchiato." She perused the short menu. "Uh, no, double shot Americano."

Thomas' eyes felt as big as moons, his heart bigger. This gal was beautiful—eyes like the color of the sky, perky nose, and built. "Are you a local?" he asked, putting out his hand. He knew better. Of course, she wasn't a local; she was God's little Christmas present.

Suddenly, there was a commotion at the roll-up door.

"Heavens, Fred, it's too early to get a pop at the Western," said an older lady who bustled up to the line, eyed Thomas and the blonde, and elbowed her way in front.

The old lady looked vaguely familiar. The one time his parents made him go to church, maybe? Ah, under her fold-out plastic rain hat he recognized Mrs. Rhinehart, one of the women in his mother's gardening club, Digging with Dolores. "Mrs. Rhinehart, hello."

Mrs. Rhinehart opened and closed her umbrella quickly, spraying water on Thomas' gray sweatshirt. "Pardon me, sonny boy. I was here first." She charged ahead.

"Not on your life," the blonde said, nudging her hip into the older woman. "Beauty before age." She leaned toward the counter, blocking the old lady.

"Uh, no, it's age before beauty, miss," Mrs. Rhinehart said, pushing back.

"Are you, like, kidding me, Grandma?" Almost a foot taller than Mrs. Rhinehart, the blonde looked down onto the elder woman's scalp. "Don't you recognize me? I'm Ellen Lipsak, poster girl for ARF, Animal Rescue Foundation."

"So? I'm Mrs. Rhinehart, Mrs. Fred Rhinehart. Go to the back of the line."

The clerk behind the counter, about to take orders, backed up in the tiny shop.

"Look lady, I don't care how old you are. Get your elbows out of my ribs."

"Get offa me!" Mrs. Rhinehart shrieked.

Justin, from the picnic table, whispered, "C'mon, Thomas. Show us what you're worth."

Thomas stepped aside, practically knocking over a small metal rack full of copies of *The New York Times* and the *Point Reyes Light*. Chivalry eluded him; he had no idea what to do next. Besides, both of these women were armed: Mrs. Rhinehart with her umbrella and purse and Ellen Lipsak brandishing her own giant bag.

"I've killed little old ladies before—you won't be the first," Ellen spat.

"Liar," Mrs. Rhinehart shouted.

"Wanna bet?"

Mrs. Rhinehart tightened her knobby knuckles around her umbrella handle and lifted it over her head.

The light rain intensified.

Thomas watched as the women circled each other in front of a pair of Adirondack chairs. The women gave dirty looks to anyone who wanted to intervene.

"You ... you ..." Mrs. Rhinehart was incensed.

"Put a sock in it," the blonde said, still circling.

Something caught the corner of Thomas' eye; an old man, round and tall, rolled into the open-air café. He had an air of resignation about him. His jacket was unzipped and his hat, an old fedora, was askew. When he saw what was going on he picked up speed. The rain came down harder.

"Mildred. Dear."

The old lady stopped, poised, her umbrella over one shoulder, her purse over the other. "Fred?"

"Come on, sweetheart, your favorite show is on."

"What? I'm in a fight. Stay out of it, buster."

Ellen, seeing an opening, charged forward.

Mrs. Rhinehart, in total surprise, stumbled back.

"Mildred! Be careful." The man charged into the fray, wrapping his bulk around his wife's shoulder and pulling back at the same time.

"But ... but ...but," Mrs. Rhinehart stuttered. "Fred, don't."

Ellen set down her bag, ordered, gathered her coffee and change at the counter, turned back around. "Steamed milk, ma'am?"

"Uh, okay, sure," Mrs. Rhinehart blinked. "Goes well with whiskey." She pulled out her flask.

The man led his wife to the bench. "Boys?" Both Thomas and Justin gave up their seats and leaned against the inside wall of the barn.

"Oh my, oh my." Mrs. Rhinehart fluttered her hands. "I haven't had this much fun since Mrs. Ferguson's cow chased you out of our front yard, Fred. Too bad you tripped."

"That was fifty years ago, Mildred," Fred said, dropping his head in his hands.

"You got pets?" The blonde sat down with everyone else at the picnic table, handed over a mug of steamed milk, took a sip of her coffee. "Hey, how long you guys been an item?"

"Too long," Fred said. His wife swatted him on the arm.

"Just kidding," Fred said. "I'm Fred." He put out his hand.

"Ellen Lipsak. From New Jersey. Nothing comes between me and my coffee, sir, not even someone as pretty as your wife."

"I told you I still had it, Fred." Mildred beamed.

Ellen leaned forward. "So, what kind of animals do you have, folks?"

Thomas took a quick look at Justin, shrugged his shoulders, and started walking toward the back of the barn where a door led to the street.

"Not our day," Justin said.

"Chivalry's dead," Thomas sighed. "I was so close."

"Chivalry's not dead to me, boys," Ellen Lipsak said, running up to them and slipping an arm through each of theirs. "So, you guys know of any place where we can have some fun?"

"Like Madame Bovary looking for an empty house?" Justin asked, not believing his luck.

"You bet. If there's a party on, who needs coffee?"

From the Sheriff's Calls Section of the Point Reyes Light
November 20, 2014

OLEMA: At 6:48 p.m. deputies removed a small bag of carrots from the road.

Carrots

"Oh, Doris," Mildred exclaimed as she turned over the last page of the *Light* and sat down in a chair for her weekly cut and curl. "Someone out there lost their carrots. You think they're going to starve?"

Doris let out a laugh. "Were there any other groceries left? A carton of milk, perhaps? Oranges, cheese or cold cuts?" She smoothed her hands on her smock. "On second thought, there wouldn't be anything. The coyotes probably ate everything. "

"Don't be silly, Doris. Coyotes don't eat carrots. Nobody eats carrots," Mildred said. "And nobody drinks carrot juice either."

"But I do!" Little Beatrice piped up. She'd been hiding in the back of the shop behind some beauty racks reading a year's worth of *Sensationally Sexy and Over Fifty.* Little hair left, having trouble with her balance—and hating those horrible knobs on her fingers—she could still hear. A little bit. "I love carrots!"

"No need to shout, Mrs. Fisher," Doris said. "Were they your carrots?"

"You know I can't drive anymore. My helper, Jonas, he drives a sidecar." She came out from behind the magazines. "Do you think Jonas had an accident—and all that's left of him are carrots? He's late to pick me up, if you have to know." She sat back down in a huff.

"Isn't that him, then, Beatrice? In the sidecar? At Toby's. Across the street?" Mildred asked.

Beatrice got up and peered out the window. "Nope, he doesn't know any blondes."

"Beatrice!" Mildred cried. "He's a boy. They love blondes."

"Oh dear," Beatrice cried, sitting back down.

Mildred looked Beatrice up and down, turned to Doris and whispered. "Don't you think she belongs in a home, dear? She's nutty at ninety-six."

"I heard that!" Beatrice shouted, brandishing her rolled-up magazine over her shoulder. "I'll give you some Sheriff's Calls from the Light." She stood and marched over to Mildred.

Doris got between them. "Mrs. Fisher, Mrs. Rhinehart, please."

"Wacky old lady steals headline! Again!" Beatrice thwacked the top of Mildred's chair, making Mildred's smock flutter and fall. "Ferocious beast eats carrots, terrifies pedestrians!" She slammed the magazine down onto a side table, making it clatter to the floor. Combs, brushes, and bottle of blue Barbicide disinfectant fluid went flying.

"My goodness!" Mildred exclaimed, holding onto the arms of her chair for dear life.

"Frumpy broads no more! Little old ladies take over Point Reyes Station!" Beatrice stormed to the front door of the shop. "Carrots be damned. Come on girls, we have nothing to lose but our shoes!" And brandishing her magazine, Beatrice marched out of the salon, down the ramp to the sidewalk, and without looking, walked right out onto Route One.

Doris ran out. "Mrs. Fisher! Mrs. Fisher!"

"What about my hair?" Mildred hollered. Folds of tin foil covered her scalp. "You can't leave me like this—Doris!"

But Doris was running to Mrs. Fisher who was now in the middle of the street, yelling at the world. "Save yourself! You still have time!"

"Mrs. Fisher?" Doris placed her hand on Mrs. Fisher's shoulder. "Cars may be coming, dear, and I do think that everyone has already heard you."

Beatrice blinked through watery eyes. "It's not? The end of the world? Carrots? Well then, why would they have a Sheriff's Call about carrots? They don't have a Sheriff's Call about me!"

"They will now," Doris answered, stopping an oncoming Plymouth in one direction and a BMW in the other. She guided Mrs. Fisher back to the sidewalk.

A police car came fast, lights flashing and siren blaring. The siren reverberated after the cruiser pulled over to the curb. Officer Linda Kettleman stepped out. "Doris, everything okay here? Mrs. Fisher, you're scaring the tourists."

"Did you answer that Sheriff's Call about carrots, Officer Kettleman?" Beatrice asked.

Mildred, at the door to the salon, lifted her hands and waved. "Great to see you, Officer Kettleman! The cavalry arrives! I love a party!"

"No, ma'am. The Sheriff's calls are just the daily report ..." Officer Kettleman muttered. "We don't report all of it, you know."

"There's been a murder?" Mildred shouted. "Who is it this time? Can I come to the Public Safety Building and confess? You found out so early, so quickly, I didn't mean to kill him."

"Mrs. Rhinehart, Mrs. Fisher," Doris called out. "Let's go in, shall we?" She gently guided Mrs. Fisher back to the first chair.

"Hey, that's my spot!" Mildred snapped.

"Not so fast," Officer Kettleman said. "Mrs. Rhinehart, whom did you kill?"

"It was my husband, Fred. He didn't like his eggs. Shirred eggs, Officer, and he wouldn't eat them."

"That's cause you can't cook, you old bat!" Beatrice lunged at Mildred but she no longer had her magazine. She reached for the scissors on Doris's counter.

"They'll be none of that," Officer Kettleman said, setting her bulk between Mrs. Fisher and the scissors. "What's gotten into the two of you?"

Doris stood back. About time the cops got involved in her little shop. The ladies had been bickering for months.

"It all started with carrots," Beatrice said. "Someone left carrots in the road."

"Ah," Linda said.

"It's your fault too," Mildred said. "Getting us so excited over a vegetable. Confine your calls to real crimes and leave the veggies alone."

"Oh brother," Officer Kettleman dropped into a vacant seat. "How do you do it, Doris, without losing your mind?"

"I was wondering the same thing myself, Officer," Doris answered, picking up a smock. "But think about it a sec. I'm not the person calling the cops about carrots. Now lean back. I need to wash your hair."

From the Sheriff's Calls Section of the Point Reyes Light, January 8, 2015

STINSON BEACH: At 2:15 p.m. a woman said a man with a "spattering" of silver hair had nearly hit her while she was climbing into her car; she had flipped him off and then he had returned and said he should have run her over.

GT Premium

"That's what happened, that's what happened, sir, I swear," Edna Ferguson said.

Bernard frowned. It seemed like people were being a lot more rude these days. "Mrs. Ferguson, ma'am." Bernard pulled out his steno notebook and pencil. "Start from the beginning, please."

"It's Ms. Ferguson, sonny. Never found anyone worth carrying his name."

"Yes, of course, Ms. Ferguson. My apologies. Again, what happened, exactly?

"He followed me down Panoramic. Guess I was going too slow for him. He kept creeping up on my rear bumper, flashing his lights. He wanted me to go faster or pull over. Where the hell am I supposed to pull over? It's cliffs all the way to the water."

"You were right to go slow, Ms. Ferguson." Bernard scratched his bald spot. He was none too happy about losing his hair at thirty-two. It wasn't Dad's fault—he had leonine hair—and perhaps it was Mom's, but when he'd talked to her about it, she'd let out a snort. "Didn't you learn anything in biology, Bernard?" He decided not to call her this weekend.

His feet hurt. He'd been on duty since 6 a.m. "And after that?"

"I pulled up to the fire station, to make a complaint, and the bastard slowed and stopped behind me. I got out of the car, but I was scared, and even though the fire station door was only twenty feet away, I couldn't take the chance, so I climbed back in."

"Did you get his license-plate number?" Bernard asked, thinking he'd call Dad instead and see how Mom's cold was, but he would just put Mom on the line. Bernard thought the invention of the cell phone hadn't been that good an idea.

"Hell no. I was afraid for my life. He pulled up next to me while I had the door out and was threatening me, officer ... officer."

"Please, take a breath."

"I'm a usually kind person, but I did not have Ralph with me—"

"Your husband?"

"My Glock."

"And you have a license for this handgun?"

"A concealed carry. A G Twenty-six. Where the hell are the cops when you need them?"

"What happened after that, ma'am?" Hell. She looked like his grandma, white hair, Peter Pan white collar on sunflower blue dress, sensible shoes, and packing. Dear God.

"He looked like one of those movie stars—you know the one for beer? XX beer—that's not a dirty movie, deputy. Do you mind if I have a cigarette? This whole thing has made me nervous. Silver hair, lots of hair. In his fifties."

Bernard only wished he'd have hair in his fifties.

"What's a girl to do? After I got back inside the car, I gave him the finger and drove off. I hid behind the market, way up one of those single-lane roads, and was about to turn around, when he comes climbing up the hill after me."

"In his car?"

"Of course in his car. Late-model Mustang. Guy thinks he's a jock. That's when he threatened to kill me. Oh God!" She burst into tears. "I knew I should've had Ralph with me."

"Anything else you can remember about the car? Color? New? Convertible? Bumper stickers? This is assault, Miss. You could have been hurt. Fighting with people in cars is a dangerous business. Best not to start."

"He's the one who tried to run me off the road! I'm an unarmed woman, deputy. Isn't it your job to protect and serve?"

Bernard, chastened, pulled out his radio. "Do you know if he went up or down Route One?"

"I was shaking so hard, I couldn't tell. Officer, you've got to do something!"

Bernard barked into his radio. "It was a Mustang."

"Candy-apple red," Edna said, feeling somewhat satisfied. "Two thousand fifteen."

Bernard repeated the info into the radio.

"GT Premium."

Bernard looked at tiny Mrs. Ferguson. "Anything else you want to tell me, ma'am?"

"About cars?"

"About anything."

"He's my brother, Officer," she said, shading her eyes from the sun. "And he's been pissed ever since our mother died and I got everything."

From the Sheriff's Calls section of the Point Reyes Light
January 8, 2015

BOLINAS: At 12:14 p.m. a foster parent reported that a teenager was not listening.

Hope and Traffic

"At least they're not talking about me this time." Thomas giggled into his chocolate milk. He was outside Toby's, at the coffee bar, on his second date with his new girlfriend Marlene, who was humming to herself and sipping espresso.

She finished her bear claw and tapped her finger on one of the computer repair ads in the *Light*. "What do you think about these guys, Thomas?"

"Computer problems?" Thomas asked. "I can fix it for you." Dad was real peeved the last time Thomas "fixed" his machine, but Thomas had made the PC work twice as fast, and except for the little glitch with the Internet connection, Dad was back at work in the Creamery building within the hour.

Marlene flipped the back page of the paper over and closed it.

There was a smattering of locals and tourists hanging around the coffee bar, enjoying the afternoon sunlight and it was warm. "I'm bored," she said. "Let's do something."

"Something" and "dates" was not a combination where Thomas excelled. He eyed Cheda's across the street. More often than not, entertaining girls by going for rides ended up with embarrassing afternoons with Dad's BMW once again going into ditches and Thomas having to call Tiny at Cheda's again and Dad not being happy at all.

"Let's take a walk," he said with an ease he didn't think he had and Marlene said yes, and they were off.

Thomas was grateful. Maybe, if he was lucky, he'd go out with her long enough to get farther than he did with his last girlfriend. There was hope, wasn't there?

Hope and traffic and a lot of cars, but they made their way between the Creamery building and Stellina restaurant, passed by the brick building at the edge of town, and stood by the Giacomini wetlands proper where Thomas took a breath and Marlene's hand at the same time.

"I love this view," he said.

"Me too."

"Could you believe that thing in the paper? That a teen wasn't listening?"

"My parents would never call the cops about something as silly as that," Marlene said.

"What a wonderful world that would be," Thomas answered, a little out of his depth. He wished that was true. Dad called if he blinked funny or didn't eat all his cauliflower.

He studied Marlene. She was a looker, all right: jet black hair, almond eyes, slender legs that went on forever, and work boots. His kind of gal. Not like that dingbat Lulu who wore spike heels day and night. Spike heels that looked like they could kill him. Work boots showed someone sensible, someone who wouldn't fight, someone cute, someone who might like him.

They walked down the narrow path toward the creek. "A girl drowned here once," Thomas said, not wanting to say it, not wanting to put a damper on his day, or Marlene's, but he had to. She'd been nine.

"Unusually warm for January," Marlene said, taking off her jacket.

Thomas wished she'd take off more. He put his arm around her and she leaned in, leaned down to unlace her boots. "Can you hear all that racket?"

"Of course," Thomas answered, hoping she was only talking about birds. Lulu had talked to everyone, real or imaginary. He wasn't at all sure where Marlene was going with this. She took off one boot and showed off one argyle sock with a big hole in the heel. An in! If he had another date he'd buy her some socks and she'd think he was a hero.

She took off her other boot, both socks and leggings. God, she looked cute. Goosebumps rose on her skin.

"Marlene?" Thomas asked.

"I've always loved the water," she said, and, facing him, took off the rest of her clothes.

Thomas' mouth went dry. He closed his eyes. Opened them again. Holy shit. He felt like he had a fever, but he wasn't sick and he wasn't dead. His heart had taken over his body. Suddenly warm, fragile, hot and eager.

She stood by the water's edge and leaned forward. "Watch my dive!"

"No! Don't! It's shallow!"

Marlene didn't listen. She plunged in.

Thomas couldn't stand it. Why did people near him dash into the water and disappear? He stood up, took off his shirt, shoes, socks and pants. He'd saved Justin, but that had been sheer luck. Now, Marlene? He ran to the edge of the water, raced in up to his knees.

"Marlene!" he called. "Marlene!"

Silence. Birds called. A heron caught a fish, flew away. A head rose up out of the river about twenty feet away. Marlene? Was it deep enough to drown? He went in deeper, up to his shorts and everything froze. That head dropped underneath the water, popped up again, but it was not Marlene. It was a seal, with a black nose, whiskers, big brown eyes. It snuffled and dove.

"Marlene!" It was a narrow creek, but long. Which way'd she go? There were no air bubbles on the surface of the water. He remembered the poor little girl who got lost in the mud; and he went in the whole way, relieved it was only four or five feet deep in the darkest stretches.

"Marlene?" he yelled and gasped for air.

"It's not far, Thomas!" she called, and he looked downriver. She'd come up on the opposite side, onto a short sandy bank where a tributary creek, the Olema, came in.

She was standing there, naked, her long brown hair cascading down, covering her breasts, her arms outstretched, waiting for him. "You think you can make it?"

Shivering with cold and excitement, Thomas swam the rest of the way, pulled himself up on the bank and held her close. She was warm, her body making his heart race along with other parts of him. She was nasty and wonderful and tasted like cherries, her mouth on his, searching, searching.

"Thomas!" A voice called from above, through the bushes.

Thomas's hands roamed her body and, wishing like hell the voice would go away, pulled her close and kissed her deeply, something he'd been wanting to do for a while.

"Best be careful, son! That might be poison oak."

Thomas was confused. "Dad? What are you doing here?"

"Thomas!"

"Go away!" Thomas cried. "I'm busy."

"You're late," his father said. "Once again, you're not listening."

He reached for Marlene, for her silky soft skin. His hand touched wood, rough wood. He opened his eyes.

"Dad?"

"Your mother and I told you we'd meet you at the Market at one-thirty and you've been here all that time."

"Marlene?" he asked.

"Do I look like a Marlene to you?"

"Uh, no," he said.

"Your girlfriend? She left ages ago," his father said. "But she said to give this to you." He pulled a slip of paper out from under the chocolate milk.

Thomas opened it.

"Next time, lover boy, stay awake."

From the Sheriff's Calls Section of the Point Reyes Light
January 15, 2015

NICASIO: At 7:32 p.m. someone saw a cow.

Get the Cow

"You mean to tell me people call the cops when they see a cow?" Mildred asked. "Just imagine, up and down San Geronimo Valley, people pulling over and dialing nine-one-one and saying, Officer, a cow, lots of them and they are all over the place."

Fred rubbed his eyes. Their cat Ginger had walked on his face all night and he hadn't slept well, not in the least. Stuffing one of Mildred's muffins into his mouth he took a bite and cracked his tooth.

"Mildred! Did you drop rocks in your muffins? Again?" He worked the sharp corner of his tooth with his tongue.

"I washed the lettuce three whole times, Fred."

"And you put lettuce in the muffin mix?"

"Of course not."

"Then where'd you get this?" Fred held the rock between his thumb and his index finger. "Mildred! I've told you and told you to stop baking. We can buy better pastries at the Bovine." Another thousand bucks and his health insurance didn't cover chips and cracks in his teeth.

"That's not a pebble, that's a walnut."

"Hardened, baked beyond belief, and petrified. And you want me to eat it?"

"If my food doesn't agree with you, don't have any."

"Oh, that'll be the day. Maybe we can get catered meals. I'll take it out of our housekeeping money."

"Don't you dare!" Mildred rushed over to the spare sugar bowl and lifted the lid. "Two quarters, a nickel, and ..." She poured it out. "A five-dollar bill. Go on, Fred." She threw the money at him. "You cook for a change."

Fred, bewildered, looked at the five-dollar bill at his feet. In his day, as a kid, a five spot went far, but today? "Two fancy coffees at Toby's, a piece of pizza, or a beer at the Station House? I'll take it."

Mildred wiped her flour-covered hands on her apron. "So that's how it is, then. You get all the money to waste on these fancy coffees. What about me?"

"You don't drink coffee."

"Neither do you."

"But I do drink beer." Fred slipped the bill into the front pocket of his Oxford cloth shirt. Tonight, he'd watch a little baseball, have a Negra Modelo, watch the girls at half-time and pretend, for a sec, he was young again and not married to Mildred.

"You're a little argumentative for a Wednesday." The half-eaten muffin was on the table beside him. "Let me see."

She pried it apart with skinny fingers. Some parts were cooked perfectly; other parts were kind of chunky and rough. There was another muffin on his plate. "This one's okay," she offered, holding it out to him.

Fred eyed the muffin—poked it. "That one's not cooked ... and that other one," he was on a roll, "is full of rocks. Dear."

She looked down at her hands.

"Have you been potting plants in the kitchen again? Maybe you left a worm in our tuna noodle casserole last night? Or a roly-poly. A spider, perhaps? These are not walnuts." He jabbed at the muffin with his big fingers. "I can see the difference between a walnut and a rock and this is a rock. You're trying to kill me."

"And all the people are trying to kill cows," she said defiantly, sitting straight up in her chair.

"What people? What cows? Are you off your meds?"

"What I'm thinking, Fred," she sniffed, "is what if the cow was in the garage? On the front lawn? On our porch? In your car?"

"Seems to me they could've said something more definitive in the paper about the cow," Fred said.

"Cow plops seem plenty definitive to me," Mildred said. "I bet there were lots of those."

"Well, yes, of course," said Fred. "That's most definitive." He thought a sec. "So is the pebble that broke my tooth." He held out the rock.

"I don't believe you. Show me! Show me!" Mildred cried. "Open your mouth and let me see."

"Not on your life." Fred closed it fast.

"Dr. Davies says you need to floss more."

"Of course he'd say that," Fred answered. "Now, my wife, my dear wife, what did you see in the paper?"

"Cow, someone saw a cow."

"In the road."

"Could be."

"Could be in the back of my sixty-seven Buick Galaxie," Fred said, wishing he still had the car.

"That would make a picture. Shall I get my camera?" Mildred went over to the credenza and pulled out her old Polaroid."Good. I still have some film. Can you go get the cow?"

From the Sheriff's Calls section of the Point Reyes Light
April 23, 2015

OLEMA: At 7:50 a.m. someone said his or her missing cell phone was pinging in the Pacific Ocean.

The Phone

"It's true, I can hear it," Lulu Garcia said to Thomas. He was standing under the big map in Olema rolling his eyes while Lulu held the receiver and grinned. They'd been trying to decide where to go, until Lulu saw the pay phone and made him pull over.

"Lulu," Thomas said, trying not to sound sorely aggrieved, though he was. "The salt water would flood the electronics and it wouldn't work."

Lulu slammed down the receiver. "Then why is it ringing? Hunh?" She leaned out one hip. "Explain that."

Thomas wasn't sure where the ringing in a cell phone came from anyway—a recording in a central office or a ringing in his own phone, or the one he was calling. He didn't have a clue. But he did have common sense, more than Lulu on one of her best days. She was a looker, sure, blond, pretty, and a great body—but brains? Not much. He looked her over, from her high-heel flip flops to her little rose-colored pout. "No, Lulu."

"You're an ass, Thomas. Like I said, I was there, with you, at Limantour, and you said, hold out your phone, and I did, and a wave came—and foop, my phone fell in the water. It's all your fault. Buy me a new phone—or help me find mine."

"Lulu, I don't have that kind of money. Call your insurance company and they'll get you another."

"What do I know about insurance? I'm only sixteen."

"All the more reason," Thomas replied.

"You can be a real jerk."

Thomas bristled.

"All my girlfriends think so."

He shifted in his high tops. He wasn't a jerk. He'd taken Lulu out, after all, surprising all of his friends. He felt sorry for her. She should be proud of him for that. "They do? But I'm a nice guy."

Lulu gave him one of her looks.

"Okay, okay, never mind. Let me take you back to Forest Knolls."

"To that stinky trailer park? No thanks," Lulu snapped. "Take me to Limantour. We can use your phone to find mine. Like when you've put yours down and can't remember where, so you call yourself? This time, you can call my phone. See, just like that and all our problems are solved. Unless," she narrowed her eyes, "you want me to tell my girlfriends the truth about you? Your secrets?"

Thomas groaned. Had they really slept together? How come he'd been so stupid? A bet with his best friend Justin? He'd heard of guys who did that, but not him. They'd been loaded. He looked at Lulu, sexy Lulu. What the hell had he told her? "Secrets?" he croaked, his mouth dry.

"Un-hunh." She shoved out her other hip, clicked her purse open and shut. "I haven't forgotten, you know."

"What secrets?" he asked. Had he told her he loved her? For sure, no. He'd not said the 'L' word to any girl, ever. That he was gay, which wasn't true, and no one really cared anyway. "Something to do with a car?" he asked, searching his mind for answers.

"Come with me to Limantour and I'll tell you what you'd rather I forgot," Lulu said, climbing into Thomas's dad's BMW.

"I'm not taking you to the beach to chase after a dead phone," Thomas replied, shoving the car keys deeper into his pocket.

"Then let's go back to school, and I'll tell Dr. Wilkerson that you pulled me out of class to take advantage of me, an innocent girl." Lulu blinked her false eyelashes and stared at Thomas.

Should he call her bluff? Blow her off? Hell no. He'd be sorry.

"What? It was your idea to cut school," Thomas replied, looking from Lulu to the pay phone to the road to Limantour, to the road home. "Shit. You drive a hard bargain, Lulu Garcia."

"I'm a nice girl. I want to stay that way."

"Hunh?"

"You telling me my reputation's not stellar? What about you, lover boy? How many times have you been towed? Shall I call Tiny at Cheda's? Or your dad? He'd be real happy you skipped school." She closed her hand over his iPhone 6 that was sitting on the dash of the convertible.

"My dad's out of town," Thomas said, feeling somewhat relieved.

"Bet he answers his phone, buddy boy." Lulu laughed. "As I recall, your password is a simple one, one-two-three-four, something even you can remember."

"Goddamnit, Lulu." Thomas pulled the car key out of his pocket, slid behind the wheel. "I never thought you'd stoop to blackmail."

"Me? I'd never do anything of the sort." Lulu blinked her eyes. "Now, let's go to the beach and find my phone." She flipped out her hair, held out Thomas' iPhone. "See? Just like I told you—it's still ringing."

From the Sheriff's Calls Section of the Point Reyes Light, May 7, 2015

TOMALES: At 1:15 p.m. heart trouble was reported from a red Camaro parked outside the post office.

Heart Trouble

"Do you think the car was sick?" Alice asked. She was sitting near the stranded boat behind the Inverness store with Beth-Ann who was smoking. Alice hadn't taken to it yet and wasn't sure if wanted to.

"Heart trouble was the reported cause of the Camaro's demise." Beth-Ann's voice sounded like narrator in a horror movie. "Authorities suspected that it was the run-in with the Jaguar that did in the little red car." She took a drag on her cigarette. "Ever since the movie came out—years ago—there have been times in the darkest of nights when the tiny hamlet of Inverness comes alive with the noise of talking cars. The local deputies haven't yet been able to figure it out."

"I bet," Alice said.

"The red Camaro had a long and fruitful life in the village of Tomales. Occasionally, she'd go to Petaluma, but mostly she stuck around getting washed. She liked the feel of polish."

"I wouldn't mind someone looking after me," Alice said. "But maybe not with polish."

"Boys aren't all they're cracked up to be," Beth-Ann said in her real voice. "Their hands can be calloused and they can be rough."

"The car, tell me about the car."

"The Camaro always wished for the big time. Lexuses, Mercedeses, and all kinds of SUVs poured through Tomales, leaving that little Camaro hungry for company and adventure. The fateful night was a dark one, for a gibbous moon is a small one. She saw a Jaguar speed through town. It was late but she didn't care. From the battery on a cell phone the little Camaro charged up her cigarette lighter—into the ignition system and kaboom—she came to life. Pumping herself up with courage, she plowed through a white-picket fence and followed those red lights through town and on the way to Bodega Bay on Route One."

Alice leaned on her hand and listened intently.

"North of Bodega Bay, the road gets narrow as it follows a cliff edge with a big drop-off to the ocean, as you know. The Camaro fell in love with the black Jaguar, who went faster and faster, blowing through the commercial district and hitting the straight-aways at fifty. The Camaro hurried to keep up. It was tough for her, knowing when to slow down but not wanting to. That Jaguar was hot. Coming around a sharp turn, in the gloom and fog, the Camaro lost the Jag. She wondered if he'd gone to Jenner at a hundred miles an hour. Pulling off to the side of the road, the Camaro, its engine ticking cool, thought about her options. Go for it or go home? She thought long and hard for a full half-minute.

"Unable to stand still any longer, she was about to speed up when she heard the whoop whoop of helicopters and tuned her radio to KWMR. "Car ran off a cliff in Bodega Bay," the news said. The little Camaro trembled in her pull-out. Sadly and slowly, she cruised back to Tomales, and backed in slowly behind the ruined fence, and turned herself off."

"That's a sad story," Alice reached for a bit of seaweed that was on the log beside her. In the mud flats beyond, a turtle headed for water.

"The little Camaro never went anywhere after that. Weeds grew up inside her chassis, her wheels went flat, and day after day she dreamt about that Jaguar. She wasn't getting polished anymore and dust and bird poop peppered her once-bright exterior. A smidge of moisture had crept inside the car, and mold blossomed as winter descended and the rains began. She started to have heart trouble, but her owners ignored her pleas and her horn sputtered and died. When the deputies were called, on a bright Sunday morning right after church in May, they arrived just in time to give her last rites. The little Camaro gave up her dreams and her life before the sun went down."

"Oh dear," Alice said.

"And that's what's going to happen to you if you don't date, Alice," Beth-Ann said stubbing her cigarette out on the log. "Come on. My brother Matt has a friend over. He can do anything."

"Like what?" Alice asked, not really sure. She didn't want to have weeds growing between her toes, but she didn't want to get in trouble either.

"Its okay, Alice, trust me," Beth-Ann said. "My brother says he's built like a truck. You do like trucks, don't you?"

**From the Sheriff's Calls Section of the Point Reyes Light
June 11, 2015**

INVERNESS: At 4:49 a.m. a woman called 911 and stated that a chimpanzee was calling.

Not That Unusual

"Really? The newspaper said that?" Beth-Ann asked, arranging her hair. She'd tried the latest fashion, part in the middle and let your hair go, but it was always getting in her face and making her crazy. "Alice, look again, read it to me."

The teenagers were sitting out in the sun outside Toby's, a shared cappuccino between them. It's cheaper this way, Beth-Ann had said but the cappuccino, after Beth-Ann had had her share, looked like swill to Alice.

"I bet the chimpanzee was surprised when he heard a voice on the other end of the line," Beth-Ann said.

Alice wasn't sure what to say. Her best friend was usually cool and calm and knew everything, but today she thought her friend was just plain loony. "There was no chimpanzee, Beth-Ann."

"How do you know?" Beth-Ann buffed her nails. "My mother says there are all kinds of wackos in this town. Her best friend Mrs. Friedman has a Rhesus monkey for a pet. Keeps it in her pantry. That's a lot smaller than a chimp. There's this wire mesh cage. Sometimes she walks around with the monkey on her shoulder."

"Everyone knows about Liz," Alice said. "She's nuts. She had a llama too, and a goat."

"Not that unusual for West Marin," huffed Beth-Ann who was playing with her cigarette pack in her purse. Too many people meandering around in front of Toby's for her to smoke—someone would tell Mom.

Disappointed, she pulled her hand out, dropped her chin and looked at Alice. "Wouldn't it be nice if there was a real chimpanzee in Bolinas? Point Reyes, perhaps? Tomales?"

"It would have to be in Bolinas." Alice giggled. "All the crazies live there." She eyed a boy across two tables. Coffee-stained skin, dark brown eyes. He was looking at her. She tingled all over, her eyes feeling bright. She stood up straight. "But who would call the sheriff at a quarter to five in the morning?"

"I saw what you just did. You tell me you don't know how to flirt," Beth-Ann said. "Not bad, not bad at all." She scanned the small crowd. "But that guy—" she pointed to a man in his 80s, with cane, and snickered. "He's more your type."

"Thanks a lot. That's my Grandpa. Give me a minute," Alice answered, making her way to Toby Giacomini's red-painted rocker on the porch in front of the store.

While Alice was gone, Beth-Ann applied fresh lipstick, adjusted the foot bed in her three-inch heels, and eyed the small gathering. That guy Alice had pointed out was cute—too cute for Alice. In his mid-twenties, buff, wearing a bicycle jersey, bright yellow. She could pick him out of a crowd in a hurry, that was for sure. She eyed him and gave him a little wave.

"You feeling okay, Grandpa?" Alice asked, giving him a peck on his super soft cheek.

He put his knobby hand on her arm. "I thought I'd find you here. Do me a favor will you, honey? Go inside and get your Grandma. Too many people in there for me."

"Sure, Grandpa." Alice walked inside the double glass doors. She wondered if it was one of Beth-Ann's friends who had called the sheriff and said they were a chimpanzee. She went inside the store, back into the art gallery, and still no Grandma. Grandpa would be sorely miffed if she wasn't thorough, so she headed into the adjoining barn. The smell of fresh hay filled her nostrils. All around her bales of hay, as tall as mountains, climbing to the rafters where barn swallows flew and chirped and called to one another.

She found Grandma perched on a wooden stool, her face up against a little window, peering into a tiny chicken coop where chicks were making a racket. Grandma leaned closer, closer, her wingtips edging the corner of the stool.

"Grandma!" Alice called.

Mildred jumped off the stool and onto the ground, grasping her chest and barely squeaking out the words, "Oh God, child, you scared me silly." She pulled out a handkerchief and dabbed her sweaty brow.

"Grandpa's looking for you." Alice offered an elbow. "He's out front, in the rocker."

They walked back out into the sun. Beth-Ann's cappuccino was there but no Beth-Ann. They rounded the baskets of blue lake green beans and found both Grandpa still in his chair and Beth-Ann leaning over and talking to him.

"I wasn't gone more than a second, Fred, and you send out the National Guard," Mildred said. The old fart was listening to Beth-Ann tell stories and thinking he was young again.

"Yoo-hoo! Fred!"

"Hush," Fred lifted his head and frowned. "Beth-Ann is telling me a story about a chimpanzee."

"It was one of you girls, wasn't it?" Mildred narrowed her eyes and cut them at Alice, making her feel very small. "Making jokes with our Sheriff's Department. You should be ashamed."

Alice and Beth-Ann said together, "We didn't make the call."

Fred sat there, extremely delighted. "What call? Anytime I'm surrounded by young women, any day, beats playing solitaire." He looked at Mildred who scowled. "You included, of course."

"I bet it was him, Beth-Ann," Alice said. Fred's cell phone was in his lap, ringing.

"Pick up the phone, Fred," Mildred said. The two girls leaned closer.

"I don't hear anything," Fred replied.

Mildred picked it up and thrust it in his hands. "Just what I thought, girls, we have found the joker in our midst. There's the phone number right here, Sheriff's Department."

"Can't anyone have any fun around here?" Fred bellowed, grabbed his cell phone and climbed, with difficulty, out of the rocker and marched across the street to the Western for a pop.

*From the Sheriff's Calls Section of the Point Reyes Light
June 11, 2015*

BOLINAS: At 12:50 p.m. children were reunited with their mothers.

Priscilla May

"Well, I should say those mothers would be relieved," Mildred said, checking her new do at Doris's salon. Things were uneven, still, and she'd asked Doris twice to fix it.

"So where were the children before they got reunited?" Hortense exclaimed, not knowing what she should worry about first, the children or her hair. "Were they at a fair? School? Lost?"

"They were on a field trip," Mildred went on. "In Muir Woods. One of the girls got separated. Another fell in the creek."

"You're making all that up," Hortense said.

"You think?" Mildred asked.

"Mrs. Rhinehart. Cut, perm, or trim?" Doris asked.

"Just a wash." A wash was safe, wasn't it? "Hair's my loveliest feature, don't you think, Doris? Fix the cut while you're at it, please. It's still uneven."

"Of course, Mrs. Rhinehart." Doris agreed, a little too loudly. "Now lean back."

As soon as Mildred's head was comfortable in the sink, she thought about her arch enemy Hortense's hair. It looked shaved, and had a word in it, at the scalp. Did the word say "Help" or "I'm hot?" Mildred couldn't remember. The warm water dribbling over her ears made her swoon.

Hortense, on the other side of the salon, stood up in a hurry. "Get me my phone, Doris. I've got to call the sheriff."

"Anything the matter, Mrs. E?" Doris asked. "You look pale. Need a glass of water? Tea?"

"Heavens no. All I can say is," Hortense pulled up to her full height of 5'-1". "It's those children." She took her cane, marched to the center of the shop, and banged it on the floor. "Girls," she addressed the three women in the shop who looked up from two-year-old *In Style* magazines. "In our day—my day.... Well, you younger girls just wouldn't understand."

Younger girls, thought Doris. Her youngest customer had just applied for Social Security.

"Our children didn't have to be 'reunited' with their mothers," Hortense went on. "They were never lost. They were with us." She checked for satisfactory smiles from all around.

"My kids didn't have to stick to me like glue to be safe," said one of the "younger" women, Priscilla May. "I let them roam all over the Mesa. We never had to lock our doors and the kids turned out all right."

Mildred narrowed her eyes. "So you had the perfect kids, didn't you, Pricilla May?"

Priscilla May beamed.

"Yet, as I recall," continued Mildred, "it was your younger son Billy who kept getting into trouble. All those suspensions," she clucked her tongue. "And the whole town knew the day I put a stop to letting your Billy date my Martha."

"I don't remember a Martha," Doris said.

"Alice's mother," Mildred snapped. "My daughter. So," she fixed her beady eyes on Priscilla May. "What should we say? How's your husband? Has he finally decided to attend AA? It's about time."

"Well, I never." Priscilla May threw down her smock and marched out the door.

Doris sighed. "Mrs. Rhinehart ... I wish, I only wish, you wouldn't ..."

"That old bat is such a liar."

"Mrs. Rhinehart," Doris said. "Honestly."

Hortense, not altogether surprised, patted her hair, the shaven side and the long side. Maybe it wasn't so bad. She hoped the ladies in her bridge club would think she was both hip and cute.

"So, where were the children?" Mildred asked both Hortense and Doris. "Why 're-united'? Why a sheriff's call?" Mildred marched around the tiny shop. "The longer I live in this town, the less living here makes any sense to me at all."

The door burst open, the little chimes muffled as the door hit the wall with a bang. It was Linda, Officer Kettleman. "Anyone seen Priscilla May?"

"She was just here," Doris answered, dying to cut a chunk of Mrs. Rhinehart's hair. Chasing her customers out of the shop, indeed.

"We've hunted all over town," Linda continued. "Her children are worried."

"Oh dear," said Doris. "She couldn't have gotten far."

"She left here ages ago," Mildred said.

"Trying to cause more trouble, Mrs. Rhinehart?" Doris asked. "Priscilla May just stepped out, Officer Kettleman."

"That old bat was muttering about some found children," Hortense piped up.

"Those children were found," Officer Kettleman said. "Re-united with their ..."

"Mothers!" Mildred and Hortense said together.

"They had just gone down to the creek to see the newts," Linda explained. "The kids wanted to take them home but I had to advise against it. All your daughters would have been surprised with the new house pets. Took me some time to convince them."

"We should have given one to Priscilla May!" Mildred clapped her hands.

"Where'd she go?" Linda asked.

"Check the Western," Mildred said. "That girl just loves the sauce."

"Mrs. Rhinehart," Doris said, "No more stories, please."

"I'm not the one hiding in a bar," Mildred said, holding out one bony, knobby finger. As she pointed, a figure emerged from the Western next door. It was Priscilla May, weaving a little bit, strolling down the street and patting her hair.

From the Sheriff's Calls section of the Point Reyes Light
June 11, 2015

WOODACRE: At 5:08 p.m. a man said his neighbor had just threatened to shoot him and his dog and put him in a barrel and send it out to sea.

The Threat

"If my neighbor keeps this up, I'll be ordering an AK-Fifteen and take him out first," David Baker said to the sheriff as he stroked his wire terrier. She was nuzzling on his lap, and he couldn't bear the thought of someone hurting Scooches.

"Maybe it was a prank call, Mister Baker," Linda Kettleman said. It was tourist season and they were out in droves, though come to think about it, she couldn't remember a time of year when it wasn't tourist season.

"Look, he's as mean as a box of six-inch nails, ma'am," David said, refreshing the web site grabagun. com. "He's always threatening me and Scooches. My dog wouldn't hurt anything—she's only twenty pounds."

"You want me to come out?" Linda asked. Despite the dark clouds in town, it had been a quiet day, and Walt was busy studying his new book *Gardening for Dummies*.

"If it's not too much trouble."

David was peering out his kitchen window when he saw the cruiser slide up to his front door. He'd found the perfect gun—the American Classic Amigo, .45 caliber, in hard chrome, for $ 635.66. In hopes that the deputy would think he was a nice man, he switched the website to Jackson and Perkins, and filled his screen with flowers and bulbs, but he knew, he knew without a shadow of a doubt, that that Amigo would be his new best friend forever. Even with the two- day shipping cost of $ 85.95 it was worth every penny.

"Thank you for coming, Officer," David said through his screen door.

Linda noticed that the house was surrounded by woods—the whole way up the narrow rutted driveway. Where were the neighbors, anyway? She couldn't see anything through the bishop pines heavy with lichen. "May I come in?" The balding short man with the piercing black eyes and weasel nose opened the door.

The dog, a terrier, barked at Linda, making her head hurt. Damn little dog was going after her pant cuffs, which were expensive.

"Scooches, go lie down."

The dog stopped mid-bark, climbed onto an overstuffed chair, buried its nose under its paws, and went to sleep.

"As you can see, Officer, my Scooches is no threat, no threat at all." David wondered where he was going to set up his blind to take out that asshole Blake next door.

"And your neighbor, sir?"

"A quarter of a mile away." David couldn't remember why he'd called the sheriff at all.

"Well, what's his problem?" she asked, knowing that she'd have another story to tell Walt.

"Oh, you'd think my neighbor would not be a problem, Officer, uh, Officer Kettleman," David said, satisfied. Good. At least he could still see something without his glasses. "But he sneaks up on me at night. He pulls up in my gravel driveway, and uses a bullhorn—a bullhorn, Officer! —and yells at me. Says rude things. Upsets Scooches. 'Go back from where you came from, you jerk!' he shouts at midnight, Officer. I'm at my wit's end."

Scooches, upon hearing her name, opened one eye, noticed she wasn't being called into duty, and went back to sleep.

"I'm an innocent man, Officer." David hoped he looked stern. He'd set up some booby traps on that asshole Blake—cut off his power, jammed his cable connection, thought about putting tacks on his driveway. He wasn't normally a vengeful man but the asshole had started it with his incessant calls to the cops about Scoochie. "He threatened to shoot me, Officer."

"Well," Linda answered. "I need to go see him. This is a serious charge."

"I should say so," David added. "But I don't think he's home—look."

Out the living-room window, in a patch of green, Officer Linda Kettleman saw an orange truck peel out onto a shared driveway.

"It's our easement that's causing the problems," David said.

"With a truck like that, I can track him down in town," Linda said, taking her leave.

A moment later, David closed and locked the door. Blake had been warned. The cops had been called. He'd done all the right things. Now he was free to take matters into his own hands.

With Scooches at his heels, he took a walk along the perimeter of his property. He'd built tall fences and enormous gates and installed a set of security lights that blinded everyone within twenty feet of his property line. He'd put up wind vanes, set with old hubcaps that clattered when it blew. Neighborly? Not really, but this was war. Blake was a blot on the universe who had to go.

It was two days later when they found David. He'd been trying to string a second set of electrical wires but forgot to ground the system. He'd fallen off a high ladder. They found Scooches curled up by his master's chest, tucked up next to his rifle and his stiff, cold hands.

Linda hadn't the heart to attend the funeral. But she did something for the old guy. She adopted Scooches, who proved to be a faithful, though a somewhat over-enthusiastic companion for her and Bernadette. As for Blake, the neighbor, she went to see him the day after the funeral on a fine late-spring afternoon.

Blake, at least eighty, with sparse white hair, answered the door on the first knock. The house was spartan, clean, and tiny. "I don't know what the problem was with David, my neighbor, poor guy." Blake lowered his head and prayed. "He was a peculiar man. Always after my asparagus. The first time I tried to bring him cookies as a peace offering, he threatened to shoot me, so I stayed away. God rest the souls of confused men like that, Officer. I'm truly sorry what happened to him."

Blake rested one gnarled hand on a copy of the *Point Reyes Light* that was perched on a side table by the front door. "It's such a shame. Nice man, but a teller of tall tales, I'm afraid."

"Thank you for your time, sir," Linda said, and turned to leave. Out of the corner of her eye, she caught a glint of light, and took a second look. In front of the picture window Blake had a spotting scope and nearby stacks of *Birdtalk* and *Audubon* magazines.

Satisfied and on her way back to her cruiser, she was looking forward to taking Scooches out for an overdue walk. Checking her photos on her iPhone and climbing into the car at the same time, she didn't notice the red dot in her rear-view window that soon zeroed in onto the back of her head.

**From the Sheriff's Calls section of the Point Reyes Light
July 2, 2015**

WOODACRE: At 5:50 p.m. a man said his mother-in-law from Clearlake had phoned to say she would send a thug to beat him up.

Thorn in My Side

"Another good reason I'm not married," Stanley Farnum said to his buddy Robert Fitzhugh. He puffed on a cigarette. They were sitting out in front of Toby's on a sunny afternoon, even though he knew smoking wasn't allowed. When he saw an Officer heading across the parking lot toward the coffee bar, he slipped his hand under the table.

Robert, who was married, wasn't ready to say what he thought, at least not right away. His mother-in-law wasn't a bowl of cherries but hire someone to come beat him up? He didn't think so. "I would never marry anyone like that." Which, of course, he had.

Stanley watched a pair of scantily clad teenagers hop onto the Stagecoach bus. "If I was younger, Robert, if only ...."

"You sound like a dirty old man."

Stanley laughed. At 70, he was an 'oldish' man, but dirty? Never. He showered twice a day. "Where's the wife, then, Robert? Staying with her mom in Clearlake, planning your demise?"

"You have an evil mind, Stanley. If you must know, she's shopping at Walmart."

"In Clearlake?"

"I guess. They like to shop. What's it to you?"

"Another something I love to hate, Robert. Shopping, big box stores, the whole commercial fiasco pandering to consumer idiocy."

"Which explains your worn-out blue jeans and threadbare socks?"

"Shop at home, shop quick—and hey—would you take a look at that." Stanley eased his heavy chin into his hands and suppressed a whistle. He'd got in trouble for catcalling so he stayed quiet.

"You marry one of those nymphets, you'll get a mother-in-law like mine and then, wham, bam, thank you ma'am, you'll be a marked man. Mark my words, Stanley."

"But I can look, can't I?" Stanley asked.

"If you can stand it." Robert looked too, all the time, but he found it too depressing, a man of his age lusting after young things. And Betsy found his staring rude. But she was out of town. What would she know?

"I bet that wife of yours, and her mother, are right now calling some thugs. You got home too late from the Western last night. They got wind of it, and bam, you're dead."

"People don't do that kind of stuff, Stanley."

"Wanna bet?" Stanley replied. "Guys with guns go into movie theaters and kill people. Go to church and kill people. Why kill strangers? Why not your own family members? They can be annoying, too."

"Betsy's mother Ethel has never been my favorite, that's true," Robert grumbled.

"Thorn in your side ever since you got married, Robert. Every time we get together, you complain about her. She gave me the skinny the last time she was in town while you and Betsy were shopping at the Palace Market. Her mom thinks you could do better at the Sanitary District."

"It may be shit to you but it's our bread and butter," Robert smirked. That old saying always drew a smile. "I keep telling Ethel my pension is safe ..."

"She says you're not a very good provider."

"The District has great cost-of-living raises."

"That you don't treat Betsy right."

"I treat her like a queen."

"That you could use more household help."

"She doesn't work. It's not that hard to vacuum."

"Doesn't matter, though, what I say. You're not good enough for her daughter. That's more or less what she said."

"I love my Betsy, my little angel."

"But not her mom, don't you. You hate her mom! Don't you, Robert!"

"Stanley!"

"It's true, isn't it?" Stanley stirred his coffee with the blade of his pen knife. "So, my feeling is, why not get the jump on them, Robert? Proactive, not reactive. Is that right? They are planning on sending a thug out to beat you up. Send a thug after them first."

"Eighteen years I've had to put up with it all.'You didn't buy the best champagne for the wedding, Stanley. You don't take her out to dinner enough. You're falling short.' 'Didn't your mother teach you any manners?' Oh – it just burns me, all those endless criticisms. Nag, nag, nag."

"As if you deserve it, my man," Stanley said easily, softening his voice. "You're a good man, Robert."

"Exactly," Robert replied.

"A great worker."

"I got my commendation last month. Best overall attendance, twenty years."

"Good provider, too."

"Nice house, I got her a nice house."

"And now her mother sends thugs to—thugs! To beat you up."

"That's not entirely true."

"What part, Robert? That you don't hate your mother-in-law?"

"I do, I do," Robert said, feeling itchy. "They get back tomorrow." He sunk his head into his hands. "Two weeks of Ethel in the house and I think I'm going to lose my mind."

"Exactly." Stanley was quiet a moment. "You want me to do it? As soon as they come back from the airport, when they're tired and maybe not so sharp? Say, at your place on the Mesa. You can keep Betsy in the house and I'll jump your mother-in-law as soon as she gets out of the car."

"In front of the house?"

"Of course."

"In front of the neighbors?"

"You don't have any neighbors."

"In front of God, then? I don't want her hurt." Robert's head swam. He'd never had such a horrific thought. He was a nice guy, normally. Mostly. Usually. Always? Well, maybe not always.

He thought of Ethel. In his kitchen, going through his papers, criticizing his garden or half-dead roses, complaining about his stacks of *Guns 'N Ammo*. Wanting him to take her out for target practice. He'd practice on her.

Robert took a sip of his cold, bitter coffee. "No, no, no, Stanley. No, don't do anything. Listen," he tappedon his best friend's arm. "When she's here, making me nuts, would you come meet me at the Western, for a beer, maybe three?"

"That all you want, Robert?" Stanley asked, putting his cigarette out on the bottom of his shoe. "Are you sure?"

***From the Sheriff's Calls section of the Point Reyes Light
July 23, 2015***

DILLON BEACH: At 6:18 a.m. a wife called, crying.

The Race

"What do you think that was about, Doris?" Mildred asked. She'd come in for her weekly do and the salon was quiet for a change.

"I have no idea," Doris lied, but she wasn't going to tell. Many days this month she'd woken up crying— unsure what it was about. That she hadn't had a boyfriend in ten years? That her son was about to start fourth grade? That she couldn't seem to make ends meet? The list was endless. She sighed.

"Maybe the wife needed a haircut and her husband wouldn't pay for it," Mildred said. "Maybe she needed new whitie-tighties and he said her five-year-old underpants with the broken elastic were fine. Men can be so clueless." She rested her face in her hands.

The bell on the door sounded as one of Doris's regulars, Hortense, came in with her cane. A little older than Mrs. Rhinehart, Mrs. E. was sharp and crackling and sometimes could be a lot of fun— when she was in the right mood, that was.

"Have a seat, Mrs. E.," Doris said.

Hortense wormed her way into one of the beauty chairs, eyeing her arch-enemy reading the *Light*. "What's happening, Mildred? You're frowning again."

"Some wife is crying, Mrs. E. Mrs. Rhinehart's trying to figure out why." Doris clipped Mrs. Rhinehart's hair loosely around her ears. Mrs. R. thought her ears were her best feature.

"If I was a wife, I'd be crying all the time," Hortense said with a huff.

"Hey!" Mildred shot up. "My Fred—he's a good man."

"Does he make you cry, Mildred? Does he understand common decency? Like if you feel like staying in bed or not doing the dishes or he sees you throwing the laundry out the window. Wouldn't he say something? Anything? Mildred?"

"Fred's never made me cry," Mildred repeated.

"But you must admit you threw laundry out the window. Bess Masterson at church told me that only last week and Fred was hopping mad, because his underwear fell into poison oak and he had to use a mop handle to rescue his whitie-tighties."

"Another reason to not be married, then, Mrs. E.?" Doris called, playing the devil's advocate. Some days, with their endless chatter, her girls at the salon made her want to misbehave.

"I guess I was confused. You ever get confused, Hortense? Forget your socks? Why you went downstairs to get something? What day it is?"

"Another good reason I live in a one-story house," Hortense spat, pleased she had the upper hand. And yet. And yet. "There are a lot of reasons husbands make wives cry, Mildred. I'm not counting your Fred amongst one of those." But she was, she knew she was. Fred was too big, too fat, and too opinionated in her estimation. "And of course, my Michael, gone these twenty years—God rest his soul." She crossed herself. "He never intentionally hurt me or a fly, or a child, or a dog." She burst into tears.

"There, there, Mrs. E." Doris brought out her half-empty tissue box. Seemed like more and more these days her "girls" were working themselves into a tizzy.

"Bet the woman's husband made her split the check," Mildred said. "That would make me mad too."

"They do that these days, you know, the Milleniums," Hortense said.

"Not 'ums' 'als'," Mildred corrected. "Millennials."

"Sounds like a disease to me," Hortense said.

"Those girls and boys have nothing but money. None of 'em would ever bat an eye at a date trying to split a check. Men in our day would never dream of such a thing."

"If chivalry's gone, I'd be crying too," Mildred said.

"My Fred."

"Is always kind."

"Of course."

"Loves his beer."

"Well, yes."

"And his recliner."

"And Alice. Of course, Alice." Mildred said. "What's not to like about that girl?"

"Tell her not to get married, poor thing. Some boy, or husband, will make her cry. She's a sensitive thing, I've heard," Hortense said.

"What? You think no woman should get married? What about children? What about furthering the human race?" Mildred exploded.

"It is a race, isn't it, girls?" Doris said, reaching for a comb.

The other two women gasped. For them life was supposed to have slowed down, not speed up. There should have been plenty of time for hobbies like crocheting hats for the homeless, collecting blankets for feral cats, or playing bridge. But now, now, life hadn't turned out that way. It had accelerated. Aging wasn't a linear progression; it was changing by the hour. Mildred wrapped her hand over her mouth.

"If you keep that up, Doris, you're going to make me cry. It's always a race, isn't it, girls?" She turned her head, slightly weeping into a hanky she had tucked in her blouse.

"Now you did it," Doris said, whispering to Mrs. E., tucking a smock around her and opening and closing the scissors with a snick-snick sound. She spoke louder. "All of it, none of it, near the ears, off the ears, from the top, a bowl cut, flip or bob? What'll it be this time Mrs. E.?"

Hortense sighed. "I was married for thirty years, Doris. Husbands say the strangest things. They don't know enough about the weaker sex. They make us cry all the time."

"I know," Doris said, clicking her scissors. "But they don't mean to."

"But they do!" Mildred stood up and banged her cane on the floor. "Men are as mean as snakes. They say the meanest things."

"I knew she was lying about Fred," Hortense whispered to Doris.

"Me too." Doris reached for the comb. "I knew it all the time. Now, Mrs. E. what's it going to be?"

From the Sheriff's Calls Section of the Point Reyes Light
July 30, 2015

FOREST KNOLLS: At 2:59 p.m. a resident reported an on-going problem with a neighbor who doesn't like his or her trumpet playing.

The Trumpet Player

"What am I supposed to do, Officer, play a kazoo? What would Michael Tilson Thomas say? A kazoo at Symphony Hall? The Maestro wouldn't like that at all." Matthew McKinney sat down in a heap on one of the chairs outside the Lagunitas market, as close to Forest Knolls as you could go unless you wanted to be in the forest.

Officer Linda Kettleman, by now a two-year veteran, sat down beside the perp. "Your neighbor called us, Mr. McKinney. We need to pay attention. A peaceful environment is all we can hope for. We all like quiet."

"But I don't play in the middle of the night. I only wail on Benny here," he tapped his trumpet, "when the mood hits me. I'm a musician, ma'am, we don't get up until noon, so after my coffee, my meditation, I start practicing around four. Sometimes five."

"Not what I heard," Linda said. She only wished her place was quiet. Bernadette had taken to wanting to 'play' from two to four in the morning, and used her strong little lungs to prove it.

"Without Benny here, I'd die," Matt McKinley said, his eyes on Sir Francis Drake Boulevard disappearing around the corner. "It's the only thing that keeps me alive, since, since my girlfriend, Marjorie May, moved back to Memphis a year ago."

Not even thirty, Linda thought. Alas, heartbreak hurt just as much whether you were younger or older. She couldn't remember the last time she'd let anyone near her heart, except for Bernadette. That brown-eyed bouncing baby was starting nursery school in a few weeks. At last.

Matt McKinley itched his full head of thick black hair.

Linda liked his mustache. Thick and bushy and trimmed, for goodness sakes. "So, Mr. McKinney——-"

"Matt."

"Mr. Matt. How can we compromise with your neighbor?"

"Shoot him. Shoot the old bat."

"That's no help. Think again." In her two years on the force too many of her perps wanted to settle disputes the easy way. Too many times she'd heard 'Put him out of his misery,' or 'Drive that son of a bitch out of town.' "Let's see if we can be helpful."

"I'll play here," Matt McKinley said suddenly, standing up, setting his trumpet on his lips and blaring a tune he made up on the spot. He wasn't in tune, and the sound the trumpet made squeaked and sputtered.

"Perhaps if you could take some lessons, Matt?" Linda asked. She had kept herself from blocking her ears out of politeness, but they hurt.

Matt pulled down his trumpet. "You don't like "Rhapsody in Blue"?" he asked, his green eyes sparkling. "How 'bout "Taps"?"

Linda put her hand gently on his trumpet. "Not here, Matt."

His face clouded. Motorcycles blew past them down the road. "Music is better than motorcycles any day."

"That may be true, but Mr. McKinney." Linda's walkie-talk buzzed. "Please. Be considerate. Rent a studio. Play in the forest away from people. And when you play, hold out that last note a little longer, all right?"

"Have you taken music lessons, Officer?" Matt asked.

"Not since high school, Matt. And I'm not telling you when that was." She heard an urgent call come in through her walkie-talkie. "I've gotta go."

Matt decided to head to the Cheese Factory in Nicasio, overlooking the pond, and took off for Nicasio Valley Road.

But when he got there, and started to play, all the picnickers and tourists packed up their snacks, walked to their cars and pulled out. Except for one. An elderly man, not using a cane but needing to, ambled over to Matt.

"That's quite a trumpet, you have there, young sir," he said, leaning on a picnic bench.

Matt smiled. "A few more weeks' practice and I'll try out for the Symphony."

"And how long have you been practicing, son?"

"Six weeks. You wouldn't think three little buttons would cause so much trouble." Matt removed the mouthpiece from the trumpet and rubbed his lips. "Hard on the mouth."

"May I?" the elderly man asked, taking the trumpet. He pulled his own mouthpiece from his pocket and before Matt could say anything, the older guy was playing sweet and low, big and brassy, his tremolos carrying across the green valley and into the hills beyond.

Matt watched him, his eyes lost in the tunes of sadness, melancholy and heartbreak. Tourists in cars going 60 miles an hour down Point Reyes Petaluma Road slowed, pulled into the parking lot. Others stopped on the side of the road, their windows down, engines off.

Linda Kettleman, hearing a call that there was a disturbance, drove on by, slowed, stopped, turned off her computer, her walk-talkie and her cell phone, got out of the car, leaned against the door, and stayed lost in thought of a time long ago and far away.

The old man played until the parking lot was full, the road jammed, the picnic area full of families shushing their children, staff at the Cheese Factory outside, aprons on. No one cheered or said a word as the notes rolled on. Cows and calves wandered down to the pond. Crows, cawing in a copse of trees, silenced their arguments, flew down to a rail fence near the old man blowing the trumpet, folded their wings and settled down.

The world stopped, full of music and longing as the old man played into the gathering dusk, until parents led their children back to their cars and staff, called from an open white door, reluctantly headed back inside to work.

Matt remained. The cars left one by one. The crows took off in a rush of wings.

The man put down Matt's trumpet.

"How did you—? My God, you make it look so easy. I'm Matt." He put out his hand. "Matt McKinney."

"Fisher. Fisher Williams," the man said, shaking Matt's hand. "Practice, boy, all it takes is practice. And gigs, lots of gigs. And more gigs."

"Amazing doesn't cut it, I mean ..." Matt sputtered. The trumpet was still warm in his hands. He looked around for a car. "Mr. Williams."

"The Fish. Everywhere you can play, play. Everywhere you can go, go? Get it?"

"You walk here? Take a bus? Can I give you a ride?"

"Me? I don't need no ride," Fisher said, wiping sweat off his forehead. "I need a new life," he said and disappeared up a hill and was lost in the valley beyond.

Matt sat there, as darkness fell, cradling his trumpet. "Practice, that's all it takes?" he asked, and inserted his own mouthpiece and began to blow.

The trumpet glowed a warm light against the gray darkness, vibrated while Matt tried again and again to get a pure note, until, hours later, the notes came out sweet and whole, like liquid gold, that was, and Matt's music floated up into the night.

In the morning the staff found him, exhausted and cradling his trumpet under one of the picnic tables, wan and cold in the harsh morning light. They tried to take his trumpet, coax him out from under the bench, give him water and cheese.

"I have met my master," Matt said, "and he has come to me. Leave me until dusk until I play again."

And that is why, in the summer, if it is near dusk, you can find Matt, plaintively practicing, his trumpet against a glowing sky, and sometimes if you are lucky and very very quiet, you will also see the master. He has his own trumpet now and they occasionally play duets. The neighbor in Forest Knolls moved away and bothers no one. Michael Tilson Thomas, came out to Nicasio at dusk, with his husband, and returned to San Francisco a happy man—for he thought he had found his new soloist. But Matt preferred the open hills to the rehearsal carrels, the streetcars and the schedule.

The old man would have none of it, he walked to the hills, never looked back. He wasn't seen again until the following spring, at Walker Creek Ranch, teaching some children how to play, alive and well and looking twenty years younger.

And as for Matt, he moved to Bolinas, bought a place on the Mesa, sound-proofed it but plays outside as all his neighbors amble over to listen to his music.

He plays until the glow of the sun hits the roof in the morning, or kisses the horizon on its way to tomorrow, or his mouth gets sore, whichever comes first.

From the Sheriff's Calls Section of Point Reyes Light

August 27, 2015

BOLINAS: At 3:12 p.m. someone, sifting through a pile of belongings found dumped on Dogwood, discovered letters written to a woman who had died fifteen years earlier.

Dear Teresa

"Dear Teresa," Alice read. She lifted her eyes and looked straight at Beth-Ann. "Hey, listen to this."

Beth-Ann, who was tapping tobacco from the end of a Camel—my, she felt bold today—looked up from her task. "Who's Teresa?"

"Just listen." Alice squinted at the tight handwriting. "By the time you read this, I will be long gone. But just remember, dear girl." Alice unfolded the next page of the thin blue airmail letter. "You've always been my daughter and I will love you forever."

Beth-Ann took a deep drag of her Camel and coughed hard. "I swear I'll bring up a lung. Jesus Christ, how can anyone smoke these things? Whatever you do, Alice, don't ever let me smoke crap like this again." Beth-Ann ground out the cigarette with the heel of her high heel shoe.

"So maybe you'll stop smoking altogether?" Alice asked.

Beth-Ann answered with a snort.

Some days Beth-Ann was just high maintenance. "Well?"

"Maybe, yes, I could try, sure, what the hell, if you say so. Shit, you sound just like my parents." Beth-Ann rolled her eyes. "What's with the letters?"

"They're dated 1995," Alice said.

"That wasn't so long ago," Beth-Ann replied.

"You weren't born yet."

"Oh, that's right." Beth-Ann threw her Camel cigarettes into a trash can and reached for her cloth bag, the one that held her stash.

"Not here, Beth-Ann. Jeesh, have you lost your mind?" Alice waved her away. "If you need to smoke," she added, "do it away from me."

Beth-Ann, with a frown, stepped behind some trees.

Alice saw a ring of smoke emanating from around the trunks. She went back to her letters. This one was from Lisette.

"My heart goes out to you in your time of sorrow, Teresa. I can't imagine what it would be like to lose a child."

Alice looked up at the sky, at the tree Beth-Ann was trying to hide behind. A child? A teen? Like her? Oh God. She clutched the letter and read on through reddened eyes.

"P.S. It's been a long time since I've seen you, my dear. Maybe I'll come see you in the spring when the poppies are blooming and hope is in the air, but for now, write and write often. P.P.S. If letters are tough for you, how about or a phone call?"

Alice folded the letter carefully, put it back in its envelope. She pulled another one out of an orange-colored Camptrails backpack full of letters.

"Teresa. We'll be up next week with the boys. They love the beach, as you know. Is it a far walk for them? At eight and ten, they can be quite independent. Are you still playing the flute? We'll be there a week from Wednesday. Love, Lisette."

Alice felt better. Even though she was being nosy, at least reading this letter didn't felt like an intrusion. She checked out Beth-Ann sitting on the ground, leaning against a tree.

Alice tucked away another letter. Should she call Mom with her treasure? Should she look for Teresa? Wouldn't she want these letters? She scrabbled around in her purse for her cell, but the battery had gone dead. She thought of asking Beth-Ann but knew better than to try to talk sense into her when she was stoned. Feeling again a little like an intruder, Alice slid out another letter, this one postmarked Paris, France.

"I'm sorry I missed your mother's funeral, Teresa, but cash is at an all-time low. I'm trying to get into the Sorbonne, but my French isn't very good. Still, it's coming along, Dieu merci for that, and I'll get there someday, I hope. Your mom would be proud. Much love, your cousin Lisette."

Alice looked up. Twenty years ago. What would Lisette be doing now? A teacher, perhaps? A French teacher? A businesswoman? A mom, with a French husband and two or three kids about to enter college? She wondered where she'd be in twenty years. Tied to a dishwasher with three babies, a dog, two cats, and a turtle? Or in Paris, herself? Turning to another letter, she heard a rustle behind her.

"You still at it, Alice?" Beth-Ann asked. "Those letters don't belong to you."

"But they were here in the dumpster. Beth-Ann, dope is supposed to make you mellow."

"You're still snooping."

"Just one more letter, all right? Just one? Then we'll ask your mom what to do with them."

"I'm hungry," Beth-Ann mumbled.

"I just want to find out if Teresa has a boyfriend or not. Sounds like she's a nice person."

"And then?" Beth-Ann was unsteady on her feet.

"Then we'll go get ice cream or something." Alice's fingers closed around another blue envelope, this one unopened. She looked at the date. December, 2000. Why hadn't Teresa opened this last, final letter?

"I trust you find yourself close to God's hands now, Teresa. He has been a comfort to me in my time of difficulties. Your father called me a few weeks ago with the news of your diagnosis. The same thing happened to my cousin—and she, but .... How are you feeling? Can you get out and see the ocean, the flowers, the bees? Do you have any help? If you need anything, please call, my number's in the book. Just down the street. Preacher Catherine can come by. Am I being too intrusive? I don't know how to do this. May God bless you. Much love, Lisette."

Alice, her eyes brimming with tears, looked up at Beth-Ann.

"What happened to her? Cancer? Brain tumor? Did she have a boyfriend, Beth-Ann? Did she have lovers?" Alice cleared her throat. "Did she run on the beach, make out by the fire, camp at Samuel P. Taylor State Park? Swim at White House Pool? Did she do everything on her bucket list?"

"I'm not old enough for a bucket list," Beth-Ann said. "I'm only fifteen."

"Poor thing," Alice said, putting the backpack down.

"But I'm not too old for a swim," Beth-Ann said. "Let's go to White House pool."

"It's not a real pool, you know, it's just a bend in the river," Alice said.

"So?"

"But I didn't remember to bring my suit," Alice said with a frown.

"A suit? No one wears a suit at the pool," Beth-Ann replied. "No one wears anything at the pool."

"What would Teresa say?" Alice asked.

"She'd say life's too short for a suit," Beth-Ann said, taking her hand.

From the Sheriff's Calls Section of the Point Reyes Light June 18, 2015

POINT REYES STATION: At 1:59 p.m. a man believed George Bush was stalking him. (It wasn't clear from the press log which Bush.)

He Was Here, the Younger

"Junior or Senior?" Bernard asked. He was sitting at his desk, twirling his pencil. Linda was off and Walter was hiding behind his plants.

"Junior or Senior what?" the caller argued.

"Bush," Bernard answered. "You called, said someone was stalking you. I'm just wondering if it's the elderly President Bush or his son, W."

"A bunch of creeps if you ask me."

There was a silence as Bernard heard the sound of a chair sliding against a wooden floor.

"I think you better come over. Whoever it is, they're staring at me through the kitchen window."

"And you're located where?" Even though the caller—an older guy, it sounded like— mumbled directions, Bernard understood. After climbing in a cruiser, heading up the hill to the Mesa, he found the mailbox and the dirt road, followed the line of cypress trees and pulled in to the driveway.

But when he knocked on the iron door, rang the bell, and walked around hollering hello, there was no answer.

He was heading back to the cruiser, about to chalk up the fifth crank call for the week, when he heard footsteps and turned.

"You don't look at all like one of the Bushes," a man claimed. He was holding a shotgun aimed at Bernard's middle.

"I'm with the Sheriff's Department. Don't you see my uniform, my patrol car?" Bernard asked. "Please, put down the gun."

"Show me your badge."

Bernard made a move to draw his weapon when a blast shot off through a stand of trees. He froze.

"Keep your hand away from your weapon, buster, and we'll get along just fine," the perpetrator said, coming over. He was wearing flared blue jeans, a ragged blue chambray shirt, and a colorful vest, and had long hair down to his waist. "Cole. Cole Conway. You can't be too careful in these parts."

Bernard eyed the shotgun.

"One shot. But I'll break it if you want, Officer." He cracked the action and showed Bernard the empty receiver. "Never mind Betsy. Come on around the back and I'll show you footsteps."

"You been living here long time?" Bernard asked, gathering his wits and feeling sweat trickle down the back of his neck.

"Got it in '05," Cole answered. "It was my Dad's." He led the way through an overgrown patch of blackberry bushes. Fresh poison oak, oily and wet, peered through the vines. Bernard did his best to keep his distance. Underfoot, dry dirt led to moist earth.

The house was small, red with white trim and small wooden windows. Bernard thought he knew all the houses in town, but this was a new one. They turned the corner to a huge view, Tomales Bay shimmering in the noonday sunlight, Inverness Ridge hanging tall. Once again, he was reminded of why he moved to West Marin. But he had to keep his focus. The old guy could still be armed.

"There. Look." Cole Conway pointed to footprints in the mud, by a kitchen window.

Men's oxfords from what Bernard could guess. But the Bushes? That was a stretch. "Want to come to the station and make an identification?"

"What for? Everyone knows what the Bushes look like," Cole said. He lifted a string from around his neck, and showed off a small leather bag. "My hoochie bag is supposed to ward off bad guys. Maybe it's not working today."

"No problem here then, Mr. Conway," Bernard answered. "I'll be going now." Bernard let him go ahead. Ever since he'd been clonked on the head two months before he'd been wary of all perps.

"He was here. The younger," Cole sputtered. "He was leering, with that high-pitched voice of his and his pokey ears. I wouldn't —mistake the President, Officer."

"I should say not," Bernard replied. "But what would he be doing here in Point Reyes looking in your window?"

"You don't believe me?" Cole narrowed his eyes. "That's what they all say. Even that girl cop ... Miss ... Miss."

"Kettleman."

"She suggested therapy. Therapy, my ass. If you ask me, the Bushes need therapy, forcing us to go to war."

"I'll say," Bernard answered. "Before you get in the cruiser, I'll need to pat you down."

Cole, standing back, his face wild, reached for his pocket.

"No! Don't! No sudden moves!" Bernard shouted, reaching for his holster.

Cole Conway got real still, his eyes as big as a horse's. "A pencil. I'm just reaching for a pencil."

"Why a pencil? I'll get you one." Bernard said, reaching into his vest pocket.

Cole's hand was fast. He pulled out a knife, a small knife. With a flicker of a finger he released the blade. Snap.

Bernard touched his walkie-talkie. Didn't say anything. At the station they knew real well what five clicks meant.

Cole circled Bernard. The cruiser was twenty feet away. His hand hovered above his holster. Could he draw fast enough? Wary, he watched Cole's hands.

"It was my sister. She put me up to it. 'Call the cops, Cole. Make them come. Make them get rid of the Bushes. Make them get rid of the TV."

Bernard studied the man's eyes. "PCP? Angel dust? What'd ya take, Cole?"

"It's the Bushes! Ruining this country! Sending us to war!"

"Did you lose a brother, a son, over there, sir?" Bernard asked, keeping an eye on the knife.

"My sister's never been better," Cole said.

"And she lives with you?" Bernard asked.

"Who else would call the cops on the Bushes?"

"It was your voice on the phone."

"Of course! Of course!" Cole circled, gesturing with his knife, forcing Bernard back toward a copse of trees. "They'll be after me next."

"Your sister's a vet, sir?" Bernard asked.

"They took away her soul, Officer. They destroyed my sister, my lovely sister."

"I'm so sorry, Cole."

"She swears every day when she reaches for her bad leg, the one that's held together with screws and rods, and stands up, looks out the window."

"Can I see her?" Bernard asked, coming closer.

"She thinks they're coming to get her good leg. I'm not the only one who's armed, Officer."

191

A shot rang out, pinging the cruiser. Bernard turned, ducked, and ran. The blade of the knife nicked him on the ear as he dove for the trees. Holding his ear, blood covering his hand, he pulled his weapon.

Another shot rang out and Cole fell to the ground. At the same time sirens and lights filled the air. Bernard crouched, stuffed a handkerchief on his ear, and held his fingers to his eyes, pointed at the house as the gun rang out again.

By the time Walter and two other officers fanned out into the trees, and surrounded the house, they found the woman cradling her crying baby, two shotguns by her side and a bullet hole through the center of her forehead.

From the Sheriff's Calls Section of the Point Reyes Light, August 13, 2015

NICASIO: At 3:13 p.m. someone watched a man exit his car and walk down the middle of the road, barefoot, shirtless and dressed in white jeans. He was gazing at the trees.

Wings

"What are they calling me for?" Mildred asked.

"This isn't about your brother. Henry doesn't own any white jeans."

"Oh, my dear little wife, hand me the phone," Fred said, cupping his hands over his ears as her voice got louder and louder. "No need to shout."

"Turn down your hearing aids!" Mildred said, slammed the phone into his hands, and stormed out the bedroom door.

Fred had been taking a nap. Feeling groggy, he put the phone next to his ear. "My brother doesn't drive, and he certainly doesn't go shirtless or barefoot." The officer asked him, only too kindly, to come to the station, and at the same time Mildred charged through the door, her Easter hat on, her purse over her arm, twirling the keys.

At the station, Office Linda Kettleman helped them into a cruiser and with lights flashing; the three of them sped out of town burning up the asphalt along Route One.

Mildred, excited, clutched her purse and whispered, "Faster, faster," while Fred, in the front seat, asked the deputy to give him more information.

"It could be Henry," he muttered, feeling sad. Henry had been doing better lately, or so Fred had thought. Henry had been taking his meds and living in a studio in Inverness Park. He even had enough money for a cup of coffee every Thursday when they met at the Bovine.

"He may be gone by the time we get there," Linda said, "or he may be confused, on the side of the road, or lost."

"Or worse," Fred said. A moment later, he brightened. "Maybe it's not Henry."

"Oh, it's him, all right," Mildred said from the back. She would have clocked him on the shoulder, but there was a wire-mesh grill between them. "That old fool should be in a rest home."

"Like you?" Fred said, under his breath. She didn't hear him, which was good, or was it that he hadn't heard her? He didn't know the difference.

They pulled up in front of Rancho Nicasio, at the Square. The afternoon was a cool one, as the clouds blocked the sun and a hush had come across the landscape. The little church stood sentry over the peaceful setting.

Fred stuck his hearing aids deep in his ears. He'd have to be on double alert to hear his brother in the silence. "I'll take a walk to the church," he said, easing himself out of the front of the cruiser. Linda had already stepped out.

"Hey! What about me?" Mildred cried, stuck in the back where there were no door handles. "Somebody could die back here!"

Fred opened the door. "I'll take the church; you want to wander around the Square?"

"I'll bet a whole quarter I'll find your brother first," Mildred said, and climbed over a rail fence into tall grass.

Fred liked the little church. He checked the front step. No clothes, no shirt, but a gathering of bread crumbs near the front door. Henry—or whoever—couldn't have gone too far. Otherwise, birds would have eaten the evidence. He wandered back behind the church, steering clear of blackberry bushes and softly calling, "Henry? Henry, is that you?"

"I made the call a little over an hour ago," the proprietor of Rancho Nicasio said when Linda came through the door to the bar. "He was barefoot, shirtless, and mumbling something about his beloved. Gone these twenty years." The proprietor, a guy with a handlebar mustache, wiped down the bar. "We get plenty of interesting people out here, Officer, but usually not someone that old, showing off his pecs, with a full head of white hair. He headed outside."

"His name's Henry," Linda muttered, and gave him her card. "Call me if he comes in, please."

The door banged open. Mildred came to the bar. "Drinking already, Officer Kettleman?" She threw her purse and coat on the counter. "Whiskey, neat, and make it snappy, bartender. My brother-in-law's missing and it's chilly out there."

Linda left Mildred at the bar, climbed back into the cruiser and drove around the Square, knocked on the doors of the few houses, then took a ride at least four miles out of town in all three directions, going slow and calling Henry's name. She didn't see any pedestrians at all. Disappointed, she drove back to the Square and checked the bar again. She looked in the church, feeling despondent. A man in his 80s, shirtless and shoeless, could get cold and disoriented if he wasn't brought inside soon.

Fred tiptoed around the back of the church, muttering to himself, calling out Henry's name and fiddling with his hearing aids. It was brushy back there, tall grass pulling at his pants. A coyote yipped in the distance. "Henry?" he called. Nothing.

Linda pressed on the latch to the front door. It would be locked, surely, but it opened with a whisper. The sanctuary looked inviting. She walked the pews, checked the floor and hiding spaces, and left the door unlocked as she walked out. "Henry?" she called out to a darkening sky.

At the back step, Fred sat his bulk down. What would Mom say? Even though she'd been gone forty years, she always insisted that Fred take care of his older brother. "He's special," she'd say. "He needs a little more than you do, my beautiful boy." I failed, Fred thought, and pressed his head into his hands.

Something swished the grass near his feet. "Henry?" He looked up to recognize Marmalade, the orange parish cat, whose picture had recently been in the *Light*. Fred stood up, and on creaky legs meandered into the church. The front door was open and candles flickered on a table by the door. Fred wasn't a religious man, but he could use some help today. He sat in a pew, begged God's forgiveness, and prayed the best he could, using shreds of phrases he remembered from Sunday school. A few minutes later, he felt a hand on his shoulder. "Linda? Officer?" he asked and opened his eyes.

"Imagine my surprise. There I was feeling out of sorts, and bang, here's my little brother, sitting in a church, for God sakes. Fred, have you lost your mind, or have you been saved?"

It sounded like Henry, and looked a bit like Henry. But he wasn't wearing his usual clothes, beat-up blue jeans and red and black Buffalo plaid flannel shirt. He had on a thick puffy white top. "You okay, big brother?" Fred asked.

"God asked me to put on wings," Henry smiled and smoothed the feathers on his arms. "You like?"

"We've been worried about you," Fred said. "How'd you get here? Are you wearing shoes?"

"God's little sandals," Henry replied, showing off his feet. "White pants, angel wings, and sandals. Seems like I'm ready for the Holy Ghost."

"You're ready for the asylum, buddy boy," Fred said, taking his arm. But the arm felt ethereal, as if nothing was there.

"Oh, it's me, all right, Fred," Henry laughed. "I'm no ghost. The Holy Father called and I came running. I listen well, these days, Fred and I listen to Him."

"For heaven's sake," Fred sighed. "Anything broken? You off your meds?"

"Never felt better, little brother." Henry twirled in the candlelight. "Mom would be proud, don't you think?"

"Will you come see Mildred?" Fred asked, feeling he'd lost control of the situation. She'd know what to do. "She's at the bar."

"Drunk, I bet," Henry said. "I swore off booze when the Lord called."

"Jesus," Fred said, putting his head into his hands.

"He called too, but I didn't answer," Henry said. He looked up at the ceiling. "But he's watching over me. "And if you sit in the pew with me and pray, maybe he'll listen to you too." He grinned. "C'mon, Fred, make me happy for change."

Fred would've gotten up and dragged Henry out of there but Henry was a bigger man.

"Come, sing a hymn with me," Henry said.

Fred's head swam.

"You remember 'You Have a Friend in Jesus,'" Henry said. "Sing, little brother, just sing."

Feathers fell from Henry's costume onto Fred's lap, but he sang, in a crackly, gravelly voice, and he sang the next hymn as the door burst open, and he sang again while Henry squeezed his fingers ever tighter and insisted, "The next verse, Fred. Don't forget the next verse," and Fred kept singing, as his voice rose with his brother's and two female voices joined them, one his wife's, Fred thought, but she slurred her words and a fourth voice joined them.

Henry loosened his grip on Fred's fingers.

Fred opened his eyes. No one was there. Goosebumps ran up and down his arms. The church was empty except for one white feather on his lap.

The door opened.

"Fred?"

It was Mildred. "You coming, sweetheart? Your brother's in the car. We just found him there, grinning in the back seat, his flannel shirt in his lap. It's getting late, and my roast has been cooking all afternoon."

"Yes, dear," Fred said, clearing his throat. It felt a little constricted. "I'll be there in just a minute."

From the Sheriff's Calls Section of the Point Reyes Light
August 13, 2015

CHILENO VALLEY: At 6:57 p.m. the driver of one of the vehicles in the aforementioned accident fled on foot through a field, his blue boxers showing under his green shorts as he headed for shelter in a red barn.

Jackson Pollock

"Colors! Again!" Beatrice declared. "Just think of all those colors—blue, green, red— primary colors, Lucas. You can paint the whole world with primary colors."

Lucia rolled her eyes. An LVN nurse, she was Beatrice's day nurse—that's when her bunions weren't killing her and she could get a ride out to Inverness Park from her new son-in-law Buddy Boy. She wished she could remember his name. Miela had told her a million times. "Yes, Mrs. Fisher. Colors! How wonderful. Do you want your paints today?"

Beatrice brightened. Grabbed the sides of her walker, stood up. "Yes. Please, Lucas, of course. Paint!"

Lucia, bristling at the name Lucas, pulled herself up to her 5'-2" frame and headed off to the studio. She shouldn't have mentioned anything about paints and now Mrs. Fisher was going to bury herself in them. Oils, of course, which meant a tin of turpentine. If only Mrs. Fisher would use acrylics, but she wouldn't hear of such travesty. Perhaps, this time?

"Come to your studio, then, Mrs. Fisher?" Lucia called, hoping for less clean up.

"And leave 'One Life to Live'? What? Then I won't find out who Samantha marries. Heavens no, bring my paints in here." Beatrice narrowed her eyes. What was Lucas thinking? Maybe it was time to get a new boy.

Lucia brought in the paints, a tin of turpentine, a jar full of brushes, a palette, and rags. She set them in front of Mrs. Fisher on a TV tray and Mrs. Fisher sat up, looking her up and down.

"Forget something Lucas?" she snapped.

Lucia studied her collection. "Nope. Everything's here, ma'am." She gave Mrs. Fisher a thumbs up.

"And what do you expect me to paint on? My teeth?"

Oh dear God, Lucia thought, she was losing it. She brought out canvases of many sizes, set them by Mrs. Fisher's walker, and waited.

"All right! Let the festivities begin," Mrs. Fisher trilled and picked up a brush. She squeezed a glop of red on her palette, tapped her brush through it and swept a swath of red across a canvas. "Start with red, always start with red, boy." Mrs. Fisher squinted at her canvas and spread great brush loads of color across it, peering under and above her thick glasses, dipping her brush in turpentine and covering her canvas with that as well.

The painting didn't really look like Jackson Pollock—no drips and splatters—and it didn't look like Kandinsky with great splashes of color, or Mondrian either. Lucia sighed. She wished she could remember more from her art-history class in high school but it had been summer and warm and she'd kept dozing off. She headed back to the kitchen to do the dishes. Mrs. Fisher liked them done by hand and there were a lot of them.

She was listening to the dialogue from the TV— "Samantha, no—you couldn't! No please don't shoot. Samantha!" —when Lucia heard a crash. She looked into the sink. Nothing broken there. Tried to hear over the noise from the TV. Something was out there clattering. Had Mrs. Fisher fallen from her walker? She ran to the living room.

Mrs. Fisher had flipped over her walker and, still standing, was waving her arms in the air, her paint brush flailing about, throwing paint everywhere. "Oh Lucas! Sam's shot the sheriff! Isn't that wonderful? Join me in the closing credits. I love this song."

"Oh dear, Mrs. Fisher," Lucia replied. There was paint everywhere—drips on the sofa, across the carpet, along the front and back of Mrs. Fisher's smock, even on the ceiling and the TV.

"It's a joy to be alive, Lucas!" Mrs. Fisher pirouetted, flung her brush in the air, and threw it at the wall. Mrs. Fisher saw Lucia's crestfallen face. "It's my house, Lucas! I don't give a shit!" she exclaimed and headed off to her bedroom.

"Oh, Mrs. Fisher, you feeling all right?" Lucia called after her while surveying the ruination of what had once been a pretty living room. She picked up a rag.

"And don't touch a thing, Lucas!" Mrs. Fisher shouted. "If Jackson Pollock can do it, so can I!"

Lucia looked down the hallway at the small old lady peering around a door, her nightie clutched close to her chest. "Bring me some tea, won't you, my dear?"

Lucia left everything, except the turpentine. That she closed and set outside the front door. A staunch environmentalist, she didn't take well to petroleum smells. She closed all the inks, made up some hot water, brought out Mrs. Fisher's best china, cups, and saucers, and set them on doilies on a silver tray. Mrs. Fisher's cat Peaches followed her around the house, so she fed her first and, tray in hand, and meandered down the hallway as the cat kept rubbing at her legs and threatening to take her down.

She found Mrs. Fisher in bed, with a bed jacket on, fluffing up her pillows, and reaching for Peaches, who made her way onto an opposite pillow, curled up and fell asleep."Quite the morning, Mrs. Fisher."

"Of course, of course, it's always that way when I paint." Flecks of red, blue, and green paint peppered her arms and cheeks. Her gray eyes were as bright as Lucia had ever seen. Was she taking her meds correctly? Should she call the doc?

"Thank you, my dear Lucas. Have a seat, boy."

Lucia lifted a stack of records off a nearby hardback chair and set them on the floor.

"Bet you think I'm a nut, Lucas."

"Not at all, Mrs. Fisher," Lucia lied.

"Oh, come off it." Mrs. Fisher took a sip of her tea."Nice—just the way I like it. Now. Have you seen this?" She waved one knobby finger at a picture book on her dressing room table. "That's my name on the cover, girl." She snickered. "My cover, girl." She pressed smooth the ruffles on her bed jacket and leaned forward. "Now tell me again about that accident. The driver had on blue shoes ..."

Lucia looked at Mrs. Fisher. She called her girl, she was lucid? Then she picked up the art book, felt its heft. Opened the page. Fabulous rich-colored paintings on every page, gallery openings, photos of famous people and one of a familiar face with those same gray eyes. She was about to mention that, no, the driver was wearing blue boxers not blue shoes, when she glanced up at Mrs. Fisher, the book heavy in her lap, a lifetime. "That's right, Mrs. Fisher, blue shoes."

"Green barn?" Mrs. Fisher asked.

"Of course," Lucia smiled. "The Green Barn."

"And a red shirt," Mrs. Fisher exclaimed, clapping her hands.

"That's right, Mrs. Fisher."

"Never forget, little girl." Mrs. Fisher smiled. "I may be old but I remember everything, Lucia. Absolutely everything."

**From the Sheriff's Calls Section of the Point Reyes Light
August 13, 2015**

STINSON BEACH: At 3:06 p.m. two dogs were barking at passersby from a car.

Bolinas Prefix; 868

"Barking dogs? Really?" Alice asked Beth-Ann. "All dogs bark in cars. What were these people thinking who made the call? I bet they never had a dog of their own."

The girls were sitting on the beach, by the naked-lady statue. Alice wanted to go swimming, but the waves were a little high, the water was cold, and reading the *Light* was much more fun.

Beth-Ann chewed on a fingernail. She had a month before she had to move to Davis to live with her dad, and she wanted to spend as much time as she could wiggling her toes in the sand and spending time with Alice. She was going to miss her best friend.

"I guess," Beth-Ann said. She didn't want to talk about dogs; she wanted to talk about boys. "Are you going to call him?"

"Call who?" Alice answered, digging a hole with her foot.

"You know who, Kevin. I saw him making eyes at you in history class, third period. Alice, you've got to do something. About your hair. Wear makeup. Flirt. Let him know you care."

"Kevin's a dweeb, Beth-Ann."

"Not really. He likes chemistry, you like chemistry. It's a match made in heaven."

Alice couldn't care less about boys. The whole dating thing was foreign to her. Hair? Her hair was fine. Makeup? She'd been to Macy's with Beth-Ann once and all the little cases had been so expensive. She didn't have that kind of money.

"You going to swim, Alice, or spend all day reading the paper?"

"If you come with me," Alice said. "You know the Buddy System."

Beth-Ann looked at her freshly manicured toes, the red polish glittering in the sun. "I suppose."

Alice pulled off her sweatshirt.

"Wow, Alice, I didn't know they made bikinis that small."

"Come off it, Beth-Ann." Alice's swimwear was not a bikini at all. It was a pair of shorts, a little too tight, and a sports bra. "My mom—didn't, hadn't. Leave me alone." Alice ran to the water, not looking back, and strode in to the tops of her thighs. Jesus, the water was cold. That doggone Beth-Ann. Alice always felt small around her. Would life be easier or harder with Beth-Ann in Davis? Lonely, no doubt, but better? She wasn't sure.

Beth-Ann followed and stepped into knee-high water. "Alice, it's a terrible thing, trying to make me swim. The water's too cold. They're bugs and fishes in the water, and all this squishy stuff. Gross." She walked out and went back to her towel.

Boyfriend or no boyfriend, Alice wasn't going to let Beth-Ann think she was a wuss. She strode in boldly, waist high, shivering and thinking warm thoughts, forcing her body to enter slowly, deeper, deeper.

"Have fun!" Beth-Ann shouted from the shore.

Alice glanced back. Beth-Ann was talking to some boys. Screw her, screw the boyfriends, screw it all. Alice dove in. The water streamed over her as she swam hard, trying to warm up her body, her pits where she was the coldest, or her head, which she brought down underwater and opened her eyes. She'd always loved the water. She swam a little bit more, then popped up. The waves were steeper here, and wider, and when she spun around to see the shore was a long way off. How'd that happen?

She'd heard about Great White sharks patrolling the shallow waters of Stinson Beach and swam harder, keeping her head above water so she could keep an eye on the shore. It was still a forever long way off. Harder and harder she swam, pushing against a current that was pulling her toward Bolinas Lagoon. She cried out "Help." But her voice died in the wind.

She stopped spinning and focused on one house on shore. She told herself, swim, rest, and keep your eye on the house. It was tiny. Still annoyed with Beth-Ann, she used that energy to swim, swim, rest, and swim. Was the house a little closer or farther away? She couldn't tell. She wasn't cold anymore, and if she didn't allow panic to overwhelm her she'd be all right.

Head down, stroking hard, she hit something with her hand. A shark? She recoiled. Fifty feet from shore and she was going to be bit by a shark? She looked down into the water. It wasn't a shark. It was a surfboard. A guy in a wetsuit.

"What are you doing all the way out here?" he asked.

She treaded water, hard, trying to stay warm. "Current. Got caught. Have to swim. Long way," she choked.

A long arm bent down. He was on his knees now. "Grab my arm and when I say, kick, kick, and kick hard."

She heard his command and tried getting up on the surfboard. The top of it was rough, which hurt her skin. She couldn't hold on.

"Again," he commanded. "Try again. Kick as if your life depended on it."

Alice grabbed his arm with her hand and tightened her other hand on the surfboard. Then she kicked as hard as she could and got her chest up on the board. "Good. Good. Now, climb up. I'll help you."

Alice, feeling like a floppy fish, though a grateful one, eased herself up on the board— her chest, the top of her legs, then one leg and the other until she was crouched on the board, behind him. "Thanks," she sputtered.

Together, they paddled to the beach. She held tight to the board as they crested the waves and ground out the last twenty feet from shore. She climbed off and shook his hand.

"Thank you again," she chattered, now shivering.

"Not a good idea to swim that far," he said, tucking his surfboard under his arm. He looked like a black fish to Alice. "You must be freezing. C'mon, I'll get you a towel."

And before Alice could say no, he'd wrapped her in a fluffy towel. A golden retriever, on a leash and attached to his gear bag, jumped up and down as they came near.

"I'm Tim," he said, "and your name is?"

The golden was wagging so hard, his whole backside was involved, his long tail swishing Alice's legs.

"I'm Alice," she said, petting the dog.

"Meet Betty," Tim said.

Alice noticed a shadow approaching on the sand. It was Beth-Ann, marching over.

"You must be awfully cold," Tim said folding Alice in the towel a little tighter and rubbing her arms and shoulders. With the activity and the wagging tail, Alice felt warmth in ways she didn't think possible.

"I live in Bolinas and commute to Drake," Tim said. "Surfed all my life—but I've never rescued a mermaid before."

"You okay, Alice?" Beth-Ann asked, noting the cozy scene with Alice, the boy, and the dog.

When she drew closer, the dog started to bark.

"Easy, Betty," Tim said.

Alice gave Beth-Ann a little wave.

"That your friend? You should get in warm clothes, Alice," Tim said, holding his arm around Alice and walking toward Beth-Ann.

Betty loped along ahead.

"I'm no mermaid," Alice answered, forever grateful. "Not even really want to be one."

"If you want to swim again," Tim said, "give me a call. Four-oh-six-seven."

"No prefix?" Alice asked.

"My grandfather's number," he said. "Now, of course, you have to add eight-six-eight and four-one-five. What a pain." He headed inland, waving over his shoulder.

"And you thought you didn't need boys," Beth-Ann whispered once Alice was near. "What did you think you were doing, going swimming way the hell out there?"

Alice wouldn't, couldn't, tell her why she'd gone. She repeated Tim's number to herself and waved good-bye.

The girls walked by a car at the end of Brighton Avenue. Two Chihuahuas were barking like crazy.

"Irritating little farts." Alice said. They passed the car and the barking ceased. "I'll say it again, Beth-Ann. Calling about barking dogs is no reason to inform the sheriff."

"Oh God," Beth-Ann said. "I was about to call them myself when I saw you so far out there, and then there was that guy ..."

"Tim."

"Yes, Tim." Beth-Ann opened her car door and handed Alice a warm jacket. "Just how do you do it, Alice?"

"Not on purpose," Alice replied and under her breath whispered 868-4067.

"I bet," Beth-Ann said, turning on the car and the heat up high. "You know, you have a knack." She shifted into drive. "Next time, though, how about meeting boys the easy way?" she asked. "On land?"

***From the Sheriff's Calls Section of the Point Reyes Light
August 13, 2015***

STINSON BEACH: At 8:23 p.m. a resident said a neighbor had scattered little bits of paper scrawled with the word "devil."

Midnight Came with a Crash

"They're after me, I know it," Elizabeth McPhail said, while nervously fingering the phone cord to her black rotary-dial telephone. "Officer—please, you've got to do something."

Linda Kettleman adjusted the ear piece on her cell phone and sighed. Third nut this week, there didn't seem to be any end to them. "Do you need help, ma'am?"

"Satan's behind this, I'm sure," Elizabeth exclaimed, pacing her tiny bungalow high above the beach. On a clear day, she had a view of the ocean: now it was foggy and she couldn't see her own fence, much less the water five hundred feet below.

"Satan, ma'am?" Linda asked, curious. "And where and when did you find the papers?"

"All over my yard. It's a fenced yard, Officer. With security cameras and my big dog Josie who barks all the time. I thought they'd given her poison, but she's dreaming here beside me, her big paws twitching to and fro. Do you think she's dreaming about the devil too?"

"I doubt it," Linda replied.

"They've been after me for years. Sneaking into the house in the morning, putting salt in my tea, butter in my soup, devils, all of them. Making life miserable for an old widow like me." Elizabeth sobbed.

"Do you want me to come out, ma'am?" Linda asked. What could she do? Review the little pieces of paper? Sometimes it took hardly anything to push the local residents right off the edge.

"Yes, please do. And make it snappy." Satisfied, Elizabeth marched back into the kitchen and laid out the notes like little soldiers. There were ten of them. She set them in a row, the word "devil" on each one, bright and red as blood. She bent down to look carefully, but her reading glasses kept slipping off her nose. She tossed them back on their chain, slammed open the front door, and went up to the gate.

They were seven feet tall, wooden, and heavy, and blocked everyone's view of her property. She opened one onto a quiet single-lane street. No one was out, not even old Mr. Stritch who lived across the street and was forever puttering in his front yard. He had a 1972 beige teardrop Saab. Down the road it was a different story, with the teenage twin boys, Bill and Steve. Their cars were haphazard, covered with duct tape and much loved. Were they the perpetrators who liked to scare little old ladies like her?

A few minutes later she saw the cruiser pull up. Feeling obligated to please, she asked the officer, "Would you like something to eat or drink? I make a mean pecan pie."

Linda Kettleman shook her head. "The notes, ma'am?"

Examining the handwriting, drawn in a bold fashion with a red magic marker, she told Ms. McPhail in no uncertain terms that they were a prank. "Anyone after you, ma'am?"

"Everyone, Officer," Elizabeth said.

"If it happens again, call us. Here's my card." Linda handed over her info, took the notes, put them in a plastic bag, and headed back to the cruiser. It was going to be a long night if the fruits and nuts in town kept this up.

Back in the house, Elizabeth set up her shrine. Against the devil. She'd tried the Hindu god Ganesh—the elephant with all the hands—but that had brought dog droppings to her door. She'd tried Jesus on a cross outside her gate, but that had been turned upside down and splattered with mud. This time she was more careful. She set out five candles, a statue of Mary, a cloth picture of Vishnu, a small ceramic Buddha, and, turning off all the lights and holding a rosary and praying, she fell asleep in her chair.

Midnight came with a crash.

She awoke suddenly, candles sputtering on their ceramic dishes, Buddha knocked over, and by her feet, a red pitchfork.

"Oh God!" she yelled and picked up the pitchfork. It was hot. She threw it against the wall where it burst into flames. Or had it? She looked closer, the remains of a bottle of Jack Daniels still in her hand. No. The plastic pitchfork had clattered to the floor, still and cold.

Elizabeth turned on all the lights, blew out her candles, dressed in a bathrobe, and carrying the pitchfork, opened her front door and then the gates, and stared out onto a dark road. Not a light was on. Somehow she could see, though. Was there a little glow from the pitchfork? She stumbled to the twins' house and pounded on the door. No answer.

Standing there in the dark, holding a plastic red pitchfork and feeling unhinged, she was about to turn around and go back home when a hand closed in on her shoulder. She screamed.

"Oh heavens, Ms. McPhail. It's just me, Norma, the twins' mom. We were just coming back from the movies. What a surprise, to see you standing at our front door.

Why, Ms. McPhail, you're trembling like a leaf. And what's with the pitchfork? Practicing for Halloween? Boys, the lights."

The road exploded into daylight. Elizabeth felt foolish and small in her pink pedal pushers, her bunny slippers with fluffy toes, her nightie fluttering in the breeze, and a plastic pitchfork in her hand.

"Someone's been scaring me silly, Norma, and I'm sure it's your boys. They're leaving notes with the word 'devil' all over my yard and breaking into my house. Making my life miserable. I've already had the cops out here once. I'll call them again."

"You'll do nothing of the sort, Ms. McPhail," Norma said, patting her hand. "You've had a scare. Poor thing."

Elizabeth dropped the pitchfork and put out her hand.

"Come inside. Shall I call your doc? Boys, make up a pot of chamomile tea."

Elizabeth felt herself being dragged into a modern house with tall ceilings, enormous windows, and a huge fireplace. She followed Norma into the kitchen.

"Midnight, too, Ms. McPhail," Norma tut-tutted. "Are you doing all right? Worried about something? Can't sleep?"

"It would be a lot better if I hadn't received all those notes," Elizabeth snapped.

Bill and Steve were sitting at one end of the granite kitchen counter, pecking away at their cell phones.

"Boys?" Ms. McPhail said. "Any explanation?"

"We didn't do anything, we just got back from five days at Dad's," one of them said.

"Goodnight," said the other. They ran up a flight of stairs at the back of the house.

Elizabeth felt uncomfortable. She didn't belong here in this house with white wall-to-wall carpet and fancy art on the walls. Even with the boys upstairs there wasn't a book or paper out of place. And no TV. Anywhere. "Thank you for your tea, Norma," Elizabeth said, rising up from her stool. "You've been very kind."

"I'm just trying to be a good neighbor, Ms. McPhail. Call us anytime you feel threatened," Norma offered, opening the heavy oak front door. "Or if you need anything, of course ..."

Elizabeth, confused, wrapped her bathrobe tighter around her. She looked for the plastic pitchfork to throw in the trash but couldn't find it. Tomorrow, she'd find it for sure. The darkness enveloped her now, crossing over and covering her like a shroud. But she found her house, her gate, all right. Out in front, attached to the upside-down cross, was the pitchfork, glowing red, slowly burning down the gate.

From the Sheriff's Calls Section of the Point Reyes Light
October 1, 2015

INVERNESS: At 11:17 p.m. deputies contacted an adult couple that had been having loud intercourse. They had disturbed other guests at the hotel who feared the woman was being "raped". The woman stated she was "very happy" and "needed no assistance". The deputy informed the couple that the hotel walls were thin and they had disturbed the other guests. The couple stated they were done for the night.

The Chifforobe

"Oh Fred!" Mildred exclaimed and held the newspaper to her chest. "Oh my God, Fred, we were never like this."

Fred rolled his eyes. He had wished they'd been like that, indeed. He thought a moment. He couldn't remember the last time when —

"Take my hand, Fred, its muddy here," Mildred demanded. They were walking on Chicken Ranch Beach on an early Saturday morning and the tide had been high in the night, moving all the trails and sand around. "I could say they were rude, those people," she said ambling by a collection of shells and seaweed.

Fred, treading carefully around wet spots, followed his little wife. They were on a new exercise regimen—taking walks two times a day. It gave Mildred another chance to chatter—as if she ever stopped—but it gave him time to take a break from both baseball and beer. Not his idea.

"We did that," Mildred said. "We were staying at your father's house in Tomales."

Fred could hardly remember his childhood, much less his parents' place. Red? Gray? In town or out? All he remembered was the kitchen with what his parents

215

called the icebox and his mother's pinto beans. He wished he could say something about her cooking, but alas, she couldn't cook either.

"Your father sent us upstairs to two different bedrooms—on opposite sides of the house. As if, as if," Mildred went on. She stopped at a creek. A foot wide? Two? No worries, she had Fred.

He put out his arm. "Sounds somewhat familiar," he said.

"We couldn't stand being apart."

"We were used to it," Fred said. "We never lived together before then like kids do today. What are you going on about, dear?" It was getting chilly. Was a storm coming? His feet were tired. Mildred, however, was striding down toward the Bluewater, the kayak rental place.

"Dear! Wait up!"

"What were we, twelve?" she asked. "I always liked you, Fred Rhinehart."

"Twelve? No. Sixteen. Your parents were out of town. They let you stay with mine."

"We could have stayed alone. We were teenagers, not children."

"My parents were no fools," Fred said. "Decorum. You know, think about what the neighbors would say. There were wack jobs like Mrs.Willis, even then."

"Still. What did they know? I wasn't wearing flannel nighties back then, Fred."

Fred wished he could remember what she had been wearing. Whatever it was, there seemed to be a lot of it.

"It was two a.m."

"The witching hour," Mildred said, taking his hand.

"If only we could feel that way now," Fred mumbled. His wife would not be pleased if she heard him. She was continuing to talk into the wind, then turned suddenly, startling him. "I'm not the one who practically knocked over the Chifforobe."

"Wasn't my fault. You started it," Fred said.

"Started what?" She looked at him with a pained expression.

"Daisy started barking. My parents ran down the hall and you were laughing."

"And ever since, Fred, you have been a source of great amusement."

"It wasn't fair. There was no place to hide," Fred added. "One hallway, one window, one broken door in the Chifforobe."

"I still stuffed you in. You were thinner then, buster."

Fred picked up a ball a dog had left. Daisy had loved the chase. So, indeed, had he.

"And if you hadn't sneezed."

"Dusty in there," Fred said. "I remember the smell. Musty, and tight."

"So," Mildred took Fred's hand as they re-crossed the tiny creek on their way back to the bridge. "Your parents were a little miffed."

"A little?" Fred grabbed her hand a little tighter. "I recall something more potent than that. They grounded me for a month."

"So? Distance makes the heart grow fonder."

Fred thought so. He'd love Mildred a whole lot more if she lived down the street.

"It was hard," Mildred went on. "We were so much in love."

"Yes," Fred said. "We married that fall. You looked great in your wedding dress."

"Sure came off easy later that night," Mildred said. She'd downed her flask and was feeling frisky.

"Shall we try again?" Fred asked, leading her back over the bridge. "I'm sure your wedding dress still fits."

"Loose. Probably, is more like it. So, Fred—do you think we woke the other guests at the hotel that night?"

"I don't recall," Fred blushed. He'd remembered all of it. Someone had pounded on their door. "It was you who made all the noise, dear, with your whooping and hollering." He guided her into his VW.

"I'm too ladylike to make those kinds of noises," Mildred clucked, pulling on her seatbelt. It was stuck. "Could you?"

Fred leaned down and fastened it for her, giving her a kiss on the way back to his seat.

She closed her eyes and moaned.

"So, it was you," he said, feeling that kiss. First proper kiss he'd had in over two years. "Oh dear, shall we go home and disappear?" He felt flushed all over.

"And have someone call the cops?" She pounded on the dash with her hand. "What are you thinking, Fred, have you lost your mind?"

And Fred, slowly turning the car around, only wished he had.

**From the Sheriff's Calls Section of the Point Reyes Light
August 20, 2015**

OLEMA: At 5:44 p.m. something was found on Bear Valley
Road.

The Russian

"What do you think that 'something' was, Beth-
Ann?" Alice asked.

"I have no idea," Beth-Ann replied, swinging her
backpack up over her shoulder.

The girls were walking down Levee Road, and
although there was only a little traffic, the few cars going
over sixty still scared the beejeesus out of Beth-Ann. She
heard the whine of a truck engine revving up behind
them and pushed Alice toward the bushes.

"Jeesus, that was close," Alice said, feeling shaky.

In a few minutes, they crossed a footbridge and
entered the woods proper. To Alice it was a wonderland.
A hundred feet from the road they couldn't see the cars,
much less hear them. They were surrounded by brush
from their ankles to a canopy over their heads. At the
first sign of a cut and a bench, they headed in, away from
the path, and sat down by Lagunitas Creek. A heron, on
the opposite side, took off in a whoosh of wings.

"Someday, some way, someone's going to build a
decent bridge, so we can walk all the way to town safely,"
Alice said, taking off her backpack and setting it down on
the bench.

"We'll be old ladies by then," Beth-Ann answered.
She slipped her bandanna from her hair, shook it, and
retied it across her forehead.

To Alice she looked like a pirate. She knocked
sand out of her shoes and pulled out her copy of the *Point
Reyes Light.* "So, why would a 'something' make it into the
Sheriff's Calls?"

Beth-Ann shrugged.

"If it was a dog, they'd say."

"That's right."

"And if it was a wallet, they'd say too, as they've done before," Alice said.

"You've been reading a lot of these." Beth-Ann grinned. She pulled out a doobie and matches. "Do you mind?"

"My grandmother is nuts about the Sheriff's Calls. It's the only thing that gets her out of bed. That and the beauty parlor."

"I wish I had a grandma who was still around," Beth-Ann replied, speaking slowly, to keep the smoke in her mouth as long as possible. "What do you think it was? That 'something'?"

"Something like ... soup." Alice giggled. "A book, an iPhone, a passport, a gun."

"A gun? Wouldn't they say? Besides, who'd leave a gun on the sidewalk?"

"Who said it was in town?" Alice was enjoying the game. "What if it was robbers, at the Palace Market, and they got into their Chevy, and the driver misplaced his keys, and they all ran away and one of them dropped a gun?"

"No. Too convoluted. Too much work to make that sound real," Beth-Ann said. "No, it wasn't a gun."

"How about a person? Or someone left a child?" Alice asked, feeling a little worried. If they didn't get home soon, would Mom get anxious and call the cops?

"No, it was found on Bear Valley Road," Beth-Ann said. "Where the tourists go. Something like a cell phone? Something valuable?"

"In that case, then, nothing funny about losing a cell phone," Alice said. Her phone was the lifeline to everything she held dear—Mom's number, Grandma's, Beth-Ann's, and all her music and photos.

Beth-Ann grabbed Alice's arm. "What's that? I heard something."

"Something? Like what?" Alice whispered.

Both girls turned at the same time.

Two dogs, a beagle and a pointer, came rushing toward them, the beagle smaller, but definitely in charge. Both barking ferociously.

Beth-Ann and Alice jumped on top of the bench and yelled, "Get away! Get them away!"

"Boris! Karloff! Get over here!" A man's voice broke out of the bushes and the dogs immediately stopped barking and ran back to the trail where the man was standing. "Sorry about that," he said, tipping his straw hat.

"They scared the shit out of me!" Alice exclaimed, still holding her backpack in front of her. "You Russian?"

"Oh, hell no. Boris Karloff was an actor and I like calling his name," the man said, coming closer. "He was English, but pretended to be Russian." He tied his dogs to a tree and directed them to sit down. "I'm Yevgeny," he said. "My parents were revolutionaries, but me, not so much. You live around here?"

Alice swallowed hard. They were at the end of a dead-end path and no one knew where they were. To each side of them was poison oak, to their back was the creek, and in front of them a Russian guy. He looked just about thirty, with dirty blond hair, a scruffy beard, a beat-up backpack, and shorts that reached to the bottom of his knees.

"So," Alice offered, "did you see the newspaper?" She held it out with trembling hands to put something between her and him. "It says that the cops found something on Bear Valley Road." She passed the paper over and slid down away from him, giving him a little room on the bench. A path of escape, she thought, though a narrow one.

"How silly," Yevgeny said, pulling off his hat and running his hand through his hair. "You girls live around here?"

There was something about him that gave Alice the creeps. A tourist? They never came here. She shrugged her shoulders.

"Tomales," Beth-Ann said. "My dad, the sheriff, we're waiting for him. Where're you from?"

Yevgeny laughed. "The Central Valley."

"We were thinking," Alice said, "that maybe that something was a suitcase, or a phone."

"I wouldn't think so," Yevgeny said. "I bet that something was a ... gun."

Beth-Ann and Alice looked at each other for a second and bolted, away from the bench, just barely squeezing by Boris and Karloff who were snarling and barking. They dashed down the path, across the bridge. Levee Road never looked so good.

"Wave down the first car you see, Alice!" Beth-Ann yelled. "I'll go across the street and do the same."

"No. Stay here with me!"

A tow truck, going fast, came barreling toward her. She waved her arms and the truck stopped in a squeal of brakes and a lot of banging from the back. Alice looked at the driver. It was Tiny, heading back to Cheda's. She waved.

"There's a bad guy in the woods!" The girls tried to climb into the cab.

"I'll call the Sheriff." Tiny jumped down. "Where is he?"

"He's got dogs," Beth-Ann said. "Big dogs. He's Russian!"

"Get in."

She hoped Tiny would drive them to Inverness Park, home to Mom and her collection of *House Beautiful* magazines, but Tiny ran across the bridge, leaving them alone in the truck.

"What if the man kills Tiny?" Alice asked a second later. "Come on!" She grabbed Beth-Ann's hand and dragged her back into the woods. Alice expected to hear barking and growling, but heard nothing. Had Tiny already been killed?

Beth-Ann and Alice stopped at the first cut off and peered around the bushes to look. Yevgeny didn't have Tiny at gunpoint at all. The two guys were laughing and shooting the breeze.

"Everything okay?" Beth-Ann asked.

"It's my grandmother's cousin, Yevgeny, from Oakdale," Tiny said. "Here for a visit."

The dogs, Boris and Karloff, stood up and growled.

"Quiet," Yevgeny ordered and the dogs lay down. "It's okay, girls," he smiled and waved. "I'm the something everyone's been looking for."

From the Sheriff's Calls Section of the Point Reyes Light
September 3, 2015

NICASIO: At 7:17 p.m. a ranch hand reported a man and a woman with a white Mercedes doing a nude photo shoot. They had told the caller not to block their car.

The White Mercedes

"I sure wish I'd been there," Justin said to Thomas. They were sitting in the Commons, the little park next to the yellow house in the center of Point Reyes Station. The bike racks were overflowing.

"Thomas? You listening? Naked people. Nicasio. Ready to roll?"

"Not a sight I would've driven by," Thomas replied. He jabbed at a picnic table with his pen knife. He was still sore about Marlene. He would have done anything to have seen her naked.

"The guy didn't—you know, the photographer— didn't tell the ranch hand to get out of the way or ask for privacy. But why would the ranch hand block their car?"

"To see more, I guess," Thomas carved a big "M" in the table, making it deeper with each stroke. "They have all these naked women in magazines and on TV. Now, in public. Do you see that kind of thing in Cambridge?"

"Nah. All the interesting stuff happens out here in West Marin."

"All the interesting stuff happens to you," Thomas said bitterly. It was true. All the cool stuff went to Justin. Learning to drive a tractor at 12, the sports car his parents gave him at 16. All Thomas got was a broken down VW diesel truck that shook like crazy and sputtered smoke.

"So, what's been going on since I left?"

"Dazzling lights of downtown Kentfield where they roll up the sidewalks at seven. Or rich couples coming out here on the weekends to their favorite restaurants."

Thomas didn't want to mention his date with Marlene, where he'd fallen asleep and she'd dumped him the next day. Since then he'd been feeling a little low. "It's the same. Bicyclists still ride side by side and clog all the roads."

"In Cambridge bicyclists are everywhere, at night, in the rain, on every doorstep, on every pathway, lights on, not so much. They're crazy. You still have that old ten-speed your parents gave you? It's a classic."

On this subject Thomas stayed mute. He had just bought—with his savings from stocking shelves all summer for the Palace Market—the best bike he could afford, a candy apple red cruiser. He liked it. He wouldn't say anything; Justin would call him a wimp.

"Do you think we should go out there, Thomas?" Justin asked. "To Nicasio, I mean?"

"And drive around looking for naked people?" Thomas laughed. "Like they would just pull off the Petaluma-Point Reyes Road in their car, in front of the reservoir, perhaps, and take off all their clothes?"

"Oh, I wish," Justin said. "My kind of people."

"Your kind of people are college students, hot girls, and techies, not hippies communing with nature, or fancy New York photographers looking for a great backdrop."

"We can pretend to be fishing."

"I've never seen you gut fish, Justin. Or bait a hook."

"I'm a babe magnet, Thomas—even you say so. And I know some families in Nicasio."

"The family? The ranch hand?"

"Uh, no." Justin's heart sank. He wanted to do something with his best friend, something other than hanging around their little town, waiting for dad to call. "Stay here if you want, Thomas, I'm only here for a few days. I need to see water."

"From what you tell me the Charles River is full of water."

"Big water. Water that's not surrounded by buildings. Water where I can see hills. My mom's sick. If you don't want to go, I'll take her."

"We could both take her," Thomas answered. He'd heard about Justin's mom from his dad. Things did not sound good. That's why Justin had come home. "We could act like gentlemen."

"That's an idea," Justin said. "But no foul language. She sits in front."

"Of course," Thomas said, thinking hard. His parents were both in good health, he had never thought about mortality before, not like this, not so close to home.

"You think she's up to it?" Thomas asked. It didn't seem appropriate.

"We'll see," Justin said, getting a text. "Just what I thought, she'd love to go."

"To see naked people?" Thomas asked.

"No. Water, you dingbat. She wants to see the reservoir."

From the Sheriff's Calls Section of the Point Reyes Light
October 1, 2015

OLEMA: At 9:48 a.m. a woman hiking the Bolinas Ridge Fire Road with her sister and three dogs said a man had run past them wearing only socks, running shoes, and a red baseball cap. He had not made any obscene gestures.

Happy Hour

"Well, I'm certainly pleased about that," Mildred said, patting her hair on the way out of Doris's salon.

"Pleased about what, babycakes?" Fred asked, longing to go into the Western next door for a beer. It was only 11 a.m., but it was happy hour somewhere and he needed his Negra Modelo.

"Don't you read the paper, Fred?"

Fred hadn't read anything but *Racing News* and *Baseball Forever* for ten years. "What is bothering you this time, dear?" He'd learned long ago—maybe year two in his marriage to Mildred—that he had to say, 'Yes, dear,' to whatever Mildred wanted. It had been a good plan, now after fifty years, it was worth the risk to do something different. "Let's go have a pop!" he called brightly. "I'll give you my cell phone and you can call your sister. Here's a nice bench outside. Right here."

Mildred stared at him long and hard. No matter how long they'd been married, Fred still didn't get it. "No."

"No for the bench or no for the pop?" Fred asked, confused.

"I don't drink soda, I don't drink beer, and I don't lounge around bars on Tuesday mornings."

Fred sighed, took his wife's elbow, brought her to the passenger side of his '57 VW, and opened the door. As she climbed inside she took her cane from him at the last minute, then knee-capped him with it.

227

"Ow! What was that for?" Fred kept an eye on the cane, and once she got it firmly planted inside the car, he shut the door. "What's the matter with you?"

"You were not listening," Mildred said, and pulled down her mirror to check her hair. Doris had done it right this time, mostly white with just a shock of blue over her ears. Reverse osmosis, Mildred had said and Doris, with the cup of blue die in her hand, replied, "Whatever," and applied the paintbrush in just the right place.

"Listening about what?"

"Oh, okay, for Heaven's sake." Mildred opened her paper and pointed to the Sheriff's Call that had made her blush. "This."

Fred couldn't really make out the tiny lettering, even while squinting, so he just laughed and smiled at his little wife.

"This, you dingbat." Mildred shot her finger through the paper.

"I can't read anything when you tear it, dear," Fred said patiently, and put the car into first. It purred as he drove down 'B' Street. "Home, then?"

"Not until we stop at the Public Safety Building."

"What for? Your corns are bothering you? Or your bunions? You don't like the way Doris did your hair? Or is Mrs. Willis bugging you again?"

"Just drive, you big lunk, and stop making fun of me." Mildred tapped her feet on the floor mat. Actually, he was right. Her bunions were killing her, and the new sandals she'd bought from Zappos—a place Doris had told her about—didn't fit. "You don't understand me at all, Fred." She dropped her head in her hands, though she was mostly pretending. She was fine, really, just disappointed by Fred's lack of support. "It wasn't me who saw that runner on Bolinas Ridge Trail."

Fred sped up, happy his wife was still chatting, having forgotten about stopping at the Public Safety Building. He rattled across the Green Bridge and lowered his speed from 40 to 25 along Levee Road. A line of tourists and locals formed behind him. It was a good day, too, no goddamn bicyclists clogging the road and he could enjoy his view of the marsh by himself—that is, aside from Miss Busybody beside him. It was nearly noon, time for his peanut butter sandwich, a glass of milk, two double-stuff Oreos, and a nap. That is, if Mildred found herself in the garden again as he hoped.

"The runner was naked, Fred."

Fred slammed on his brakes. "What? Where?"

Tires squealed behind them.

"Not here! Not here!" Mildred was afraid to turn around and look. "Can't you hear their tires squealing behind you? Pull over! We're going to get hit!"

"But I'm not the one who's naked," Fred replied, patting his tummy, his unbuttoned Oxford cloth shirt and thick leather belt with a classy Heinz 57 brass buckle.

"Don't you hear their honking?" Mildred frantically pulled at her car door. "Pull over. Now! Or I'm getting out."

Fred slowed down close to the pedestrian bridge as twenty cars sped up around him, horns blaring.

"They're a fine bunch of fools, aren't they?" Fred said, wiping his sweaty brow with the back of his hand. "Crazy weekend drivers."

"It's time to take away your license, buster."

"Oh Mildred, not you too." Fred leaned over the wheel and thrust the column stick into neutral. "What's your problem, dear?"

"You never listen to me," Mildred sniffed, pulling out a handkerchief. "All you're interested in is baseball."

"Makes perfect sense to me," Fred mumbled.

"Put in your hearing aids, Fred!" Mildred shouted.

"Oh for God's sake." Fred dug into his shirt pocket for the little plastic eggs. He was pleased he found them so quick. He stuck them in, gave his wife a proud grin. They were loose in his ears.

"Those are for your phone, you fool!" She pulled out the paper, opened it to Sheriff's Calls, and was about to put her finger on the tear when she noticed something out of the corner of her eye. It was a red baseball cap, weaving in and out of the bushes down the path through the woods. "It's him!" she said, grabbing Fred's arm.

"Who?" Fred replied, focusing his eyes on movement—that could be a jackrabbit, a coyote, or a dog.

"The naked man!" Mildred squealed. "It's the naked man!"

"And so it is," Fred answered, as a man wearing only running shoes, socks, and a red cap bolted out of the woods and onto Levee Road.

"Good Lord. The world's gone crazy!" Mildred said, holding her hand over her eyes. "Wouldn't that be ... uncomfortable?" she asked, staring at the man.

"Now will you join me for a drink, my sweet? If we hurry, we'll beat him to the Western." Frank cranked the wheel and made a tight U-turn.

"Make it a double, Fred. It's happy hour somewhere."

***From the Sheriff's Calls Section of the Point Reyes Light
October 22, 2015***

POINT REYES STATION: At 5:10 p.m. deputies couldn't find a person who wanted to file a missing person report.

The Missing-Person Report

"What do you think it means that they couldn't find the person who made the call about a missing person, Beth-Ann?" Alice picked her way carefully along the narrow sand spit that was Shell Beach. The tide was up. Her best friend Beth-Ann looked so cool, swinging her purse over her shoulder, while Alice felt awkward and weird carrying the belly-pack purse her mother insisted she use. In two years, she could do whatever she could afford, Mom had said. Alice had no intention of waiting that long. Maybe, now that she was sixteen, she could work at the Station House or something. She'd heard the tips were great.

"Don't move!" Beth-Ann shouted.

Almost falling, Alice looked down. A sharp piece of glass poked up from the sand, inches from her toes.

"I told you we should've worn shoes." Beth-Ann picked the glass up carefully and placed it in a plastic bag. "Be careful. I pick glass up here all the time."

"Thanks." Alice looked carefully before she took another step. Between the water rising and the dangerous sand, she wasn't sure where it was safe to go. What would she have done without Beth-Ann, bled to death?

"The tide's rising," Beth-Ann said. "Come on up to the grass there. Otherwise, we'll both vanish—just like my mother's last boyfriend, who ran off with the silver."

"Your mom had silver? Like, that she polishes?" Alice had only seen that in the movies.

"No, not really, but he did disappear," Beth-Ann said. "Second one this year and I really liked this guy."

231

"Richard, Robert, Henry, Trevor?" Alice asked, trying to remember. Names were elusive to her, hiding in the back of her brain like answers to English exams, which only appeared when exams were over. It wasn't fair. She studied, too. She was no slacker, like that dumb Samantha Taylor, who cheated.

"Trevor used to take me fishing," Beth-Ann said when they reached the car. "It's a good day for a walk. Grab your sandals and let's go to the next beach."

"I can't see you fishing," Alice said, slipping on her raggedy shoes. "So what happens if you land a big one? Does the fish try to pull you into the water—and make you drown?"

"A ten-pound trout? Not likely. I'm too heavy as it is," Beth-Ann said, wending her way through the path beyond Shell Beach.

"Just think of the headline in the *Light*. Teenage girl eaten by man-eating trout."

"It's such a pretty place," Beth-Ann said, looking through the trees at the calm water.

"It's full of great white sharks."

"I don't fish for sharks and I don't fish in Tomales Bay."

"It's still dangerous." Alice sat on a damp log overlooking the water. "I love it here. But looks can be deceiving, Beth-Ann. Just up the middle of the bay, they saved fifty-four kayakers on Hog Island. They were out at night to look at the bio-luminescence when the wind came up and they took shelter wherever they could. In the dark! And last week someone drowned. And someone else ..." she gulped, "... disappeared."

"Oh, Alice," Beth-Ann said, leaning on her friend's shoulder. "Life's taken a bit of a dark turn for you lately, hasn't it?"

Alice, her eyes rimmed with tears, stared at the water. She'd never known Beth-Ann to be so thoughtful. Cool, yes, boy crazy, yes, well-dressed—way better dressed than Alice would ever be. And afraid of nothing. "I guess," she said.

"So, who's this missing person?" Beth-Ann asked.

"Three men in a skiff started out at the mouth of Tomales Bay. They capsized. Coast Guard saved one, the second one drowned, and ..." Alice sputtered, "... they never found the other."

"Oh dear." Beth-Ann put her arm around Alice's shoulders.

A seagull dropped in front of them, swirling above the smooth waves, swooped, grabbed a fish and took off.

"How can they see fish in the water? On a cloudy day like this?" Alice asked. The seagull swept over their heads and headed inland, behind them.

"Let's say Mrs. Willis has gone missing. Would you file a report on her?" Beth-Ann asked.

"My grandmother sure wouldn't. She hates Mrs. Willis."

"So do I," Beth-Ann said. "Scaring you so bad, you dropped your cell phone in the creek."

"No one would call the cops if Mrs. Willis disappeared," Alice replied, standing up. Her shorts were wet. "Come on, this trail goes on forever. Let's walk to Heart's Desire." They crossed one beach and entered the woods again.

"What if it was Doris, my grandma's hairdresser? What if she disappeared?"

"Everyone in town would go searching for her. She's the glue who holds this whole place together." Beth-Ann ducked under a branch. "Look, there's a seal."

Alice looked out onto the calm water. A ripple came and went. "I didn't see anything."

"Just wait, Alice," Beth-Ann said. "Wait and watch with me. The seal will be back."

Alice looked out over the Bay. It was a gray foggy day. Clouds hug the ground and a layer of fog had dropped below the hills above Marshall. "I'm going to miss you when you're gone, Beth-Ann."

"It's only Davis, Alice. I haven't lived with my dad for years."

"A million miles away," Alice said, picking at her hangnail. "For someone without a car. And I'll be stuck here with that dumb Samantha Taylor."

"You could come visit," Beth-Ann said. "My Dad's always liked you."

"With my grades in English, Mom would never let me go," Alice said. "She wants me to study every weekend."

"Shit, with your grades in math and chemistry, you'll make the Dean's List."

"Not with a C minus in English."

"My dad—he'll drive me to Point Reyes."

"That's what they all say."

"No, really, he will. He said so. We can still hang out. Somehow." Beth-Ann looked out onto the water.

"Somehow, sure. What the hell. I guess we can be friends on Facebook."

"We already are."

"Make video calls?" Alice asked.

"We already do," Beth-Ann said.

"Giggle 'til midnight?"

"Sure. Later, even." Beth-Ann laughed.

"But during the day, you'll be meeting cool guys—way more than there are around here. I'll be a nobody," Alice said. "Just a friend from Inverness."

"My best friend from home," Beth-Ann said. "My BFF."

Alice smiled, unconvinced. Still, Beth Ann wasn't moving for a month, the morning was still young, it was Sunday, and she'd finished her homework. But not her reading. Slogging through *Pride and Prejudice* hung heavy on her mind.

Beth-Ann touched Alice's arm. "Look."

Out on the Bay the surface of the water broke. Alice studied the growing mound of water as something emerged. Something with whiskers and a big snout. Something that snorted. She laughed and it dropped. "It just disappeared."

"But it'll be back, just like me," Beth-Ann said. "I won't disappear. You won't have to file a missing-person report on me. All you have to do is call. I'll hop up just like that seal."

"Not if you have a big date," Alice said, feeling better.

"If it's Saturday, or Friday, and," Beth-Ann said. "... maybe Wednesday."

"Any old day. I thought so," Alice said.

"But ... what if it's you, out on a date?" Beth-Ann asked. "Will you call me then?"

From the Sheriff's Calls Section of the Point Reyes Light
October 22, 2015

STINSON BEACH: At 10:45 a.m. a man who had taken an outdoor shower was running naked on the beach.

Darlene

"Are all the Sheriff's Calls like this, Doris?" Darlene Easton asked, pointing to the entry in the *Light*. She was having her hair cut at a beauty salon in Point Reyes Station and had just moved to town.

Doris clicked her scissors. "Um, well, hmm. Not all the time, Darlene." Doris put down her brush and picked up her comb. "Sometimes we have cows in the road. It is a farming community, you know." If she told her new customer that there were lots of loony people in town, would she walk out the door and never come back? Or would she continue to want all the gossip? There was no telling. "Not, not really," Doris lied. It would take more than all the fingers on her right hand to count the times naked people had run around Point Reyes.

Darlene was middle-aged, with a spattering of gray just above her ears. She seemed to like it short, which pleased Doris no end.

"Is it always this quiet on a Monday?" Darlene asked, looking out on an empty street. A car went by every five minutes—about as different from L.A as she could imagine. "Where's the nightlife in this town?" she asked, and leaned forward and pulled out her iPhone.

Doris lifted one hand and gestured over her shoulder to the bar next door. "Back there."

"The restroom? Why, that's disgusting," Darlene said. She was a private investigator, a P.I., trying to retire. Ten years of perps in LA was ten years too long. "Why are you smiling, Doris?"

"Not the restroom, the bar, the Western. It is back through that door or you can go around to the front. They have live music on the weekends. During the week, it's open all day and you can play pool."

They heard the thunk of pool balls.

"See?"

"What's the crowd like there? Farmers? Ranch hands?"

"Locals," Doris answered. "Good old boys. Everyone wears jeans. You want something fancy, go to the Station House across the street. Or to Tony's or Nick's Cove in Marshall. There's all kind of places where they play live music, if that's what you want." Doris picked up her blow dryer. "And how would you like your hair?"

"Wild," Doris said. "Use lots of product. I like a firm look, kind of like a space cadet."

"I wouldn't think you were serious." Doris laughed.

"Maybe, just a little bit. Hell, I wanted quiet, so I moved here, so quiet is what I'll get."

"Just read the *Light*, Darlene. There's not much quiet there. You'll see."

"From what I've already read, you may be right," Darlene giggled. She had made the right decision, coming to this quiet hamlet. "You do toes too?"

Doris pulled out her pedicure tub. With no one else in the shop, Doris could take her time while Amanda Eichstadt was broadcasting on KWMR.

The door burst open, ringing the chimes and startling both Doris and Darlene out of their reveries. It was Mrs. Rhinehart.

"Doris! Quick! The girls are coming. You've got to do something! I was following some instructions on the Internet and I used—well, never mind what I used. Look at my hair! It's orange, Doris!"

The old lady cascaded into Darlene's foot bath, making the water slosh and spill. Darlene lifted her head from reading *Sensationally Sexy After Fifty* magazine. "What the hell?"

"Pardon me! Pardon me!" Mildred exclaimed, pulling over a chair. "Doris! They're coming this way! I'd bleach my own hair to get the color out, but I'm sure I'd get it in my eyes. Oh Doris, I'm so ashamed."

Doris looked at Darlene, lifting her hands from the water. "Do you mind?"

Hell, Darlene didn't mind. This was exactly the kind of action she'd been looking for. And entertaining too. Besides, her bare feet were quite happy in the pedicure tub.

The old lady yanked off her head scarf, while Doris pulled out a smock and let it drift over her tiny frame. Oxford shoes peeped out from the bottom of the chair and above, stockings, knee-high. Darlene averted her eyes.

The door crashed open again. Doris, sensing a fight, covered Mrs. R's face and hair with a towel and placed another smock over her feet.

"You seen her?" another elderly woman asked. "My son just gave me an iPhone, and he said I could take photos, and I thought it would be grand. Mildred, orange hair, the *Light*. That would beat Art Rogers's photos any old day, wouldn't it, girls?" She looked at Darlene. "And who are you?"

"Darlene," Darlene answered, putting forth her hand for a shake. "I'd get up, but, you know." She wiggled her toes in the bath.

"Who's under the towel?" The second old lady asked. "Is that Mildred?"

"Darlene's daughter," Doris answered. "Now, do you mind, Mrs. E., I have customers waiting."

"But what about my picture?" Hortense Elliot t asked.

"You want a good photo?" Doris asked. "Go on down to Stinson. There's been another sighting."

"Of whom? Of what? A killer whale? Another surfer? Mildred?"

"A naked man," Doris said, pulling out her pedicure kit, sponge, towels, cuticle remover and polish. "Color, Darlene?"

"A naked man!" shrilled Hortense Elliott. "I'm out of here! That's way better than Mildred with orange hair." She turned and ran out of the shop. "Come on, girls," she shouted to the other ladies who were peering out through the picture window. They all ran down the ramp, purses high on their arms, got into an old Nash and disappeared down the block.

Mildred pulled the towel off her head. "Thanks, Doris. It was tough to breathe under there."

"Mrs. Rhinehart, can you wait a moment and I'll take care of Ms. Easton here first, and then remove the color from your hair?"

"Don't you dare!" Mildred looked in the mirror again, adjusted her orange curls. "I kind of like it." She reached for her purse. "Put me in for next week then, Doris." She stood by the door. "Where was that naked man again?"

"Stinson," Doris said. Mildred flew out the door.

"My kind of town," Darlene sank back in her chair and lifted one foot. "Fire engine red, Doris, I think I'm going to like this place."

Almost Famous

"Oh Fred, dear Fred." Mildred gathered the straps of her apron, threw it on the counter, and sat next to him on the threadbare sofa. She leaned forward and looked at the TV screen. "So, what's on?" she asked, nursing a cup of chamomile tea.

"Baseball's over for the season," he said, and sipped his Negra Modelo. "It's not a new beer," he said. "I've been working on this one all day."

"Me too," she said. She pulled her flask from her pocket. "Nothing much to do since we've been banned from the *Light*."

"What do you mean?" He set down his half-empty beer. As for the chips he'd set out, he suddenly wasn't very hungry. "So you weren't kidding? No more Sheriff's Calls? No more comments about Mrs. Willis and her stupid dog? What about Alice?"

"She's fine. In school. It is the middle of a workday."

"So, what's the matter?" Fred didn't like to see his little wife upset.

She sniffed. "It's just that—that lady. The one who published a book about us? Us, Fred? She doesn't want any more stories. We were famous for a little while."

"You'll always be famous in my mind," Fred said.

"That's because we've been married forever. I better be famous in your mind. It's the rest of the world I worry about."

"You had your time in the sun, dear. The book made the bestseller list for nonfiction in the I.J."

"For non-fiction," Mildred sniffed.

"But that's even better. Don't you see? That means you're real." Fred took a sip of his beer. Lukewarm, but good anyway. Maybe it was time to put a second bottle in the fridge.

"Of course I'm real," Mildred said, patting her hair. "But ... but...my limelight ... its fading fast. Soon Alice, Thomas, and Henry, he may disappear too."

"Not Henry. Henry's too big to disappear. And where will all our relatives go, then?"

"The lady!" Mildred cried. "She said no more stories about us! No more Sheriff's Calls stories."

"You mean I might disappear too?" Fred asked, mouth agape. The beer in his hand was flabby and flat. Not the way his body was, though. That was round and chubby, and real, for God's sake. "I'm not disappearing."

"Just like Tinkerbell in Peter Pan. She was fading away ... only the children could save her."

Fred looked down at his body. None of it seemed to be disappearing. As a matter of fact, he'd had to go and buy a bigger belt, only last week.

"So, if we pray, Fred, if we get down on our knees?"

"You're not religious in any way, my dear. And it's not good for your knees." Mildred, on the other hand, had been shrinking for years. Paper thin now, if she turned sideways, you might miss her.

"Look at the TV. Look at the paper. Our little light is going out, Fred."

Fred opened the newspaper, the *Point Reyes Light*, and turned to Sheriff's Calls. "Still—the same number of calls, the same mayhem, confusion, the usual reality-challenged people making the same calls to the Sheriff."

"Cows. Are there cows in the road, Fred?" she asked, weaving her fingers together as she sat on the edge of the sofa.

"Of course, cows. Three cows went back inside a fence the same way they came out."

"And drivers? Drivers still going off the road?"

"Right into a ditch. Want to see?"

"Teenagers behaving badly?" Mildred asked, turning on the oven.

"Of course."

"Cops?"

"All over."

"Oh sweetheart, I thought ... I was so worried. If there are no calls, there is no me, is there? Is there a me?"

"You going to drive into a ditch? Party all night in front of Smiley's? Have an altercation with a cat? Fight with Mrs. Willis?"

"Mrs. Willis? Of course."

"Then you have nothing to worry about, sweetheart. As long as there are Sheriff's Calls, you'll always have me."

"Really?" Mildred wiped an eye.

"And you'll always be you."

"Oh. I wasn't so sure I really wanted to be me. I'm getting a little old, I guess."

"Guess not, you gorgeous thing. Want to dance?"

"Then I am real," she said with finality.

"And me too." Fred swallowed the rest of his beer. She had startled him today.

"So there will always be Sheriff's Calls—whether that lady wants us or not. Right, Fred. Right?" She batted her eyes. "There will always be an us?"

"My darling, of course. Come in close, now. You and I will be here always, paper or no paper. And always is a long long time. Shall we start it with a dance? A waltz?" he asked, taking her hand and leading her out onto the floor.

From the Sheriff's Calls Section of the Point Reyes Light
January 13, 2016

SAN GERONIMO VALLEY: At 5:18 p.m. a motorist said a white man with a shaved head had flagged him down to say he had escaped from kidnappers. Deputies placed the latter on mental health hold.

Tapioca

It was Darlene's second date with Bernard since she'd moved to Point Reyes two months earlier. She was in his car, a 1997 Honda Accord, on their way to dinner at Frad's and a movie. She'd always admired men who could drive a stick, but when he slammed on the brakes and downshifted, grinding the gears, it made her cringe.

She knew it wasn't a flat but she wanted to humor him. He had a kind and gentle nature, not so good for a cop but good for her. A lot better than those P.I. loser types in LA. "Doesn't sound like a flat, Bernard; otherwise we'd go kthunk-kthunk and be all crooked." Years ago she'd made the mistake of helping out on another date, when he'd had a flat. That had been her last time out with him. He was kind of cute.

"Nope, not the tire, Darlene." Bernard set the emergency brake.

This time she kept her hands to herself and hated feeling helpless. She looked up from perusing the Sheriff's Calls in the *Light*.

"There's a guy in the middle of the road," Bernard said. "Wish I had my cruiser. I'll only be gone a minute."

After ten years in LA Darlene had had her fill of all night stakeouts chasing sleazeballs. In the fall she decided to move to the country, write her version of the Great American novel, and enjoy life. But sitting still did not fit well—not when there was some action going on. "Anything I can do?" she asked, her head out the window.

"Nope. Got this," Bernard replied.

Darlene put down her paper and strained to hear, but they were just out of earshot. Bernard, a 30ish cop with thinning hair, was standing on the side of the road talking to a white guy with a shaved head. Skinheads? Gang member? There was always something interesting going on with Bernard. Darlene got out of the car.

"And there I was, standing right here, on the side of the road. I should've told my sister, she knows about these types of things," the bald guy muttered, rubbing his hands together.

He was wearing khaki pants, a khaki shirt, but no identifying insignia. Not Park Service, that was for sure; they wore a darker shade of green. Darlene came closer, staying on the back side of Bernard's car so the bald guy could see her, but Bernard couldn't. He had his back to her, was scratching his bald spot with one hand and reaching for something with the other.

"There were five of them," the bald man said. "Short guys."

"Your name, sir?" Bernard pulled out his badge.

"I didn't do it. I didn't do anything, Officer. Don't arrest me."

The bald man was trembling, but Bernard wasn't intimidating, not really, just a bit tall. He was kind of goofy and had a soft side as big as the moon. Darlene had picked up on that right away.

"Name, sir?" Bernard asked again.

"Templeton. Templeton Fortescu," the bald man sputtered. "The guys were all small—short like your girlfriend back there."

Bernard turned and frowned when he noticed Darlene. She gave him a little wave.

"I got this, Darlene," Bernard said.

Well, sort of. That Bernard. The old guy was like, quaking in his shoes. "Templeton," Darlene said, walking over to him and putting out her hand. "It's been too long." The bald man blinked. "There were five of them, and only one of me. The two of you wouldn't stand a chance. They were so ... pretty," he sputtered. "Gray."

"A family of grays, then?" Darlene asked. "Squirrels?"

Bernard rolled his eyes. "Darlene, I'm the cop here."

"Of course I remember you," Darlene cooed. The bald guy looked her in the eye. Relaxed, some.

"So, you've seen them too?" he asked, bright-eyed.

"Meth, dope, crack, oxy—what'd ya take, Mr. Fortescu?" Bernard asked.

Running roughshod over a perp was no way to make them talk. Darlene would have to talk to Bernard about that some other time. "I'm so sorry, Mr. Fortescu, that must've been quite a surprise."

Mr. Fortescu grabbed Darlene's arm. "They were quick. I gave them all I had, fifteen cents. They screamed at me so I handed over my cell phone and they threw it in the road."

"That's terrible," Darlene said, trying to pull away, but the guy had a grip like a prize fighter. Bernard stepped in closer, pried Mr. Fortescu's hand off her wrist.

"If you don't mind, Mr. Fortescu?"

"My wife made me do it. We were in the kitchen, eating leftover mac and cheese, and next thing I know, she's telling me about this car, this vehicle, says people are crying out on the road, and could I save them. My sister's delicate, Officer."

Darlene pulled out her cell phone and pressed record, fascinated. "Your sister or your wife, Mr. Fortescu?"

He shook his head when he saw the red light. "No. Please. Mr. Blinky makes me nervous. You can't record me. They'll take my soul. They said ..."

"Who said?" Bernard asked.

"The gray guys! All I tell you about is gray guys!"

"Like the man in the gray flannel suit?" Darlene asked. "You a movie buff?"

"My wife would say so, but she's not here. And what's it to you? You're missing the point."

"Which is?" Bernard asked. "Who left? Who stayed? Your sister, what happened to your sister?"

"Their skin was gray," Mr. Fortescu said. "And you don't believe me. Like your pants, Officer. Slate gray."

"I see." Darlene stepped closer. "Did they take your virtue, Mr. Fortescu?"

"What virtue?" Mr. Fortescu laughed, his belly hanging over his belt buckle taking the brunt of it.

"Did they take anything else, Mr. Fortescu?" Darlene asked.

"They tied me up. By then my wife had come out of the woods ... our house is just up there ... Officers ... and ... and...," he broke up, sobbing. "Then, they took her!"

"There, there, Mr. Fortescu," Darlene said. "Perhaps you can come with us."

"So we can take care of you, put out an APB on your sister," Bernard said. "Or was it your wife?"

"I don't have a sister. Aren't you guys listening at all?"

"Of course, your wife, Mr. Fortescu," Darlene said. "How can we help you, then?"

"Don't bother." Mr. Fortescu came over to Bernard's car, leaned against the hood, took a look at the sky, held one hand over his eyes to shade them from the sun.

Bernard rested a foot against the fender. "And then?"

Darlene put her hand on Mr. Fortescu's back.

"You'll never find her," he sobbed. "She went, with them. The group. The five of them. Happy, a smile on her face, skipping, laughing. About fifteen minutes ago."

Bernard pulled out his cell phone, called the station, and was about to request a cruiser when Mr. Fortescu tried to yank the phone out of his hands.

"Now, now, now, Mr. Fortescu, we'll have none of that," Bernard snapped.

"That's what did it, Officer," the bald man said. "The signals. They'll swallow you up, just like what happened to Gladys." His face went white and he wobbled a little bit, pulled himself up again.

"Mr. Fortescu, you feeling all right?" Darlene asked. "Your wife, then, she still at home?"

"Making tapioca," Mr. Fortescu replied. "I've always loved tapioca."

"Should we call ahead and ask them to make it for you at the police station?" Bernard asked.

"But there's no stove at the police station," Mr. Fortescu replied. "Only at the fire house. Everyone knows that."

"My dear Mr. Fortescu," Darlene said, taking his arm and opening the door to Bernard's car. "It's been a kind of a tough day for you, hasn't it?"

"My wife's just been abducted by aliens. I should say so, Miss."

"You two must've been very happy together," Darlene said.

"Me? What? Gladys. Happy? Um ... yeah, sure, but that was before ... well, you know... She was okay, until ... until..." his eyes grew soft.

"What happened exactly, Mr. Fortescu?" Bernard asked gently.

"The spaceship came. It was long and had wheels and made a funny sound."

"The 68?" Bernard asked.

"How'd you know?" Mr. Fortescu asked. "They got in behind her, shoved her up the steps. She's not that small, but she smiled when she got on board."

"I see. And when was this, then?" Bernard asked. "I'll call Marin Transit."

"Don't bother. She called me from Tulsa. A year ago. She lives with the grays."

"Did you get her number? Going to get her back, then?"

Mr. Templeton tucked himself near Bernard's ear. "She says it's the best sex she's ever had."

"I see," Bernard said, his face pinking up.

"That's why I'm waiting here. For my bus. A man has needs, Officer." Mr. Templeton looked long and hard at Bernard.

"Looks like we're all set here," Darlene said, having heard everything. "Mr. Templeton, I hope you get lucky tonight." As for her, she already had her answer. This time she wasn't going to wait until the third date.

From the Sheriff's Calls Section of the Point Reyes Light
November 5, 2015

CHILENO VALLEY: At 6:14 p.m. a silver Mustang, screeching and braking wildly, drove into a ditch.

God, Give Me a Miracle

"Mildred, no! I said STOP!" Fred shouted.

His pretty little wife, her mouth pursed, let go of the wheel just as it dropped off the shoulder. "Heavens to Betsy, Fred, you don't have to yell."

"'Let me drive', you said, 'I can do it,' you said. And now look." Fred climbed out of the car with difficulty as the door scraped on underbrush and he could barely slip by. "What do you think you're doing?"

"Driving," she said, re-applying her lipstick. Whatever the time of day, whatever they were doing, whenever she needed a pause, she applied lipstick. The rear-view mirror was askew, so she did the best she could. Pause, indeed. Being married to Fred, she needed all the pauses she could get.

He was out in front of the car, looking down.

"Well, give us a push, dear," she said, adjusting her glasses. "Come on."

Fred would've if he could've. "I'm not Superman, honey. I can't lift up the car or turn back time."

"Wasn't that cool, running the world backwards to save Lois Lane? So, what can you do that's heroic to save me?"

"I told you not to take the wheel," he sighed, coming around to her side. The door creaked open. There was a bit of a gash through the fiberglass of the left bumper where she'd hit a fence five minutes before, but under the circumstances, the car looked pretty good. He could fix it with duct tape, but it was Mildred's sister's Mustang and she liked her things neat.

"You okay?" he asked his wife, proffering a hand.

"Now what are we going to do? We're all the way out Chileno Valley Road. No one around. 'Let's take a ride, you said. 'Let's see the country.' I've seen as much grass as anyone would ever need to."

"Mildred, the car's in a ditch. Can't you see? Can't you feel it, the way it's tilted?" He caught his breath. "I need to get back in, maybe I can back us out."

"Call nine-one-one. I'm not moving." Mildred felt something damp on her forehead and pressed her fingers to her scalp. Bug bite? Flea? Tick bite? What was it? Whatever it was, it was wet. She brought her hand to her face and studied her fingers. Damp and red with blood. "Fred?" she asked. "Fred? Something strange is going on here."

Fred stumbled, looked in his pockets for his phone. Not in his jacket, not his placket pocket. He pulled out a handkerchief, pressed it in Mildred's hair, patted for the wound.

"It's such a silly thing, Fred, you know? Driving? You just toodle along, then, bam. You stop. Don't you think that's, uh, odd?" She kept pressing her fingers back in her hair, then onto her face.

"Oh sweetheart, sweetheart, what are we going to do?" Fred opened the passenger door, pulled out more tissues from a box at the console. He searched for the cell phone. It had been in his pocket, but Mildred had asked for it. "The cell, dear. Where'd you put it?"

"Spring is such a pretty time of year out here, Fred. Don't you wish it was spring?"

"The phone?" Fred asked.

"No need to shout."

"And?"

"It's on my lap. Here." She closed her bloody fingers over the phone. Looking bewildered, she moved her head from side to side.

Fred folded his handkerchief into quarters, wiped off the phone, and tried to hand the cloth to Mildred. When she didn't make a move to take it, he pressed it into her hand. He backed out of the car and opened on the passenger side door.

"Where are you going?" she asked.

"I'm right here," Fred replied. "Just outside the car. Now, lean forward."

"Do you think Alice is all right?" Mildred asked, going a little gray.

"No need to worry about Alice at a time like this. Here, let me see."

"I'm bleeding like a madwoman, Fred! Do something! I could die right here and all you're doing is handing me tissues."

Fred gently and slowly examined his wife's scalp and hair, turning pink and red at an alarming rate.

"Don't pull my hair!" she shouted.

"I'll be gentle," he murmured, touching her with the tips of his fingers. Placing a tissue on what he thought was the wound, he punched in 911.

No reception.

"God, give me a miracle!" Fred yelled. "Come on, you stupid phone!"

"No need to shout in the store, Fred. We can get vegetables when you're feeling better."

He examined the phone. One bar.

"They say the end is painful, but I say—what's the diff? World's going a little foggy today."

Fred marched back to the road, ready to flag down somebody, anybody. He saw a mailbox across the street, but the house was down a long drive, and he wasn't going to walk that far.

He punched in the number again.

"Nine-one-one," a voice said.

"We're on Chileno Road!" Fred shouted. "Twenty minutes out! Car's in a ditch ... and my wife's been ..." He listened but heard no response. The phone had died. "Wait! No! Hold on one second!"

No bars, no battery, no nothing.

He went back to check on Mildred. "Darling, does it hurt?" He tried to staunch the blood, but it was everywhere, behind her ear, on her hands, the dash, her face, her lap.

Hearing a car, he stepped back out on the road, waved both arms. Two boys were heading west in a light blue Ford Fairlane. They turned around and stopped fast, the front of their car inches from the back of the Mustang.

Fred ran to the car, yelling, "It's my wife! She's hurt! I've called nine-one-one, but—"

"I've got this." One of the boys grabbed a first-aid kit from the trunk of his car.

"She's not making a lot of sense," Fred said, steering the teen toward Mildred. The kid looked, maybe, twelve, but old enough to drive? Had the DMV changed the rules? "Do you know what you're doing?"

The boys, one blond, one with skin the color of mocha, went to work on Mildred.

"Why, hello boys," Mildred said. "You look like my sister's kids, Bert and Ernie. But they live in Livermore. What are you doing all the way out here?"

One held her head while the other talked to her gently, patting her hand and telling her she was going to be all right. Fred wished he had that kid's skill. He never should have let her behind the wheel.

The blond kid set gauze on Mildred's scalp, close to her forehead, and the other cleaned her face and hands but not her lap which held a mess of blood-tinted tissues. She looked better.

"You like cupcakes, boys?" Mildred asked. "I make great cupcakes. Fred, over there, he won't eat any, but he's fat, anyway, and doesn't need them. I bet you kids love cupcakes. Blue velvet or lemon?"

The blond kid exited the car, and went to talk to Fred.

"She always this way?" he asked.

"I tried calling nine-one-one," Fred said, "but my battery died."

"No need, we already called them," the blond kid said.

Fred felt like the tomato soup Mildred used to make and leave on the kitchen counter to ripen. Forgotten, useless and just too old.

The other kid stayed with Mildred. Fred watched them talk. The kid had an easy way with her. Fred could see Mildred nod and smile, and when she got afraid, the kid held her hand again.

"Who are you guys?" Fred asked.

"That Manuel, always had a thing for grandmothers," the blond kid said.

Sirens split the air as the EMT van swerved and stopped. The paramedics took over and the boys got out of the way.

"She was talking about cooking," Manuel said, standing next to Fred.

"Don't squeeze me so hard! What are you guys, a bunch of lunatics?"

Fred could recognize his wife's voice anymore.

"Any of you ever had a mother? No, I didn't think so. I'm a little old lady and don't you forget it. Hands off, you bunch of gorillas."

"We did the best we could," Manuel said. "She wasn't bleeding that much, just a bump on the head. Those can be a concern."

"I know that," Fred stuttered.

"We're studying to be paramedics," the blond kid said.

"Ready, Mr. Rhinehart?" one of the paramedics asked. "She's asking for you."

"If you like," Manuel replied, "we'll follow the ambulance."

"You've been very helpful, I'm sure there are things you need to do," Fred said, digging into his pocket for the keys.

"I'll take the Mustang, and Frank will follow in the Ford," Manuel explained.

"You seem like nice boys," Fred said. "I have no patience for teens who lack direction. Been studying long?"

"Fred! No. Wait!" Mildred yelled. "You forgot the groceries!"

"How hard do you think she hit her head, sir?" One of the paramedics asked.

"I'm not sure," Fred said, squeezing into the back of the van. "What is your sister going to say, Mildred? Oh God." He put his head into his hands.

"I'm bleeding to death and all you care about is a stupid car?"

"Fred, say hi to Tim," Mildred said, holding onto one of the paramedics. "He's kind of cute, don't you think?"

"She'll be fine, Mr. Rhinehart, don't you worry," Tim said, trying to extract his arm.

"Those teenagers were raised right, Fred. You could learn a thing or two from them," Mildred said.

Fred watched out the rear-view window. Both boys climbed into the silver Mustang.

"Don't pay any attention to them, you big lunk, I'm the one going to the hospital."

"And they're the ones driving away in your sister's car."

From the Sheriff's Calls Section of the Point Reyes Light, November 5, 2015

STINSON BEACH: At 7:14 p.m. a woman reported the theft during the last year of skulls, lights and gravestones from a shared storage shed.

Electric Rain

"Sssh," Calvin said as he stood behind a storage shed with his new girlfriend Dana Goodyear. She'd sidled up to him only last weekend at Toby's and he'd been so happy that she accepted his invitation for a date he'd agreed to do the "little favor" she'd asked him to do. Now, with his hands full of Halloween stuff, he wasn't so sure.

He'd been a little less adventurous since the raccoon bit him on the finger and he'd had to go to the hospital for rabies shots, but now, a girl, a real live girl was interested in him. How could he resist? It'd been too long since he'd gone out. At 33, he was way overdue.

"Come on, Calvin. The owner could have seen us already," Dana said, popping her face out the passenger side window of her Dad's 1979 gray Chevy Camino.

"Why do you want all this stuff, Dana?" Calvin lifted the Camino's lid and lay the gravestones in carefully so they wouldn't make a sound. They weren't stone, and certainly not bronze, but some kind of composite plastic and they were heavy.

"Hush," Dana said and started the car. "Get in and let's go!"

They were at the far end of a gravel drive, near a mailbox, but they hadn't turned around first, or backed in, and the tires made a crunching sound on the gravel driveway as Calvin made a careful three-point turn. Just as he straightened the wheel and headed to the road, the lights came on in the house behind them and Calvin gunned it.

The road from Stinson to Olema was winding, tight, and followed the contours of Bolinas Lagoon, so no matter how much Calvin wanted to go faster, he was stymied—take the corner too tight and hit the cutbank or go too wide and end up in the water. Despite Dana's insistence that he pick it up he stuck to what he thought was a safe speed, headed up Route One, and disappeared inside the Thirteen Turns. It was a winding way through a grove of eucalyptus trees and he had to slow down even further.

Almost through the last turn, they heard a siren.

"Faster! Faster!" Dana pumped the floor with her feet.

Back on a straightaway, Calvin took his first turn down a driveway. It went around a bend. He killed the engine and the lights, got out of the car, and looked back at the main road. Heard a few cars shoot down Route One. Finally saw blue and red lights pass by.

"What, are you crazy, Dana? Do you know how many times I've been in trouble with the law? You didn't tell me we were going to steal anything!"

"It's for my mom," Dana said. "She's a waitress at the Station House. This stuff's been covered in dust for years—and Mom needs it for her costume party."

"But Dana, Halloween was last week."

"You want to break my mom's heart? She's got breast cancer."

"No, no, never mind, Dana. Gee, I'm so sorry," Calvin said. "Anything I can do?"

"Sit and wait with me, if you would. Until we're sure the cops are gone."

Calvin waited. Waited until the night was full of peepers, waited until he heard owls hooting, waited until he couldn't stand it anymore.

"Thank you," Dana said, finally, as they pulled back out onto Route One. "You'll make my mom very happy."

Back in Point Reyes Station, he pulled up to Dana's house. He helped her with the gravestones, which felt heavier than when he picked them up at the shed. Luckily he had brought a coat, it was chilly out.

Dana held the kitchen door open with her hip as Calvin did as he was told. Last trip, he held two skulls in his hands and looked them over under the back-door light. They weren't plastic. They were real! Real bone. "That's it for me," he said.

"Oh no, no, Calvin, just give me a sec." Dana made her way around stacks of cardboard boxes in the kitchen and lit candles. "'Member when I came to see you in Bolinas?" she asked, placing the skulls on the kitchen counter. "I didn't know how much I'd come to love this area. Want a beer? A joint?"

Calvin wasn't sure. Dana was pretty, with that long slash of dark hair, black as ink eyebrows and red as blood lipstick. She was ... interesting. Weird and interesting. And sexy as hell.

He leaned against one of the counters, lit the joint and held his breath, eyed Dana. Was he going to get lucky tonight? He'd done the favor. He felt like an ass, thinking such thoughts, with Dana's mom's condition. He cleared his head, popped a beer. Cool liquid ran down his throat, tickling his tonsils. Tasted good. He wondered if Dana would taste good too.

"She'll be so surprised, my mom, that is," Dana said, running her hands across one of the tops of the skulls. "A child, maybe, Calvin, this one's kind of small."

Her perfume wafted over him. Smelled like lilacs. She grazed his shoulder with her fingertips. He cracked open another beer.

While he watched, Dana transformed the kitchen. She set the gravestones against the wall, festooned the cabinets with lights, stroked the skulls again with her palm, and touched Calvin's cheek with the same hand.

He felt warmth, a little more than he might expect on a cool night. Was she thinking the same, on their first date? Where was her bedroom? She lit incense.

He sat down at the kitchen table, while she grabbed a jar of peanut butter and celery, his favorite snack.

A flicker of red light caught his eye. A laser pointer? Where was the laser pointer? Had he been drinking too much or not enough? Dana had her back to him and was humming to herself while looking out the window.

Calvin blinked. Must've been the reflection from the lights he'd stolen, red and green, Christmas lights, a few days after Halloween, that she'd plugged in. The flicker of lights again, brighter now, red, dark red.

The letters on the gravestones seemed to hum, brighter now, then darker now. Had they looked like that earlier? Too much pot, probably. He took a bite of celery. He sucked on a tablespoon of peanut butter, slowly, savoring the salt.

"Thanks for getting the stuff," Dana said, sitting down next to him and turning out the kitchen lights.

There were enough candles to burn down America, Calvin thought. He'd go down in warmth tonight, for sure. How to start this thing? With a kiss? He extended a hand.

Halfway to her face he felt a stabbing pain on the scar of the back of his hand. Where he'd wrecked his motorcycle two years ago on black ice in Inverness, coming down the hill. The scar burned when it was cold out, but it hadn't been that cold tonight. A light rain started to fall.

Another flash of light. This time he followed it. The smaller skull, the child's, seemed to float above the counter. "No, no thanks, no more pot for me, Dana."

She was closer now. He extended his upper hand, the other hand. No pain. Of course, no scar. He touched her cheek. Electric rain surged through him. Power like he'd never felt before. Nothing stopping him now. He rose, but felt a crack in his knees, staggered back to his chair.

"What the hell?" he exclaimed. "I've never felt so odd, Dana. Your house grounded properly? I swear I got a shock right now."

"Electricity's off," she said slowly. "I've also disconnected the phone." She grinned a slow, sweet smile, tossed her hair over her head. "It's just us chickens now."

"My cell phone?" Calvin croaked.

"The devil's playground," Dana whispered, coming over to him. Leaning down.

"You seen it?" Calvin stuttered. "My phone?"

"You don't need it now," Dana said and closed in on him with a kiss.

They found his body wrapped in a shroud just inside the post office, leaning against the letter boxes. When they moved him, he'd been leaning up against box 66, but someone had written, in magic marker, a third six. Two skulls lay in his lap, one large, one small, and his head was wound with lights that went on and off until they found the cord and pulled it.

A plastic gravestone lay at his feet, with his name crudely carved in front. Calvin Dunn, RIP, 1982-2015.

The coroner told the *Point Reyes Light* that it seemed as if Calvin had been struck by lightning, which was odd as there hadn't been a storm, just a sprinkle of rain.

No one reported it in the papers, not even the *Point Reyes Light.* The editor thought the news would upset everyone in the tiny community and keep the tourists away.

From the Sheriff's Calls Section of the Point Reyes Light
January 15, 2016

INVERNESS: At 11:58 p.m. a second mysterious note had been left downtown.

The Note

"The mysterious note, it's got to mean something," Alice said, smoothing down the Bovine Bakery's copy of the *Light*. She eyed Violet sitting on the adjacent stool. Violet had just moved to Inverness. Mom, who knew Violet's mom and had a soft spot for an outsider, had insisted Alice hang out with Violet all day. Alice had frowned, argued, and finally agreed. One time and one time only and the car for an afternoon. The girls had been together since nine and the day had been going downhill ever since.

They were perched on their stools, nursing cold cups of cocoa, watching the world go on outside. There hadn't been a long line when they'd arrived, but now it snaked around the corner.

"Maybe it's a ransom note," Violet ventured.

"So, who or what would they be ransoming?" Alice asked. "A stash of pot? A person? A child?"

"It's got to be a spy. A dead drop. CIA," Violet said, feeling bold. It was the first time she'd hung out with Alice and she didn't want to blow it.

"I think you've been watching too much TV, like *Homeland*."

Violet felt shut down. Be confident, dear, her mother had said. Speak up. "Carrie Mathison would get to the bottom of the mysterious note," Violet said. "She'd corral the guy in the playground, and while he was waiting for one of the outhouses, she'd sidle up to him, and we'd know, we'd just know he was the one, but then he'd slip away."

"Yeah, yeah, okay," Alice replied. "And then leave a note. 'Life has become a dangerous affair.'"

"Or ... or," Violet thought a sec. "'The milk of eternity. Drink.'"

"That's just plain silly." Alice stirred her cocoa with a piece of pasta, the bakery's choice of stir stick. Violet was no Beth-Ann. "My Grandma likes whiskey."

"You think the note says that?" Violet asked.

Alice tried not to roll her eyes. Be nice, Mom had said. Pretend you're new in town. You might like her. "Don't think so, Violet."

Violet's face clouded but when six motorcycle guys pulled up, revving their engines, she perked up right away. They killed their engines and climbed off their bikes, stood outside the bakery, looked in the picture window. Violet pulled her face back. She'd been staring. Some day she'd get a ride on a Harley.

"The note should say something about love," Alice suggested.

"Like those motorcycle guys?" Violet asked. "They look like love to me." The line had moved fast and now one of the guys was standing a foot from her, inside the shop, his leather jacket covered with insignia, Hell's Angels, Devils Camp.

"How could a love note be mysterious?" Alice noticed her reflection in the window. She had a white mustache from the whipped cream and quickly wiped it off. "Unless it said this: 'Love comes at midnight.'"

"But why leave a note at all?"

"I dunno," Violet said. "But it's got to be something to get the cops involved."

Both girls slid off their seats. They walked out into a bright day, full of tourists, bicyclists. Another roar went up as twenty more motorcycles swallowed the town.

"How can I miss you when you never go away?'"
Violet giggled.

"That's a line to a song. Wait, wait," Alice hesitated, "how 'bout, 'Drop Kick me Jesus Through the Goalpost of Life.'"

"A song? That's a song?" Violet asked.

"For real." Alice said. They walked over to the Commons, the tiny park by the yellow house, took their seats under a large cypress tree.

"You know, Point Reyes Station is, like, a huge town, compared to Forest Knolls. Now, there's a hick town."

"And that makes Point Reyes Station a booming metropolis?"

"Hey Alice, you know any cute guys?" Violet asked.

"The only guys I know are too old, too weird or don't like girls." Alice said. She didn't know what to do with herself with Beth-Ann living in Davis. She could fill her time doing homework, but that didn't feel right, and watching movies or something, but that didn't feel right either. Hanging out with Violet felt like a kitty kiss, abrasive and way too wet.

"How 'bout one of those motorcycle guys?" Violet asked.

Alice didn't feel like laughing. Guys didn't like her. And guys wouldn't want to spend the day along Lagunitas Creek skipping rocks. Not without hurting somebody, usually.

"You got family here?" Violet asked, coming around and plopping herself down on Alice's other side. "My Grandma died when I was a baby. But I didn't know her, so I guess it's okay."

"Mine's around," Alice said. "She lives up on the Mesa with my Grandpa."

"What's she like?" Violet asked.

"Wonderful," Alice said. "Funny, opinionated and loves me to pieces." Two bicyclists came around the corner, crashed into each other, picked themselves up and walked into the bakery. They were dressed in yellow from their caps to their socks. Alice wondered what it would be like to look like a cartoon. Maybe she could be the road runner, or Bugs Bunny. Or her luck, Huckleberry Hound. She looked over at Violet. Maybe she'd been kind of mean. "My Grandma's in her eighties. If she ever asks you if you want a cupcake, say no."

"Not much like those Grandmas on TV who make cookies and pies?" Violet wished she'd had a grandma.

"Not if you like them burnt," Alice replied.

"My mom says she's going to take me out fishing," Violet said. "I guess it's okay." She chewed on a fingernail. "As long as I don't have to kill them with my fist, like that guy on the Discovery channel. He's kind of cute, though."

"But gutting them? Draining blood?"

"So what else is there to do out here?" Violet asked.

"My Grandma loves the beauty parlor."

"Ooh. Get your hair done like Lady Gaga. And a pedicure! And a manicure. You'd look girly."

"I don't care about stuff like that," Alice said.

"Well, maybe that's it, then," Violet said. "Maybe that's why the guys ..." the minute she stopped talking she knew she'd made a mistake. Alice's face fell.

"Maybe that's nothing. Let's get out of here," Alice said. The weather was warm, for January. The girls took a walk, passed by the brick building and were soon on the path that led down to the water. One the way, they saw the rock with the inscription, Wiebke's View.

"Nifty, hunh?" Alice said. Flat land forever, ponds, marshes, a white barn in the distance, and, beyond, Inverness Ridge rising against the sky. "What a spot."

"Alice, I appreciate you spending the day with me. I know you're doing it because my mom asked. I won't bother you again," Violet said.

"You don't have to do that," Alice lied. "It's just that—my best friend—she just left town."

"I heard," Violet said. "I'm sorry. I make a lousy substitute."

"You're all right, Violet. Kind of quiet, like me," Alice said.

Violet beamed.

"Beth-Ann was always cooking up goofy things. And she smoked."

"Pot?" Violet asked. "My sister Pam's always asking me to, but ..."

"And she loved the Sheriff's Calls."

"Like the ones about those naked guys who show up in the paper all the time?"

"How'd you know?" Alice's eye caught something white, a folded paper beside the rock. She picked it up.

"Everyone loves the Sheriff's Calls," Violet said. "Even my Dad who lives in Memphis. He asks me to read them to him over Skype."

"I do that with Beth-Ann," Alice said.

"If only I could be so lucky to meet one of them—one of those naked guys," Violet giggled. "What you got there?"

"Maybe it's the mysterious note they were talking about," Alice replied.

"'Free drinks to the first person to hike from Palomarin to Bear Valley?'" Violet was on a roll. "'Carwash at Cheda's, bring your tractor? Your best friend is moving away but you're going to be okay?'"

Alice lifted the paper, gazed at Violet's eager sweet face. "It doesn't say anything like that... she stuttered.

"Bet it does."

"It says something better," Alice caught her breath. "It says: Love awaits."

From the Sheriff's Calls Section of the Point Reyes Light, March 5, 2016

FOREST KNOLLS: At 3:59 p.m. a woman said her caretaker had used her credit card.

All Together Now

"You didn't have to call the cops, Mrs. Fisher," Lucia said to the small woman brandishing her cane.

"You used my card, you ungrateful girl."

"Oh, Mrs. Fisher!" Lucia cried, eyeing the tall man with sparse hair, standing in the doorway to Mrs. Fisher's cottage. He was pulling out a small notebook. If they only knew, she had a record, but it had been ages since she'd stolen the pen from CVS pharmacy, when she'd been a kid, and was just about to return it when the security guard had caught her and reported her to her parents.

Beatrice closed and opened her eyes. If she was quick enough, she'd catch the dream again, that dream when she was a young girl of twelve, a blondie, and her big brother was going to take her to the beach. Was that him, then, at the door? He looked bigger, somehow.

"You all right, ma'am?" The cop asked. "You look a little wobbly."

"You get to be almost a hundred and you'll be wobbly too, buster. Lend me a hand. The floor's coming up a little fast."

"Mrs. Fisher!"

Beatrice Fisher, a woman of short stature to begin with, seemed to shrink before Lucia's eyes. She leaned against the wall and slowly, without affectation, slid down to the floor. Luckily she didn't hit her head.

Lucia stooped down and pulled Mrs. Fisher's head and shoulders away from the wall, while the cop scooched down on Mrs. Fisher's other side. Her head felt loose on Lucia's shoulder.

Lucia raised her eyes and looked at the cop, who held his fingers against the older woman's neck and shook his head.

The funeral was a busy one. The little old ladies from Doris' salon, Hortense, Mildred and two others stood at attention, weeping while listening to the local minister give a eulogy about a woman he'd never met. The ladies were dressed in their best Sunday dresses, Mildred in yellow and white, Hortense in pink, their hair perfectly coiffed. It was an odd contingent. Thomas, wearing his father's tweed jacket that hung to his knees, stayed by the back door, shyly holding Marlene's hand. Linda held her two-year-old Bernadette on her hip and chatted with Lulu. Tiny, the tow-truck driver, in clean blue jeans and a new pair of tight-fitting cowboy boots, straightened his tie and wiggled his sore toes. Tim, the surfer, looked in on the tidy crowd. Alice had called him, finally. He eyed her across the room. She smiled behind her hand.

Darlene stood by Bernard and handed him a tissue when his eyes grew moist. Doris held her son's shoulder, while Lucia, feeling a bit awkward, cried silently into a hanky she'd tucked into her purse. Henry would've come but he couldn't find his shoes. Violet was too shy to be a part of the gathering despite Alice's pleas and Walter, distraught over his dying ficus, had gone to the nursery in Tomales instead.

Ellen Lipsak watched through the window.

"Well, that's it then. Beatrice bites the dust," Mildred said as they walked into the fellowship hall for the reception.

Mildred pulled Alice close to her. "Honey, do what you can to make my passing as easy, will you, child?"

Fred eyed the crowd, grabbed a handful of nuts, and hoped it would be over soon, so he could head back to the Western for a pop.

"Grandma, you're never going to die," Alice said, holding her. Grandma had gotten a little smaller, a little frailer. "Don't leave me, not now, not ever."

Mildred smiled. "Not on your life, honey bunny, not on your life. Not as long as you need me, Alice."

FINI

Air Force Writing Guide

Air Force Writing Guide

How to Write Performance Reports, Letters of Counseling, Awards, and More

MSgt R Parker

Military Writer Press
2010

Dedicated to the men and women serving in the Air Force
around the world, far from home and family

Table of Contents

INTRODUCTION

The purpose of this book is to compile information collected over the years from the Air Force Writer website that may be of use to our comrades in arms. The Air Force Writer website is an enlisted community resource that accepts and shares information with Air Force members. I would like to thank the dozens of Airmen who contributed material for the website and this book.

This book is not an official reference for procedures, rules, or regulations. Although general procedures are listed where appropriate, this book is only intended to help with writing tasks not undertaken before by providing examples. The pub or instruction always takes precedence.

This information is provided for educational purposes only. Any reference bearing resemblance to real persons, living or dead, is purely coincidental. Although every effort has been made to ensure accuracy, no warranty or guarantee, expressed or implied, as to the accuracy, reliability or completeness of furnished information is provided. The author and publisher are not responsible for damages resulting from the use of this book.

Corrections should be sent to editor@airforcewriter.com. Any corrections or improvements will be included in this book's next edition.

The Enlisted Performance Report

It's an unfortunate fact of Air Force life that no matter how hard you work or how many hours you put in, your accomplishments won't be recognized unless they can be accurately represented by the words contained on a single sheet of paper -your EPR. Performance reports are among the most important documents you're likely to encounter during your military career. That single sheet of paper affects your chances for promotion, your assignment options, training opportunities, and your entire future in the military. No other document has as much effect on your Air Force career or your life. It's important that you take the time to do a good job on your own and your troops' EPR.

If you're the ratee, make sure that when your supervisor asks for input or EPR bullets for your EPR that you provide as much information as you can. Providing material for your EPR is not doing your supervisor's job. It's an opportunity to have some influence on your EPR and career! It's almost as if your supervisor handed you a blank check and told you to fill in whatever amount you want. Because EPRs have a lot of weight in determining if you get promoted and a promotion means an immediate raise of thousands of dollars a year. I don't know about you but I could definitely use the money. So when my supervisor gives me a chance to have some input on my performance report, I'm taking it!

But often, when the time for the annual performance review rolls around, a lot of people find it difficult to write or provide input for their evaluation. I think the hardest thing for most of us is to come up with 15 accomplishments to fill all the blocks on the AF Form 910. The things we do every day seem pretty routine and just don't seem important enough to put in an EPR. But they are. The work that all of us do every day is indispensable to the Air Force's mission. It just takes a little thought to bring it to light and express its full impact. To help in identifying your noteworthy achievements, take a look at our sections on example EPR bullets. If you know what you want to say but just can't find the phrase that sounds right, check out the section titled Performance Report Phrases. Maybe you'll find what you're looking for there.

Writing an EPR is not hard. If it's your first time writing one, it might be confusing at first but once you're finished, you'll wonder what all the fuss was about. I know a lot of people groan about EPRs as if they were as hard to write as a college term paper. They like to give the impression that in order to write a good one, they have to lock themselves away somewhere and work through the night, or maybe all week, without food or water, to produce the holy grail of performance reports. And if they do, it's because that's what they *want* to do. They *want* to be dramatic and are probably the kind of people that make a big deal out of every little thing in their life anyway. Because writing an EPR is not hard at all. In fact, it's easy. If you think about it, common sense will tell you that, if a large organization is trying to develop a rating system that's going to be used by a wide variety of people, in order to make it effective, they will make every attempt to make it as simple to understand and use as possible. And they have.

An EPR is simply the documenting of a person's performance for a specific length of time -usually a year. All large organizations have a method to rate and record the performance of their employees and the AF Form 910 is the Air Force's method. The EPR is used to document performance but also serves as a public record of your career. They can be used to prove where you were and what you were doing (approximately) at any time during your career.

Everyone in the Air Force has their careers and performance recorded this way and, if you're a supervisor, you'll be responsible for doing it for the people you rate.

In my opinion, the reason the EPR has a reputation for being so difficult is because the people who process the EPRs *make* it difficult. Supervisors routinely review EPRs submitted to them, mutilate them until they're bleeding red ink, and return them to the well-intentioned writer for editing. It's a fact of Air Force life that no matter how well you write and how well you comply with current guidance, some raters will not be satisfied with *any* EPR you submit. This is due to any number of reasons:

- Even a rater with good intentions tends to view other writers' work as inferior. Because they don't write with the same tone, it just doesn't sound quite right and will be returned for editing.

- Some raters feel that the EPR submission process won't be recognized as the tough, exacting definition of a ratee's career that it's supposed to be if EPRs aren't continually returned for improvement.

- Some raters appear to take pleasure in routinely returning EPRs for rework as an indication of their power and station and superior writing skills.

- Sometimes an EPR has to be viewed in the context of all the other EPRs being written in the squadron.

- And, of course, many EPR drafts *do* need improvement.

Whatever the reason, rejected EPRs are just a fact of life. Everyone receives rejected EPR drafts and you shouldn't get bent out of shape over it. If you start the process expecting to see your draft EPR returned for further editing, it will be much less painful.

This brings us to the topic of the "80 percent solution". My advice is: don't kill yourself trying to make your first EPR draft perfect before sending it to your supervisor for review. I learned, through experience, that it served no practical purpose to labor over an EPR draft until every bullet statement, every sentence was "perfect". My carefully chosen words would be lost on my supervisor and he would just slash and mark up the EPR and return it with specific, if garbled, instructions written in the margins (with plenty of explanation points!!!). You can, if you want to, turn in a "finished" draft but, most NCOs agree that it's a waste of time and recommend the 80% solution: get the product in pretty good shape, 100% complete, but don't waste a lot of effort on poetic nuances to get it just right. Your supervisor most likely won't understand the fine touches and will just mark it up with red ink. *After* he returns the draft to you, *then* do your best work.

You can expect your supervisor to return your draft EPR several times for editing with the justification being that someday, somewhere, at some mysterious, fabled Review Board in the Sky, Senior NCOs will be reviewing stacks of EPRs to determine who gets the dream job of the century. And if your EPR isn't just right, it could mean that someone else will get that dream job instead of you. It could mean that, because you didn't take the time to use exactly the right word or list your bullet statements in exactly the correct order, your rival, who *did* use the right word and who *did* list his bullets in the correct order, will get the job instead. I don't mean to dismiss their concerns entirely but in my 24 years in the Air Force I have never seen it come down to this level of granularity.

I don't mean to totally dismiss people who place a lot of importance on EPRs. Because they *are* important. They are a significant factor, often the biggest factor, in whether you get promoted or not. Yes, promotion does depend on other factors (testing, time in grade, etc) but the promotion points of the EPR will almost certainly make the difference between getting promoted and *not* getting promoted. When I was a young airman, I used to think EPRs weren't important and I'd get promoted by testing but I'm here to tell you, that's a hard way to go. For some career fields, it may be impossible to get promoted without a good/five EPR. So I'm not saying they're not important. I'm just saying they're easy to complete. And complete accurately.

One of two forms is used for documenting performance of enlisted members. Use AF Form 910 for ranks AB through TSgt. Use AF Form 911 for MSgt and above.

EPRs are, by nature, competitive. Although their primary goal is to record the ratee's performance for the reporting period, these records will be used to compare Airman against each other. They will also be used to justify eligibility for assignments, decorations, and promotions. A well-written EPR will showcase both what the individual accomplished and the impact of those accomplishments and make sure the subject is eligible for any opportunities he has earned.

In summary, EPRs are easier to write than most people think. If you have all the information you need, which is the RIP and a list of the ratee's accomplishments during the rating period, you can produce a pretty good draft in an hour or so depending on your ability.

Completing the AF Form 910

SECTION I. Ratee Identification Data

Blocks 1 through 10 are self-explanatory. This information is contained in the EPR shell (also known as a "RIP") which is generated by the personnel section (of your unit or the base). The information entered in these blocks must match what is on the RIP. If the details don't match, work with your supervisor or MPF to figure out what the problem is.

SECTION II. Job Description

Block 1. Duty Title. Normally the work center has a series of approved duty titles. Use the one approved for the ratee's rank and position. The duty title is also listed on the RIP.

Block 2. Significant Additional Duty(s). List any assigned additional duties (such as Equipment Custodian, ADPE Monitor, etc).

Block 3. Key Duties, Tasks, and Responsibilities. Every shop or office has a set of standard Job Descriptions (depending on rank) for the Key Duties, Tasks, and Responsibilities fields. If the officially sanctioned blurb needs editing for grammar or accuracy, there is no law against it although your supervisor must approve the changes. The Job Description entries must be in bullet statement format:

- *Manages* $1.1 B in communications infrastructure at the Louisiana missile tracking center
- *Processes* communications outage reports for US Northern Command theater operations
- *Analyzes* communications requirements and determines and engineers efficient comm links
- *Assists* theater operations participants in resolving procedural and operational issues

If the ratee supervises any troops, state that fact on the first line of the job description. Note that all bullet statements in the Key Duties, Tasks, and Responsibilities block have to begin with a present-tense verb.

Note: to be competitive, entries in this block should describe a level of responsibility greater than that for the duties listed in the previous reporting period's EPR. The goal is to demonstrate and document growth in the ratee's abilities. If the workcenter limits the Job Description block to a standard blurb commensurate with your rank, there's not much you can do about this. If possible, list significant additional duties that indicate the trust and confidence your NCOIC places in you.

SECTION III. Performance Assessment

This is the most important section of the EPR. This is where the ratee's accomplishments are documented by the rater. The following categories must be addressed by the Rater and the Additional Rater:

- Primary/Additional Duties (4 lines)

- Standards, Conduct, Character, & Military Bearing (2 lines)

- Training Requirements (2 lines)

- Teamwork/Followership (2 lines)

- Other Comments (2 lines)

- Additional Rater's Comments (3 lines)

In addition, if required (if the ratee didn't meet standards), Fitness must also be addressed

Airmen are often asked to provide their own bullet statements. This is not unusual and it's in the ratee's best interest to provide the most information possible. After all, your rating will be influenced by the information you provide.

Coming up with enough accomplishments to fill the EPR form can be hard. At times it can seem almost impossible. The quickest way to come up with enough material for your EPR is to brainstorm. List all the ratee's accomplishments on a separate sheet of paper. Jot down everything that might qualify as an accomplishment. Don't leave anything out. Include volunteering for the Air Show and Meals on Wheels, giving to the Combined Federal Campaign, and anything else you can think of. If you're still coming up short, if your work center has a log or calendar, review it to remind yourself of projects you completed or fires you put out. Then, when you have at least fifteen accomplishments (to fill all the required sections), go back to the form and start fitting them in. If you try to think up accomplishments individually, edit them for readability, and make them fit in the space provided as you go along, your progress will be much slower.

One thing that's very important to remember when you're putting together a list of accomplishments is to not be modest. If you're new to Air Force performance reports, you might be reluctant to claim credit for any achievements that you weren't 100% responsible for. Don't be! Most work center accomplishments require the efforts of several people and are the result of teamwork. If you had any part in an accomplishment, even if it was just making a couple of phone calls, you are allowed to claim it as your own and summarize it in a bullet statement. A work center supervisor will often reuse the same bullet statements, over and over, in several different EPRs so it's not unexpected or out of the ordinary. As a rule of thumb, if you had any part in an achievement, from documenting the situation in a log to turning a wrench, you can claim it. So claim everything and let your supervisor sort it out. And don't worry that your supervisor will scrutinize your inputs and dispute your claims. It doesn't happen. A supervisor is much more concerned with getting enough material for your EPR than with analyzing which person contributed the most to this or that accomplishment.

The format required for entries throughout the EPR is the "bullet statement" format. If you don't use this format, your EPR will be returned for editing. See the section on bullet statement format for more information.

Make sure you write your bullet statements in plain English using common words that anyone can understand. Avoid jargon and strive for readability. By jargon, I mean words or phrases that are only understood by people in your career field. You might understand what "retrofitted weep holes" means and how important it is but most people would not. It's very important that your EPR be understandable to anyone who reads it because it's the main source of information for selection for NCO of the Quarter, promotion, and other personnel decisions. The old Senior NCOs who review EPRs to make these decisions are from a variety of career fields. So make sure it's understandable to anyone so that you're selected for the opportunities you've earned.

If abbreviations or acronyms are used, they must be "defined" the first time they are used unless they are commonly understood and approved. See the section on

23

Approved Abbreviations and Acronyms for reference. The list of acronyms approved for EPRs varies by Command but the list in this book is a compilation of several Commands' lists and should be 99% accurate for your location. The goal is clarity and readability.

Note: All entries in the Performance Assessment Section must have occurred during the reporting period. The reporting period is the span of time between the EPR's beginning and end dates. It's not permissible to use an accomplishment, no matter how significant, if it occurred before the start date of your current report. It is permissible however, to include events that started in a previous reporting period and continue into the current reporting period or events that have just started and have not been completed yet.

1. Primary/Additional Duties

Place an X in the block that accurately describes the Ratee's performance. This means, of course, that you are responsible for rating the person's performance and how well it met established standards. As the rater, although you may accept guidance from peers and supervisors, this decision is yours alone.

All the bullet statements in this section should concern the ratee's performance in their primary (or additional) duty - not participation in the Meals on Wheels program or work with the annual base Dining-in.

There's only room for four single-line bullet statements in this section so make them count. Two line bullets are allowed but since there's only four lines in which to list all the ratee's accomplishments, unless you have a really special two-line bullet in mind, it would be more effective to list four individual, single-line accomplishments.

Examples:
- Managed 11 personnel work center in direct support of U.S. Space Command--exceeded all assigned goals!
- Directed emergency repair of air conditioning at Air Force Network site; rescued $5M in critical equipment
- Reacted quickly under pressure, reprogrammed C-5 display unit on divert acft; $9K flight computer saved
- Utilized existing equipment and spare parts to assemble rack--saved work center $26K in material costs

There are only four lines available for describing our accomplishments. Make sure your *best* accomplishments are

25

listed! After your brainstorming section, review your list of primary duty accomplishments and rate them from most significant to least. List the best or most significant accomplishment first, at the top. The next important accomplishment would be second from the top and so on.

The best accomplishments are those that can be shown to somehow support your unit's goals or mission. If you have trouble remembering your work center's goals (which is very easy to do when you're engrossed in the day to day details of making things happen), google your squadron's home page. Usually the squadron will have their goals listed right on the first page. Try to relate your accomplishments to your unit's or your work center's goals.

The overall goal of the EPR is to, as accurately as possible, describe a person's performance. To that end, every statement should be "qualified"; every claim should be supported by a quantity or be as specific as possible. See the section on Bullet Statement Format for more guidance on the entries in this section.

Whatever bullet statements are used, they should support the rating marked. For example, if the Clearly Exceeds block was marked, the bullet statements in this section must describe performance that clearly exceeded standards. Your chain of command will insist on this. They aren't as demanding when it comes to the lesser ratings, but overall five ratings must be supported by bullet statements that justify the rating.

2. Standards, Conduct, Character, & Military Bearing

Place an X in the block that describes how well the ratee meets Air Force standards. This means, of course, that you are responsible for rating the person's performance and how well it met established standards. By established standards, we mean standards that an Airmen of the same rank in the same unit would be expected to meet. Ratees should be compared with their peers. As the rater, although you may accept guidance from others, this rating is your responsibility to decide. If the Additional Rater does not agree, he or she may indicate their disagreement by marking the Non-Concur block in Section VI.

The comments here must support and justify the rating, are limited to two lines, and must describe how the ratee adhered to or exceeded standards.

The accomplishments listed can be from a broad spectrum of service, generally anything not duty or training related but somehow enhancing the military community. Essential topics are dress and appearance and conduct on and off duty. Higher ranks (SSgts and TSgts) are expected to be managers and, as such, bullet statements for these ranks should address enforcement of standards and military customs and courtesies.

Examples:
- Mature leader; won't compromise standards, enforced highest AETC standards of conduct
- Participated in Airman Leadership School renovation; improved quality of life for over 2,600 students

27

- Immaculate uniform--strict adherence to AFI 23-201--sets example for peers and subordinates
- Guided, counseled Airmen on uniform standards--raised section morale/performance

For more examples, see the Standards, Conduct, Character, and Military Bearing section.

Note: As with all bullet statements, generalities should be avoided. "enforced highest AETC standards of conduct" is a laudable achievement but it would be better to state *how* this result was manifested, such as "his section recognized for lowest number of incidents in sq".

To be competitive, Staff Sergeants and Tech Sergeants should list bullet statements that demonstrate maturity and an ability to enforce standards. Enforcing standards can be something as simple as consistently requiring Airmen to report to work on time, keep their ancillary training up to date, or keep their uniforms looking sharp. Enforcing standards can also be the supervisor meeting his responsibilities by counseling Airman who don't comply with standards and documenting non-compliance.

3. Fitness

Place an X in the block that describes whether or not the ratee meets Air Force fitness standards. Mark the Exempt block only if the ratee is exempt from all four components of the fitness assessment. If the ratee does not meet standards (score 75 or above), the rater must make a comment (limited to a single line) and the EPR will automatically be a Referral EPR. If the ratee does meet standards, do not enter any comments.

Comment examples for Does Not Meet:

- Failed to meet standards in push-ups and crunches

- Did not meet body composition requirements, exceeded standards on other components

- Made aggressive progress in short time on only category not previously qualified

- Unable to meet standards in aerobic fitness; scores are improving in all areas

4. Training Requirements

Place an X in the block that describes how well the ratee meets training requirements. The comments here are limited to two lines, and must describe training-related accomplishments.

The focus is on On-the-Job training, ancillary training and readiness. In addition, for SSgts and TSgts, addressing more advanced training requirements like PME, off-duty education, technical growth, and upgrade training is appropriate.

Note that some types of accomplishment are not authorized to be mentioned in the EPR or this section:

- Commenting on the ratee's attendance or graduation of a mandatory PME school is not allowed. There is an exception: if the ratee earned some kind of special recognition while attending PME school, then recognizing that achievement is allowed.

- Commenting on any type of WAPS test score or board results is not allowed.

Every other form of training is fair game, including CDC completion and scores.

Examples of Training Requirements bullets:

- Completed largest set of CDC requirements to date, 3 months ahead of schedule; excellent progress!

- Shop qualified in less than half normal time--enthusiastic and fearless; ready for increased responsibility

- Pursued off-duty education--completed four credits towards CCAF Transportation Management degree

- Exceeds all training requirements; evident by a 98 percent on his 7-Level, End-of-Course examination

See Training Requirements section for more Training EPR Bullet examples.

Remember: If the Clearly Exceeds block is marked, the bullet statements is this section must describe a level of performance that exceeded standards. If you don't have anything that clearly exceeds standards, you might want to sign up for a college class or start work on a new qualification and then list that as one of your bullets. It's allowable as long as you sign up or start before the EPR's close-out date. And most squadron's require your EPR so early that this is almost always possible.

5. Teamwork/Followership

Place an X in the block that describes how well the ratee works with others. While the Primary/Additional Duty section listed the ratee's concrete accomplishments, this block is used to describe and rate an Airman's more subjective qualities.

Listing actual achievements does provide some insight into a person's abilities but it doesn't provide the whole picture. A list of achievements doesn't give any indication as to the character or personality of the ratee. An Airman might have a long list of impressive accomplishments but be an unruly member with a bad attitude. He or she might be an expert in their field but the absolute worst at sharing experience or getting along with others. This kind of anti-social behavior can handicap a work center's ability to be productive.

These social qualities are very important, fully as important as a person's technical skills. So, in addition to describing a person's professional and technical skills, we need a way to convey to the reader his social skills, his integrity, character, loyalty and other qualities which are not apparent when merely reading a list of accomplishments. This block is where this is done.

The comments here are limited to two lines and must support the rating. The accomplishments documented here should involve team building, support of the team, and followership.

To be competitive, SSgts and TSgts should also address Leadership, Team Accomplishment, and Recognition of others (management-related aspects of teamwork).

Examples of Teamwork and Followership bullets:

- Participated in Airman Leadership School renovation; improved quality of life for over 2,600 students

- Qualified himself on shop's new eq, trained all members of shift; multiplied mx effectiveness

- Instituted on-the-job CDC tutor program resulting in 6 airmen upgraded ahead of schedule, reduced failures to zero!

- Volunteered off-duty time for air show--prevented work center manning shortage; hardy character

- Led self-help project to upgrade shop telephone system--improved capability, safety, saved AF $14K!

See Teamwork/Followership section for more Teamwork bullet examples

6. Other Comments

Consider Promotion, Future Duty/Assignment/Education Recommendations and Safety, Security, and Human Relations.

MPFM 07-44 states "Comments in the Other Comments block are optional; however if used, bullet format is mandatory. Comments are limited to two lines. This section may also be used to spell out uncommon acronyms. NOTE: Stratification is prohibited for AB – TSgt."

Although comments in this two line block are not officially mandatory, to be competitive, they deserve *at least* as much attention as the other sections. This is where the rater gets to express his opinion of the ratee. It's difficult to get a complete picture of an Airman's personality, performance, and potential from the abbreviated bullet statements listed in the other sections of the EPR. An Airman might accomplish a lot but was it on his own or was it because he was pushed by his supervisor? The supervisor can attempt to clarify that confusion in this block by using appropriate adjectives such as motivated, mature, or influential.

Adherence to the rule requiring each statement to begin with a past-tense verb, is not as iron-clad in this section. Raters may deviate from the Spartan rules required in the rest of the EPR as necessary to express the character of the ratee. Note that stratification (comparing performance with peers) is not allowed for Airman through TSgt.

The last line of this block should contain a solid job recommendation and/or promotion recommendation. Make sure you qualify any claims to greatness. For example, in order to claim an Airman is "Best in Wing", the ratee must have won a Wing-level award (Wing NCO of the Quarter, Wing Maintenance NCO of the year, etc.) and that accomplishment should be listed somewhere in the EPR.

Note that this block, by being optional, may be used by the rater to signal less than perfect performance. A review of a top Airman would normally require all sections in the EPR to be filled out while a mediocre performance may be indicated by leaving the optional section blank. If your rater actually uses this block to spell out acronyms (as allowed IAW MPFM 07-44), maybe you should start looking into a job transfer. See the Supervisors Code section for other methods of signaling substandard performance.

Examples of Other Comments bullet statements:

- Reduced chronic maintenance backlog by 50% with 99% accuracy, best repair rate in five years

- A key unit member with unmatched dedication to duty and personal performance--our choice for BTZ!

- An earnest airman, exhibits rare discipline in working towards completion of qualification training

- Mature and confident airman with extraordinary knowledge and initiative--immediately promote to SSgt!

- On site only six months, already 75% qualified on work center qualification training tasks

- Driven NCO with outstanding results. Continue to entrust with increasing responsibility--Promote now!

- Maintained $6M of fixed asset property account with 100% accuracy rating; best rating in six sections

- The most conscientious, loyal, and dedicated NCO I've served with in 20 years-- STEP to TSgt Now!

See the Other Comments section for more examples.

Note: If you want to go the extra mile, don't leave a lot of white space (unused space) at the end of a bullet statement - in any block anywhere in the EPR. Officially, white space is OK. Because the goal is to accurately describe the ratee's performance with no unnecessary clutter, inevitably white space will naturally occur. But, if you want to go above and beyond, if you want to demonstrate that your troop is important to you and worthy of a good rating, this is where you can demonstrate a little extra effort. Reword the statement so that there are no more than five or six spaces at the end of each statement. Make that block as full of text as possible to give the impression that you wanted to say more but there just wasn't enough space to do it. When future reviewers of the EPR see how well it was written and how someone labored over it, it should make them realize that this person was considered to be above average and deserving of the extra effort.

SECTION IV. Rater Information

This information is self-explanatory and contained in the EPR shell or RIP generated by the personnel section (of your unit or the base). The information entered in these blocks must match what is on the RIP. If the information on the RIP is not correct, it is your responsibility to make sure it gets corrected.

SECTION V. Overall Performance Assessment

Check the appropriate box in the Rater's Assessment row. Do not check the box in the Additional Rater's Assessment row. The Additional Rater will check the box he or she thinks is appropriate when you send the EPR to them for review.

Defend Your Rating. Sometimes the Rater's rater will try to get the rater to change the rating. The rater has total independence in evaluating the ratee's performance; he or she may rate the individual as they see fit. If the Additional Rater does not agree with the overall rating, he or she may indicate this fact by marking the block (in Section V, OVERALL PERFORMANCE ASSESSMENT) they deem appropriate.

Record the date of the last feedback session.

SECTION VI. ADDITIONAL RATER'S COMMENTS

In this section the Additional Rater, the rater's rater, enters information that will express his or her opinion of the ratee. Often the ratee has to provide enough bullet statements to fill all the required sections on the AF Form 910 including the Additional Rater's Comments block. There are only three lines. There is no prescribed format as to the order and character of the bullets in this section but traditionally, the first line in the Additional Rater's Comments block is an introduction where the Additional Rater describes the ratee's overall performance. The second line is for listing the Ratee's best accomplishment. The last line is a summary of the performance and a promotion statement. The Additional Rater's comments can't repeat any of the bullets entered earlier in the EPR. It has to be all new material.

Suggested format:

Introduction: a single line for the Additional Rater to describe the ratee's overall performance

Accomplishment: the ratee's best accomplishment

Summary: a single line for the Additional Rater to summarize the ratee's performance and make a promotion statement.

Example:

- A task-oriented, conscientious NCO--consistent efforts increased site efficiency by 30%
- Oversaw replacement of Tech Control Facility, complex task--cutover with zero downtime!
- Exceptional performer--further challenge with most difficult tasks--promote ahead of peers!

Note that the above suggested format is only a suggestion and that some reviewers prefer only three more duty-related bullet statements in this section. In general, the more factual the information and accomplishments, the stronger the EPR. The flowery and unsubstantiated introductory statement shouldn't be used at the expense of a valid accomplishment. It would be better to list a strong accomplishment on the first and second line and let the last line summarize overall performance and provide a promotion statement. See the Additional Rater's Comments section for more examples. For more information on promotion statements and the importance of including them, see the section titled, The Supervisor's Code.

If the Rater qualifies as a single-evaluator, meaning because of his rank he is also the Additional Rater, using the Additional Rater section is not mandatory. In this case, type in the section, "This section not used".

SECTION VII. FUNCTIONAL EXAMINER /AF ADVISOR

If applicable, place an X in the appropriate box.

SECTION VIII. UNIT COMMANDER /CIVILIAN DIRECTOR

The Commander marks the Concur block and signs.

SECTION IX. RATEE'S ACKNOWLEDGEMENT

After the EPR has been accepted by the Additional Rater and has been processed and signed by the Commander, the Ratee must sign the report in order for it to become a valid record of performance and be accepted by MPF. Signing does not indicate agreement with or acceptance of the rating. It merely indicates the Ratee is aware of the record. If the Ratee is not satisfied with the rating received, he or she is still entitled to submit an appeal IAW AFI 36-2401.

Bullet Statement Format

There aren't many things as frustrating as having the report you labored over for hours abruptly returned for editing because it's in the "wrong" format. The goal of this paper is to help avoid that problem when it comes to EPRs. The required format for entries in the Air Force EPR is the "bullet statement" format.

Bullet statement format is merely the use of short sentence fragments to describe something. The goal is brevity and normal sentence structure requirements, such as conjunctions and punctuation, are not necessary. The reason for this is economy of space. There's not many lines in an EPR and using this format allows the writer to communicate more information in the space available.

Job Description

When completing the Job Description section of the EPR, use bullet statements that fully describe the ratee's duties:

- Manages $1.1 B in communications infrastructure at the Louisiana missile tracking center
- Processes communications outage reports for US Northern Command theater operations
- Analyzes communications requirements and determines and engineers efficient comm links
- Assists theater operations participants in resolving procedural and operational issues

These job description bullets should begin with the action that is being described. Start the bullet statement with a present-tense verb whenever possible (Manages, Directs, Supervises, Repairs, etc.). Normally you won't have to write your own Job Description. The work center usually has two or three standard versions of the work center's duty description that can be copied and pasted and management usually prefers that you use the accepted version. One version is used for ranks up to SrA or so and another one is used for NCOs and supervisors. Most people just leave the Job Description blank and let their supervisor fill it in since they have access to this information.

Performance Assessment

When completing the Performance Assessment blocks and the Additional Rater's Comments block, where the ratee's accomplishments are documented, the bullet format is different than the format used in the Job Description block. In the Performance Assessment blocks, the bullet statements should have two parts:

Part 1. Describes the accomplishment.

Part 2. Describes the accomplishment's positive effect or impact or result

Example: Washed over 99% of stored aircraft--reduced corrosion problems by 75%

Note that bullet statements are limited to two lines. But, even though we're allowed two lines to elaborate on each accomplishment, to give the best impression, the EPR should consist mostly of one-line bullet statements like this:

- Traced problem on faulty interface panel to burned resistor, replaced--restored monitoring capability
- Delivered over 75K gals of JPTS; supported five temporarily assigned U-2s--zero delays to vital mission
- Mastered all facets of PACAF's largest distribution element in record time--reduced workload on undermanned team

In addition to having two parts, the bullets statements in the Performance Assessment section are different that those in the Job Description section in that they should begin with a past-tense verb (rather than present tense).

The reason for this abbreviated style of writing is that, in the past, a lot of people had problems remembering or even identifying their accomplishments over the previous year. When it came time to fill out their EPR, typically they could only come up with three or four accomplishments and because that would fill up only about half the space in an EPR, they would have to add a lot of extra and unnecessary adjectives and big words to describe their accomplishments-- just to fill the required space. The end result was a lot of fluff and hot air that didn't say much but sounded nice. The requirement for bullet statements helps to prevent that kind of writing and makes the report more factual.

Although the goal is a single-line bullet statement, sometimes it's difficult to adequately describe a complex and important accomplishment in a single line. In that case, by all means, use two lines. Just don't use too many two-line bullets or it might appear that you don't have many real accomplishments and you're trying to fill space. The format below is commonly used for two-line bullet statements (although variations are acceptable).

- Oversaw long overdue, complicated preventive maintenance inspection on equipment
-- Trained six techs on alignments, prevented future maint delays, ensured continued ops

It consists of the main bullet on the first line and a sub-bullet on the second line. The double dash before the sub-bullet on the second line indicates that it supports the line above. The single line bullet and the two-line bullet format can be mixed as required. Liberties may be taken with this format. A bullet can consist of two or three or more fragments and the accomplishment can exceed one line and run into the second line like this:

-Provided valuable assistance to depot maintenance team; replaced azimuth motor's electric brake assembly--enabled depot team to proceed with analysis of autotrack failure

Note that when wrapping a bullet into the second line like this, the double-dash isn't required to identify the result or impact. A semicolon may be used to separate the accomplishment and result instead. The goal is conservation of space and short, compact, meaningful statements. Bullet statements don't have to follow strict grammatical rules. For example, substituting commas or semicolons for "and" and omitting articles such as "a" or "the" will help you shoehorn an accomplishment into a single line.

Bullet statements describing accomplishments (for the Performance Assessment Section) should begin with the action that is being described. Start the bullet statement with a past-tense verb whenever possible (Managed, Directed, Repaired, Authored, etc.)

Registered over 3K participants...
Identified, isolated loss of radar to fault in...
Repaired broken nose-wheel...

Don't start a bullet statement with adverbs as in "Quickly and efficiently registered..." or "Expertly and unfailingly identified...". Yes, there's nothing technically wrong with saying it that way and it may be just what you want to say but the Air Force frowns on unnecessary adverbs and adjectives. And this kind of thing suggests that the accomplishment isn't significant if you have to resort to this kind of word inflation. But, if being quick and expert is somehow above and beyond and needs to be emphasized and you can get away with it, use it!

Clarify what the individual did; be specific as possible. Review every word and evaluate whether it's too broad. If another word can narrow the meaning, use it instead. Don't leave room for doubt. Examples: "Participated in..." could mean anything from "showed up for" to "directly managed the operation." Make sure the EPR states what the person actually did. Another example is "Active member of Base NCO club" which could mean anything from just paying their dues to planning and organizing special events. Be specific and support statements with facts.

The overall goal of the EPR is to, as accurately and completely as possible, describe a person's performance. To that end, every statement should be "qualified"; every claim should be supported by a quantity or an extent. For example, consider the bullet statement:

Treated sick dogs and cats--prevented spread of communicable disease

There are a lot of details that are missing. How many sick dogs or cats were treated? Whose dogs and cats? What kind of dogs and cats? What communicable disease? What was the risk if not treated? If the answer to any of these questions isn't inspiring, then it's not important. Don't mention it. But it's by asking these questions that we find the gems. For every bullet, ask Who, What, When, Why, and Where. When we ask these questions we find that 95 of the 100 total pets on base were inoculated. That's quite an accomplishment so the number of dogs and cats should be listed --95% of base pets treated. Where was the disease spread? What was its effect? It might be more dramatic and hard-hitting to say, "confined spread of fatal infections to off-base community, spared 95 lives" rather than "prevented spread of communicable disease". Study every bullet and make sure it accurately and fully expresses the accomplishment.

Use numbers, dollars, percentages, etc where you can. They help quantify results. Percentages have more impact if you clarify the scope: "increased reporting by 10 percent" could mean an increase of one if the baseline is ten. "Increased reporting 10 percent—from 900 to over 990" has more impact.

Write every bullet statement so that anyone can understand it. The EPR will be reviewed at boards consisting of NCOs from a variety of career fields so it must be understandable to a broad audience not only someone from your career field or squadron. If it's not understandable to anyone, you're limiting the effectiveness of your statements and your EPR.

Don't leave a lot of "white space" or unused space at the end of a bullet statement. Officially, white space is allowed. Since the goal is to accurately describe the ratee's performance with no unnecessary adjectives, white space will naturally occur. But, if you want to go the extra mile, if you want to demonstrate that your troop is important to you and worthy of a good rating, this is where you can demonstrate a little extra effort. Reword the statement so that there is no more than five or six spaces at the end of each statement. Fill the blocks with text. Make it look as if there wasn't enough room for you to write everything you wanted to say about this fantastic troop. When future reviewers of the EPR see how well it was written and how someone labored over it, it should make them realize that this Airman was viewed as a person worth the effort. Note that this step, the elimination of white space, is not practical until the EPR has already been reviewed and approved.

Don't write meaningless bullets. "dedicated NCO--allegiance to mission inspires peers" does sound grand but it isn't very specific. Without an action and a result nothing is really said and the bullet is only the rater's opinion; it's not backed up by fact.

Different organizations have different requirements as to format. Most require the bullet statements to start with a single dash (-) and supporting bullet statements (sub-bullets) start with a double-dash (--). Most units use a semi-colon (;) or a double-dash (--) to separate the accomplishment and its result. Check with your supervisor or orderly room for your unit's required format.

EPR Bullet Statement Examples

Primary and Additional Duties

- Accomplished 225 of 300 upgrade/qualification tasks; 75% completed on three airframes--ahead of peers

- Accurately initiated 45 routing/adjustment forms--100% contract compliance/saved $35K in double payments

- Acted as liaison between HQ PACAF and HQ AETC--guided disputes between AF personnel and HQ AETC to mutual success

- Admitted over 90 patients; 100% record accuracy--laid error-free foundation for all subsequent documentation

- Advised installation commander on environmental, safety and health (ES&H) issues--integral to Wing mission success!

- Advised military members on formal training classes needed to progress--no lost advancement opportunity

- Agile Combat Support!--Reviewed, prepared over 3K troops in less than a week for deployment--100% met requirements

- Ambitious Airman; completed 4 CDC volumes 2 months ahead of schedule; maintained outstanding 94% VRE

- Analyzed over 300 exploited documents (1,000+ translated pages); provided critical intelligence to tactical commanders

- Assisted in delivering over 75K gals of JPTS--supported five temporarily assigned U-2's--Zero Delays

- Assisted in install of fiber optic cable based network for Operation Deployed Arrow--provided Army contingent full access to air tasking order data, increased force readiness

- Assisted in redesign of tool system--resulted in service-wide award for innovation

- Assisted in water main repair at AAFES; 48 hrs around-the-clock ops--minimal impact to 16K weekly patrons

- Authored over 200 DOCEX reports--solely responsible for rising success of derivative missions!

- Briefed current intelligence during internal training--meticulous detail; increased awareness for 60 personnel

- Briefed over 12,000 deploying troops on the tarmac on destinations and expected conditions--enhanced readiness!

- Briefed several theater commanders and dignitaries on time-sensitive intelligence during operation--enabled cohesive effort

- Building custodian for $5M passenger terminal--presented excellent first impression of AMC travelers

- Built flawless workstations and server databases for local system training exercises, Lightsabre 08 and Joint Warrior 09--directly responsible for zero failures!

- Compiles detailed after-action reports which shape future deployment strategies throughout the entire USAF

- Completed TCTO 1A-131-1668 on all aircraft--completed in less than half allotted time

- Conducted daily heat stress evaluations; protected over 12,000 workers and children in three day care centers

- Conducted numerous interior/exterior sweeps of Pax terminal during latest CERE--enhanced terminal security

- Conducted over 30 extensive classes on NBC warfare defense for personnel deploying to Desert Storm--multiplied effectiveness

- Conducted security patrols on four deep wells/two reservoirs; protected potable water for 2.8K MFH facilities

- Connected remote users to Air Operations Center via Secure Internet Protocol Network--enhanced post defense readiness

- Consolidated S1 operations from three locations into centralized hub--created continuity, increased functionality by 40%

- Constructed bulletin board displays; provided 13,000 annual patients with preventive eye care information

- Contributed 20 off-duty hours to environmental data migration; updated 10 hazmat shop folders; exceeded AMC goal by 10%

- Coordinated 125 sorties with CAOC; mitigated airspace conflicts between US & allied aircraft--zero incidents

- Coordinated 13 priority fly-in cals--actions guaranteed 437th SOG AC130 gunship mission and deployment

- Coordinated ground operations for Silver Shield mission supporting Gen. Flintstone--textbook operation

- Coordinated Wing Commander's change of occupancy; zero discrepancies noted during move-in

- Created database/tracked ventilation equipment in two hundred facilities--improved air quality/production

- Created intuitive TO index by function and equipment; increased workcenter maintenance effectiveness

- Created unprecedented plan for ANGuard medical support to homeland defense--dramatic improvement in state response!

- Dedicated to excellence--orchestrated relocation of clinic's diagnostic equipment--eliminated excessive patient travel

- Dependable airman; deposited over $20K of passenger terminal's funds--100% funds accountability!

- Deployed 45 days to Nicaragua; completed $256K in projects--new school/clinic raised QoL for 600 locals

- Deployed as primary C2IPS/CTAPS system administrator for Exercise Iron Cobra--established CTAPS network in Air Operations Center in record time--excellent mission support!

- Deployed superstar! Safety NCOIC of EAMS, ensured safe movement of 77K passengers/80 million lbs cargo

- Deployed to Osan AB, Korea during Kadena runway closure--aided operations by creating a smooth transition

- Detailed the DV vehicle for the AMC Commander--continues to set the highest standards possible

- Detained military member for DWAI, discovered two concealed weapons; ensured safety of all on-scene patrolmen

- Developed a cross-training program and self-directed work atmosphere that improved employee productivity by 95%

- Developed file systems for all DCO staff agencies and three maintenance squadrons; increased efficiency

- Developed new research methodology--improved the accuracy and timeliness of reports by 25%

- Developed training program that improved skills of observation teams, produced 33% increase in capabilities during operations

- Developed, conducted training for workcenter members--highest ratio of shift qualified personnel ever!

- Diligent, tireless operator--identified unobserved enemy movement--led to mission generation, success, with no losses

- Directed 2-person team to repair 18" storm drain; cleared 330 lbs of debris--avoided flooding to 7 facilities

- Directed C-17 fuselage/pod repair; replaced two chafed structural components--finished in 36 vs 72 hr ETIC

- Discovered KC-135 cell pinhole leak; applied patch-- eliminated depot requirement, $10K in repair cycle costs

- Dispatched to simultaneous domestic disturbance calls; sound judgment delivered safety to all concerned

- Disseminated daily image reports and indexes via SIPRNET--100% accurate, correctly formatted and ahead of schedule!

- Electronically mapped 400 water main valves; KMC database updated--ensured quick id/isolation possible

- Enabled network monitoring within AOR--increased workcenter diagnostic skill--reduced repair time by 75%

- Energetic in administrative duties; monitored key flight functions and enthusiastically accepted additional duties

- Engineered, established first-ever interface between two proprietary VTC systems--enabled SOCOM planners to communicate in real time with AOR commanders

- Engineered rerouting of 600 pieces of OIF mail weighing over 12K lbs--same-day lift/averted 48-hour delay

- Ensured 100% of assigned tasks completed on time, no continuity loss during multiple leadership changeovers

- Ensured safe working/living environment for 30K military members--largest American military community overseas

- Established fire department at bare-base location in Yukekova, Turkey—obtained necessary equipment; operational in 7 days!

- Established procedures and originated Wallace Air Station forms--a first!

- Executed JTF Network Ops orders; forced 230 SIPRNET scans/password resets--solidified network defense

- Exhibited extensive job knowledge during exercise Fulchi Lens 04; single-handedly solved numerous printer malfunctions

- Expertly bore-sighted systems--accuracy made live-target firing unnecessary--saved over 10K in ammo

- Expertly evaluated over 120 job orders; developed short/long range goals, an astounding 80% completion rate

- Expertly troubleshot KC-135 faulty #1 tank to broken ground wire--saved over $8K on unnecessary valve replacement, launched on schedule!

- Extensive technical knowledge--expert troubleshooting ability decreased equipment down time by 40%

- Identified and detained individual for DUI and driving without a license; keeping the streets safe for all

- Identified broken pin on a KC-135 main tank boost pump cannon plug--expert repair saved over $5K for unnecessary pump replacement

- Identified cracked UHF antenna, repaired--restored communication, immediate launch--mission multiplier!

- Identified error in C2IPS installation guide--submitted change, resulted in bulletin that prevented loss of critical data and operational capability world wide

- Identified fault of transient C-130 to left External fuel level control valve--replaced, record turn-around

- Identified right Benson tank sump leaking before apparent to crew--repaired, resealed sump from inside tank--enhanced air safety

- Identified two leaking nut-plates on an outboard main top panel after flight--applied temporary repair--restored for flight until permanent fix can be made

- Identified, corrected dozens of long-standing personnel issues--restored 100% visibility on DEROS allocations

- Identified, isolated loss of radar to fault in Common Integrated Processor--reseated card to restore--saved $2600

- Impacted unit mission! Effected 594 KC-135 fuel system repairs--wing flew 6.5K FY04 hours; 9% above goal

- Implemented a phase training program; reduced required training time of newly assigned personnel by one year

- Implemented a proactive program to reduce tool shortages; over 800 man-hours saved during a six month period

- Implemented air strike procedures that increased efficiency and reduced man hours by 50%

- Increased face-to-face time spent by medical providers with patients by 25 percent; efforts lauded by superiors

- Initiated the transition of personnel records from paper files to a database, provided a more user-friendly and efficient system

- Innovative tech--designed and built portable training simulator/test equip cabinet using existing spare parts--saved work center $3K

- Installed pressure tank/6K ft of line from water well to base camp--improved shower/laundry water pressure

- Instructed personnel on AF policy and AF PT/Eval/Urinalysis programs and consequences--reduced failures by 90%

- Isolated and repaired digital flight control system malfunctions on F-16; launched on time, prevented mission failure

- Isolated cross-talk noise problem on site tactical interface panel to faulty shield grounding--restored interface capabilities with tactical systems worldwide

- Led 3-person water main repair crew; directed damaged line exposure/fix--prevented $4K vs contractor cost

- Led 5 file server re-builds; 232TB of critical data moved--4k users file retrieval access time slashed by 30%

- Led environmental health assessment teams in Georgia Republic ISO Operation IRAQI FREEDOM--reduced hazard to deployed troops--zero food/water-borne illnesses!

- Led fire hydrant replacement; ensured 100% fire coverage for AAFES warehouse--$200M in assets protected

- Led outpatient dispensing line redesign; smooth-flowed work; increased productivity 45%--metric proven

- Led tank reseal team--reduced fuel leak delayed discrepancies to 0.5 per aircraft--exceeded MAJCOM goal by 50%

- Led the Wing in pollution prevention initiatives---30% reduction in long-term hazardous waste/material storage!

- Lost and Found representative; efforts resulted in recovery of over 1200 lost bags--unparalleled customer service

- Maintained air pressure tanks at two facilities; suppression sys 100% operational--lives/$9M assets protected

- Maintained an $18 million fixed asset property account with a 96.8% accuracy rating-best rating out of nine sections

- Maintained an impressive 100% fully mission-capable rate for Oct 09; shattered AETC record of 98%

- Maintained land mobile radio system--guaranteed critical communications at all times--always prepared!

- Maintained over $1.5 million in weapons, munitions, and other support equipment--flawless accountability of critical armor assets ensured readiness

- Maintained squadron personnel mobility folders, scheduled pre-deployment requirements; ensured 100% readiness

- Maintained/operated the Microwave, Display, and Computer Test Stations--ensured thorough, calibrated F-15 maintenance

- Managed 20 personnel workcenter in direct support of U.S. Space Command--exceeded all assigned goals!

- Managed and maintained internal office suspense-- streamlined office--reduced late reports 75%

- Managed Blood Alcohol Test program for 62 squadrons; ensured chain of custody and 100% accurate results

- Managed flightline Snow/Ice Removal program--kept airfield operational/no delays despite 50% reduction in snow removal assets

- Managed ROI process of patient records for copying; reduced customer wait-time by 40%--increased efficiency

- Managed Technical Order accounts and commercial manuals for two functional areas--prevented maintenance delays due to lack of technical references by providing necessary resources

- Masterfully rerouted more than 20K lbs of delayed Baghdad destined mail--improved total uplift by 48 hours

- Meticulous attention to detail; orchestrated the transfer of over 6000 pieces of classified ; 100% accountability

- Meticulously managed/researched/filed over 10 feet of medical documentation; perfect accountability!

- Modernized section's outdated process for tracking safety issues--logging rate now at 100% for first time

- Monitored and processed over 11,000 enlisted and officer performance reports--reduced late reports from 30% to 5%

- Monitored, coordinated multiple work crews via radio as dispatcher; reduced unnecessary trips 30%

- Moved 12,000 passengers and 500 short tons of baggage with zero aircraft delays--extremely proficient!

- MX expert who rebuilt interphone cord; 90 min fix accomplished in 30--82 pax & 12 cargo tons moved to Iraq

- Outstanding troubleshooter--resolved over 200 Network Control Center trouble tickets per month via telephone

- Overcame all challenges while deployed to Operation DESERT STORM--assisted short-notice relocation of Air Ops Center to Eskan Village--data interruption less than one hour!

- Oversaw 150+ data backup & restoral tasks; seamless information redundancy resulted in 100% data recovery

- Part of unit's Confrontation Management Team, minimized escalation of events by over 3K protesters during series of anti-American protests--ensured safety of base populace

- Performed annual modem characterizations; verified equipment performed within optimum parameters; ensured compliance with DISA standards

- Performed as observer/controller during five exercises; integral to overall success of SF assessments

- Performed end-of-runway, through flight, and phase inspections--attention to detail resulted in zero mishaps

- Performed entry control for more than 1,500 personnel into a Protection Level 1 facility during CJCS-directed Exercise DELI MOOSE 2009--ensured zero security breaches

- Performed pump tests on 14 vehicles, ensured optimum readiness of the vehicle fleet and contributed to an "Excellent" rating in the Nov 09 UEI

- Performed RWP on 64 cadillac latrines; inspected/repaired all faulty fixtures--extended each facilities service

- Performed weekly preventive maintenance on the B-52H Automatic Pilot, Stability Augmentation System, and J-4 compass System--zero failures in 12 months!

- Planned and implemented direct internet connection for C2IPS system at JTFSA in support of SOUTHERN WATCH--increased joint intelligence and planning capability

- Planned restroom construction at Readiness Flight facility--Conducted cost analysis, recommended in-house project; saved $200K

- Prepared $12M vehicle fleet for largest typhoon ever--prevented damage, fleet 100% operational!

- Prepared flight personnel for their Standardization Evaluations; increased pass rate by 75%

- Processed 100% of customers inventories/schedules; 256 products delivered--first time met requirement this year

- Processed almost 3K Quarters notifications; informed support staffs; ensured 100% personnel accountability

- Processed over 3000 patient records requests monthly; enforced 100% HIPPA compliance standards

- Processed thousands of AUTODIN messages at Base Communications Center--accuracy rate over 99%

- Productive asset--enabled continuous mission support when 25% of the flight was deployed

- Provided 6 hours of flight instruction; taught 32 people on respiratory protection/QNFT--vital to AEF training

- Provided administrative support to another low-manned team; team player; ensured continuity of patient care

- Provided baggage/staircase support for POTUS entourage during visit to Lajes--safe and efficient operation

- Provided combat planners with accurate database array--produced over 5100 sortie air tasking orders daily--most ever!

- Provided over 30 hours of flight instruction; instructed 16 people on respiratory protection/QNFT--vital to EAF readiness

- Provided twenty-seven officers and SNCOs convoy training prior to short-notice deployment; ensured safety

- Published civilian provider formulary--enhanced 7,500 patients' care; non-stocked requests dropped 50%

- Quick-witted; when communications failed with Nellis controller, assumed control of camera suite--prevented loss of feed

- Quickly mastered all facets of PACAF's largest distribution element--reduced workload on team

- Quickly replaced a defective RC-135 engine feed manifold valve--installed new component in 5 hours--ahead of schedule!

- Rapidly and efficiently checked in 3K patients during critical manning shortage; exceptional customer service

- Received trans-load training; decontaminated/stored pallets while in MOPP4--ready for any eventuality!

- Recommended use of user-friendly thermostats and filter replacement media--modernized without expense

- Reduced overall number of trouble calls requiring on-site technician support/diagnosis by 25 percent

- Refocused office responsibilities--accuracy and timeliness of report processing increased by 90%

- Relocated, trained new Document Exploitation team in Multinational Division-Southern Area of Operations--increased AO's exploitation potential by 50%

- Removed, replaced and resealed leaking Benson tank lines--restored aircraft to fully mission capable in half normal time

- Removed/replaced damaged in-ground sewage tank for CAOC dining facility--restored facilities ops 100%

- Repaired TISEO, PAVE SPIKE pods, PAVE TAC pods--maintained in peak operating condition; always mission ready

- Replaced faulty sprinkler head at gym's sport field; achieved total zone coverage--boosted morale of 2K users

- Reprogrammed F-16 digital flight control computers, negated need for replacement-- saved over $30K in repair costs

- Resolved 235 trouble tickets; 55% above avg/20% more than closest--improved service to 100s of customers

- Resourceful--obtained two scarce regional RMS training slots--saved $7000, increased flight personnel qualifications

- Responded to emergency fuel spill, supervised crew in stopping leak, quick response prevented destruction of entire acft fleet

- Responded to suspicious package report; assisted HAZMAT team in recovering contents--prevented personnel exposure

- Reviewed, updated, corrected several key Software Installation Plans; oversight prevented critical C2 delay

- Revised examination procedures for aircrew members--incorporated low light requirements--ensured mission readiness

- Revised, updated ROI continuity books; key to excellent rating during JCAHO inspection 2008

- Revived hearing protection program--conducted noise studies in over a dozen shops--reduced hearing loss by 10%

- Saved $70K in bottled water; operated 2 water purification units--made 20K gallons daily for camp personnel

- Scheduled both recurring and emergency maintenance on work center equipment--ensured data on target at 99% rate!

- Scheduled course dates for officer and enlisted military members to attend--maximum use of available slots

- Scheduled deployments for 12 specialists; ensured maximum efficiency, 100% mission coverage

- Served as witness for OSI & Legal Office in UCMJ actions; provided bullet-proof documentation

- Set up forms and publications accounts for six branches--integral to squadron operations!

- Simulated on-line missions without interrupting real-time tasks--provided realistic training for squadron

- Skillfully replaced 11 ALCM turbofan engines; returned $9.6M assets to stockpile--enhanced integrity of fleet

- Solely responsible for correspondence, filing, and reporting during stand-up of tactical operations HQ--assured mission effectiveness from day one

- Spearheaded MFH main sewer stoppage; quickly unclogged 3 manholes--zero interruptions to 4.2K residents

- Stellar up-keep of $2.5M vehicle fleet--achieved 99% in-commission rate--mission readiness enhanced

- Stopped taxiing KC-10 from colliding with fire bottle; prevented aircraft and equipment damage

- Superb manager; programmed/executed recurring work program with impressive 100% completion rate

- Supercharged radiation safety program manager!; ensured 100% Nuclear Regulatory Commission compliance

- Superior performer! Certified over 60 items of TMDE, key to laboratory's 5 day backlog--lowest backlog in years

- Superior performer--key to delivery of over 12M gallons JP-8 aviation fuel to 110K a/c annually--maintained an impressive 15-minute avg response time

- Supported daily replenishment of F-76 fuel to special purpose vehicle fleet--guaranteed mission readiness

- Thorough maintenance practices; maintained 100% Quality Assurance pass rate from Oct 08 - Sep 09

- Tireless achiever; maintained 100% on-time departure rate for over 32 Citizen North missions

- Traced intercom system outage affecting the UHF and VHF radio systems to grounded headset--prevented mission scrub

- Traced long-standing problem between AMC system and TBMCS to configuration--correction saved over 1200 man hours per month

- Tracked inaccurate reports and returned to units--preemption reduced late submissions by 50%

- Trained 12 newly assigned personnel on CERE procedures--significantly enhanced war-fighting abilities

- Trained four personnel on baggage X-ray equipment servicing--increased uptime, reduced passenger delays

- Trained other personnel within and outside the unit on personnel management tasks--recognized by FW Commander

- Trained over 450 base personnel on basic guard duties--increased post security, prevented injuries

- Training streamlined transition of newly assigned airmen to their workcenters, reduced qualification time by 50%

- Troubleshot elusive number 2 cell leak on transient KC-135R--identified compromised seal, repacked--prevented extensive depot-level repair and costly cell change

- Troubleshot failure of aircraft's number 4 aft boost pump to put out low pressure light--traced to bad pump--replaced and deployed immediately

- Troubleshot over 400 PC and circuit outages to resolution--professional support to base

- Troubleshot transient KC-135RA number 3 reserve fuel tank problem to gravity transfer valve--prevented inflight emergency

- Unit electromagnetic radiation safety officer; scheduled initial inspections--ensured safe terminal environment

- Updated workcenter's master equipment inventory listing and PMI schedule-- review increased inventory accuracy/improved maintenance at USCENTCOM by 40%

- Utilized existing equipment and spare parts to assemble rack--saved work center $3K in material costs

- Validated/scrubbed 122 PMEL accounts; overcame personnel rotations--restored vital oversight

- Valued trainer; trained pers on high power amp maint--improved maint capability and eliminated unscheduled outages

- Versatile--directed health care operations at Enewetok Atoll health clinic--rejuvenated the ES&H council, injury rate reduced 25%!

- Volunteered to augment Ramp services during peak hours; loaded 747 cargo in summer heat--great team player!

- Volunteered to load baggage, operate step truck for POTUS entourage--showcased AMC professionalism

- Volunteered to perform visual tests at local elementary school--guarded health of over 250 students

- Worked tirelessly to prepare for inspection--directly responsible for strong rating received during HQ PACAF ORI

Does Not Meet Standards Examples

- hid serious shortfalls until it was too late to correct them

- is a motivated troop but needs further guidance in...

- an excellent technician but needs to work on tact and communication skills

- has unlimited potential but requires more experience before...

- started more projects than other members but finished fewest, need to concentrate on completion

- took advantage of sick call to avoid duties, lowest flying hours in flight for entire reporting period

- must realize the importance of finishing assigned tasks without supervision

- failed to use time wisely, consistently failed to complete duty assignments

- frequent unwillingness to cooperate in working toward unit goals affected readiness

- when reminded, can be a very productive Airman, requires periodic supervision

- a capable Airman but fails to use his abilities to the fullest

- not focused, often distracted, her accuracy rate has declined and was the lowest in the shop

- failed to comply with instructions of superiors on several occasions

- an outstanding technical resource but needs to focus on working as part of a team

- his performance was often inaccurate but wildly incorrect when under stress

- failed to use time wisely...frequently failed to meet administrative suspense

- did not make the effort required to become proficient in her duties

- did not make the effort to meet her responsibilities to the work center

- performance, although sometimes brilliant, is erratic and undependable

- did not meet expectations in...

- was indifferent to suggestions for advancement and missed many opportunities for improvement

- demonstrated lack of ability to execute his duties and depends on others for help

- was unable to qualify in key tasks and limited the readiness of the entire team

- repeatedly failed to qualify on core tasks to avoid shift work/deployment

- excellent tech, superior skills but frequently late for duty-- bad example for subordinates

- irresponsible supervisor; frequently slept on duty while subordinates worked--poor leadership

Standards, Conduct, Character, and Military Bearing

- A dynamic Senior NCO, increased communication between the ranks, increased overall satisfaction at work

- Absolutely superb leader! Commander selected to participate in $450K Charleston AFB core upgrade

- Adheres to top AFI 23-201 standards, exemplary appearance and bearing sets example for subordinates

- Attended annual Air Force Ball--positive conservator of Air Force culture in a joint environment

- Best in command! HQ AFSPC's "Financial Management Specialist of the Year" for 2008

- Briefed 60 CSAs from 5 grps on VPN upgrade; vital info disseminated--smooth transition for tier one customers

- Briefed junior airmen at Airmen Leadership School on Air Force Evaluation System--enhanced careers

- Capable professional; selected to act as Anti-Air Warfare Commander (AAWC) during critical joint exercise ANVIL TREE

- Co-chaired "Operation White Christmas"; planned, organized entire program—raised over $17,000 for families

- Co-organized base Top-3 weekend golf tournament; great morale booster for base enlisted personnel

- Continued sandbag efforts while others gave up; ultimately successful, preserved over $1M in communications equipment

- Coordinated, participated in traditional CoC ceremony, participation demonstrated concern for subordinates, ensured traditions and pride endure

- Created and implemented an innovative CDC Course status chart--ensured all troops in upgrade training were ahead of schedule--99% pass rate on all End of Course exams

- Currently enrolled in Organizational Management course; increased supervisory skills

- Dedicated health provider; chosen as AMC Enlisted Health Services Management NCO of the Year 08

- Dedicated professional who continues to develop future NCOs as a member of the SF Mentorship Program

- Dedicated! Volunteered 5 hrs to lay/spread gravel around Dorm Bldg 300-enhancing base beautification for all

- Developed and maintained an intensive physical fitness program that improved morale and reduced the semi-annual failure rate by over 50%!

- Devoted hours of off-duty time to ensure unit's tng requirements were met; all trainees fully qualified in min time

- Diligently pursing a Masters of Science Degree in Philosophy while concurrently acting as mathematics tutor

- Displayed exceptional pride in image, wears immaculate, inspection-ready uniform at all times--best example

- Dynamic leader; proven track record of maintaining and enforcing PACAF standards of conduct; vital for success

- Emceed at Chief Enlisted Manager's farewell as acting First Sergeant; ensured adherence to AF traditions

- Energetic in administrative duties; monitored key flight functions and openly accepted additional details

- Enforced strict adherence to AF Instructions--balanced efforts united team of enlisted and officers, boosted morale

- Escorted families at Black Hills National Cemetery; honored fallen comrades; enhanced public AF relations

- Established top rapport as NCOIC--contingency, ancillary tng effectiveness ratings consistently highest in sq--highly effective leader

- Exceptional NCO; superb military image made him the obvious selection for NCOIC of the unit Honor Guard

- Exemplary management skill and organizational foresight, personifies allegiance, military bearing, strong code of ethics

- Exhibited exceptional pride in workcenter, fellow Airmen, and the AF--NCOIC entrusted her with equip oversight

- Hand-picked CSW Airman! Won Airman of the Quarter third Qtr 2007--sets the standard for a true professional

- Hand-picked to instruct 50 students in advanced Installation Defense skills at the Joint Readiness Training Center

- Hand-selected to perform security for high profile mission in direct support of ENDURING FREEDOM

- Helped renovate the dormitory and living spaces for the NCO Leadership School--key to force success

- Highly skilled technician; often relied upon to complete numerous difficult jobs with minimum supervision

- Inexhaustible commitment and determination, provided sound leadership to 40 Airmen and civilians, provided quality support

- Infallible standards of dress/appearance with positive attitude--perfect representation/model for peer emulation

- Instituted new quality control inspection procedures raising customer satisfaction 25%

- Led by example, conducted bi-weekly PT sessions for 5 flights; increased sq fitness scores

- Made breakfast burritos for squadron booster club, resulting in over $200 profit for squadron

- Maintained an impressive 100% fully mission-capable rate for Oct 08; shattered AETC standard of 80%

- Maintains a fierce and steadfast belief in assigned mission, provides workcenter with clear guidance

- Managed 20 personnel workcenter in direct support of U.S. Space Command--exceeded all assigned goals!

- Mature leader; won't compromise standards, enforced highest AETC standards of conduct

- Organized 2009 Dining-in, a hallmark event for over 1,000 Airmen & their families; reinforced pride and commitment of families to AF way of life

- Organized base-wide golf tourney benefiting Armed Forces Retirement Home; fundraiser netted over $1500

- Oversaw On-the-job training program resulting in 6 airmen receiving their upgraded status ahead of schedule

- Participated in the Livestrong Foundation Bike-a-Thon raising over $5,000 dollars for cancer research

- Peerless uniform and appearance; adheres to AFI 23-201-- sets example for peers and subordinates

- Performed as observer/controller during five USAF XXX exercises; key to overall success of SF assessments

- Positively impacted the lives of over 2,000 children through efforts with the Children's Healthcare Foundation

- Provided setup/security for annual Frostbite Run event-- contributions earned $15K for unit's morale activities

- Ready to deploy on short notice, to meet any contingency, anywhere in the world--rare intensity

- Registered over 40 military and family members to vote; timely actions ensured voter eligibility

- Reviews regulations constantly; sharpens knowledge while providing an honest service to all AMC travelers

- Revitalized 12 drogue/drag chutes--repaired suspension lines/canopies--saved AF $500K in replacements cost

- Revived wc morale after personnel issues; insisted on loyalty to supervisors and peers--restored msn rate

- Risked personal safety to ensure safety of visiting unit and their mission--personified spirit of sacrifice for mission

- Security for base airshow; controlled entry for 130 media reps--ensured safe environment for over 100k people

- Selected as squadrons SNCO of the Quarter, first quarter 2004--impact on the mission was key to success

- Selected as top performer of the month for Apr 2009; displayed exemplary leadership and professionalism

- Selected for advancement to E-6 under the Stripes for Exceptional Performance Program

- Selected over peers to represent unit in several high-visibility ceremonies; an example to peers

- Selfless mentor: spent over 250 hrs guiding Boys Scouts of America youth--ensured high morals and good stds

- Selflessly gave 20 hours to organize & chaperone summer camp trip to Zama Zoo--70 children educated & safe

- Selflessly volunteered time with the Airmen Against Drunk Driving campaign; ensuring 100% safe transport

- Served as Secretary, Kaiserslaughtern German-American Association--good community ambassador

- Solved many housing, medical, & personnel issues for members; cornerstone of our team, taking care of Airmen his top concern

- Spirited! Led set up/tear down detail for ADAB Phantomween event-increasing morale over holiday season!!

- Standards and professional competence generated immediate confidence/improved subordinate morale

- Star performer! Received only stripe available from 333 MG/CC for STEP promotion to Staff Sergeant

- Superb uniform--strict adherence to AFI 23-201--sets example for peers

- Superior athlete! Destroyed AF PT test with 97.5% score; bolsters the Fit to Fight concept amongst all peers

- Superior military image led to selection as the AF representative during the CJCS tree lighting ceremony

- Superior warfighter--recognized by Exercise Evaluation Team members as Superior Performer in the May 2007 IRRE

- Takes exceptional pride in personal image and has a meticulous military appearance, positive service ambassador

- Takes pride in service, resolute in his duty--a textbook example of leadership by example

- Top Airman! Selected as 437th MX Airman of the Quarter for the second quarter 2009

- Trained four elements in preparation for Global War on Terrorism deployments--reinforced knowledge of standards

- True wingman; AADD program vol; dispatched and chauffeured--provided ## mbrs safe rides home

- Trusted by Flt Commander to lead team in risky, remote installation--completed, activated 100% reliable radar

- Turned down transfer to main base to remain behind with his team and ensure reliable comm link--impeccable character

- Utilized process improvement techniques; reduced military performance reporting delays by 75%

- Virtually eliminated late or no-show reports for training--herculean effort made to look easy

- Vol for difficult civic project under austere conditions to bolster US image abroad; improved relations

- Volunteered for and served as driver for the tour of comm squadron facilities by GTE

- Volunteered to load baggage, operate step truck for POTUS entourage--showcased AMC professionalism

- Works after duty hours to make sure Airmen are taken care of; efforts apparent in best discipline rate in Group

Does Not Meet Standards Examples

- is uncooperative when corrected and displays a consistent lack of interest in section goals

- his failure to follow orders led to the loss of his security clearance and now section is undermanned and unable to meet quota

- avoids complying with orders, regularly shows disrespect to NCOs, requires constant supervision

- cannot be depended on and is frequently late for shift. Recommend...

- demonstrated a serious lack of integrity and poor judgment without consideration of results

- compromised integrity by submitting altered documents; poor example to subordinates

- encouraged coworkers to advance by cheating for each other, poor example

- reported to work under the influence of alcohol and was unable to execute his duties as...

- was entrusted with our most critical and essential tasks but disappointed his mentors

- cannot be relied upon to maintain production rate in the absence of supervision

- cannot be trusted to oversee safe delivery of...must be supervised at all times

- was and is negligent in meeting his responsibilities causing numerous obstacles to mission accomplishment

- counseled twice for disrespect toward an NCO

- refused suggestions to attend counseling until his problems escalated to the point of making him unfit for duty

- failed to maintain fitness regimen or join squadron fitness events

- doesn't realize the critical importance of following orders and may endanger this unit

- was disciplined for assault and his off-duty actions make him unfit for duty

- exemplary performance but uniform and bearing do not meet standards and will hold this Airman back

- presents an unprofessional appearance and lacks military bearing

- complained about time spent TDY and on deployments, adversely affected morale and discipline

- lacks respect for chain of command and needs improvement in peer communications

- displayed a consistent lack of interest, initiative, and enthusiasm and is the subject of frequent counseling

- failed to render the proper respect, subject of repeated verbal/written counseling--behavior unchanged

- has not made any effort to change his behavior during this reporting period and is not fit for retention

- turned in a superb performance, maintains exemplary uniform but needs to be reminded about haircuts

- encouraged peers to disregard standard SOP and fails to follow chain of command to the detriment of the work center

Fitness

- Member has chronic medical condition impacting AF goals for fitness
- Failed to meet minimum body composition [or whatever category(s)] standards
- Is office fitness monitor and consistently scores highly on his PT test
- Made phenomenal progress in conditioning in short period of time; guaranteed success next test
- Enthusiastic participation in fitness program promises success and growth
- Scored 72.5, making significant progress in FIT program
- Scored 34.1, failed to show to scheduled unit physical training sessions
- Confident ratee will exceed standards next rating period; exceeded expectations
- Fitness decline due to medical condition; future promises above average performance
- Exempt from fitness standards on three of four categories due to pregnancy
- Makes every attempt to adhere to standards, trust ratee to exceed standards in the future
- Passes three of four categories, significant progress made on weak area
- Surpassed scheduled goals; on track to pass previously failed categories
- Reduced run time by 25%; guaranteed success on next year's run

Training Requirements

- Accomplished 225 of 300 upgrade/qualification tasks; 75% completed on three airframes--50% ahead of peers

- Achieved an outstanding 99.5 percent on his initial evaluation as a Keys and Codes Controller—highest score in shop

- Advanced toward education goals; enrolled in on-line Action Officer course and completed two credit hours toward CCAF

- All shop trainees fully qualified in minimum time-- significantly improved section's effectiveness

- Assessed sq tng needs, developed approp programs tailored to wc needs--reclaimed 10K+ man hours lost on unnecessary tng; enhanced productivity

- Attacked Commander's special interest area of CDC pass rate--regular interface with section leaders raised pass rate to 98% in less than 12 months

- Attended 40 hrs of ROWPU training; acquired skills needed to operate in an expeditionary environment--GWOT ready

- Attended in-flight welding course; 7 cores task signed off-- immensely improving flt capabilities/msn readiness

- Attended SERE Exercise with team while balancing regular duty requirements--qualified for deployment

- Awarded Bachelors Degree for Technical Management from Embry Riddle Aeronautical University; 3.6 GPA

- Certified Heartsaver AED instructor; trained 30 Airmen-- prepared to respond to life-threatening emergencies

- Completed 190 of 210 upgrade/qualification tasks; 75% ahead of peers, 30% ahead of schedule!

- Completed additional 22 credits towards MS degree in Technical Management while maintaining a 4.0 GPA

- Completed CDCs 1 month ahead of schedule; scored 90% on end of course exam--sets the example for peers!

- Completed CDCs 2 months early; upgrade trng 100%; earned 12 college credits w/3.5 GPA towards CCAF

- Completed train the trainer course--trained and certified flight personnel on job-specific tasks; zero failures

- Comptia Network+ certified; grad level tng completed 18 months early--met cyber-critical DoD requirements

- Consistently strives for improvement, working diligently towards career progression...recommend promotion

- Continuously excelled in OJT/upgrade training; scored 80% on CDC EOC exam--completed 1 month in advance

- Coordinated HAZMAT efforts of maintenance flight sections; reduced redundant effort, produced most complete MSDS library on base

- Coordinated with squadron and base training managers to manage ancillary training program for over 250 squadron members

- CPR certified--enhanced skills needed to quickly aid deployed team members; 100% qualified for deployment

- Currently enrolled at University of North Dakota--earned 9 semester hours with a 3.8 GPA

- Dedicated individual; completed cdc ontime with 85% on EOC- shows initiative towards career progression

- Dedicated to self-improvement through education; completed BS in Info Mgt; earned 4.0 GPA, graduated with honors

- Delivered trained Airmen able to join operations, ready to fight, immediately on arrival

- Designed training prog that improved subordinate observation teams skills--increased capabilities during ops by 33%

- Developed and presented tng materials on new equipment being fielded to units throughout Europe--prepared for success!

- Developed comprehensive 20-page training pamphlet for newly-assigned personnel--improved overall job knowledge and performance

- Developed insp criteria for 35th AW units; helped prepare, equip, train on individual protective equipment for ORI--members exceeded ATSO reqts

- Developed squadron Electromagnetic Radiation program--promoted personnel safety and compliance with OSHA guidelines

- Developed squadron Electrostatic Discharge program--prevented future equipment damage; likely savings of $20K

- Developed squadron Report of Survey program--streamlined investigations, recovered over $15K

- Developed training manuals, multimedia visual aids, and reference library; revitalized ancillary training program

- Devoted many hours of off-duty time to ensure the unit's training requirements were met--led by example

- Earned 19 credit hours toward Bachelors Degree in Information Systems--maintained impressive 3.2 GPA

- Eliminated ancillary training no longer relevant, redesigned needed training so requires less time--increased efficiency

- Enrolled at University of Maryland; finished 4 courses w/3.5 GPA--merited 12 college credits towards CCAF

- Enthusiastically completed Journeyman Career Development Course--outstanding 89% on end-of-course test

- Established rapport as Ancillary Tng Program mgr--contingency/ancill tng ratings highest in sq--highly effective leader

- Exceeded all training requirements; scored 97 percent on his 7-Level, CDC End-of-Course examination

- Exceeds all training requirements; evident by a 98 percent on his 7-Level, End-of-Course examination

- Exchanged language lessons; learned basic Japanese/taught English--improved important US/Japan relations

- Gave Financial Awareness training to first-term airmen; reduced flight bounced check incidents by at least 50%

- Goal-oriented; enrolled in Air University Action Officer course; 14 of 27 courses completed, 90% average

- Graduated 40-hr water purification unit training; proven under fire--kept aging units operational during deployment

- Graduated Technical Order training; assumed failing position--improved program, decreased wait for needed references by 75%

- Hazardous Material Awareness certified--enhanced skills needed to quickly identify hazardous incidents

- Helped reorganize section into efficient, streamlined shop--zero late reports for all training requirements

- Identified lack of Corrosion Control program, instituted accepted AF methods; prevented waste by eliminating structural failure

- Identified on-line availability of AF ancillary training requirements--increased qual rate by 60% sq-wide

- Identified redundant ancillary training requirements; reduced time away from primary job, increased focus on necessary skills

- Improved squadron adherence to training regiment; eliminated delays for deployment due to lack of qualification

- Improvement-oriented; enrolled in Wing Action Officer course from Air University; 10 of 26 courses completed, 95% average

- Initiated the transition of 400 personnel training records from paper files to database; increased efficiency

- Instructed six Records Management classes for squadron-- improved efficiency evident by inspection results

- Instructed unit personnel in pre-deployment training; coord w/ AOR units focused on needed trng, improved applicability

- Involved in local Head Start Program; read books to over 35 children--bettered community

- Joint Focused! Provided JIT training for 200 U.S. Army personnel tasked to augment deployed forces

- Led 20 pers thru pre-deploy trng, supervised eq issue, convoy & weapons trng, land navigation, and cultural awareness

- Led section to new heights in all process performance indicators--shop continued to exceed every goal

- Maintained a 3.0 GPA in term 1, 2 with the University of Maryland University College

- Managed unit deployment trning requirements--ensured essential personnel, sufficient deployment staffing--key to unit readiness

- Manually updated 31 systems to latest SAV edition; quarantined 35 outdated systems--protected 2.1M network

- Modernized section's outdated process for tracking safety issues--logging rate now at 100% for first time

- Motivated airman; displayed genuine enthusiasm; made steady progress in Maintenance Administration qualification

- Multi-skilled amn; contributed to all Maintenance Control sections--raised flight's Preventive Maintenance Inspection list accuracy

- Provided Land Mobile Radio training to base populace; recognized by Group Commander for superior performance

- Provided twenty officers and SNCOs convoy training prior to short-notice deployment ISO Classified Operation

- Pursued off-duty education; completed eight credit hours towards CCAF Transportation Management degree

- Qualified 36 security personnel in ID camera system operation--multiplied section efficiency

- Qualified in Personnel Program tasks, tackled Information Management training; proficiency reduced report delay

- Radiation Hazard certified--enhanced skills needed to quickly identify threats to personnel safety and mission

- Revamped six mobility procedures; streamlined readiness/ancillary tracker--heightened war-time posture of 23

- Revised Ancillary Training Program, tailored for unit members--reduced overdue qual by 30%

- Revised squadron Ancillary Training requirements, tailored for unit members--reduced overdue qualification by 30%

- Revived the Sq Report of Survey program--aggressive follow-up reduced investigation time 50%;best program on base

- Scholastic juggernaut; completed Master of Science Degree in Space Studies, held a respectable 3.86 GPA

- Selected over peers for advanced flight medicine training; enhanced skills increased workcenter efficiency 50%

- Selected over peers to attend advanced Air Base Defense skills course; enhanced skills produced streamlined SOP

- Selected over peers to attend advanced Equipment Maintenance course; new skills raised workcenter productivity 50%

- Spearheaded campaign to increase efficiency--took charge for cover train inputs and training documentation

- Superior performance in all phases of PME garnered his selection out of 22 airman as class 09-B ALS Distinguished Grad

- Tackled failing workcenter security program; raised inspection results from substandard to excellent in less than 3 months!

- Taught pre-deploy trng; despite short-notice, worked closely with trainees, staff, produced AOR-qualified Airmen on time

- Trained 16 ARC pers on 51 core/duty tasks; mbrs 100% equipped/qualified--enhanced "Total Force" readiness

- Trained 4 Amn on data backup & restoral procedures; increased task coverage; 5 lvl requirement met

- Trained 66 individuals in SABC training; immeasurably increased wing readiness posture

- Trained four XXXX elements in preparation for Global War on Terrorism deployments

- Trained junior personnel in mobilization preparation/processing; negated need for TDY tng, saved unit $25K

- Trained junior personnel in mobilization preparation; reduced processing delays, increased efficiency

- Trained personnel on forklifts (4k & 10k), warehouse tugs, and Aircraft Loading Specialty vehicles (25k & 40k)

- Trained three members in mobilization preparation-- multiplied effectiveness, 3 weeks ahead of schedule

- Troops First Attitude, constantly strived for more tng, set std for improvised training, ensured AV shop best trained group in CE

- Tutored high school students--raised students' grade from an "F" to an "A" in a mere four weeks--inspiring!

- Utilized process improvement techniques; increased military performance reporting timelines from 78% to 97%

- Virtually eliminated late or no-show reports for training-- herculean effort made to look easy

- Volunteered for CPR classes--enhanced skills needed to quickly aid deployed team members; 100% deployment qualified

- Volunteered for generator training; acquired skills needed to operate in expeditionary environment--GWOT ready

- Volunteered over 100 hours to become Self-aid and Buddy Care, Red Cross CPR certified--integral to squadron safety

Does Not Meet Standards Example

- overcame several obstacles to advancement but requires further training before workcenter qualification

- has made significant progress in qualification and may be ready for advancement

- demonstrated dedication and sincere effort to improve but limited by experience.

- negatively affected our state of readiness by...

- failed to take advantage of opportunities to advance

- counseled by the Flight Commander for having the least qualified flight in the squadron

- failure to plan ahead or manage current training requirements; reduced readiness

- his performance was below average and is in immediate need of retraining

- is indifferent to suggestions for advancement and misses many opportunities for improvement

- despite encouragement and efforts of peers, cannot qualify for duty and fails to make effort to improve

- will not use off-duty time for study or self-improvement, fails to advance in qualification

- failed to acquire the necessary skills and attributes to...

- despite the best efforts of trainers on and off-duty, was unsuccessful in qual attempt..

- demonstrated a lack of knowledge in most duties, did not comply with SOP and is a threat to the safety of this section

- despite increased assistance and training, he continued to have serious difficulty completing assigned tasks, recommend reclassification

- lacks experience and maturity and fails to understand the importance of advancement

- unable to adjust to deployment or the diverse demands of a joint environment

- probably the worst performer in our flight, cannot be depended on

- failed to meet Group standards and should not be retained

- demonstrated a lack of skill or knowledge in most of his duties

- delayed qualification to avoid deployment, manipulated system to shift responsibilities to peers

Teamwork/Followership

- Absolutely superb leader! Commander selected to participate in $954K Keesler Air Force Base core upgrade

- Active Air Force Sergeants Association team member-- recruited six members, helped sign up 120 new members

- Active and perceptive, kept chain of command apprised of racial/sexual climate, prevented obstacles to wc harmony/mission success

- Active in community--Prepared family style barbeque for 35th FW at Hirosaki's Cherry Blossom festival

- Active, dedicated SNCO mentor, led by example, encouraged equal treatment/opportunity for all members-- best climate assessment in Grp

- Airman of the Month board member--leading the way for others--supports recognition for deserving Airmen

- Best in command! HQ AFSPC's Financial Management Specialist of the Year for 2009

- Bridge the Gap program member; counsels community members in drugs/alcohol addiction recovery

- Captained the replacement of 2760 computer systems; recovered 100% of documented assets; excellent stewardship!

- Chaired Operation White Christmas; planned, organized entire program, raised over $12,000 for 95 needy enlisted families

- Conducted OPSEC training for 28 CS--62 mbrs better postured for worldwide deployments--key to readiness

- Dedicated base Honor Guard mbr; 78 hrs--displayed outstanding professionalism...commemorated war heroes

- Dedicated professional who continues to shape future NCOs as a member of the SF Mentorship Program

- Dedicated to healthy lifestyle; competed in Okinawa open wrestling tournament--won second place trophy

- Developed inspection criteria for 88th AW units; enabled units to prepare, equip and train on the use of

- Developed, coordinated physical fitness regimen for squadron--increased participation and fitness scores

- Directed ops in Collection Management Sect--handled 80+ Requests for Info/week during active ops--key to successful intel ops

- Directed unit and active duty AF personnel as team leader during Silver Flag deployment greatly improving

- Displays exceptional leadership qualities; ability to get the job done; recommend promotion/retention

- Donated 40 hours off-duty time to mentor, instruct three high school students during study halls; superb mentor

- Effective and vital for the success of AF program-leadership style overcomes any obstacle before him-promote!

- Elected 1961st CS Top 3 Sergeant at Arms--led standard conduct/order of meetings--ensured smooth changeover

- Elected Bay chief for second floor of dorm; accountable for the appearance and safety--best dorm on base!

- Everyone's dream leader; standards others strive to achieve-wingman for AFRL-promote this cycle a must

- Exceptional shift leader! Led shift in correction of 600 sensor pod and 400 support equipment discrepancies

- Expertly led the Squadron enlisted members during the AMC IGX in March 2006, his efforts were praised by

- Fitness professional; led fitness center weekly circuit training class--500 base members improved their fitness

- Fostered an atmosphere of understanding, trust, and tolerance; increased team effort--shattered all performance records!

- Generous contributor to the 2007 Combined Federal Campaign--donation contributed to smashing USAFE goal

- Hailed by TF16 Commander and Sergeant Major for his exemplary work during VTC for Task Force Targeting

- Hailed by two star General during safety board; provided support; aided in prevention of mishap reoccurrence

- Head coach of Patch high school wrestling team; taught safe/proper techniques--zero mishaps/injuries

- Helped reorganize section into efficient, streamlined shop-- zero late reports for all training requirements

- Implemented an internal Random Evaluation Program that increased external evaluation scores by 20%.

- In preparation for the ORI, organized, implemented plan where sq info on the email global was updated and correct

- Innovative and resourceful; researched and took the lead in unit's migration to the MBITR tactical radio system

- Involved in local Head Start Program; patiently read books to over 22 children ages 5 years to 7 years

- Kadena Integrated Delivery System Member--AADD NCO advisor--efforts helped cut base 07 DUI's 30%

- Key member of antenna TCTO project; upgraded 14 satellite antennas; 180-day TCTO slashed to 90 days!

- Led 3 person water 4" main repair crew; directed damaged line exposure/fix--prevented $4k vs contractor cost

- Led fire hydrant replacement; ensured 100% fire coverage for AAFES warehouse--$200M assets protected

- Led tank reseal team; reduced fuel leak delayed discrepancies to 0.6 per aircraft--bested MAJCOM goal by 80%

- Worked with Japanese Air Force/civilian authorities bus accident response; fostered strong partnership

- Managed 10 person all source intelligence production section--led, guided and directed activities of junior analysts

- Managed a team of four collection operators and five intelligence analysts in intelligence operations

- Managed six DOCEX teams in the Multinational Division-Northern Area of Operations (MND-AO)--multiplied intelligence collection ability!

- Motivated team player who recognizes unit success is a team effort; always strives to become a better player

- Motivated team player; contributed off duty time and effort to support unit's self-help project--saved est $15K

- Organized a team for the March of Dimes "Walk America" 20K march--raised over $500 to combat birth defects

- Organized and oversaw base Asian American celebration; promoted knowledge and understanding of racial diversity

- Outstanding SNCO, volunteered to act as Operations Chief replacing deployed CMSgt, outstanding job!

- Oversaw On-the-job training program resulting in 6 airmen receiving their upgraded status ahead of schedule

- Pacesetter; organized first base detention center substance abuse/addiction recovery support group

- Part of team that increased equipment readiness to 98%--10% over unit's score last year!

- Participatory leadership produced most professional mixed-gender working environment in sq; zero sexual harass issues!

- Participated in 8-hr Adopt-a-Highway cleanup; removed 500 lbs of refuse--fostered community/AF alliance

- Performed flag detail for retirement ceremony; recognized 20 years of faithful service--team member honored

- Played a leading and aggressive role in establishing continuous care packages to forward deployed members

- Primary Observer/Controller for exercise X; directly responsible for biennial inspection success

- Proven management skills set him apart from peers--transformed unit from lax to compliant-promote ASAP!

- RAF Croughton base soccer team member, played on two UK teams--fostered positive host nation relations

- Rapidly established dynamic and motivating leader image--coordinated process for Tsunami victim donations

- Received letter of appreciation--chaplain praised outstanding support/community service to Ramstein area

- Regularly participates in and oversees the weekly Meals-on-Wheels program--valued member of community

- Reorganized and upgraded Pass & ID facility on off-duty time--saved over $5,000 in labor costs

- Researched, took the lead in unit's migration to the new computer filing and tracking system; great sq support

- Reviews regulations constantly; sharpens knowledge while providing an honest service to all AMC travelers

- Revived and revised the retirement ceremony program; documented, streamlined process, raised support to 100%

- Selected to lead joint team which discovered, targeted, performed damage assessment on hundreds of key targets--critical to mission success

- Served on the 35 AMXS Christmas party Committee--raised morale for single soldiers

- Set the example for 126 Airmen--sacrificed 250 community hours--named 214th Wing 2008 Volunteer of the Yr

- Solid performer; displays exceptional leadership qualities /abilities--recommend promotion soonest

- Spearheaded youth/adult annual football game--improved morale for families/Team Hill's military members

- Stellar NCO who leads by example; invaluable asset to the XXX training mission; must promote now

- Superior leadership skills fostered most united team in MAJCOM; sq had least reported EO incidents in MAJCOM

- Supported Airman Against Drunk Driving--worked 14 hours--contributed to prevention of 7 D.U.I. violations

- Troops First Attitude, constantly strived for more tng oppty, made shop best trned group in CE; great vision/judgment

- True wingman; AADD program vol; dispatched and chauffeured--provided ## mbrs safe rides home

- Unit AADD rep; prompt response on four call-outs--key to program success--saved lives & ensured zero DUIs

- Unparalleled enthusiasm; possesses an out-in-front leadership style and the attributes of today's model NCO

- Volunteer phone bank supervisor at Easter Seal telethon; surpassed its goal--raised $32,000

- Volunteered as youth group leader at chapel--enhanced the lives of local teens through positive guidance

- Volunteered for Commander's change of command ceremony--excellent military community involvement

- Volunteered to assist local Red Cross in distributing food and clothing to flood victims in the Gulfport area

- Volunteered to set up tents for annual volksmarch--support integral to success of yearly event

Does Not Meet Standards Examples

- failure to supervise subordinates or follow procedures resulted in the loss of $2,000 worth of equipment

- unexcused absence from duty left soldiers unsupervised and jeopardized mission

- fails to understand the importance of his duties, takes advantage of every situation to avoid responsibility

- demonstrated little regard for the security and accountability of sensitive items during deployments

- participated in squadron events more than training or work--lags peers in qualification, unable to pull shift alone

- is a positive and effective leader but may need more experience before...

- exhibits strong ability to lead, should now focus on staff skills and communication

- reported for shift change late, forced entire relieved shift to work overtime, lowered team cohesion

- is sometimes unaware of operational picture and often leaves subordinates unsupervised

- leadership and managerial skills need improvement to qualify for next rank

- had poor rapport with his subordinates and was ineffectual in supervision or delegation of responsibilities

- lagged behind contemporaries in...

- was ineffective and provided no useful guidance

- failed to maintain standards and allowed his workcenter rating to decrease from Excellent to Satisfactory

- perception of favoritism affected morale and discipline within the section

- lacks initiative and managerial skills

- frequent abuse of sick call forced off-duty coworkers to cover her shift--seriously affected work center morale

- lacks enthusiasm in his duties and has no pride in his performance

- failed to develop subordinates; did not perform mandatory mid-term counseling

- failed to consistently inspect Airmen and their equipment, decreased unit readiness

- mediocre staff skills contributed to mediocre results during inspection

- did not enforce training guidelines--work center qualification/skill declining

- fails to understand the importance of his position, avoids responsibility when possible

- avoids responsibility and is a negative influence on his section

- did not make sufficient effort to qualify for deployment, increased workload on remaining shop members

- delayed qualification to avoid deployment, manipulated system to shift responsibilities to peers

Other Comments

- A compelling leader who inspires excellence in those around him. Strongest recommendation for promotion

- A dynamic and diverse Senior NCO with a decisive and proactive leadership style--would make great 1st Sergeant

- A first-rate non-commissioned officer who is willing to face up to any task and tackle the issues head on

- A model NCO, SSgt Smith sets the standard in everything he does; an all-around performer--ready for next stripe!

- A positive leadership example that consistently brought out the best in subordinates...promote now!

- A Self-Starter whose work is marked by integrity and initiative, performs with precision/great sense of responsibility.

- A well rounded individual, supports/encourages participation in squadron and community activities--wingman!

- Aided ACC firewall installation team; bolstered network security posture--thwarted over 5k network probes

- Aided Facility Management for 2 months showing great efficiency when tasked; displayed great versatility

- Aided in facility excellence program; 100+ hours of base beautification--enhanced installation appearance/QoL

- An indispensable member of our staff; responsible for several changes that improved our personnel programs

- Appearance and military bearing are above reproach, give first slot at NCO Academy. Recommended for promotion!

- Assisted critical software tiger team; 298 MDG systems patched/restored--swift response lauded by MDG/CC

- Best in command! HQ AFSPC's Financial Management Specialist of the Year for 2006; reserve seat SNCO Academy!

- Briefed weekly in-processing group on space available travel benefits--positive military spokesman

- Chaired Operation White Christmas; planned, organized entire program--raised over $15,000 for 200 needy enlisted families

- Clearly Superior--First selection for Below-the-zone promotion from the section's peer group of 12 airmen

- Co-Chaired 35th SF Sq 2008 Christmas Party--coordinated with minimal time and resources--reduced the cost for over 100 guests

- Coined by Vice CC 86th Aeromedical Evac sq; photographed prior CC's retirement ceremony--selfless airman!

- Community minded; vol/represented Hickam AFB in Waipahu May Day parade; raised $15K for Boy/Girl Scouts, YMCA

- Conducted single/unaccompanied airmen meeting every Sunday at chapel--fostered a supportive environment

- Confident and aggressive, she tackles and completes all assigned tasks expeditiously and accurately

- Consistently produces sound results; continue to challenge this NCO with more responsibility--promote!

- Consistently stays one step ahead of the game. Eagerly seeks out new assignments. Advance to TSgt

- Consummate law enforcer; professionally handled any of a variety of situations thrown in his direction

- Created Personnel Support Center CD for distribution during site visits--streamlined personnel support

- Dedicated to healthy lifestyle; competed in Okinawa open wrestling tournament--won second place trophy

- Demonstrates the confidence needed to face the USAF toughest challenges--promote when ready

- Deployed 45 days to Nicaragua; completed $250K in projects--new school/clinic raised QoL for 500 locals

- Despite increased workload, maintained qualification for Force Protection duties--ensured mission protection

- Displays exceptional leadership qualities; ability to get the job done; recommend promotion/retention

- Dynamic airman; multi-talented mechanic; readily accepts increased responsibilities; Promote Now!

- Dynamic and distinguished NCO; leads by example; sets high, attainable standards--promote immediately

- Esprit Des Corps; participated in Chiefs' 3 Mile Run; raised money for Dining Ins/Outs and awards banquets

- Exceptional performer--further challenge with most difficult tasks--promote ahead of peers

- Exchanged language lessons; learned basic Japanese/taught English--improved important US/Japan relations

- First rate professional! Shows ability and initiative to assume greater responsibility--promote now

- First to take charge! Assumed responsibility of Det's AF Assistance Fund Campaign--100% contact in 24 hrs

- First-class NCO whose can-do attitude and ceaseless determination are contagious--an excellent role model

- Fisher House, Landstuhl supporter--led all-day sq hike fundraiser --raised $3K+ to feed/shelter family members

- Flexible and versatile leader with unbounded potential, ready to assume SNCO responsibilities!

- Gave 30 hrs to KMC AADD program--saved 12 careers...built and manned unit haunted house--raised $2.4K

- Gifted technician w/unparalleled initiative; continue to challenge w/ increased responsibility--promote!

- Good work ethic; tackles any task above his skill level w/outstanding results--promotion to SrA recommended

- He continually displays unlimited growth potential and is ready now for increased responsibility

- He has impeccable military bearing and appearance. He has earned my strongest recommendation for advancement

- Head coach of Patch high school wrestling team; taught safe/proper techniques--zero mishaps/injuries

- Highly dedicated and motivated superintendent, which is reflected in his attitude, subordinates and work ethic

- Highly motivated! Energetic and diligent--demonstrated strong ability to identify, analyze and solve problems

- Installed pressure tank/6K ft of line from water well to base camp--improved shower/laundry water pressure

- Involved in local Head Start Program; read books to over 35 children--bettered community

- Leader, motivator, skilled technician--leads the pack--keep him in the front--promote to SMSgt now!

- Managed the Electromagnetic Radiation Safety Program for the 437th Fighter Squadron--zero incidents of RF exposure

- Mature and confident airman with extraordinary knowledge and initiative--immediately promote!

- Member chosen, flown to AMC Headquarters to accept AMC C& I Professional of the Year award

- Motivated to excel! Awarded a BS in Education and Workforce Management while maintaining a 3.8 GPA ALL

- Moved over 300 cases of Girl Scout Cookies to/from storage area--key to scouts raising $16K in cookie sales

- My #1 NCO; selected as Health Services Manager of the Year 2005--promote ahead of peers!

- My #1 of 5 NCOs--proactive leader--exemplary NCOIC who led the most active section in the squadron

- My #1 of 6 SNCOs; selected by Maintenance Chief as 1961st Maintenance Group NCO of the Year 08'

- My #1 of 9 MSgts! Superior performance across the board--give him bigger challenges--promote now!

- My go to NCO for ISR planning; outstanding NCO with exceptional knowledge, promote to SNCO now!

- My number one SSgt; proven, exemplary track record confirms he is ready for immediate promotion!

- Operated 2 ROWPU units; made 20K gallons daily for camp personnel--Saved $70K in bottled water contracts

- Organized a team for the March of Dimes "Walk America" 20K march--raised over $500 to combat birth defects

- Outstanding Airman with can-do attitude--always willing to do more challenging tasks with greater responsibility

- Outstanding NCO who leads by example; a solid professional ready for increased responsibility; promote!

- Participated in Airman Leadership School renovation; improved quality of life for over 2,600 students

- Participated in annual base charity fund raiser, the 24 hour marathon--increased military stature

- Participated in squadron intramural basketball--American league champions--earned 12 points toward CC cup!

- Participated in the wing's 2006 bicycle roundup event, confiscated 200+ unregistered bicycles--enhanced base appearance

- Phenomenal airman; surpassed every expectation in training and duty performance; ready for promotion now!

- Provided administrative support to 100K visitors to 2005 Charleston AFB Air Show; ensured 100% support

- Provided security for over 1000 cadets, distinguished visitors, and guests during 2009 USAFA graduation

- Quality NCO; displayed excellent knowledge , drive and initiative in completing any task-- promote now

- Recent graduate of Airman Leadership School; deserving of new promotion to staff sergeant!

- Recipient of Mission Systems Flight Superior Performer Award for March 08; promote ahead of peers!

- Reorganized and upgraded Pass & ID facility on off-duty time--saved over $5,000 in labor costs

- Selected as top performer of the quarter for 3rd Quarter 2006; displayed leadership, professionalism

- Served on the 35 AMXS Christmas party Committee--raised morale for single soldiers

- Solid performer; displays exceptional leadership qualities /abilities; recommend promotion at earliest date

- Spearheaded youth/adult annual football game--improved morale for familys/Team Hill's military members

- SrA GXXXXX is a very talented, well trained electronics and systems technician who inspires his peers

- SrA XXXXXXX is an intensely loyal and dedicated professional with exemplary leadership and communication skills

- SSgt L is a rising star with unlimited potential who is ready for positions of increased responsibility.

- SSgt Smith is a dynamic and multi-talented NCO with a decisive and proactive leadership style

- Star performer! Received only stripe available from 321 MG/CC for STEP promotion to Staff Sergeant

- Stockpile preparation team member for 09 Nuclear Surety NSI; garnered "Excellent" from ACC--promote now

- Strong community leader--chaperones school functions--regularly mentors elementary school children

- Superior leader and professional; sets high standards for his peers to emulate--ready for promotion!

- Taught Sunday School--positive spokesman for military values, responsible citizenship

- Team player! Sacrificed 8 hours to cook/clean/serve at RAF Croughton's Valentines Couples Spaghetti Dinner

- Top quality performer with unparalleled potential and solid NCO attributes; promote to TSgt ahead of peers!

- Top-notch Contingency Skills instructor--imparted his operational experience and combat skills to 300 students

- Top-notch individual--highly effective; always ensures the job gets done correctly--promote to SRA now!

- TSgt XXXX is a dynamic and energetic manager who continually displays all the traits of a First Class MSgt

- TSgt XXXXXX is clearly a top performer who is the one to choose for the most demanding assignments

- Tutored high school student--raised students grade from an "F" to an "A" in a mere four weeks--inspiring!

- United RAF Croughton Chapel community--cooked and cleaned at five soup dinners--fed more than 200!

- Visited 2 Philippine orphanages; donated over 40 hours labor on new building--solidified community support

- Volunteer phone bank supervisor at Easter Seal telethon; surpassed its goal--raised $30,000 for charity

- Volunteered 20 hrs at skate park--taught 32 teens basic skills...sorted 2K lbs of postal mail--kept msn flowing

- Volunteered 3 hours for Adopt-a-Pet at Vandenberg Team car wash; helped raise over $500--promote soonest

- Volunteered for Commander's change of command ceremony--excellent military community involvement

- Volunteered ISO RAF Croughton Youth Group--developed/sustained activities for teens--provided safe alternative for base teens

- Volunteered time for MacDill Open Window Foundation Nov 08' Thanksgiving--prepared dinner for 60 soldiers; increased morale

- Volunteered to assist local Red Cross in distributing food and clothing to flood victims in the Gulfport area

- Volunteered to work 30+ hrs with AADD; transported 12 inebriated airmen to their homes--careers/lives saved

Additional Rater's Comments

- #1 2E NCO in AF Space Command! Selected as Communications & Information Professional of the Year for 2009

- #1 of 250 38CSW Airmen! Won Airman of the Quarter for 3rd Qtr 2008--sets standard for a true professional

- #1 of five NCOs! Outstanding leader and top performer--delivered stellar results during Global War on Terrorism

- #1 of six planners! Successfully trained dozens of theater comm planners--vital to USCENTCOM mission

- A dependable NCO with some room for improvement and the potential to become an outstanding leader

- A first-rate non-commissioned officer who is willing to face up to any task and tackle the issues head on

- A positive leadership example that consistently brought out the best in subordinates...promote now!

- A positive, can-do attitude; an example to his peers and subordinates--our next MX flight leader!

- A task-oriented, conscientious SNCO--efforts lead to increasing workcenter efficiency and effectiveness

- A true professional who's always in the middle of our most critical processes--promote immediately!

- A unit leader with unmatched dedication to duty and personal performance...promote now to TSgt!

- A welcome new addition to the INSOCOM workcenter, a motivated airman with potential for growth

- A well rounded individual, supports/encourages participation in squadron and community activities--wingman!

- Absolutely superior NCO; challenge with greater responsibility--must promote immediately to Chief!

- Absolutely superior NCO; excelled in job performance, community service and leadership--promote at once

- Aided Facility Management for 2 months showing great efficiency when tasked; displayed great versatility

- All star member of my Joint Service Support Team; no personnel challenge too great; promote to MSgt ASAP!

- An earnest airman, exhibits discipline in working towards completion of qualification training

- An excellent performer; always looks for ways to improve the working environment for the MacDill team

- An exceptional NCO and capable leader; performed duties as jet engine mechanic in an outstanding manner

- Assisted critical software tiger team; 298 MDG systems patched/restored--swift response lauded by MDG/CC

- Attended Enlisted Professional Development Seminar; developed supervisory writing skills--promote now!

- Automated logistical operations reporting; resulted in a 25% increase in the rate of transactions

- Confident and dependable, quickly becoming an integral member of the workcenter. Promote.

- Consistently produces sound results; continue to challenge this NCO with more responsibility--promote!

- Consummate law enforcer; professionally handled any of a variety of situations thrown in his direction

- Created phased trning program; reduced required trning for site qualification by 9 months--increased productivity!

- Dedicated SNCO--allegiance to mission inspires peers, made this NCO invaluable team member. Promote

- Demonstrated outstanding engineering skills and maturity--exceeded standards in a complex environment

- Demonstrates the confidence needed to face the USAF toughest challenges--promote when ready (4 rating)

- Dependable, motivated, and trustworthy--a SNCO with the courage to manage without visible support

- Developed a cross-training program and self-directed work atmosphere that improved employee productivity by 95%

- Directly contributed to Det ## earning the 2008 USAFE Outstanding Aerial Mail Terminal of the Year Award

- Displays exceptional leadership qualities; ability to get the job done; recommend promotion/retention

- Driven SNCO with outstanding results. Continue to entrust with increasing responsibility--Promote now!

- Dynamic airman; multi-talented mechanic; readily accepts increased responsibilities; Promote Now!

- Dynamic and distinguished NCO; leads by example; sets high, attainable standards--promote immediately

- Eager to supervise troops! Attended Enlisted Professional Development seminar; honed leadership skills

- Eager Volunteer; represented the AF at elementary school Patriot Day event, exemplary showcase of the AFRC

- Excelled as Facilities Superintendent for over 60 days during incumbents absence--excellent performance at next level

- Excelled as Mechanical Foreman, post held by seasoned SNCO--took on new duties with uncommon zeal

- Excellent technical abilities; motivated and self-confident airman; consistently performs high quality work

- Exceptional Patient Administrator committed to successful completion of all assigned tasks-promote with peers

- Exceptional performer--further challenge with most difficult tasks--promote ahead of peers

- First rate professional! Shows ability and initiative to assume greater responsibility--promote now

- First-class NCO whose can-do attitude and ceaseless determination are contagious--an excellent role model

- Flexible and versatile leader with unbounded potential, ready to assume SNCO responsibilities!

- Good performer with potential to be an outstanding Airman and a valuable asset; promote with peers

- Good performer, accomplished tasks with minimal supervision; works well with peers; promote

- Good work ethic; tackles any task above his skill level w/outstanding results--promotion to SrA recommended

- Great technician; knowledgeable on all workcenter communications systems; promote

- Great tool room tech--maintained and updated aircraft maintenance Technical Orders per regs

- Guided 17 preventive maintenance inspections; sustained access to 21 servers--ensured service to 4k+ users

- Hard charging airman whose willingness to strive forward has set him apart from his peers--promote!

- Hard working, versatile NCO. Quickly workcenter qualified. Challenge with more responsibilities.

- Highly motivated! Energetic and diligent--demonstrated strong ability to identify, analyze and solve problems

- Highly motivated; determined to succeed in his job; completes tasks correctly first time; a real strength

- Highly qualified NCO; pivotal in uptime rate of over 99% on all strategic links; exceeded DISA standards

- Highly reliable, indispensable member of our team; well trained and knowledgeable on satellite equipment

- Highly skilled and dedicated professional, performs far beyond expectations; outstanding asset to the unit

- Highly skilled member and motivated NCO; valuable asset to the unit and vital to Air Force mission--promote!

- Highly skilled technician; often relied upon to complete difficult jobs with minimum supervision

- Impeccable military bearing paired with maturity and poise; the Airman every unit hopes to gain--promote now!

- Inspected, serviced, and repaired aircraft systems--my most dependable and knowledgeable troop

- Maintained 100% operational capability and accountability of $25 million worth of equipment--increased unit readiness

- Maintained an $18 million fixed asset property account with a 96.8% accuracy rating-best rating out of nine sections

- Managed 93 personnel in 4 demanding, busy shops: Housing Maintenance, Vertical, HVAC & Horizontal--no backlog!

- Managed airman schedules, balanced technical skills resulting in 99% aircraft launch reliability rate

- Master of his trade; I rely on his knowledge and expertise on the system configuration; promote

- Mature and confident airman with extraordinary knowledge and initiative--immediately promote to SSgt!

- MSgt <> is the epitome of a highly motivated Senior NCO in appearance, knowledge and performance

- MSgt Baker is enthusiastic, dedicated SNCO--quickly transitioned from maintenance background to staff

- My #1 NCO; selected as Health Services Manager of the Year 2007--promote ahead of peers!

- My #1 of 16 TSgts! Superior performance across the board--give him bigger challenges--promote now!

- My #1 of 5 NCOs--proactive leader--exemplary NCOIC who led the most active section in the squadron

- My #1 of 6 SNCOs; selected by Maintenance Chief as 1961st Maintenance Group NCO of the Year 07

- My go-to NCO for ISR planning--outstanding NCO with exceptional experience, promote to SNCO now!

- My nominee for promotion under the Stripes for Exceptional Performance program--promote this warrior now

- My number one Mobility line troop--can always be counted on to insure compliance with requirements

- My number one SSgt; proven, exemplary track record confirms he is ready for immediate promotion!

- Naturally encompasses the superlative qualities needed in today's Air Force; a shining example of our core values

- On site for only seven months, already 65% qualified on workcenter maintenance training tasks

- One of my best - a highly skilled/consistent stand out performer recognized by AMC IG - promote now!

- Outstanding Airman with can-do attitude--always willing to accept more challenging tasks with greater responsibility

- Outstanding NCO who leads by example; a solid professional ready for increased responsibility; promote!

- Outstanding NCO! Achievements key to site winning 2007 CE Support Center of the Year--#1 of 29 sites

- Outstanding NCO. Crisp military bearing and appearance. Exceeds standards in military courtesies, fitness, and job performance

- Outstanding team player! Propelled unit to win 2008 "OL of the Year" award--promote immediately!

- Possesses strong record of credibility, loyalty and dedication--true team player--promote now!

- Prime candidate for increased responsibilities--don't hinder this hard-charger--trust with most important tasks

- Quality NCO; displayed knowledge, drive, and initiative in completing any task--promote now! (5)

- Recent Airman Leadership School graduate; earned the John L. Levitow award. Ready to promote.

- Recent graduate of Airman Leadership School; deserving of new promotion to staff sergeant!

- Recently promoted Below-the-Zone--sustained superior performance warrants promotion to SSgt 1st time!

- Recipient of Mission Systems Flight Superior Performer Award for March 09; promote ahead of peers!

- Reviews regulations constantly; sharpens knowledge while providing excellent service to all AMC travelers

- Rock-solid performer; consistently provides high-caliber maintenance and technical direction

- Second to None in the First Command! #1 of 2,900 permanent party airmen--2008 Airman of the Year

- Selected as top performer of the quarter for 3rd Quarter 2004; displayed leadership, professionalism

- Singular initiative and ambition hastened the progress and development of our mentoring program in 2009

- Solid performer; displays exceptional leadership qualities /abilities--recommend promotion soonest

- SrA GXXXXX is a very talented, well trained electronics and systems technician who inspires his peers

- Standout amongst peers! Selected as Det ## NCO of the Qtr, 3d Qtr 05 for superb leadership/job performance

- Star performer! Received only stripe available from 1961st CG/CC for STEP promotion to Tech Sergeant

- Superb radio operator--definitely promote this outstanding and professional operator

- Superb technician; highly motivated and dependable; delivered quality service to customers; promote

- Superior leader and professional; sets high standards for his peers to emulate--ready for promotion!

- Superior NCO and communicator--828th MOC OL-A NCO of the Quarter --definitely promote now!

- Superior performer; certified over 200 items of TMDE, key to laboratory's 1 day backlog--lowest in 5 years

- Supervises two airmen; both are ahead of their peers in Career Development Course completion. Promote.

- The most conscientious, loyal, and dedicated NCO I've served with in 20 years-- STEP to TSgt Now!

- This NCO achieves optimal levels of performance & accomplishment with lasting results--promote to TSgt!

- Took command with ease; completed over 450 scheduled work requests; supervised 11 military/12 local national employees

- Top 15% of my SNCOs; superior technical expertise paired with unmatched motivation - promote to SMSgt!

- Top Airman! Selected as the 848th Missile Group Airman of the Quarter for the second quarter 1996

- Top quality performer with unparalleled potential and solid NCO attributes; promote to TSgt ahead of peers!

- Top-notch technical abilities key for mission support, ready for increased supervisory responsibility--promote!

- Utilized process improvement techniques; reduced military performance reporting delays by 75%

Does Not Meet Standards Examples

- unable to report to work on time and needs constant supervision. Retention is not advised.

- SSgt Smith is uncooperative with leadership and fails to understand the difference between "taking care of troops" and following orders. His combative attitude is counter-productive and a liability to this Squadron.

- resists suggestions for improvement and actively works against the orders of his superiors

- not fit for this type of activity, exhibits a negative attitude and should be disqualified

- has the potential to be an excellent technician but is often careless with...

- cannot work with his peers and is counter-productive

- unable to succeed without supervision but resents guidance and ignores advice

- allowed the pressures of family issues to affect her performance. Recommend release from duties and counseling until such time she can resume work without endangering others.

- does not comply with regulations and is a threat to the safety of this flight. Recommend discharge at earliest opportunity.

- did not follow orders and repeated past objectionable behavior; performance is not consistent with military standards. Demote.

The Supervisor's Code

For years, there have been persistent, whispered rumors circulating among Airmen that NCOs and supervisors possessed some kind of secret language or code, understandable only to its initiates, and were somehow communicating amongst themselves and even with unknown NCOs in the future --across space and time --to control and contaminate the careers of their subordinates. One particularly poisonous rumor was that Senior NCOs were using a covert cipher in their troops' performance reports with mysterious and often disastrous results. Until now, no real evidence has ever been unearthed to support these wild claims but now the truth can finally be told.

Few people know that the Randolph AFB Personnel Center has an annex and even fewer know its secret location: in the basement of the Alamo. There, under cover of darkness, generations of Airmen have labored in the shadows over glowing recommendations and marginal performance reports. Guarded night and day by federal agents, the very existence of this facility is known only to a few. I myself was imprisoned there for three long years. While I worked there, in the fortress of servitude, I managed to smuggle out, piece by piece, the tenets of a supervisor's code so diabolical and confusing that it would drive normal men mad. It was years before I had the courage to share this information with outsiders and years more before I was able to find someone willing to publish it. But now, here, finally, consolidated into one document, is the secret code no Airman has been privileged to see...until now!

Writing and reading performance reports is not the straight-forward activity you might suppose that it is. Performance reports are a complex mix of subtle claims, statements, and lies. Over the years, NCOs have modified the format of the performance report until every EPR actually has two layers of meaning. The top layer, the type-written statements, are immediately apparent and understandable to anyone. But there is an insidious second layer, invisible to the untrained eye, that contains even more information. The second layer is a combination of format and secret key words and phrases. Supervisors use the invisible layer to convey their true feelings while pacifying the ratee with the apparently satisfactory ratings on the surface.

Normally, the two layers should coincide in meaning and they usually do. But there are times when a supervisor might be forced to use the code to convey his overall judgment of the ratee while the actual typewritten words might convey a somewhat different meaning. For example, if a supervisor is forced to give an Airman an overall five EPR because he failed to document substandard behavior, he can still resort to the Supervisor's Code to document a less than perfect performance.

As all Airmen know, the only way to have a lasting effect on a troop's career is to sabotage his or her performance report. LOCs and LORs and other temporary annoyances come and go and drop out of your record after a couple of years but EPRs are *forever*. They are always a part of your record. Even at your next duty station. Even after you're retired. Airmen might gleefully PCS thinking they've seen the last of a spiteful supervisor but often, the joke is on them. Their supervisor may have embedded a little chunk of code in their EPR that will be noticed and noted by future raters again and again over the course of the ratee's career. It's as permanent as a case of herpes. Although it's true, as many Airmen argue, that it's the overall EPR rating that's used to calculate your WAPS score, the written content also carries a substantial amount of weight. It's used by Review Boards to choose who gets submitted for Below-the-Zone, Airman of the Quarter, and other programs. If you can't figure out why the Commander won't sign your retraining paperwork and never returns your calls, check your old EPRs.

The code is a manner of writing. It's an agreed upon set of key words that all NCOs understand to have a double meaning. Using these secret key words, a supervisor can write an apparently satisfactory EPR which when read by other NCOs in the know, paints a very different picture of the ratee's performance. Many an Airman have read their EPR and thought it to be acceptable or even commendable but were left scratching their heads wondering why they were never allowed to participate in any reindeer games.

Supervisors insert hidden meaning into an EPR through a combination of secret key words and phrases and formatting. There are two general divisions where effort is focused: the body of the EPR and the Promotion Statement.

How to Conceal Negative Meaning in the EPR Body

If you want to give an overall impression of substandard performance, start with the duty title. The duty title should not be for a position with more responsibility than the duty title listed in the last EPR. It should not suggest any kind of growth or advancement or increased experience. If possible, make sure the duty title doesn't imply authority or responsibility. NCOs know that when critical work center positions have to be filled, Airman are compared, and the most experienced, efficient, and mature Airman get the job. When an Airman is not assigned to positions of greater responsibility, it signals to any future readers that the ratee's performance was judged to be only average. Or maybe less than average.

White space is an effective yet subtle method of signaling that the ratee is a mediocre performer. White space is the inevitable space left at the end of a bullet statement. Don't make it obvious. Just 10 to 12 spaces should do the trick. Officially white space is acceptable so the ratee can't accuse the rater of sabotaging his career. But future reviewers will understand the excessive white space to be an attempt to communicate less than stellar performance.

List more community-related bullet statements than duty-related bullet statements in the EPR. Or as many as you dare. This makes it clear that the ratee didn't have any (or many) duty-related accomplishments. An EPR with too many such bullets broadcasts a negative message that only the most clueless Senior NCO would miss. To really work this angle, use community-related bullets in the Additional Rater's block too!

Fluffy, say-nothing bullets--great, flowery prose with no specific impact send the message that this person didn't really accomplish anything and the supervisor had to resort to inflated, empty bullet statements to fill the empty space. An example of a fluffy, non-competitive EPR bullet:

- Totally dedicated and focused...can juggle feathers in a hurricane; the epitome of leadership

Use inappropriate or weak epr bullets. A good rule of thumb is to ask yourself: is this bullet good enough to support the rating or a promotion recommendation? If not, use it!

To make a weak bullet statement even worse, make it into a two-line bullet with a sub-bullet supporting it! Nothing spells unremarkable performance like emphasizing a weak achievement as if it was the best one. For example:

- *Innovative customer service representative, complies with all service guidance*
-- *Adherence to published standard operating procedures reduced waiting 20 percent*

Although subtle hints of disapproval can be woven into the body of the EPR as shown above, they can be mistaken for sloppiness or rater inexperience. But there is no mistaking the intent of the Promotion Statement.

How to Sabotage the Promotion Statement

Comments from the rater or the Additional Rater are the most important part of the EPR. Promotion board members depend on this section of the EPR to provide the most revealing information about the individual they are evaluating. They are aware of the code and know that the graduations of performance documented here are universally understood. Although an Airman may have received a standard 5 EPR, the promotion statement will relegate the Airman to one of several stratums.

It's easy to slip in a seemingly acceptable but ultimately derogatory promotion statement. In real life, we understand the words, adequate, acceptable, and average, to be positive adjectives. But, in today's Air Force we are expected to exceed standards, stand head and shoulders above our peers, and be #1 of 12 airmen in the work center all the time. That's how the code works. If the rater describes the ratee's performance as anything but ABSOLUTE BEST EVER, PROMOTE IMMEDIATELY!, he or she is history.

But the rater doesn't have to resort to such transparent statements. English is a marvelously subtle language, awash in nuance and double meaning, as it is. In this "Through the Looking Glass" world of Air Force Performance Report English, up is down, hot is cold, and always means never. To give you an idea of how positive sounding descriptions can telegraph not-so-good performance, check out this ranking of promotion statements taken from a popular and authoritative Air Force Evaluation guide:

SAMPLE STRATIFICATION LEVELS

Top Level

- ✓ #1 of 7 MSgts in my division
- ✓ Top 1% of all Tech Sergeants
- ✓ 1 of my top 2 support NCOs
- ✓ Top 1% of all SNCOs I know

2nd Level

- ✓ Top 5%-10% of his peers
- ✓ Top 10% of my Senior NCOs
- ✓ Top 10% of Tech Sergeants I've seen in 20 years
- ✓ Top 5% of my star-studded cast of Airmen

3rd Level

- ✓ A leader of incredible breadth
- ✓ Impact leader—gets results
- ✓ Tested hard—passed brilliantly
- ✓ My most talented SNCO

4th Level

- ✓ Outstanding, superior performance
- ✓ If I go to war, I want him in the lead
- ✓ Exemplary! Sharp, honest professional
- ✓ A thoroughbred running full stride

Who would have ever thought that these 4th-level bullet statements are appropriate for the lowest level of performance? Not me! I would have been happy to have seen *any* of these statements in my EPR! The lesson that we should learn from this is that you can say just about anything you want about someone but if you haven't qualified the statement by comparing him or her against their peers, you might as well not say anything at all. This is a great way of disguising your intent if your aim is to produce an ineffective EPR.

Promotion Statements are the most common method of sending hidden signals. These deceptive comments have a long and checkered history and have become an Air Force tradition. They can be written strong or written like a dormant computer virus. For example:

- SSgt Smith will make a good first-line maintainer; promote when ready

Any NCO reading this promotion statement would understand its meaning immediately: the rater doesn't believe this troop should be promoted. Even though the rater is complimentary and even approves a promotion, this statement actually says that SSgt Smith is *not* a good first-line maintainer *now* but *will be* one day (sometime in the distant future probably). Furthermore, by writing, "promote when ready", the rater is clearly stating that the ratee is not ready *now*. Otherwise the rater would have written, "promote now". This is a classic example of the code. It says "promote" but actually means *don't* promote. Another example:

- Good performer with potential to be an outstanding Airman and a valuable asset; promote with peers

This promotion statement is the kiss of death. It has substandard written all over it. Good? What about "top" or "best" or "great"? Potential? Potential is one of those universally recognized key words I told you about. This phrase, "potential to be", is understood to mean that, although you have the *capability* of someday being an outstanding Airman, you are not one now. And just why you're not one now we're left to wonder. But there's no mistaking the message: You are not an outstanding Airman which is probably a polite way of saying you're sub-standard. And the statement, "promote with peers"? Although the supervisor did write, "promote", he qualified it with "with peers". This indicates that the rater doesn't think you're ahead of the pack but should only be promoted when EVERYBODY ELSE is! In real life, there is, of course, nothing wrong with being average or being promoted at the same time as everyone else. But remember, we're in the Air Force and we must adhere to the code. In the Air Force, Airmen are bulletproof and Officers are immortal. So to slander someone with a statement like Promote With Peers is like saying your ancestors are from France. If you see this on your EPR, consider pounding your supervisor.

Other examples of "not ready for prime time" statements :

- groom for SMSgt

This phrase suggests that further preparation or grooming is necessary before the person will be ready for promotion to SMSgt or that the individual is not currently ready for promotion. Subtle, eh? I thought it meant that the rater approved of the ratee and had given him his blessings but that's not what it means at all!

- Continue to challenge with...

Although this phrase literally implies supervisor approval and a ratee who enjoys challenges, it is actually supervisor code for "this person is not ready to advance and should remain in his current position" or "not ready for promotion". The logic behind this is that if a person was really high-speed, he'd be ready to graduate to more responsibility and a more demanding job.   Air Force people are always advancing, always accepting greater responsibility.   By saying "continue to challenge...", the rater is suggesting that he needs more practice at whatever it is he's currently doing. Or that he makes lousy coffee. One of those.

- Dependable NCO! Never fails to meet Air Force standards!

Personally, if I had seen this on my EPR, I would have been flattered but I would have been wrong! This is bad. It's a disguised way of saying a person only "meets standards". In real life, meeting standards is a good thing but in the secret code of the EPR, it's about as bad as being a sex offender.   Air Force people always *exceed* standards or maybe even invent their own.

- has potential for success

Even though this sounds promising and positive, it's not. When the rater writes that the person has the *potential* or the possibility of success, the rater is not saying that the ratee is a success -only that he has the *potential* to be a success. Some day. The same way a lump of dough has the *potential* to be a jelly doughnut. It's a very common way of describing inferior or lackluster performance. Subtle yet plain. Even the least experienced NCOs can understand it.

- strives for perfection in all he does

Although on any other planet, this would be received as a complimentary bullet statement, in the Air Force, it has long been a code phrase for "doesn't succeed" or "not quite ready for promotion". The reasoning behind this is that supposedly, if the ratee had actually been successful in his or her endeavors, the rater would have written "achieved perfection in all he does" or "reached perfection". The words, "strive" and "try" are understood to mean unsuccessful as in "strived but didn't quite make it" or "tried but failed". So, to slip this by the ratee, couple the code words with something grand and heroic like "always strives to exceed world class standards". He'll never know what hit him.

- knowledgeable Airman with plenty of potential; continue to challenge for excellence--ready for promotion

By now, I think you can recognize the pattern. The keyword, potential, indicates a current lack of ability. The phrase, continue to challenge, is a plea to keep this loser where he is and away from flammable materials. If the rater had thought that the Airman was capable of bigger projects with more responsibility, he would have stated something along those lines. Instead, by saying, continue to challenge, the rater is stating that the ratee isn't ready for advancement and should be kept in whatever position he currently holds. And "ready for promotion" is code for *don't* promote (see Key below). If the rater had believed the subject was ready for promotion, he would have used the phrase, promote *now*. And the overall statement is nothing but a ball of fluff that doesn't actually say anything.

To paint an exceptionally mediocre word picture of the ratee:

On the promotion statement, the last line should reflect the mediocrity of the performance compared to the last EPR. It shouldn't indicate any growth or progress or rise in authority since the last EPR. The last line should not be hard-hitting or recommend progress to the next level of leadership or responsibility.

Stratification of less than the top 50% sends a strong negative message. Find a way to compare the ratee with the lower half of the rating pool, i.e., my #7 of 15 NCOs. Although it certainly works, this is sort of clumsy and obvious. A better strategy would be to poison the job recommendation.

Raters, when favorably reviewing a ratee's performance, always make recommendations as to what future position the ratee might excel at. To handicap your ratee, recommendations for the next job should be for a job at the same or lower level of responsibility than is currently held. This is the equivalent of "continue to challenge" and shows a lack of progress or potential for progress.

No promotion statement at all or a weak one. This ominous silence speaks volumes.

To hammer home the idea that the ratee is vulture bait, recommend retention in their currently held position. An example statement would be something like:

- Best technical order tech we ever had; keep this winner managing our books!

Nothing says this person is not ready for promotion or increased responsibility like a veiled plea to keep them from leadership positions.

Make no PME recommendations. Recommending someone for PME ahead of their time is a time-honored method of endorsing the ratee for bigger and better things. Don't make a recommendation!

To confine the ratee to the lowest level of 5 purgatory, in the promotion statement, use the phrase "ready for promotion". This phrase is normally used for a "4" EPR and may not make it through the reviewing chain. Although the phrase , "ready for promotion", appears to be a positive sentiment, it's actually one of the agreed upon key phrases which means "Not Ready For Promotion". Or "consider for promotion after the rest of the free world has already been promoted. Twice." Or use the stock phrase for "3" EPRs: "consider for promotion".

Key:
>   5 - promote now, immediately, ASAP (promote)
>   4 - ready for promotion (don't promote)
>   3 - consider for promotion (never promote)
>   2 - no promotion statement (demote)

Put a community involvement bullet in last line instead of a promotion statement. Ouch!

Leave lots of white space on last line. An example of such a line might be: Met acceptable levels of performance.

In summary, using these techniques, an Airman may be condemned to a lackluster career without them even knowing it!

Performance Report Phrases

her actions exemplified the highest standards of commitment to...

provided leadership, direction, and coordination for the...

chosen for the first of more than...high-visibility missions

represents the spirit of...personifies...

supervised self-help project that...

inspired subordinates to mirror his example of quality workmanship, safety, and total commitment

demonstrated exceptional pride in...

by consistent effort and perseverance, advanced the quality of...

maintained impeccable military bearing and...

carefully managed time, personnel, and equipment resources to...

routinely chosen/selected for...

successfully completed several initiatives to...

unrelenting efforts and support was directly responsible for unprecedented progress in...

was widely recognized as...won accolades for...

innovative approach; solved a variety of problems in...

is uniquely talented and capable of...

single-handedly resurrected a demoralized and inactive Sergeants Association and...

laudable achievements include...

is an experienced and capable member of...

unparalleled ability to multitask achieved outstanding results in...

sets a sterling personal example of...

mastered all training requirements and went on to...

guided Flight to pinnacle of achievement and success in...

exceeded all standards to surpass peers in...

credited with being one of the team responsible for...

was directly responsible for the effectiveness of...

excelled as key planner for...

flawlessly orchestrated processing of...

successfully integrated efforts of all work centers to...

exhibits a special talent for...

an unusually gifted troubleshooter, provides a deep and revealing analysis...

possesses diplomatic ability to guide...

a strong background in...gave qualified, in-depth review of...

enjoys challenges and developing novel approaches to...

insatiable curiosity and relentless effort resulted in...

enforces standards while maintaining morale of...

leadership helped focus efforts of disparate group to...

participative style of management and flexible approach led team to...

demonstrates an unparalleled capacity for... and ability to...

has strong, patient resolve that ultimately...

surpassed peers and subordinates in ability to...

produced unmatched quality and quantity of deployment training to...

and stood up the first-ever...outside CONUS

his meticulous attention to detail earned him the...

her accurate calculations eliminated the need for...

as crew leader, Sergeant Smith instituted a recurring maintenance program which...

has distinguished himself through sustained, superior performance and...

displays an aptitude for increased responsibility...

commended by...for efforts and accomplishment in...

places proper and heavy emphasis on...

inventive, motivated, and extremely conscientious in...

earned widespread recognition for efforts to...

uses her extensive education and training in...to...

possesses boundless enthusiasm and determination to...

was a key member and contributed to vital interests by...

through a combination of practicality, intelligence, and common sense, was able to...

personal initiative and dedication directly responsible for...

is one of our best and most qualified technicians and...

overcame all obstacles to success despite manning and...

was responsible for substantial and significant contributions to the development of...

fearlessly accepted complex and career-risking tasks...

his "lead by example" style was instrumental in...

can be depended on produce top quality, timely...

planned, coordinated, and launched new and successful...

the cornerstone of our team and provides efficient and appropriate support to...

thrives in the dynamic and challenging environment of...

her loyalty and initiative was directly responsible for...

sacrificed off-duty time to ensure successful...

smashed the twelve-hour standard/record

initiative and technical expertise were also evident in...

enhanced the mission effectiveness of the unit by...

a confident and well spoken Airman with...

transformed a failing workcenter to a top facility in...

worked diligently to qualify himself as...

despite severe manning shortages due to unprecedented deployment support, maintained ...

our most valued and skilled team member, often recognized for...

led work center with humility, pride, and...

a leading authority in... a prime candidate for...

volunteered over 100 hours of off-duty time to provide outstanding support and service to...

exemplary character and military bearing was a factor in...

common sense and practical application of experience led to...

aggressive and decisive actions were key factors in establishing...

a mature NCO, implemented required level of discipline to restore...

dedicated to the growth and development of subordinates...

an Airman with proven experience and advanced knowledge, is uniquely qualified to...

always successfully completes assignments, regardless of complexity and...

a tireless advocate for training and support of...

attention to detail and invaluable experience played a vital role in the successful deployment of...

military bearing is beyond reproach and is...

is a motivated and proven technician who junior personnel consistently look to for guidance and...

exploits all opportunities for growth and...

natural leader who inspires confidence and trust in those around him...

a key factor in the implementation and rising success of...

technical curiosity and in-depth analysis led to...

loyalty and conviction maker her our best spokesman for...

possesses unlimited potential for...

contributed to the outstanding inter-service coordination and squadron's superior performance for...

despite rising ops tempo and increased tasking, maintained 100%...

a punctual and considerate team member who can be depended on to...

established and encouraged a "can do" attitude in his...

an ideal role model and respected leader who...

shows a remarkable ability to unite a work center in...

showed exceptional creativity and innovative use of personnel and material assets to achieve...

our champion in the management of...

aggressively tackles all challenges with...

demonstrated advanced troubleshooting technique that has become the new standard for...

consistently demonstrates superior skills, dedication, and aggressive pursuit of...

an invested and involved member, is dedicated to providing support to...

a resourceful and innovative supervisor who...

accomplished impressive results in...by...

his forward-looking and firm leadership style was responsible for...

star performer, she merits consideration for...

turned in a masterful performance as...

outstanding administrative and management skill, directly responsible for...

well prepared and is poised for achievement as...

unsurpassed in ability to...

unparalleled initiative and motivation produced....

is the inexhaustible engine that powers our cell and...

personal initiative and managerial skills overcame...

spent weeks documenting our most critical processes which resulted in...

his direct involvement and support influenced the approval and adoption of...which...

clearly demonstrated an unmatched ability to...

established a supportive but firm leadership style that propelled his Flight to...

consistent examples of integrity and loyalty won respect and support from her team and...

excels at tasks involving...

has broad and in-depth understanding of...

his actions earned the right to be assigned as...

united a diverse team of enlisted and contractors to...

performance exceeds workcenter standards of...

is a proven technical expert and an indispensable leader in...

the recognized authority and most influential in...

his expertise in management and technical ability are evident in the...

planned and executed numerous successful...

selected over peers to serve as...

brilliant manager who is committed to total...

always reliable, displays a daily diligence that...

advanced shop and unit goals by...

significantly improved the condition of...

actively supported and encouraged participation in...

successfully planned and carried out...

displays the maturity and self-confidence of a seasoned NCO...

a role model and perfect example of...

developed and implemented a new training procedure which...

personally responsible for successful management of $6 million dollars of...

extremely well organized, mission-oriented, and industrious, he is our most efficient at...

has unlimited potential with a proficiency for...

a fundamental, essential team member and key to the successful...

developed a benchmark...which has become the standard for...

extremely competent; performed all duties above expected standards and...

led a highly successful unit to...

an exceptional NCO and capable leader, performed duties as...

possesses boundless enthusiasm and excitement for...

is the cornerstone for unit and responsible for...

excelled in position normally held by Senior NCO and...

exceptional organizer and manager, she...

is a proven technical expert and exceptional administrator...

raised the bar for all efforts to follow...

consistently strives for improvement and growth...

accepts responsibility for consequences even when...

earned my complete trust and confidence when...

forged an inexperienced workcenter into an efficient and cohesive team...

meticulous attention to detail was directly responsible for 100% readiness of...

inexhaustible source of...

organized and directed ... which substantially increased the squadron's full mission capability rate/readiness

greatly increased productivity while...

dedicated long hours under difficult circumstances to...

expedited critical conversion to...

motivated subordinates to perform all tasks to the best of their abilities and...

demonstrated the highest standards of...

highly motivated Senior NCO who is committed to accomplishing the mission and taking care of...

assumes additional workload regardless of size, complexity, or...

always in focus and is exceptionally well organized and...

her merits deserve selection for...

frequently depended on to solve difficult system discrepancies in...

demonstrated outstanding technical ability when...

leadership was instrumental in...

led in the expedient recovery/rescue of...

managerial ability was evident when...

his mechanical skills were conspicuous when...

outstanding leadership, professional skill, and ceaseless efforts secured...

ensured a seamless conversion to...

instrumental in forging a strong partnership with...

his astute attention to detail resulted in...

provided the link in reaching out to our...

her efforts helped bridge the relationship between...and identified opportunities for...

went above and beyond the call of duty, selflessly...

through superior performance, expertise and "can do" attitude improved the...

pushed production of...to an unprecedented level of...

his superb management skills ensured...

was pivotal in producing...

was key in conveying system policy and principle to...

his contribution to the...section/workcenter saved the Air Force...

her quick reaction potentially saved the Air Force more than...

efforts of...contributed to the overall mission in support of both Operation...and...

which provided vital oversight to over...

outstanding leadership abilities coupled with his skill and keen knowledge of...were directly responsible for...

provided valuable oversight as one of...

and provided vital expertise as...

made major contributions to the effectiveness and success of...

was integral in developing...

streamlined the procedures for...

provided valuable support during the...

was an invaluable team player in...

further distinguished herself by...

keen attention to detail was crucial in the development of...

increased the effective and timely management of...

was instrumental in overhauling the...

was essential in the establishment of the...

organizational skills, knowledge, and can-do attitude expanded the capabilities of...

quickly adapted to changing/fluid environment and short lead times to...

has a common sense approach and superb judgment which...

set an excellent example for his subordinates by...

stepped into the demanding role of...

superior analytical and technical capabilities allowed him to...

was the driving force behind the...

responsible for an overall increase in productivity command-wide and...

skillfully directed...and safeguarded...which was vital to...

her dedication to duty resulted in her selection as...

in this important assignment, his outstanding leadership and devotion to duty were key factors in...

his decisive actions prevented and saved...

his keen insight and savvy management skills guided the team to...

tackled the most demanding...requirements which directly contributed to...

contribution to the mission and the U.S. Air Force have been invaluable to...

his technical abilities were showcased when...

her superior performance proved invaluable during...

were instrumental factors in the resolution of many problems of major importance to the...

provided much needed guidance and supervision during the...

was selected to fill a critically-manned Tech-Sergeant position managing an operational flight of...

demonstrated flawless Command and Control of response forces during...

became the "gold standard" for other Air Force programs and...

which culminated in an outstanding rating of...

in this capacity she...

professionalism and dedication to duty produced lasting contributions to the...

was hand-picked for and excelled as...

established a solid, comprehensive program and created the framework for...

unmatched diagnostic abilities and expert repairs directly resulted in...

balanced daily duties with increased force protection requirements under austere conditions which...

led...military and contractors in the support of...

was essential to the Wing's overall "Excellent" Operational Readiness Inspection rating

displayed exceptional aircraft system knowledge while performing as...

superb maintenance skills were evident when...

deployed in support of...and...

his efforts led to the establishment of...

significant contributions helped propel the...to best in Air Force, best in United States Strategic Command

earned an astonishing/unmatched four excellent ratings during...

her determination in...aided in the Wing's "Outstanding" rating during the semi-annual COMSEC Inspection

innovation made him a recognized expert in...

his comprehensive operational expertise was successfully leveraged by/to...

integrated doctrine into the practical daily operation of...

despite...provided critical input to the...

rare talent and experience combined to...

his focused efforts multiplied the effectiveness of...

developed and sustained an unprecedented rate of...

introduced a new vitality that...

motivated his peers and subordinates to...

revitalized the efforts to...

inspired his peers to new levels of...and...

provided unparalleled support of...

Positive Adjectives

On the following pages is a list of positive adjectives for use in EPRs and awards. Adjectives should be chosen wisely. There's never enough space to say everything we'd like to say about our troops' performance so it's important to make the best use of the limited space available and make every word count. For example if you wrote that a person was, "the epitome of efficiency and effectiveness", although it sounds nice, those two words mean roughly the same thing. You could have used another adjective that more expansively described the person's character such as "*dependable* and efficient".

A

able
above average
acclaimed
accomplished
active
adaptable
adept
admirable
advanced
advancing
aggressive
agile
alert
ambitious
amicable
analytical
articulate
assured
astute
attentive
authentic
authoritative
aware

B

balanced

beneficial
best
bold
bona fide
brave
bright
brilliant
bulletproof
busy

C

calm
capable
careful
cautious
certified
commanding
commendable
committed
compassionate
competent
confident
conscientious
conservative
considerate
consistent
contributing
cooperative
courageous

courteous
creative
critical

D

daring
decisive
dedicated
deliberate
dependable
detail-oriented
determined
diligent
diplomatic
discreet
dominating
driven
dutiful
dynamic

E

eager
earnest
educated
effective
efficient
eloquent

enabling
encouraging
energetic
energized
enterprising
enthusiastic
essential
excellent
exceptional
experienced
expert

F

facilitating
fair
faithful
famous
fearless
firm
flawless
flexible
focused
forceful

G

generous
genuine

giving
goal-oriented
gung-ho

H

handy
hard working
hard-charging
hardy
healthy
heavyweight
helpful
heroic
honest
honorable

I

idealistic
illustrious
imaginative
impartial
impeccable
important
impressive
incandescent

incomparable
incredible
indefatigable
independent
indispensable
industrious
inexhaustible
influential
informed
ingenious
innovative
insatiable
insightful
inspired
intelligent
intense
intent
interested
intrepid
invaluable
inventive
invested
involved
irrepressible

J

just
judicious

K

keen
key
kind
knowledgeable

L

lasting
laudable
leading
learned
legendary
legitimate
level-headed
limitless
logical
loyal
luminous

M

masterful
matchless
mature

memorable
methodical
meticulous
mighty
mindful
moderate
modest
momentous
monumental
moral
motivated
multi-skilled
multi-talented

N

nation-wide
necessary
neighborly
new
nimble
noble
non-partisan
notable
noteworthy
no-nonsense
nurturing

O

observant
one-of-a-kind
open-minded
opportunistic
optimistic
orderly
organized
original
out-performing
outspoken
outstanding
overpowering

P

paramount
passionate
patient
patriotic
peerless
perceptive
perfect
persevering
persistent
persuasive
phenomenal
pleasant
poised

polished
popular
positive
powerful
practical
practiced
praiseworthy
precise
predominant
preeminent
premier
prepared
prestigious
principled
proactive
productive
professional
proficient
progressive
prolific
prominent
promising
prompt
proper
protective
proven
prudent
punctual
purposeful

Q

qualified
quick
quick-thinking

R

rare
rational
ready
realistic
reasonable
receptive
recognized
record-breaking
relentless
reliable
remarkable
renowned
reputable
resilient
resolute
resourceful
responsible
results-oriented
revolutionary
robust

S

satisfactory
scholarly
schooled
scrupulous
seasoned
secure
selected
self-assured
self-confident
self-motivated
self-reliant
selfless
sensible
serious
sharing
sharp
significant
sincere
single-minded
skilled
skillful
smart
sober
sociable
soldierly
sophisticated
sound
special
spectacular

spirited
stable
stalwart
steadfast
steady
stellar
sterling
strong
substantial
subtle
successful
suitable
superb
superior
supportive
supreme
sure
surpassing
sustaining
systematic

thriving
tireless
tolerant
top
tough
towering
traditional
trained
traveled
triumphant
true
trustworthy
truthful

U

ultimate
unadulterated
unafraid
unbelievable
undaunted
understanding
unfailing
unimpeachable
unique
unlimited
unmatched
unparalleled
unrivaled
unstoppable

T

tactful
talented
tenacious
terrific
tested
thorough
thoughtful
thrifty

V

valiant
valorous
valuable
valued
venerable
venturesome
versatile
veteran
victorious
vigilant
vigorous
virtuous
visionary
vital
voluntary

Z

zealous

W

warrior
watchful
well-grounded
well-qualified
well-spoken
wholesome
willing
wise
working
worthy

Approved Acronyms and Abbreviations

The goal of the EPR is to convey accurate information as simply as possible. To accomplish this, familiar, everyday words should be used and words and phrases that are not universally understood should be avoided. In addition, acronyms and abbreviations that are not widely known should not be used. EPRs will be read by people from a wide variety of career fields so they must be written using words that are understandable to everyone.

When using acronyms, there is a rule that requires all acronyms and abbreviations to be "defined" before using them. Defining the acronym before use means to spell out the word or phrase along with the abbreviation or acronym after it in parenthesis --like this:

Window Washer (WW)

After "defining" the acronym, the acronym, WW, may then be used alone throughout the rest of the document with the assumption that it is now understandable. In order to conserve space in the body of the EPR, the most efficient way to define acronyms you plan to use is in the admin blocks of the EPR (Organization, Job Description, Duty

Title). That way you don't waste space in the body of the EPR where space is more critical. Note that when you define a term, you don't simply list the word and its abbreviation or acronym. It must be used appropriately in a sentence or as the appropriate entry for a block. So it's not always possible to define the acronym or abbreviation in the admin blocks.

Minimize the use of acronyms that aren't commonly understood across the Air Force. If the rater decides that it's worth the space to introduce a new acronym to the EPR reader, it must be spelled out the first time it is used (as noted above) on each side of the EPR. Writers should critically question whether using the uncommon acronym or abbreviation contributes to the readability of the EPR and make every effort to use ordinary English keeping in mind that promotion boards are drawn from all Air Force career fields. If the acronym or abbreviation is used only once or twice, consider whether defining the term is actually conserving space. It may be more efficient to spell out the word every time and avoid using the acronym or abbreviation.

Most Major Commands or Wings have their own standards concerning what is acceptable on an EPR. If your organization has a list of approved abbreviations and acronyms, you should use it. If not, this guide serves as a general reference.   Note that some words are never abbreviated. Never use abbreviations or acronyms in the Duty Title. It must be spelled out in all capital letters.

There are exceptions to the above rule requiring all acronyms to be defined before using. Some abbreviations and acronyms are so common that everyone understands what they stand for and to define them would be a waste of time and valuable EPR real estate. The following pages list commonly accepted acronyms that do not have to be defined before using them. This list was compiled from several MAJCOM lists of approved acronyms and abbreviations and only lists those terms that were common to each list.

Acronyms and Abbreviations that do not have to be defined before using on the EPR

A

A1C	Airman First Class
AB	Airman Basic
ACC	Air Combat Command
ACSC	Air Command and Staff College
AD	Active Duty
ADT	Active Duty Training
AEF	Air Expeditionary Force
AETC	Air Education and Training Command
AF	Air Force
AFA	Air Force Association
AFAM	Air Force Achievement Medal
AFB	Air Force Base
AFCM	Air Force Commendation Medal
AFI	Air Force Instruction
AFIC	Air Force Intelligence Command
AFIT	Air Force Institute of Technology
AFMAN	Air Force Manual
AFMC	Air Force Materiel Command
AFOSH	Air Force Office of Safety and Health
AFOSI	Air Force Office of Special Investigations
AFPC	Air Force Personnel Center
AFR	Air Force Reserve

AFRC	Air Force Reserve Command
AFRES	Air Force Reserve
AFROTC	Air Force Reserve Officer Training Corps
AFS	Air Force Station
AFSC	Air Force Specialty Code
AFSOC	Air Force Special Operations Command
AFSO21	Air Force Smart Operations for the 21st Century
AFSPACECOM	Air Force Space Command
AFSPC	Air Force Space Command
AGR	Active Guard and Reserve
ALS	Airman Leadership School
AMC	Air Mobility Command
Amn	Airman
ANG	Air National Guard
AOC	Air Operations Center
AOO	Area of Operation
AOR	Area of Responsibility
ART	Air Reserve Technician
ARC	Air Reserve Component
ARPC	Air Reserve Personnel Center
ASAP	As Soon As Possible
ATO	Air Tasking Order
ATSO	Ability To Survive and Operate
AU	Air University
AWACS	Airborne Warning and Control System
AWC	Air War College

B

BAS	Basic Allowance for Subsistence
BDE	Basic Developmental Education
BPZ	Below Promotion Zone
BRAC	Base Realignment and Closure
BPZ	Below Promotion Zone
BTZ	Below the Zone

C

$C2$	Command and Control
$C3I$	Command, Control, Communications and Intelligence
$C4$	Command, Control, Communications and Computers
$C4I$	Command, Control, Communications, Computers and Intelligence
$C4ISR$	C4, Intelligence, Surveillance and Reconnaissance
CAOC	Combined Air Operations Center
Capt	Captain
CC	Commander
CC, ACC	Commander, Air Combat Command
CCAF	Community College of the Air Force
CDC	Career Development Course
CD-ROM	Compact Disc Read-only Memory
CE	Civil Engineer

CENTCOM	Central Command
CFC	Combined Federal Campaign
CGO	Company Grade Officer
CHAMPUS	Civilian Health and Medical Program of the Uniformed Services
CIA	Central Intelligence Agency
CINC	Commander in Chief
CJCS	Chairman, Joint Chiefs of Staff
CMSgt	Chief Master Sergeant
CMSAF	Chief Master Sergeant of the Air Force
Comm	Communications
COMSEC	Communications Security
CONOP	Concept of Operations
CONUS	Continental United States
CPR	Cardio-Pulmonary Resuscitation
CSAF	Chief of Staff, US Air Force
CSAR	Combat Search and Rescue
CY	Calendar Year

D

DAV	Deployment Assistance Visit
DE	Developmental Education
DEERS	Defense Enrollment Eligibility Reporting System
DIMHRS	Defense Integrated Military Human Resources System
DoD	Department of Defense
DRU	Direct Reporting Unit

DSN	Defense Switched Network
DUI	Driving Under the Influence

E

EET	Exercise Evaluation Team
EPR	Enlisted Performance Report
EUCOM	U.S. European Command
EPA	Environmental Protection Agency

F

FAA	Federal Aviation Administration
FAV	Functional Assistance Visit
FCC	Federal Communications Commission
FDA	Food and Drug Administration
FMC	Fully Mission Capable
FOA	Field Operating Agency
FOD	Foreign Object Damage
FOIA	Freedom of Information Act
FOUO	For Official Use Only
FY	Fiscal Year

G

GPA	Grade Point Average
GPS	Geographic Positioning System
GSA	General Services Administration
GSU	Geographically Separated Unit
GWOT	Global War on Terrorism

H

HHQ	Higher Headquarters
HQ	Headquarters
HSI	Health Services Inspection

I

IADT	Initial Active Duty Training
IAW	In Accordance With
IDT	Inactive Duty Training
IG	Inspector General
IMA	Individual Mobilization Augmentee
IMPAC	International Merchant Purchase Authorization Card
IP	Instructor Pilot
IR	Individual Reservist

J

JAG	Judge Advocate General
JCS	Joint Chiefs of Staff
JFC	Joint Forces Commander
JFCOM	U.S. Joint Forces Command
JTF	Joint Task Force

K

K	Thousand (as in dollars)

L

LAN	Local Area Network
LIMFAC	Limiting Factor

M

M	Million (as in dollars)
MAJCOM	Major Command
MPA	Military Personnel Appropriation
MPE	Military Personnel Element

MPF	Military Personnel Flight
MSgt	Master Sergeant
MSM	Meritorious Service Medal

N

NAF	Numbered Air Force
NASA	National Aeronautics and Space Administration
NATO	North Atlantic Treaty Organization
NBC	Nuclear Biological and Chemical
NCO	Non-commissioned officer
NCOA	Non-commissioned Officer Academy
NCOIC	Non-commissioned Officer in Charge
NET	Not Earlier Than
NLT	Not Later Than
NVG	Night Vision Goggles

O

O&M	Operations and Maintenance
OCONUS	Outside Continental United States
OEF	Operation ENDURING FREEDOM
OI	Operational Instruction
OIC	Officer in Charge
OIF	Operation IRAQI FREEDOM
OJT	On-the-Job Training
OPlan	Operations Plan

OPR	Office of Primary Responsibility
OPR	Officer Performance Report
OPSEC	Operations Security
ORE	Operational Readiness Exercise
ORI	Operational Readiness Inspection
OSD	Office of the Secretary of Defense
OSHA	Occupational Safety and Health Administration
OSI	Office of Special Investigations
OTS	Officer Training School

P

PACAF	Pacific Air Forces
PACOM	Pacific Air Command
PCA	Permanent Change of Assignment
PCS	Permanent Change of Station
PIRR	Participating Individual Ready Reservist
PM	Program Manager
PME	Professional Military Education
POC	Professional Officer Course
POC	Point of Contact
POTUS	President of the United States
PRP	Personnel Reliability Program
PT	Physical Training

R

R&D	Research and Development
RAV	Readiness Assistance Visit
RC	Reserve Component
RED HORSE	Rapid Engineering Deployable Heavy Operation Repair Squadron
RMG	Readiness Management Group
RNLTD	Report Not Later Than Date
ROTC	Reserve Officer Training Corps
RPA	Reserve Personnel Appropriation

S

SAF	Air Force Secretariat
SAV	Staff Assistance Visit
SDE	Senior Developmental Education
SEAD	Suppression of Enemy Air Defenses
SECAF	Secretary of the Air Force
SECDEF	Secretary of Defense
SIOP	Single Integrated Operational Plan
SIPRNET	Secret Internet Protocol Router Network
SITREP	Situation Report
SJA	Staff Judge Advocate
SME	Subject Matter Expert
SNCO	Senior Noncommissioned Officer

SNCOA	Senior Noncommissioned Officer Academy
SOP	Standard Operating Procedure
SORTS	Status of Resources and Training System
SOUTHAF	Southern Air Forces
SOS	Squadron Officers School
SQ CC	Squadron Commander
SQ	Squadron
SrA	Senior Airman
SSgt	Staff Sergeant
SSS	Senior Service School
STANDEVAL	Standardization and Evaluation
STEP	Stripes for Exceptional Performers
STRATCOM	US Strategic Command
SWA	Southwest Asia

T

TDY	Temporary Duty
TMO	Traffic Management Office
TR	Traditional Reservist
TRICARE	TRICARE
TSgt	Technical Sergeant

U

UAC	Unit Advisory Council

UAV	Unmanned Aerial Vehicle
UCI	Unit Compliance Inspection
UCMJ	Uniform Code of Military Justice
UE	Unit Equipped
UHF	Ultra High Frequency
UIF	Unfavorable Information File
UMD	Unit Manning Document
UN	United Nations
US	United States
USA	United States Army
USAF	United States Air Force
USAFA	United States Air Force Academy
USAFCENT	United States Air Forces Central Command
USAFE	United States Air Forces in Europe
USAFRES	United States Air Force Reserve
USAFRICOM	United States Africa Command
USCENTCOM	United States Central Command
USEUCOM	United States European Command
USJFCOM	United States Joint Forces Command
USMC	United States Marine Corps
USN	United States Navy
USSOCOM	United States Special Operations Command
USSOUTHAF	United States Air Forces Southern Command
USSOUTHCOM	United States Southern Command
USSPACECOM	United States Space Command
USSTRATCOM	United States Strategic Command
USTRANSCOM	United States Transportation Command
UTA	Unit Training Assembly
UTC	Unit Type Code

V

VA	Veterans Administration
VHF	Very High Frequency
VIP	Very Important Person

W

WAPS	Weighted Airman Promotion System
Wing CC	Wing Commander
WMD	Weapons of Mass Destruction
WRM	War Reserve Materiel

Non-Standard Abbreviations

Ironically, although each Command goes to great lengths to standardize and publish a list of abbreviations that may be used in an EPR without first being defined (see previous section), there is no official guidance on what non-standard abbreviations may be used in the Performance Assessment blocks of the EPR.

Non-standard abbreviations are the shortening of words in order to make a bullet statement fit a line.

Although there is no official list, the following are common "abbreviations" found in accepted EPRs. Although there are no rules and any word may be abbreviated, writers are cautioned to use non-standard abbreviations only when necessary to preserve readability.

This is by no means a complete list. Practically any word used in the body of the EPR may be abbreviated and in a variety of ways.

Air Force	AF
Aircraft	a/c
Aircraft	acft
Available	avail
Building	bldg
Combat	cmbt
Commander	CC
Construction	constr
Contractor	cntr
Coordinated	coord
Drop Zone	DZ

Electronic	elec
Evaluation	eval
First	1st
Flight	flt
Greater than	>
Group	grp
Hours	hrs
Identified	ID'd
Largest	lrgst
Lead	led
Less than	<
Maintenance	maint, mx
Man hours	mhrs
Man hours	man-hrs
Member	mbr
Million	M
Million	mil
Mission	msn
Movement	movmt
National	nat'l
Operations	ops
Patient(s)	pt(s)
Plus	+
Pounds	lbs
Preparation	prep
Program	prgm
Project	proj
Rounds	rnds
Runway	rwy
Squadron	Sqdrn
Squadrons	sqs

Square foot	sqft
Subject Matter Expert	SME
Support	spt
System	sys
Thousand	K
Training	tng, trng
Transfer	xfer
Weather	wx
Wing	wg
With	w/
Without	w/o
Work Order	W/O
Year	yr

Referral EPR

Normally, writing a referral EPR is the last thing a supervisor wants to do. A referral EPR is serious business and is very often the first step in ushering an Airman out of the Air Force. In my experience, referral EPRs are almost always downward directed. What commonly happens is that an Airman becomes involved in an incident that attracts the attention of the Commander or the First Sergeant who order, through the chain of command, that this person be given a referral EPR. It's an uncomfortable and unfamiliar spot for a supervisor to be in. You care about your troop and don't want to see him get in serious trouble yet, as a supervisor, you must enforce standards. It's a tough spot to be in. Ultimately, we have little choice. References are:

AFI 36-2406, Officer and Enlisted Evaluation Systems

AFM 33-326, Preparing Official Communications

A referral EPR is an EPR with at least one of the rated categories graded as Does Not Meet and/or the Overall Performance Assessment in Block 5 is rated as Poor (1) or Needs Improvement (2). An EPR can have an overall 4 rating and still be a referral EPR if one or more of the rated categories is marked as Does Not Meet. It's called a referral because Air Force policy makers decided that a ratee who gets a Does Not Meet rating may not be suited for active duty and should have his or her performance reviewed by senior management. Note that when a person receives a referral report, they are ineligible for promotion testing, PCS, or awards. The official definition of a referral report, per AFI 36-2406, Officer and Enlisted Evaluation Systems is:

3.9.1. Refer a performance report when:

3.9.1.1. An evaluator marks "Does Not Meet Standards" in any performance factor in section V (OPR), or places a mark in the far left block of any performance factor in section III or marks a rating of "1" in section IV (EPR).

3.9.1.2. Comments in the report, or the attachments, are derogatory in nature, imply/refer to behavior incompatible with or not meeting minimum acceptable standards of personal or professional conduct, character, judgment or integrity, and/or refer to disciplinary actions. This includes, but is not limited to, comments regarding omissions or misrepresentation of facts in official statements or documents, financial irresponsibility, mismanagement of personal or government affairs, unsatisfactory progress in the WMP or FIT program, confirmed incidents of discrimination or mistreatment, illegal use or possession of drugs, AWOL, Article 15 action, and conviction by court martial.

In addition to the above reference, MPFM 07-44, paragraph 16, adds the overall rating of 2, Needs Improvement, as being an automatic referral EPR:

16. Definitions of overall EPR performance rating to be used on both AF Form 910 and 911:

a. Poor (1): Performs at an unacceptable level. Disciplinary action is not required, however, the report will be a referral.

b. Needs Improvement (2): Meets some, but not all, performance standards. Disciplinary action is not required, however, the report will be a referral.

For standard EPRs, comments are limited to the space provided on the form but for referrals, attachments may be used. Non-specific or vague comments about the individual's behavior or performance are not allowed. For example, statements such as "Due to a recent off-duty incident, this member's potential is limited" do not explain the behavior or how their potential is limited. The behavior that is considered to be inappropriate must be described. If comments contain references to Article 15 actions or any other punitive actions, the conduct or behavior that led to the action must be specified. For example, a report should not simply state that "SrA Smith received an Article 15 during this period." Instead, the conduct that caused the punishment should be specified with the resulting action included, such as:

- SrA Jones failed to meet standards in push-ups and crunches

- Did not meet body composition requirements, exceeded goals on other fitness components

- During this reporting period, SrA Smith sexually harassed a female coworker for which he received an Article 15

- TSgt Wanda was removed from her position as NCOIC and given a Letter of Reprimand after repeatedly making sexually suggestive and harassing comments to a subordinate

- SSgt Smith received an Article 15 for DUI on base

The focus of the comment should be on the conduct or behavior. It is up to the writer where to place these comments. They are commonly entered in the Standards, Conduct, Character & Military Bearing block. It is not necessary to fill the block with other comments as is done with normal EPRs. The object is to document bad behavior and if that can be accomplished in a single line, that's enough. But the other categories must be filled as usual. They should be filled with factual information. If the ratee has otherwise strong bullets, include them where appropriate. If the overall rating is a 3 or lower, management may require that the tone of the whole EPR reflect this. In this case, a ratee's accomplishments may still be included but adjust their impact.

If you have questions as to whether comments are appropriate, consult the base staff judge advocate and MPF career enhancement personnel. That's their job and they'll be glad to help.

If, after the referral EPR is submitted, the Additional Rater upgrades the ratings (changes to Meets Standards or higher) and/or invalidates the referral comments so that the conditions defined in paragraphs 3.9.1.1. or 3.9.1.2. no longer apply, the non-concur block is marked and comments are made supporting the disagreement in the rating. The report is then no longer considered to be a referral EPR; however, retain original referral correspondence with the report.

Who Refers a Report? An evaluator whose ratings or comments cause an EPR to be a referral report or any evaluator who determines that the report should have been referred, may refer the report to the ratee. In the latter case, the subsequent evaluator refers the report on behalf of the previous evaluator.

Referral EPRs must be shown to the ratee and the ratee must be given an opportunity to rebut the EPR before it becomes a matter of public record.

Procedures

RATER. If the referring evaluator, normally the rater, has written an EPR with ratings that make it a referral EPR, he must prepare a memorandum to accompany it. The memorandum is used to inform the ratee that the attached EPR is a referral EPR and to document acknowledgement and routing. One copy of the memorandum must be provided for each copy of the EPR. After the close-out date of the report, hand-deliver the memo and a copy of the report to the ratee and obtain the ratee's signature and date to acknowledge receipt. The signature only verifies receipt of the memorandum on the date indicated; it does not signify agreement with the report or indicate whether or not the ratee will provide rebuttal remarks. The referral memorandum will instruct the ratee to provide any rebuttal comments to the person who wrote the EPR. Provide a copy of the signed memo to the ratee. The content of the referral memorandum is dictated by AFI 36-2406 and is shown below.

RATEE. The ratee may provide comments about the report to the evaluator named in the memorandum within 10 calendar days or as the evaluator named in the memorandum approves. Additionally, the ratee may ask the MPF career enhancement section to provide guidance in preparing rebuttal comments. The ratee may have another individual prepare comments on his or her behalf (such as an attorney). However, when this is done, the ratee must include a statement confirming the document is to be considered as the ratee's response. This statement may appear somewhere on the rebuttal document or be attached as a separate statement.

NOTE: If the ratee's statement is provided as a separate attachment, it will be considered one of the 10 pages to which the rebuttal is restricted. Rebuttal comments are limited to 10 pages. These may not reflect on the character, conduct, integrity, or motives of an evaluator unless fully substantiated and documented. Any documents or attachments submitted become part of the report filed in the personnel record.

The ratee gives original rebuttal comments and any attachments to the evaluator named in the referral memo no later than 10 calendar days after receipt of the referral memo. The ratee may request more time from the evaluator named in the referral memo.

The ratee may choose not to comment on the referral EPR. Once the time limit has elapsed, the evaluator named in the memorandum completes the report and forwards it up the chain of command. Failure to provide comments does not prevent the ratee from appealing the report in accordance with AFI 36-2401 once the report becomes a matter of record.

RATER. Upon receipt of the ratee's rebuttal, or when 10 days have elapsed, the evaluator completes the report. The Evaluator considers the ratee's comments, if provided, and prepares an endorsement to the report stating "*I have carefully considered* (ratee's name) *comments to the referral memo of* (date)." If comments were not received within 10 calendar days, endorse the report with the statement

"*Comments from the ratee were requested but were not received within the required period.*" and then forward the report to the next evaluator.

If the ratee chooses not to provide a rebuttal at the time of receipt, the evaluator endorses the report with the statement "*Ratee elected not to provide comments to the referral memo of* (date)". The referring evaluator then forwards the original report and referral memorandum to the next higher evaluator for appropriate action.

Rater's Rater. The next higher evaluator then forwards the report to the Commander's staff. The commander completes the review and may comment on the report, using an AF Form 77. However, the additional rater or the reviewer, as applicable, is the individual named in the referral memorandum and will review the ratee's comments. If the commander is normally the next evaluator on the report (i.e., the additional rater or reviewer), place comments in the appropriate section of the EPR and only use an AF Form 77 if additional space is needed.

Referral Memorandum

MEMORANDUM FOR (NAME OF INDIVIDUAL)
(Ratee's functional address)
FROM: Unit/OFFICE SYMBOL
SUBJECT: Referral Enlisted Performance Report

1. I am referring the attached Enlisted Performance Report to you in accordance with AFI 36-2406, Military Performance Evaluations, paragraph 3.9. It contains comments and ratings that make the report a referral as defined in AFI 36-2406, paragraph 3.9. Specifically, my ratings of Does Not Meet Standards and comments in section III, items 2 and 6 pertaining to your failure to meet and enforce both weight and dress and appearance standards in yourself and your subordinates, causes this report to be referred.

2. Acknowledge receipt of this correspondence by signing and dating in reproducible ink. Your signature on this memo merely acknowledges that a referral report has been rendered; it does not imply acceptance of or agreement with the ratings or comments on the report. Once signed, you are entitled to a copy of this memo. You may submit comments to rebut the report. Send your comments to (*name and functional address/office symbol of next evaluator*) not later than 10 calendar days from the date you receive this memo. If you need additional time, you may request an extension from the individual named above. You may submit attachments (limited to 10 pages), but they must directly relate to the reason the report was referred. Pertinent attachments not maintained elsewhere will remain attached to the report for file in your personnel record. Copies of previous reports, etc., submitted as attachments, will be removed from your rebuttal package prior to filing the referral report since these documents are already filed in your records. Your rebuttal comments and any attachments may not contain any reflection on the character, conduct, integrity, or motives of the evaluator unless you fully substantiate and document them. Contact the MPF career enhancement section if you require any assistance in preparing your reply to the referral report.

3. It is important for you to be aware that receiving a referral report may affect your eligibility for other personnel related actions (i.e. assignments, promotion, etc.). I Recommend you consult your first sergeant, commander and/or MPF if you desire more information on this subject. If you believe this report is inaccurate, unjust, or unfairly prejudicial to

your career, you may apply for a review of the report under AFI 36-2401, Correction of Officer and Enlisted Evaluation Reports, once the report becomes a matter of record as defined in AFI 36-2406, Attachment 1.

Signature of referring evaluator (the rater)
Charles S. Beenadict, SSgt, USAF
Flight Simulator Shift Supervisor

Attachment:
AF Form 910 (or 77 or 911, as appropriate)closing 31 Jan 09
  (closing date of EPR)

CC: MSgt Smithers (Name of Next Evaluator/Additional
  Rater)

1st Ind, Dennis L. Franko, SrA (Ratee's Name and Rank)

MEMORANDUM FOR: Lawrence J. Smithers, MSgt (Name
and Functional address of next evaluator)
1977CDG/SCMM

Receipt acknowledged at _____ (time), on
_____ (date).

(RATEE'S SIGNATURE)_____

Dennis L. Franko, SrA, USAF
123-45-6789 (SSN of ratee)

Referral EPR Rebuttal

When someone receives a referral EPR, it makes that person ineligible for promotion testing, PCS, and awards. In short, it puts a real damper on a person's career. Of course, they are not fatal. They can be overcome but it takes hard work and time. It's better not to receive one at all. When an Airman receives a referral EPR, it's his right to respond with a rebuttal challenging the referral EPR. Because of its serious effects, unless undeniably deserved, a rebuttal should be submitted.

This is no time for fooling around or making a half-hearted gesture. Referral EPRs are serious business and you don't want one. The first step in rebutting a referral EPR is to identify exactly what is being described as substandard behavior. If it's a single incident which caused one Performance Assessment block to be marked to the far left (Does Not Meet), focus on countering that assertion. Approach it from every angle you can think of. Compare your actions with the actions of your peers. Did they receive a similar rating for similar conduct? If not, you might have a good basis for a rebuttal. Don't be shy in pointing this fact out. This is your career on the line and it's not only your right to defend yourself, it's your obligation.

Keep in mind that the people who will receive, read, and judge your rebuttal are the same people who want to give you a referral EPR in the first place. So the tone of your rebuttal should not be antagonistic. It should present facts in a logical order which lead to the conclusion that a particular rating is not justified. And if the low rating is no longer justified, the report ceases to be a referral EPR.

Rebuttal comments, including any attachments, are limited to a total of 10 pages. Submitted comments can't describe the character, conduct, integrity, or motives of a rater/ evaluator unless fully substantiated and documented. All attachments become part of the report filed in the personnel record.

Referral EPR Rebuttal Example

MEMO FOR 1922nd CS/CCF

SUBJECT: Rebuttal to Referral EPR, SrA John Wayne, dated 19 Sep 08

To whom it may concern,

I am writing in response to a referral EPR I received on 20 Sep 08. I strongly disagree with the rating of Does Not Meet in the Training Requirements Performance Assessment block of my EPR. I understand that I received this rating because I failed my CDC End of Course test but there are extenuating circumstances that my supervisors may not be aware of. I believe that when these circumstances are explained, their perception of my performance and, by extension, my rating, will change.

Although I didn't pass the End of Course test, I only missed the passing grade of 65 by 3 points. This was despite taking the test 6 months after I finished my last CDC volume. I finished my last CDC volume in Feb 08 but my supervisor didn't schedule me to take the test until Aug 08. By then I had forgotten much of what I had previously learned. In addition, 5 days before I was scheduled to take the test, I was moved from mid-shift to day shift. It takes time for the body to readjust to a new schedule and I was unable to get a full night's sleep the entire week before the test. I did not have adequate rest and that contributed to my failure.

In addition, although a CDC End of Course test failure might suggest a failure to prepare or a lack of motivation, my performance at work indicates I continually make satisfactory progress in my training requirements and in my work. I finished every CDC volume either ahead of schedule or on time. I am over 75% qualified on our work center tasks which is well ahead of schedule. I was recognized as maintainer of the quarter earlier this year.

I feel that the Training Requirements category refers not only to an Airman's test scores but to his efforts and training progress as well which, as shown above, have been exemplary. For that reason, I request that the decision to rate my performance as Does Not Meet be reconsidered based on the information above. I sincerely appreciate your consideration.

Respectfully,
SrA John Wayne, USAF

Performance Feedback

Performance feedback is a private counseling session between the supervisor and the ratee during which the supervisor explains what is expected regarding duty performance and how well the ratee is meeting those expectations.

The forms used for initial and periodic feedbacks are AF Form 931 for AB through TSgt and AF Form 932 for MSgt and above.

The Performance Feedback Worksheet may be handwritten or typed by the rater. The completed form should outline the issues discussed during the feedback session. Due to the amount of writing it would require to record everything discussed during the session, it is not practical to record every word or topic discussed. However, every attempt should be made to capture key concerns. Later, if the subject receives a rating that is less than expected, he or she may claim that the issue affecting the rating wasn't discussed during periodic feedbacks and therefore not fair. Ratees must understand that, omission of an issue from the form does not, by itself, constitute proof that the issue was not discussed.

Section II, Types of Feedback. In the appropriate box, indicate whether the feedback is initial, midterm, ratee requested or rater directed.

Section III, Primary Duties. The rater lists the ratee's specific duties. These entries include the most important duties and correspond to the job description used in the EPR.

Section IV, Performance Feedback. The rater addresses the same categories of performance as listed in the Enlisted Performance Report. The feedback form lists a rating scale for each category of performance and the rater marks the appropriate box for each area. If a particular topic is not applicable, the rater marks the "N/A Initial Feedback" block. If the feedback session is the initial one, raters are not required to assign a rating to any area but must outline their expectations.

Section V, Strengths, Suggested Goals, and Additional Comments. Use this section to provide insight and guidance, gained from the rater's experience, that might help the ratee progress in their career. There is no minimum amount of writing required but an honest effort to provide meaningful feedback should be attempted.

Initial Feedback Examples

Primary Duties

- Receives and prioritizes requests for maintenance, coordinates scheduled and unscheduled service

- Maintains tools and references necessary for immediate, accurate, and dependable repair of aircraft

- Analyzes and repairs reported instrument malfunctions or failures

- Supervises, instructs 4 Airmen in operations and maintenance of non-alert aircraft

Primary/Additional Duties

- Timeliness is important. All members must be present 15 minutes prior to shift change to allow time for briefing.

- All shift workers are expected to be 100% qualified in one year.

- Follow instructions, always have safety observer when appropriate, and always use T.O.--Safety first!

- Attending school during duty hours is acceptable but only after shift-qualification.

- CDCs and shop qualification are primary goals

- no participation in extracurricular events such as Honor Guard until 50% qualified

- make sure adequate clothing and equipment on hand for self and subordinates

- be aware of safety hazards --battery room, generators, fuel storage areas

- all members must work shifts and maintain shift qualification

Standards, Conduct, Character & Military Bearing

- lead by example, Airmen are watching you

- maintain clean and serviceable uniforms, set the example

- although exceptions are acceptable, breakfast and ironing uniforms should be done at home not at work

- watch conduct off-duty; incidents can cause loss of security clearance and affect career

- make effort to include all Airmen in opportunities for advancement

- demonstrate to subordinates, by example, proper way to accomplish goals-no short cuts

Fitness

- must participate in all squadron runs/events unless on shift-work or on day off

- expect self-discipline, it's up to you to make sure you maintain fitness standards

- failure to meet fitness standards will immediately affect career and opportunities

- recommend workcenter work out together to ensure participation and progress

- up to one hour, three times a week allowed for PT

Training Requirements

- 100% qualification expected in one year, progress will be evaluated in 3 and 6 months

- everyone is expected to watch their own ancillary training and keep it current

- off-duty education is encouraged, check with supervisor before committing to schedule

- ask for help if needed, if necessary, more instruction can be provided

- CDC failures are serious and may result in discharge

- recommend volunteering for one of the section's additional duties

Teamwork/Followership

- be considerate of all team members, show respect to senior NCOs, support the squadron when able

- report disagreements or problems to supervisor first so we can work them out before they affect work

- you are responsible for members of your shift, ensure their training is up to date

- don't be an information hoarder, if learn how to perform a task, share with your coworkers

- due to manning, no schedule changes or leaves without coordination with supervisor

- if not receiving adequate training, let supervisor know

- we are pulling for you and want you to be successful

- we are a team, work is not a competition, goal is quality not quantity

- identify safety hazards encountered to supervisor

- follow the direction of shift supervisor, read all workcenter OIs and policies

- your contributions and ideas are welcome; we're all working in the same direction

- if see a better way to do something, point it out--fresh view notices things we might not

Other Comments

- welcome to the shop--staff is here to support you

- Squadron quarterly award program recognizes effort, recognition helps justify EPR rating

- workcenter participates in quarterly and annual award program and AF-level Security Forces award

- make sure enroll in Senior NCO Academy correspondence course and complete by time limit

- Commander and First Sergeant have an open door policy, use discretion

- safety is paramount --safety first!

- EPRs are competitive...ratees are compared against peers

- participation in squadron functions, charities such as Habitat for Humanity, Meals on Wheels encouraged

- base agencies and opportunities for spouse include Family Advocacy Program

- if have spare time, areas that need someone to study, manage, and improve are maint documentation & ACS

- squadron periodically has need for someone to manage sq level duties (Report of Survey, etc), if interested, speak up

Periodic Feedback Examples

The Initial feedback explained the Air Force and workcenter rules and expectations to the new ratee. The mid-term/periodic feedback documents how well the ratee met those expectations. The mid-term evaluation is more subjective than the initial and the ratings will vary depending on the rater. The ratings marked are normally considered to be the ratings the ratee can expect on their EPR unless behavior changes in the interim.

The Performance Feedback Worksheet may be handwritten or typed by the rater. The completed form should outline the issues discussed during the initial feedback session.

Note that because of the amount of writing it would take to record everything discussed during the session, it is not practical to record every topic discussed. However, every attempt should be made to capture key concerns. Later, if the subject receives an EPR rating that is less than expected, he or she may claim that the issue affecting the rating wasn't discussed during periodic feedbacks and therefore not fair. Ratees must understand that, omission of an issue from the form does not, by itself, constitute proof that the issue was not discussed or provide grounds for contesting a rating.

Primary/Additional Duties

- Timeliness has improved, always dependable, good example to peers

- qualification rate is good--keep up the good work. Concentrate on critical workcenter tasks

- always check log at beginning of shift, our efficiency depends on communications across shifts

- have shown enthusiasm and provided outstanding support to team--continue to progress, always remember safety

- most Airmen finished CDCs by 6 months, focus on completion, 1 year max allowed

- performance in primary duties is satisfactory, cut back on Honor Guard events to pull ahead of peers

- increase effort to keep accurate inventory of tools and equipment; losses may be charged to supervisor

- remind Airmen of safety hazards --two incidents in last year

- thanks for filling in when workers were DNIF --will try to compensate for overtime

- this is your shop, if see room for improvement, something that needs to be done, do it --set example for team

Standards, Conduct, Character & Military Bearing

- good job mentoring shift workers--continue to lead by example

- uniforms are perfect...encourage subordinates to emulate your example

- workcenter discipline is good balance of standards and morale; has helped efficiency

- don't encourage disrespect by ignoring incidents; correct improper actions on the spot

- conduct off-duty still important; one incident can ruin a year's progress, caution subordinates

- all airmen under your tutelage have shown healthy attitude and progress--keep it up

- everyone on shift must be on time, more than twice late should result in written counseling

- cannot tolerate disrespect toward NCOs--if have problem, see me or other NCOs or First Sergeant if necessary

- subordinates copy your example, look to you for guidance, must display behavior above reproach

- am counting on you to discipline troops who don't meet standards; their failure is your failure

Fitness

- must make effort to participate in squadron runs, won't affect fitness score

- shop scores are on par with squadron, is good but we can do better

- encourage subordinates to participate in fitness routine

- failure to maintain fitness standards will immediately affect career and opportunities

- base has several free fitness alternatives -check gym for available programs

- recommend participation in workcenter/squadron PT to demonstrate compliance with program

- personnel working shifts are excused from participating in regular squadron PT but won't be exempt from test -prepare!

- up to one hour, three times a week allowed for PT

Training Requirements

- qualification is on schedule, focus on critical tasks

- qualification rate is best in workcenter, exceeded standards

- redouble efforts on ancillary training --workcenter is lagging

- congratulations on successful class, self-improvement coupled with best training records in shop earn top spot

- training NCO and supervisor continue to be available at your convenience if needed

- if fail CDC test again, may be discharged; don't risk career, ask for help if need it

- above average CDC score --way to start your career -now focus on task certification

- your work as Sq Report of Survey monitor cut process time in half; excellent squadron support

- is difficult to justify 5 EPR without evidence of progression or attempts to increase qualification

- if not 100% qualified after one year, have not exceeded standards and so do not meet requirements for 5 rating

Teamwork/Followership

- count to ten and think about what is said before responding; disrespect can snowball into big problems

- if unable to see eye to eye with rater, see me for help; don't let problems fester

- training for shift workers has not improved, may be worse; must concentrate on this weak area now

- appreciate your management of the schedule, a thankless job, but cannot allow illegal leaves

- we are on your side and only make suggestions that are in your best interest

- you are a good fit for our team and get along well with staff, keep up the good work, use influence with peers

- no problems noted with following instructions but try to show more initiative, it's your shop too

- your contributions and ideas have benefited the site; thanks for your sincere efforts

- share knowledge with subordinates, prepare them to take over your position

- qualification rate for shift members must improve before end of year or cannot support 5 rating

Other Comments

- participation in sq events will help in recommendation for quarterly awards, awards help justify EPR rating

- participation in squadron functions, charities such as Habitat for Humanity, Meals on Wheels encouraged

- flexible and versatile leaders are needed to maintain supportive and nurturing environment

- my go to NCO for document planning; outstanding tech with exceptional knowledge, share with subordinates

- support NCOIC and his decisions, help maintain positive morale

- lead by example, junior members are watching, have more influence than realize

- if interested in schools, seminars, let staff know

- demonstrate confidence--you are in charge of maintenance and must inspire belief in reaching goals

- remember: base agencies and opportunities for spouse include Family Advocacy Program, etc

The Letter of Counseling (LOC)

We know how to recognize good behavior. We write solid EPRs, express our gratitude in Letters of Appreciation, or submit deserving members for medals. But how do we deal with bad behavior? What instruments are available for counseling Airmen and correcting improper behavior? There are a range of options available from verbal counseling at the lower end of the spectrum to administrative discharge. In general, most of us only have to deal with those options appropriate for correcting behavior at the work center level. Those options, in order of rising level of seriousness are:

- Verbal Counseling
- Letter of Counseling (LOC)
- Letter of Admonition (LOA)
- Letter of Reprimand (LOR)

Verbal counseling, LOCs, LOAs, and LORs at the work center level are a form of correction appropriate for correcting habits or shortcomings which are not necessarily criminal or illegal, but which can ultimately affect job performance, work center morale, and discipline. Any supervisor can issue Letters of Counseling, Admonition, and Reprimand for conduct both on and off-duty. More serious offenses should be referred to the First Sergeant. The reference that specifies the rules surrounding administrative counseling is AFI 36-2907, Unfavorable Information File (UIF) Program. See Chapter 3, Administrative Counselings, Admonitions, and Reprimands.

Verbal Counseling

The lowest level corrective tool is verbal counseling. This is the unscheduled spoken guidance that supervisors provide every day such as, "You need a haircut" or "Your boots need shining". This type of counseling is normally not formally recorded unless the supervisor finds that the Airman failed to follow his or her direction.

If the offending Airman failed to follow the supervisor's spoken guidance, the next step would be either a formal Letter of Counseling or another verbal counseling depending on how patient the supervisor is. If the supervisor chooses to give the Airman a second verbal counseling, this time it would normally be documented in a Memo For Record.

A Memo For Record is merely an informal record or note to remind the supervisor that he spoke to the Airman about a certain topic on a specific date. It's only for the supervisor's use and the offender doesn't have to sign it. Normally the offender doesn't even know it exists. That gives the Airman two chances to clean up his act. It also provides evidence of the person's offensive behavior if needed to justify more serious action.

If the Airman still doesn't correct his or her behavior after being verbally counseled, it's the supervisor's responsibility to the work center to write a formal Letter of Counseling. Note that there is no requirement to verbally counsel an Airman before writing an LOC. It's up to the individual's supervisor.

Letter of Counseling (LOC)

A Letter of Counseling is merely the recording of an infraction. It's written by the supervisor and is a method of describing unacceptable behavior in a way that the receiver cannot fail to understand. Often, Airmen don't realize or understand the seriousness of their behavior. A formal letter of counseling is a way to get their attention and let them know their behavior is not acceptable and explain the possible consequences. The offender is required to sign the Letter of Counseling indicating that he or she was counseled and is aware of the situation. Signing the LOC not only certifies the counseling took place, it also protects the subject. If the subject's signature wasn't required, supervisors could be sending these documents to the squadron every day without the subject's knowledge.

In the grand scheme of things, a Letter of Counseling might seem to some people to be no more significant than pencil shavings but it marks the beginning of the transition of the attempt to correct bad behavior from the work center, where a troop has friends and supervisors who care for him, to the squadron, where things get more serious and impersonal.

Some supervisors build in another level of correction; although they actually write the LOC and have the person being counseled sign it, they don't send the LOC to the Squadron. No one knows about it but the supervisor and the offender. But it's there, lying in the supervisor's desk drawer like a coiled snake ready to strike if disturbed. If the offender again refuses to change his or her behavior, then the

LOC (and the MFR if one was written) is forwarded to "the squadron".

When an LOC (or similar paperwork) is forwarded to the Squadron, it is understood that the supervisor recommends that the commander file it in the troop's Unfavorable Information File (UIF).

A formal Letter of Counseling is normally recorded on an AF Form 174, Record of Individual Counseling. It provides a record of counseling and is useful for supporting more serious corrective action if needed. It may also be used as a reference when completing performance evaluations. If you don't have an AF Form 174 on hand, the counseling may be recorded on plain bond paper or squadron letterhead. The format isn't as important as the documenting of improper behavior.

Letter of Admonition (LOA)

A Letter of Admonition is more severe than a LOC. It's used to document clear violations of standards. While a Letter of Counseling is used to explain standards and reconcile behavior, the Letter of Admonition is used to document intentional disregard for established rules of conduct. A Letter of Admonition is normally issued after an LOC has been written and objectionable behavior has continued. Like the Letter of Counseling, the offender must sign the letter indicating awareness of the supervisor's direction.

Letter of Reprimand (LOR)

A Letter of Reprimand is more severe than a Letter of Admonition (LOA). It's also used to document clear violations of standard and is used for more serious offenses. It may also be issued when other, less severe methods, such as a Letter of Counseling or Letter of Admonition have failed to correct behavior.

LOC Format

A formal Letter of Counseling is normally recorded on an AF Form 174, Record of Individual Counseling, but if you don't have an AF Form 174 on hand, the counseling may be recorded on plain bond paper or squadron letterhead. If using bond paper or letterhead, the format is the same for Letters of Counseling, Letters of Admonishment, and Letters of Reprimand. The only difference is the subject line. See the example below. When writing a Letter of Counseling, the following information should be included:

- What the member did or failed to do and the associated dates

- What improvement is expected

- That continued violations of standards will result in more severe action

- That the individual has 3 duty days to submit rebuttal documents to the initiator. When calculating the response due date, the date of receipt is not counted, and if the individual mails their acknowledgment, the date of the postmark on the envelope will serve as the date of acknowledgment

- That the person who initiates the LOC, LOA, or LOR has 3 duty days to advise the individual of their final decision regarding any comments submitted by the individual

- That all supporting documents received from the individual will become part of the record

- The document must include a Privacy Act statement. Written administrative counseling, admonitions, and reprimands are subject to the rules of access and protection as outlined in The Privacy Act of 1974. The same rules apply to any copies kept by supervisors or in the individual's UIF or Personnel Information File (PIF).

The format isn't as important as the documenting of improper behavior. Although failure to include all the information required above could technically prevent the use of the document as support for further, more severe actions, I have never seen a document disallowed because of it. In real life, supervisors with enough balls to recognize, correct, and document bad behavior are relatively rare. Most of us tend to look the other way as long as possible. We don't want to write up our "friends" or subordinates. We often force our Senior NCOs to assume more responsibility for managing or disciplining our troops than we should. So, on those rare occasions when a supervisor does meet his or her management responsibility, their actions, even if poorly documented, will generally be welcomed and supported by the First Sergeant and the CSS. The important thing is your signature as a supervisor and your willingness to live up to your responsibilities as a supervisor.

Letter of Counseling Format (Bond Paper/Letterhead)

MEMORANDUM FOR (NAME OF INDIVIDUAL)

FROM: Unit/OFFICE SYMBOL

SUBJECT: Letter of Counseling (or Admonishment or Reprimand)

1. It has come to my attention that on (date here), (insert the offense here and include as much detail as possible).

2. In the Air Force, failure to go (or other offense) is a crime. Many Airmen have been given Article 15s or court-martialed for similar misconduct. This work center, this squadron, and indeed, the entire Air Force cannot function when its members become undependable. You have proven that you cannot be depended upon, and consequently, you have damaged this unit's mission capability. I expect you to work diligently at redeeming yourself and proving that you can be relied upon in the future. This behavior will not be tolerated. If conduct of this type is continued, more severe administrative action will be taken, not limited to Article 15.

3. PRIVACY ACT STATEMENT. AUTHORITY: 10 U.S.C. 8013. PURPOSE: To obtain any comments or documents

you desire to submit for consideration concerning this action. ROUTINE USE: Provides you an opportunity to submit comments or documents for consideration. If provided, the comments or documents you submit become a part of the action. DISCLOSURE: Your written acknowledgment or receipt and signature are mandatory. Any other comments or documents you provide are voluntary.

4. You will indicate receipt and understanding of this letter in the space below. You have 3 duty days in which to provide a response if you choose. A response is not required.

SUPERVISORS NAME, RANK, USAF
Supervisor

1st Ind, Name of Individual

TO: Unit/Office Symbol

Receipt acknowledged at _____hours, on _____2010.

I understand that I may submit a response within three duty days.

_____

Name of Individual, RANK, USAF

Letter of Counseling Format (AF Form 174)

Reason For Counseling: FAILURE TO OBEY

Block 9. SUMMARY OF COUNSELING

During the ORI on 31 Oct 09, at shift change, you were told by TSgt Smith that we would comply with MOPP 4 requirements at Bravo Site whether anyone came out to inspect us or not and you acknowledged his direction. Early on 1 Nov 09 we went into Alarm Blue while we were at S-24 and you failed to comply with MOPP 4 requirements. You have violated Article 92 (failure to obey).

AFMAN 10-100 Airman's Manual and the Osan Air Base ATSO Guide exist as standards to be complied with. Members of the Air Force, regardless of rank, must meet standards of performance and regulations at all times. Your actions have brought discredit upon yourself and the United States Air Force. Your actions require me, as well as your section supervisor, to seriously question your integrity and capability as a Munitions Storage Crew Member. I will not tolerate this type of behavior from a member of the Munitions Storage Section. Further violations of standards will result in more serious administrative action.

Block 10. RECOMMENDATIONS AND ADVICE OF COUNSELOR

I recommend that you realize the seriousness of your actions and their consequences and follow instructions and adhere to the Air Force Core Value, "Integrity First". This means to do what is right even when no one is looking. Examine your career objectives and determine which course of action you will follow. You will acknowledge receipt of this letter by signing in the designated block. You have 3 duty days in which to submit any information in rebuttal to these charges.

Privacy Act statement: AUTHORITY: 10 U.S.C. 8013. PURPOSE: To obtain any comments you desire to submit (on a voluntary basis) for consideration concerning this action. ROUTINE USES: Provides you an opportunity to submit comments or documents for consideration. If provided, the comments and documents you submit become a part of the action. DISCLOSURE: Your written acknowledgment of receipt and signature are mandatory. Any other comment or document you provide is voluntary.

Block 14. SUMMARY OF COUNSELEE'S COMMENTS

I acknowledge receipt of this communication on 10 Nov 09. I do / do not intend to submit information in rebuttal to these charges. I understand I have 3 duty days in which to submit my rebuttal.

The Privacy Act Statement

The Privacy Act of 1974, Title 5 U.S.C. § 552a, establishes a code of fair information practice that governs the collection, maintenance, use, and dissemination of personally identifiable information about individuals that is maintained in systems of records by federal agencies. A system of records is a group of records under the control of an agency from which information is retrieved by the name of the individual or by some identifier assigned to the individual. The Privacy Act prohibits the disclosure of information from a system of records absent the written consent of the subject individual, unless the disclosure is pursuant to one of twelve statutory exceptions. The Act also provides individuals with a means by which to seek access to and amendment of their records (Freedom of Information Act), and sets forth various agency record-keeping requirements.

When To Give Privacy Act Statements. Give a PAS orally or in writing to the subject of the record when you are collecting information from them that will go in a system of records. NOTE: Do this regardless of how you collect or record the answers. You may display a sign in areas where people routinely furnish this kind of information. Give a copy of the Privacy Act Statement if asked. Do not ask the person to sign the Privacy Act Statement. (Ref AFI 33-332 Para 3.3)

Per AFI 33-332, Privacy Act Program, Para 3.2.1, A Privacy Act Statement must include four items:

- **Authority:** The legal authority, that is, the U.S.C. or Executive Order authorizing the program the system supports.

- **Purpose:** The reason you are collecting the information and what you intend to do with it.

- **Routine Uses:** A list of where and why the information will be disclosed outside DOD.

- **Disclosure:** Voluntary or Mandatory. (Use Mandatory only when disclosure is required by law and the individual will be penalized for not providing information.) Include any consequences of nondisclosure in nonthreatening language

Authority

Title 10, U.S.C., Section 8013. IAW AFI 36-2608, Military Personnel Records System, Para 4.1, the files in a PIF (Personal Information File) are maintained and kept under authority of Title 10, U.S.C., Section 8013, and solely by offices or levels of command where there is a requirement for them in the performance of day-to-day business. PIFs must be set up using the AF Form 10A, kept up to date, correct in content, and safeguarded to ensure the PIF is not misused or that unauthorized access occurs.

Title 10, U.S.C., Section 8013. IAW AFI 36-2907, Unfavorable Information file Program, title page, "This instruction requires you to maintain information protected by the Privacy Act of 1974. The authority to maintain this information is Title 10, U.S.C., Section 8013. System of Records Notice FO35 AF MP L, Unfavorable Information Files (UIF), also applies."

References:

AFI 33-332 Privacy Act Program

AFI 36-2608 Military Personnel Records System

Letter of Counseling Examples

Using AF Form 174

Reason For Counseling: FAILURE TO OBEY
Block 9. SUMMARY OF COUNSELING

During the ORI on 31 May 07, at shift change, you were told by SSgt Smith that we would comply with MOPP 4 requirements at Bravo Site whether anyone came out to inspect us or not and you acknowledged his direction. Early on 1 June 07 we went into Alarm Blue while we were at S-24 and you failed to comply with MOPP 4 requirements. You have violated Article 92 (failure to obey).

AFMAN 10-100 Airman's Manual and the Osan Air Base ATSO Guide exist as standards to be complied with. Members of the Air Force, regardless of rank, must meet standards of performance and regulations every day. Your actions have brought discredit upon yourself and the United States Air Force. Your actions require me, as well as your section supervisor, to seriously question your integrity and capability as a Munitions Storage Crew Member. I will not tolerate this type of behavior from a member of the Munitions Storage Section. Further violations of standards will result in administrative action.

Block 10. RECOMMENDATIONS AND ADVICE OF COUNSELOR

I recommend that you realize the seriousness of your actions and their consequences and follow instructions and adhere to the Air Force Core Value, "Integrity First". This means to do what is right even when no one is looking. Examine your career objectives and determine which course of action you will follow. You will acknowledge receipt of this letter by signing in the designated block. You have 3 duty days in which to submit any information in rebuttal to these charges.

Privacy Act statement: AUTHORITY: 10 U.S.C. 8013. PURPOSE: To obtain any comments you desire to submit (on a voluntary basis) for consideration concerning this action. ROUTINE USES: Provides you an opportunity to submit comments or documents for consideration. If provided, the comments and documents you submit become a part of the action. DISCLOSURE: Your written acknowledgment of receipt and signature are mandatory. Any other comment or document you provide is voluntary.

Block 14. SUMMARY OF COUNSELEE'S COMMENTS

I acknowledge receipt of this communication on 10 June 07. I do / do not intend to submit information in rebuttal to these charges. I understand I have 3 duty days in which to submit my rebuttal.

Reason For Counseling: FAILURE TO COMPLY
Block 9. SUMMARY OF COUNSELING

During the ORI, on the morning of 11 Jun 08, you drove to and from Charlie Site at an excessive speed and then continued to run two red lights on the way back to Osan Air Base. You failed to follow simple but critical traffic rules and have shown total disregard for the safety of others and for the property you have been entrusted with. Your actions have broken Article 92 (failure to obey).

USFK Pam 385-2 Guide to Safe Driving in Korea is a regulation that must be followed. We are guests in this country and ambassadors of American culture. Your actions have not only embarrassed you, but also your unit and the United States Air Force. Your conduct requires me as well as your section supervisor to seriously question your integrity as a Munitions Storage Crew Member. This type of behavior from a member of the Munitions Storage Section will not be tolerated.

Block 10. RECOMMENDATIONS AND ADVICE OF COUNSELOR

I recommend that you comply with regulations and set a positive example for others. Review your career objectives and understand how your actions can influence your future. You will acknowledge receipt of this letter by affixing your signature in the designated block. You are advised you have 3 duty days in which to submit any information in rebuttal to these charges.

Privacy Act statement: AUTHORITY: 10 USC 8013. PURPOSE: To obtain any comments or documents you desire to submit (on a voluntary basis) for consideration concerning this action. ROUTINE USES: Provides you an opportunity to submit comments and documents for consideration. If provided, the comments and documents you submit become a part of the action. DISCLOSURE: Your written acknowledgement of receipt and signature are mandatory. Any comment or document you provide is voluntary.

Block 14. SUMMARY OF COUNSELEE'S COMMENTS

I acknowledge receipt of this communication on 20 June 08. I do / do not intend to submit information in rebuttal of these charges. I understand I have 3 duty days in which to submit my rebuttal.

Reason For Counseling: Failure to Obey Order or Regulation

Block 9. SUMMARY OF COUNSELING

Investigation has disclosed that you were disrespectful to SSgt Jones, your supervisor, by refusing to follow her directions, saying "kiss my ass" or something similar, and walking away while she was talking to you. This incident occurred around 0700 on 12 July 2009 at the POL main work center.

Block 10. RECOMMENDATIONS AND ADVICE OF COUNSELOR

You are hereby counseled that such behavior is not acceptable. I will not tolerate disrespect from anyone in this organization toward any of their supervisors. Your disrespect and failure to recognize authority has been detrimental to unit morale and the discipline of this organization. You must not repeat such conduct. If you do, it will be answered with more serious consequences. You will acknowledge receipt of this letter by signing in the designated block. You are advised you have 3 duty days in which to submit any information in rebuttal to these charges.

Privacy Act statement: AUTHORITY: 10 U.S.C. 8013. PURPOSE: To obtain any comments you desire to submit (on a voluntary basis) for consideration concerning this action. ROUTINE USES: Provides you an opportunity to submit comments or documents for consideration. If provided, the comments and documents you submit become a part of the action. DISCLOSURE: Your written acknowledgment of receipt and signature are mandatory. Any other comment or document you provide is voluntary.

Block 14. SUMMARY OF COUNSELEE'S COMMENTS

I acknowledge receipt of this Letter of Counseling on 13 July 09. I do / do not intend to submit information in rebuttal of the facts presented here. I understand I have 3 duty days in which to submit my rebuttal.

How to Present an LOC

Infractions should be addressed as soon as possible to help the offender realize that his actions are serious and objectionable. If conduct doesn't improve, the matter can then be escalated to higher levels of authority.

The goal of presenting a Letter of Counseling is communication. Sometimes we just don't express ourselves clearly, there are misunderstandings, and we don't quite see eye to eye. The Letter of Counseling is intended to clear up any confusion and to improve or correct behavior. The intent is *not* to aggravate what may already be a tense situation by causing embarrassment. A Letter of Counseling should be delivered in private with only the offender and the supervisor present. The supervisor should explain the behavior that led up to the requirement to formally document it and then allow the offender to read the LOC. The offender is then required to sign the document indicating he has read and understood the contents. Signing an LOC is not an admission of guilt. It merely indicates that the subject of the LOC acknowledges that he was spoken to about the behavior described in the letter.

Presenting an LOC can be awkward whether you're a new supervisor or a 20 year veteran. It helps to think of the process as an impersonal task that must be carried out in the best interest of the counselee and the work center.

Before presenting the LOC, reexamine the circumstances and make sure you have a valid reason for issuing an LOC. Because if you don't have a valid reason for documenting substandard behavior, the counselee will often protest to the Commander or First Sergeant and force you to withdraw the LOC which would make you look kind of silly and the atmosphere in the work center even worse than before. If you're not sure if an LOC is deserved or supportable, ask your supervisor, NCOIC, or First Sergeant for advice. It's common to be so close to a situation that you can't be sure if you're biased or not.

When delivering an LOC, don't tell the person being counseled that you wrote the LOC because the NCOIC told you to or because the other NCOs in the shop demanded it. You have to take responsibility for your actions. If you say you're doing it because someone made you, it makes you look powerless and makes it appear to the counselee that you don't agree with the documentation. And if you don't agree with the documentation, that implies his behavior wasn't really objectionable and that the LOC is more a result of office politics than bad behavior. This will give the counselee the idea that he can challenge the LOC and make you withdraw it. So maintain a united front by presenting the LOC as if it's your idea. You don't have to actually state that it's your idea but do not ever say you're presenting it because someone else told you to or that you don't agree with it.

If you truly don't agree, avoid mentioning that fact to the person being counseled. The way I do it is to politely ask the person to come to my office or some private area and then, when inside, I say something like, "I don't know if you're aware of this but there has been an issue with...". Explain that you're not taking sides, but that it's your duty, because of your rank or position, to document work center issues and facilitate a solution. Allow him or her to give you their side of the story and listen. Most people, if they're reasonable, will understand your position and cooperate. Make sure that, if you take this approach, that you're sincere and that you look out for the counselee's interest by also fully explaining the negative results of further, similar behavior.

If the offender refuses to acknowledge receipt by signing the letter, then the person who presented the letter should write, "member refused to sign" on the letter and then sign and date it. Do not end the counseling session yet. While the subject waits, get a witness to join you in the room. The supervisor who presented the document should then present it again to the offender, this time in the presence of the witness, so that the witness can verify that he or she refused to sign. If the subject again refuses to sign, the witness must then sign next to the "member refused to sign" statement. The counseling session should be ended and the LOC forwarded to the CSS. Professionalism dictates that neither the presenter or the witness discuss what occurred during the counseling session.

Responding to an LOC: The Rebuttal

References:

AFH 33-337 Tongue and Quill (for letter format)
AFI 36-2907 Unfavorable Information File Program

Letters of Counseling, in most cases, are well deserved. If you received a letter of counseling, give some serious consideration to the idea that you may have deserved it before challenging it and going up the chain of command. Is it worth it? An LOC is just a slap on the wrist and normally won't affect your career. However, if you believe you have been the victim of unfair treatment or of a misunderstanding, the Air Force provides an opportunity to respond. And if you received an LOC unfairly, you *should* rebut it. It's your right to provide an answer to the charges and if you don't, it will be assumed by anyone with knowledge of the LOC, that is was fairly administered and that you agreed with it.

Normally, when you receive a letter of counseling, the form has a line that you mark yes or no as to whether you intend to submit any paperwork in your defense. If you didn't check yes initially, but changed your mind and now want to submit something, you can. After all, this isn't the USSR. But any paperwork submitted must be submitted in a timely manner, generally within 3 days of receipt of the LOC.

The term commonly used to describe the response to the LOC, the rebuttal, implies a strong negative response or argument. But a rebuttal is really nothing more than a written reply. The response provided by the receiver of an LOC or other administrative reprimand should be called an LOC Response or an LOC Answer. Because that's what it is. Just as the LOC is an attempt to communicate with the receiver, so also is the rebuttal an effort to communicate with the sender and provide clarification. Often the rebuttal is in 100% agreement with the LOC. Sometimes it refutes some or all of the accusations by providing previously unknown information. But, whatever the case, you should not let the perceived seriousness that the term, rebuttal, suggests stop you from providing one.

Below is an example of a rebuttal. Use the personal letter format and since it may become part of your formal records, make sure you date and sign it. The overall tone must be civil and considerate. Not only will your supervisor read it but the Commander and his staff and your future supervisors may read it as well. The goal is to be persuasive. The first paragraph should be positive. Start off with a compliment. "I appreciate the opportunity to answer the charges against me and would like to express my thanks for the consideration shown me by my supervisor and the squadron" or something similar.

In the second paragraph, explain the situation in detail but as clearly and briefly as possible. Not many people have the patience to read two or three type-written pages. Strike a neutral tone and state the facts that led up to the LOC. Then explain why you think the LOC was unfair or why it wasn't warranted.

In the final paragraph, call attention to your positive record. If you've been in the Air Force for four years without receiving any kind of disciplinary action, say so. If you *have* been in trouble in the past, avoid mentioning your disciplinary record and concentrate on some other positive accomplishment. Mention your involvement in the Honor Guard or Meals On Wheels, etc. Be polite but firm. Mention the IG in a positive way. Don't accuse the person who wrote the LOC of lying and threaten to go to the IG. Just mention the IG in a polite way to let the reader know that you're aware of your rights and may be considering a visit to the IG. Use the last paragraph for closing comments. This will likely be the only time that you'll be invited to state your opinion on this matter so make sure everything you want to say is addressed. Let a friend proofread it to see if it's understandable to a stranger

Make two copies and keep one for your records. Give the original to the supervisor who gave you the LOC or his representative.

It's your right to go to the Inspector General's office on your base if you feel that you've been unfairly treated. If you intend to visit the IG, you should make every effort to let your supervisor know and give him or her a chance to withdraw the LOC *before* you go. Normally, if you indicate in your answer that you're considering going to the IG, the LOC will receive serious review and be withdrawn if it isn't fully supportable.

LOC Rebuttal/Response examples

A Direct Approach

MEMO FOR 1922nd CS/CCF

SUBJECT: Letter of Counseling Response, SSgt Moebius Traum

To whom it may concern,

1. My name is SSgt Moebius Traum. I work in the SCMM section and would like to address an LOC I recently received. I appreciate the opportunity to present my side of the story and would like to express my thanks for the consideration shown me by my supervisor and the squadron.

2. On 22 July 08, when I reported to work as scheduled, MSgt Lewis called me into his office and presented me with a Letter of Counseling for Failure to Go. He believed that I

was scheduled to work on 21 July 08 and that I did not show up for work. On the schedule I had, dated 18 July 08, I was not scheduled to work that day. The schedule was changed while I was on leave and no one gave me a copy or notified me that the schedule had changed and that I was scheduled to work. For that reason, I don't believe I should receive a Letter of Counseling.

3. I have been an Air Force member for over 4 years and have always worked hard to comply with all regulations and support my squadron. I have a good record and this is the first disciplinary action I have ever received. I request that the decision to present this LOC be reconsidered based on the fact that I did not intentionally violate any order or instruction. Further, I request an audience with the First Sergeant to determine if this situation warrants attention by the Inspector General's office.

Sincerely,
SSgt Moebius Traum, USAF

A More Conciliatory Approach

MEMO FOR 1922nd CS/CCF
SUBJECT: Letter of Counseling Response, SSgt Phillip Traum

To whom it may concern,

My name is SSgt Phillip Traum and I am writing in response to a Letter of Counseling I received on 22 July 08. I would like to thank MSgt Johnson for the opportunity to respond to this incident.

On 21 July 08, I did not show up for work as scheduled. On the schedule I had, dated 18 July 08, I was not scheduled to work that day. The schedule was changed while I was on leave and I forgot to check with the work center on my return to see if there was any schedule changes. We have a standing policy to check with the work center on return from leave and I admit that I failed to do so. I didn't expect that there would be any changes and I was wrong.

I have been an Air Force member for over 4 years and have always worked hard to comply with all regulations and support my squadron. I have been active on the squadron baseball team and have volunteered for numerous squadron activities. Although I technically did violate work center policy, I believe I was complying with the spirit of its intent and only made a mistake. I value my reputation and my record and don't want to see it marred by this single act. I regret my actions and request that the decision to present this LOC be reconsidered based on my promise to adhere to all instructions in the future.

Sincerely,
SSgt Phillip Traum, USAF

The Make-Them-Sorry-They-Ever-Gave-You-an-LOC Approach

MEMO FOR 1922nd CS/CCF

SUBJECT: Letter of Counseling Response, SSgt Moebius Traum

To whom it may concern,

Although I am not contesting the LOC received on 22 Jul 08, in the interest of clarification, I'd like to submit the following additional information.

On 22 July 08, when I reported to work as (I understood myself to be) scheduled, MSgt Lewis called me into his office and presented me with a Letter of Counseling for Failure to Go. He believed that I was scheduled to work on 21 July 08 and that I did not show up for work. On the schedule I had, dated 18 July 08, I was not scheduled to work that day. The schedule was changed while I was on leave and no one notified me of the schedule change. I did not intentionally fail to report for work. The unmanned shift was as much a product of a frequently changing schedule as inattentiveness on my part. In fact, over the past two months, there have been at least four instances of shift workers reporting for work on the wrong day or not at all because of frequent schedule changes in response to unscheduled leaves, short-notice TDYs, management changes, and a failure to communicate those changes to all shift workers. And, as of today, there are three different versions of the schedule posted in the work center which adds to the confusion.

It should be noted that I am the only recipient of an LOC although several co-workers have also inadvertently failed to show up for work because of unnoticed schedule changes. In addition, my failure to show up for work would not have been the issue it was if the other Airman who was scheduled to work had actually been there instead of fishing with the NCOIC. I have been in the Air Force for over 5 years and at both previous duty stations I did not miss a single day of work and was rarely late. These facts suggest that the working environment and work center supervision may be contributing factors to this on-going problem. As a gesture of my desire to improve my performance and make sure this does not happen again, I request the participation of my supervisor, our NCOIC, and the First Sergeant in analyzing the cause of and developing possible solutions to this chronic problem so that future occurrences may be avoided.

Very Respectfully,
SSgt Moebius Traum, USAF

Writing a Character Statement

Occasionally an Airman will be subject to some sort of punishment and character statements will be required in his or her defense. A character statement helps judges, Commanders, First Sergeants, and other strangers make fair decisions by providing a factual description of a person's character.

The most effective character statements are those written by someone who has known the person a long time and who can be considered to be impartial. An NCOIC or manager would usually be considered to be impartial.

Don't worry if you can't write well. The important thing is that you cared enough to write. The people who will read your character statement don't know the individual and are depending on you to accurately and honestly describe the person's character. They don't care if your writing uses bad grammar. They just want to make a fair decision based on the evidence and welcome all information. The strongest character statements are always personal and heartfelt. So the more you can write yours in your own words, even if it's in broken English, the more honest and sincere it will be perceived to be.

If you are called on to write a character statement on someone's behalf, make sure what you write is 100% factual. To do otherwise would hurt your reputation and possibly make you subject to UCMJ action.

Type your statement and print it on good quality paper. Your statement will represent both you and the subject and its appearance will have some influence. Make it as presentable as possible.

In general, character statements have three sections:

Introduction. Normally a single paragraph of only a sentence or two explaining who you are (rank, place of work, etc) and your relationship with the subject (co-worker, friend, supervisor, etc). This is important. The reader will automatically assign a certain level of credibility to the letter based on the relationship.

Body. The body is the majority of the letter. It can be one or several paragraphs. Here is where you make the case for the subject by describing your experiences with him or her and giving examples of the subject's good qualities. The first sentence should state your overall opinion of the subject and everything else written should support it.

Make sure you address the type of behavior that the person is accused of having. If the person who needs the character statement was accused of reckless behavior, you should emphasize aspects of his or her behavior that demonstrate a serious regard for safety and the welfare of others. This will suggest to the reader that the incident was a one-time, out-of-character act, not likely to be repeated. Spend some time thinking this through. The Air Force often moves surprisingly swiftly to discharge offenders and your statement will have a lot of weight in determining the outcome and may save the subject from being discharged.

Ask the subject of the character statement if they have any information that could help project a positive image such as a list of accomplishments, organizations that he or she belongs to, or any other relevant information. Ask your co-workers too. This is important.

Closing. Normally a single paragraph that reinforces your belief in the subject and summarizes your statement. Expressing a willingness to go further in defense of the subject by providing a phone number or offering to show up at any hearing will help.

Make sure you address specific traits. An effective character statement focuses on specifics. It can't be a rambling, general statement that "John is one of the nicest guys I have ever met". It must directly describe traits that support the person's character and counters the alleged bad behavior. The prosecution will methodically present arguments proving their case by focusing on specific traits.

If, for example, someone is being prosecuted for dereliction of duty, a character statement on that person's behalf should include information describing your experience with that person's earnest dedication to his assigned responsibilities.

If someone has been accused of insubordination, a character statement for that person should address your direct knowledge of that person's respect for authority and willingness to follow orders with examples if possible.

Of course, along with this focused description, you should also include your subject's other positive attributes. If possible, these additional positive attributes should overlap with or complement your main assertion. For example, a central theme of respect for authority and a natural willingness to follow orders would be supported by additional positive attributes of dedication to duty, an understanding of the need for order, and a positive attitude.

Character Statement Examples

12 Oct 2008

My name is SSgt Smith and I am SrA Morrison's supervisor. I am writing this character statement in support of SrA Morrison. I understand that he recently got in a fight at the NCO Club and is now subject to UCMJ action.

I have worked with SrA Morrison (as a co-worker and now as a supervisor) for almost two years and in that time I have never seen him lose his temper or even raise his voice to anyone. He is one of the most quiet members of our work center. I have always known him to be quietly cheerful and, to my knowledge, he has always had a good attitude and a positive outlook. He does his share of the work without complaint and appears to enjoy his job and being a member of the Air Force.

I remember one incident that may illustrate his non-confrontational nature. One day, as SrA Morrison and I were walking back to the barracks after working all day at the air show, we were stopped by a Senior NCO and accused of shirking our duties. The NCO apparently thought we were assigned to his work detail and blasted us with insults and even put his hand on SrA Morrison's shoulder as if to arrest him. Despite the unjustified provocation, SrA Morrison remained calm and answered in a respectful manner, explained our situation, and then just walked away. He doesn't like confrontations and will avoid them if at all possible.

He has never been in trouble before or involved in any kind of altercation. He has not received any discipline here in our work center, not even a verbal reprimand. Despite his young age, he is one our most mature Airmen and never has to be told what his job is or be reminded to do something. In fact, I once heard our Maintenance NCO praise him at a meeting with the NCOIC, saying he wished he had more Airmen like him.

In summary, I am shocked to learn of the behavior SrA Morrison is charged with. It is completely out of character for him and I can't help but wonder if there were mitigating circumstances. He is one of our best troops and I would not hesitate to recommend him for retention and promotion. I feel certain that our Section Chief would agree.

Sincerely,
---signed---

Character Statement Example

20 Jun 2009

My name is SSgt Johnson and, as SSgt Jones' co-worker, I have known him for over one year. I am writing this character statement in response to allegations that SSgt Jones was involved in misconduct downtown.

I know SSgt Jones to be a dependable and reputable member of our work center. Since his arrival here, he has become a key member of our team. He is one of our most reliable members and is always on time. He always has a pleasant demeanor and gets along well with all members of our shop. He never complains about the workload and takes all assignments in stride. He really is an example to our Airmen of model behavior.

He is also very competent and 100% qualified on all tasks. He won Maintainer of the Month in March and often trains new Airmen in shop qualification tasks. He is also frequently involved with his church's charity.

I was surprised and disappointed to hear about the incident he was involved in downtown because it is so much out of character for him. I have never known him to be in any trouble and he has not been the subject of any disciplinary action either in our work center or the barracks. I know that, if given the opportunity, he would not repeat that kind of behavior and will continue to be a model

243

Airman. If you have any other questions that I have not addressed or if I can be of further service, please don't hesitate to call me at DSN 234-5678.

Respectfully
------Signed---------
SSgt Stewart Johnson
735AMS/SCM

Positive Attributes for Character Statements:

- reliable, thoughtful, dependable, mature

- punctual, meticulous

- non-confrontational, calm, patient, cooperative

- efficient, resourceful, effective

- ambitious, eager to learn and advance

- satisfied, happy in position, motivated

- dependable, thoroughly follows instructions

- considerate, respectful, courteous

- fair, competent leader, responsible, mature

- honest, trustworthy, dependable

- good listener, good communicator, counselor

- hard working, industrious

- intelligent, learns quickly, motivated

- organized, methodical, orderly

- determined, driven, persevering, diligent

- generous, volunteers, helpful

- patient, level-headed, sober

- innovative, a problem-solver

- people-oriented, team player, selfless

- works independently, without supervision, has initiative, self-starter,

- thoughtful, patient, detail-oriented

- involved, invested, committed, loyal, devoted

- goal-oriented, long-term planner

Manual for Courts Martial Articles

When writing Letters of Counseling, some standard is usually cited as having been violated. Below is a list of the most common articles of the Manual for Courts Martial. See the Manual for Courts Martial for more information.

Article 85   Desertion

Article 86   Absence without leave (AWOL)

Article 87   Missing movement

Article 88   Contempt toward officials

Article 89   Disrespect toward an officer

Article 90   Assaulting or willfully disobeying an officer

Article 91	Insubordinate conduct toward a non-commissioned officer (NCO)
Article 92	Failure to obey order or regulation
	(including unauthorized use of Government credit card)
Article 93	Cruelty and Maltreatment
Article 94	Mutiny and Sedition
Article 95	Resistance, flight, breach of arrest, and escape
Article 96	Releasing prisoner without proper authority
Article 97	Unlawful detention
Article 98	Noncompliance with procedural rules
Article 107	False official statements
Article 108	Military property, the sale, loss, damage, destruction, or wrongful disposition
Article 109	Property other than military property of the United States—waste, spoilage, or destruction
Article 110	Improper hazarding of vessel
Article 111	Drunken or reckless operation of vehicle
Article 112	Drunk on duty

Article 113   Misbehavior of sentinel or lookout

Article 114   Dueling

Article 115   Malingering

Article 116   Riot or breach of peace

Article 117   Provoking speeches or gestures

Article 120   Rape, sexual assault, stalking, and other sexual misconduct

Article 121   Larceny and wrongful appropriation

Article 122   Robbery

Article 123   Forgery, writing check without sufficient funds

Article 124   Maiming

Article 125   Sodomy

Article 126   Arson

Article 127   Extortion

Article 128   Assault

Article 129   Burglary

Article 130   Housebreaking

Article 131   Perjury

Article 132	Frauds against the United States
Article 133	Conduct unbecoming an Officer
Article 134	General article
Article 134-2	Adultery
Article 134-3	Assault, indecent
Article 134-4	Assault, with intent to commit murder, voluntary manslaughter, rape, robbery, sodomy, arson, burglary, or housebreaking
Article 134-8	Check, writing worthless, by dishonorably failing to maintain funds
Article 134-11	Debt, failing to pay
Article 134-12	Disloyal statements
Article 134-13	Disorderly conduct, drunkenness
Article 134-16	Drunkenness, incapacitation for performance of duties
Article 134-17	False or unauthorized pass offenses
Article 134-18	False pretenses, obtaining services under
Article 134-19	False swearing
Article 134-20	Firearm, discharging through negligence
Article 134-22	Fleeing scene of accident

Article 134-23   Fraternization

Article 134-28   Indecent language

Article 134-35   Obstructing justice

Article 134-42   Reckless Endangerment

Article 134-44   Restriction, breaking

Article 134-47   Sentinel or lookout: offenses against or by

Article 134-52   Threat or hoax, bomb

Article 134-53   Threat, communicating

Article 134-54   Unlawful entry

Article 134-56   Wearing unauthorized insignia, decoration, badge, ribbon, device, or lapel button

Awards

In these days of inflated performance reports, awards and decorations have become even more important --not only to recognize the achievements of our troops but to give our top airmen the edge they need to get promoted. A quarterly award might be the difference between a 4 or a 5 EPR. An Achievement medal might be what it takes to get your troop promoted over his peers.

Submitting someone for a medal is one of the most satisfying things a supervisor can do. The results are so positive and far-reaching that it's almost magic. Not only do you get to express your appreciation for someone who deserves it, the person who was recommended is even happier than you. They're ecstatic that someone recognized their efforts and took the time to make the recommendation. And the promotion points are an added bonus. And... recommending someone for an award makes *you* look good. It demonstrates that you're taking care of your troops. And finally, the Commander is happy --both with you for being a top-notch NCO and about being able to hand out an award. Commanders love to present awards. It makes *them* look good and they're happy to have an opportunity to show their appreciation for their troops. The judicious award of medals is good for morale all around.

How to Submit Someone For a Medal

The Air Force Achievement Medal, the Air Force Commendation Medal, and the Meritorious Service Medal are probably the most commonly submitted and awarded decorations in the Air Force. The Air Force has streamlined the process over the last few years and it's easier than ever to submit someone for a medal. All it takes is:

Request a DECOR-6 for the nominee from either your Orderly Room/CSS or MSS/DPMPE. Check with the CSS first. Most units also require that copies of the recipient's last 3 EPRs be submitted along with the completed DECOR-6 as justification. If yours does, you might want to get them at the same time as you're requesting the DECOR-6 (while you're at the MSS) to save yourself a trip.

Fill out the Decor 6. This document takes only a few minutes to fill in and it can be handwritten.

Write the citation. This is the text that will be read during the presentation of the award. It can only be 11 - 13 lines so it's not very much work. The introduction and ending must be as directed by AFI 36-2803 so the only part left to write is the narrative, two or three sentences describing the accomplishment between the standard opening and closing statements.

Give the package (the citation text, the completed and signed DECOR 6, and the EPR copies if necessary) to your supervisor. Note that, in the past, in addition to the above, many units required separate written justification for the recommended awards. This usually meant a single sheet of bond paper or AF Form containing bullet statements describing how deserving the recommended troop was. Most units no longer require this. The prior EPRs serve the same purpose. (Ref AFI 36-2803, Para 3.2.4.3: "You may use copies of EPR/OPRs, covering the award period, to justify the AFCM or the Meritorious Service Medal (MSM).")

If your unit does require additional justification, use AF Form 642 or AF Form 2274 for documenting justification for an Achievement Medal. Use AF Form 642 or bond paper for documenting justification for a Commendation Medal. Use bond paper for justifying an MSM. Note that DISA has its own submission requirements and requires justification for an MSM on a DISA Form 530.

Reference: AFI 36-2803, The Air Force Awards and Decorations Program

Instructions & Examples

If you've never submitted someone for a decoration before it might seem a little complicated but it's not really that hard. All awards follow a prescribed format which is outlined in the applicable AFI, AFI 36-2803, The Air Force Awards and Decorations program. All that needs to be done is to fill in the details.

How to Fill Out the Decor-6

This document takes only a few minutes to fill in and it can be handwritten. The only information required is that which is available on the decoration recipient's personnel RIP:

ITEM 1A. Write the name of the decoration you're requesting to be awarded (Air Force Commendation Medal, Air Force Achievement Medal, etc.)

ITEM 1B. Write the appropriate indicator after "cluster". Check the recipient's decoration history listed in Para 6 of the DECOR6. If none of the type of award being recommended are currently authorized (have previously been awarded), write "BASIC". If 01 is listed (indicating the person being recommended currently already has 1 of the type of medal being recommended), write "First Oak Leaf

Cluster". If 02 is listed, the recommended decoration will be the "Second Oak Leaf Cluster", etc.

ITEM 1C. Inclusive dates:

FROM DATE. Because decorations are most commonly awarded during a PCS for service performed, this date will normally be the date the member arrived on station. If the decor-6 is for a decoration in recognition of a specific act (Outstanding Achievement), enter the first date of the act to be recognized.

TO DATE. This date depends on the circumstance:

DECORATIONS FOR OUTSTANDING ACHIEVEMENT - Use the last date of the act which the individual is being recognized for.

DECORATIONS FOR RETIREMENT - Use the last day of active duty. This is normally the last day of the month except for medical retirements. If the member's retirement date is 1 June then the last day of active duty would be 31 May. Persons on terminal leave are still considered to be on active duty.

DECORATIONS FOR SEPARATION - Use the actual day of separation from service.

DECORATIONS FOR PCS - Use the "projected departure date" as shown in item 6 of the DECOR6. If a firm departure date is known it may be used.

DECORATIONS FOR PCA - Last day of duty with the losing unit. Date should correspond to the date on the AF Form 2096 or other transfer document.

DECORATIONS FOR EXTENDED TOUR - This must be at least 3 years from Date Arrived Station or previous award (not counting awards for achievement or heroism). The closeout date for a decoration based on this provision will be on or after the DECOR6 has been computer generated.

DECORATIONS FOR HEROISM - Use the last date of the act or event for which the individual is being recognized.

ITEM 1D. Circle the term which represents whether the recommendation is based on heroism, outstanding achievement, or meritorious service. The term, meritorious service, is normally used to indicate a lengthy period of honorable service and is appropriate for the award of a PCS medal (which can be an Achievement Medal or a Commendation Medal). The term, Outstanding Achievement, is used to indicate recognition of a specific achievement. For a complete explanation of these categories refer to AFI 36-2803.

DECORATIONS FOR MERITORIOUS SERVICE:

A recommendation for doing assigned duties or related tasks in a superior manner. Generally, a recommendation for decoration based on meritorious service must be for a completed period of service as marked by reassignment PCS, PCA, retirement, separation, death or extended period of service. An AF Achievement or an AF Commendation Medal may be submitted for meritorious service.

DECORATIONS FOR OUTSTANDING ACHIEVEMENT:

Recognizes a single specific act or accomplishment separate and distinct from regularly assigned duties, such as successfully completing important projects or upon reaching major milestones of a long-term project or negotiations or accomplishments in a temporary duty (TDY) status. (A significant project accomplished within regularly assigned duties may meet the criteria).

DECORATIONS FOR HEROISM:

Recognizes acts of courage or gallantry. In most cases this should involve voluntary risk of life. The facts must demonstrate that the individual performed above and beyond that which would normally have been expected of any other person in the same situation. The act should also be service connected and/or on behalf of the Air Force.

ITEM 1E. Circle reason for decoration. Retirement, Separation, PCS, PCA, Extended Tour, Posthumous, Achievement, Heroism, Act of Courage.

ITEM 1F. Enter the date presentation is desired. This date is used by Career Enhancements to ensure the unit has the decoration in time for the requested presentation date. If processing a PCS decoration, enter a date before the recipient's last duty day.

ITEM 1G AND 1H. If the individual is separating or retiring, fill in a forwarding address. If the individual is PCSing and the gaining MPF (Item 1G) and gaining unit (Item 1H) are blank, type in the information as reflected on the member's PCS orders.

ITEM 2. This information should already be filled in (unit, station of current assignment, and individual's rank). If the individual has been or will be promoted during the decoration's inclusive period, make sure Item 2C reflects the new rank; i.e. TSgt Effective 1 Jan 09. If the individual has submitted a name change, use the official name reflected in the computer on the decoration's close-out date.

ITEM 3. Except for posthumous awards, enter "Not Applicable." If posthumous, ensure both surviving spouse and parent(s) are listed.

ITEM 4. If other persons are being recommended for the same act, achievement, or service, circle "YES" and submit

DECOR6 and citation for each person. If no other person is being recognized for the same act, circle "NO".

ITEM 5. This is for information only. If the information is not accurate, process a change through your unit orderly room.

ITEM 6. This is the decoration history as it appears in the Personnel Data System (PDS).

ITEM 7. The recommending officials must read this statement before signing item 8.

ITEM 8. Circle the appropriate RECOMMEND or DO NOT RECOMMEND statement and sign the DECOR6. Normally the Commander must also sign the DECOR 6.

QUALITY FORCE. Quality force considerations are essential to preserving the integrity of military decorations. Individuals whose performance and/or conduct have been less than outstanding should not be recommended for a decoration. A person is normally not recommended if, during the recognition period, they:

- Had an active unfavorable information file (UIF)

- Were not recommended for promotion or reenlistment

- Were on a control roster

- Served a suspended punishment under Article 15 of the UCMJ

- Were court-martialed

- Did not make satisfactory progress on the Weight Management Program

- Received a referral EPR

- Received an EPR reflecting performance that did not exceed minimal acceptable standards

NOTE: Exceptions to the above may be made in certain circumstances.

How to Write the Air Force Citation

This is the text that will be read during the presentation of the award. It can only be 6 - 14 lines long (depending on award and font size) so it's not that hard. Below is guidance for the most common Air Force awards, the Air Force Achievement Medal and the Air Force Commendation Medal.

General Air Force Citation Instructions:

Prepare citations on 8-1/2 by 11 inch plain bond paper (landscape) or the appropriate form:

AF Form 2274, Air Force Achievement Medal
AF Form 2224, Air Force Commendation Medal
AF Form 2228, Meritorious Service Medal

Use Times New Roman 12 point font.

Use the mandatory opening and closing sentences listed below.

Final text must be perfect with no corrections.

Citations must capture the substance of the decoration with dignity and clarity.

The narrative is a short description of the act, achievement, or service. Be specific on facts and limit to no more than two sentences, if possible. Emphasize the individual's mission contribution and use active voice and forceful verbs.

The use of common exercise or code names is acceptable in citations (Bright Star, Ulchi Focus, etc.).

Do not use any abbreviations other than Jr., Sr., II, etc. Do not use symbols (the exception is the dollar sign) and do not use abbreviations. Even common abbreviations should be spelled out (USAF, DoD, AFB, etc).

Do not use zeros in front of single-digit dates (ex. 1 Jan 09).

For compound grade titles, such as Senior Airman and Staff Sergeant, spell out the complete grade title in the opening sentence and then use the short title (Airman, Sergeant, etc) in the remainder of the citation.

Do not separate the rank from the name. They should always be listed together.

The Air Force Achievement Medal

The Air Force Achievement Medal (AFAM) is awarded to any member of the United States or foreign Armed Forces, on active duty or inactive reserve, who distinguishes himself or herself by outstanding achievement or meritorious service.

The Air Force Achievement Medal is awarded for outstanding achievement or meritorious service that does not meet the requirements of the Air Force Commendation Medal. Place emphasis on award to junior officers and airmen whose achievements and service meet standards. Do not award more than one AFAM during a 1-year period except under extraordinary circumstances. This medal should not be awarded for aerial achievement or retirement. The links listed below are to procedures and examples for writing and submitting an Air Force Achievement Medal package. Your mileage may vary.

The award of the "V" device for a contingency deployment operation is dependent upon the AOR being declared a hostile environment by the JCS, or hostile acts identified by the unified commander or higher authority. The award of the "V" device is based solely on the acts or services of individuals who are exposed to personal hazards due to direct hostile action during a contingency deployment operation. For a single event, Air Force Component Commanders may authorize the "V" device. The "V" device will not be awarded for normal peacetime acts or services.

How to Write an Air Force Achievement Medal Citation

The citation is the text that will be read during the presentation of the award. The citation has three parts, the opening, the narrative, and the closing. The wording of these sections will vary depending on the type of award. The AFI has rules on how the opening and closing can be worded as shown below. Limit the narrative to six lines using 12 point font and nine lines using 10 point font.

If the award is for a period of service (meritorious service), the EPRs written during that period are a good source of material.

Opening Sentence

OPTION 1. Senior Airman Dick W. Taylor distinguished himself by (meritorious service OR outstanding achievement), as (duty assignment and office location) OR while assigned to (office location).

OR

OPTION 2. Senior Airman Dick W. Taylor distinguished himself by outstanding achievement (at or near...)

Use one of the two Opening Sentences listed above depending on the type of act being recognized.

Opening Sentence Option 1 is, in general, for PCS medals. Option 1 should be used for citations written to recognize lengthy periods of service (years). It's normally used for medals awarded at the end of an assignment. In Air Force lingo, this is known as "meritorious service" which is defined as "exemplary service over an extended period of time".

Opening Sentence Option 1 should also be used for citations for "outstanding achievement". An example of outstanding achievement would be the successful completion of an important project or operation of significant duration (weeks or months) or importance.

Opening Sentence Option 2 is for recognizing acts of achievement. Option 2 should be used for short term, one-time accomplishments such as completing a small-scale self-help project or the rescue of an accident victim.

If the first Opening Sentence option is appropriate, after choosing the appropriate type of service (meritorious service / outstanding achievement), you have the choice of listing either the member's "duty assignment and office location" or the "while assigned to office location" phrase. For PCS awards (meritorious service), the duty assignment and office location option is appropriate. The "while assigned to..." option is appropriate for awards for shorter terms of service (outstanding achievement). Reference AFI 36-2803, The Air Force Awards and Decoration Program, Para 2.3 and 2.4.

Narrative Description (Achievement or Service):

Airman Taylor's outstanding professional skill, knowledge, and leadership aided immeasurably in... *This is where you enter two or three sentences describing the accomplishment such as "...establishing the first successful ship-to-shore communications method using the Air Force's newest satellite system. His dedicated efforts resulted in an increased data transfer capacity and provided a flexibility that ensured a 100% mission success rate in the United States European Command Area of Responsibility."*

Closing Sentence

Limit the closing to one sentence which will personalize the summation. Although the AFI calls for a personalized closing sentence, the closing sentence most commonly used is the same one used with the Air Force Commendation Medal: "The distinctive accomplishments of Airman Taylor reflect credit upon himself and the United States Air Force."

Other acceptable examples of personalized closing sentences are:

"His initiative saved the Air Force over $15,000 and significantly enhanced combat readiness for Special Operations Command."

"The dedication and enthusiasm exhibited by A1C Lewis were key to the success of the operation and a credit to his squadron and himself."

Air Force Achievement Medal Citation Examples

Citation to accompany the award of the Air Force Achievement Medal:

Airman First Class Hap W. Arnold distinguished himself by outstanding achievement as Theater Battle Management System Administrator, 504th Air Communications Squadron, United States Air Forces Europe, Ramstein Air Force Base, Germany. Before deploying to Joint and Coalition Exercise ANVIL TREE, Airman Arnold performed the work of an entire work center, single-handedly preparing and shipping the full theater battle management equipment compliment consisting of twelve pallets of equipment valued at over 6 million dollars. Throughout the exercise, Airman Arnold supervised 6 Airmen and managed Contingency Theater Automated Planning System configuration and databases and kept all networking records, accounts, and databases current on a daily basis ensuring 100 percent accessibility and accuracy. His unflagging and outstanding efforts were directly responsible for exercise success and increased defense readiness.

Citation to accompany the award of the Air Force Achievement Medal:

Staff Sergeant Melinda C. York distinguished herself by outstanding achievement while assigned to the Special

Operations Communications division, 437th Communications Squadron, 437th Support Group, 437th Airlift Wing, Charleston Air Force Base, South Carolina. When contractor installation problems rendered the secure telephone system for special operations inoperable, and the Department of Defense's proposed solution was months, possibly years, away, she was one of three team members who volunteered to tackle the problem. Working around training schedules and alert and flying missions, the team worked nights to finish the project in only 7 days. When all was done, the team had moved eight 50-foot electrical conduits and totally rewired the system. Her initiative saved the Air Force over thirty thousand dollars and enhanced combat readiness.

Citation to accompany the award of the Air Force Achievement Medal:

Staff Sergeant Carl M. Smith distinguished himself by outstanding achievement as a mission-essential team member of Operation Fiery Vigil, Clark Air Base, Republic of the Philippines. During this period, Sergeant Smith's superior performance and outstanding professionalism aided immeasurably in the protection of lives and equipment, and the recovery of operations at Clark Air Base following the volcanic eruptions of Mount Pinatubo. The distinctive accomplishments of Sergeant Smith reflect credit upon himself and the United States Air Force.

The Air Force Commendation Medal

The Air Force Commendation Medal (AFCM) may be awarded to any member of the United States, on active duty or inactive reserve, who distinguishes himself or herself by heroism, meritorious achievement or meritorious service. This medal is typically awarded to junior NCOs that meet the criteria for this medal.

The Air Force Commendation Medal is awarded for outstanding achievement (generally an action or accomplishment) or meritorious service (generally a period of exemplary service) or acts of courage which don't meet the requirements for the award of the Airman's Medal or Bronze Star Medal and sustained meritorious performance by crew members.

Award of the "V" device for Valor for a deployment or operation is dependent upon the AOR being declared a hostile environment by the JCS, or hostile acts identified by the unified commander or higher authority. Award of the "V" device is based solely on the acts or services of individuals who are exposed to personal hazards due to direct hostile action during a contingency deployment operation. For a single event, Air Force Component Commanders may authorize the "V" device when a single event, i.e., terrorist act, isolated combat-type incident, etc., warrants the "V" device distinction. The "V" device will not be awarded for normal peacetime acts or services.

How to Write the Air Force Commendation Medal Citation

The citation is the text that will be read during the presentation of the award. It has three parts, the opening, the narrative, and the closing. The AFI has rules on how the opening and closing can be worded as shown below. Limit narrative to eight lines using 12 point font or 14 lines if using 10 point font.

If the award is for meritorious service (a lengthy period of exemplary service), the EPRs written during the assignment are a good source of material. Below is guidance for writing the Air Force Commendation Medal citation.

Opening Sentence:

For recognizing a lengthy period of exemplary service (meritorious service) or outstanding achievement:

Staff Sergeant John A. Smith distinguished himself by (meritorious service **OR** outstanding achievement **OR** an act of courage) as (duty assignment and office **OR** while assigned to _____(office/unit) from _____to _____).

OR

For recognizing a shorter period of service, a one-time act or achievement or act of courage:

Staff Sergeant John A. Smith distinguished himself by (outstanding achievement **OR** an act of courage) (at or near) on (date).

The first Opening Sentence option above should be used for citations written to recognize "meritorious service". It's normally used for PCS citations for years of service. It should also be used for citations for "outstanding achievement" recognizing shorter periods of service. An example of outstanding achievement would be the successful completion of an important project or operation.

The second Opening Sentence option should be used for short term, one-time accomplishments such as completing a small-scale self-help project or the rescue of an accident victim.

If the first Opening Sentence option is appropriate, after choosing the appropriate type of service (meritorious service / outstanding achievement / act of courage), you have the choice of listing either the member's "duty assignment and office" or their assignment dates and office assigned to. For PCS awards (meritorious service), the assignment dates option is appropriate. The "duty assignment and office" option is normally appropriate for awards for shorter terms of service (outstanding achievement). Reference AFI 36-2803, The Air Force Awards and Decoration Program, Para 2.3 and 2.4.

Narrative Description:

For Meritorious Service or Outstanding Achievement:

During this period, the professional skill, leadership, and ceaseless efforts of Sergeant Smith contributed to the effectiveness and success of... *here's where you add two or three sentences describing the person's accomplishment.*

OR

For an Act of Courage:

On that date, Sergeant Smith arrived on the scene of an automobile accident which seriously injured the driver. Without hesitation, Sergeant Smith went to the aid of the injured victim, expertly administered first aid, and remained with him until arrival of professional assistance.

Closing Sentence:

For Service or Achievement:

The distinctive accomplishments of Sergeant Smith reflect credit upon himself and the United States Air Force.

278

OR

For an Act of Courage:

By his prompt action and humanitarian regard for his fellowman, Sergeant Smith has reflected credit upon himself and the United States Air Force.

OR

Retirement Award:

The distinctive accomplishments of Sergeant Smith culminate a (long and) distinguished career in the service of his country and reflect credit upon himself and the United States Air Force.

OR

Separation Award:

The distinctive accomplishments of Sergeant Smith while serving his country reflect credit upon himself and the United States Air Force.

OR

Posthumous Award:

The distinctive accomplishments of Sergeant Smith in the dedication of his service to his country reflect credit upon himself and the United States Air Force.

Air Force Commendation Medal Citation Examples

Citation to accompany the award of the Air Force Commendation Medal:

Senior Airman George A. Little distinguished himself by outstanding achievement as deployed Life Support element, 30th Special Operations Squadron, 437th Special Operations Wing, Joint Special Operations Air Component, Special Operations Command from 7 January 2008 to 13 June 2008. During this period, Airman Little served as the deployed Account Custodian responsible for over 600,000 dollars in critical life support equipment and was responsible for maintaining life support equipment for 13 aircrews, 4 special operation teams, and 6 MH-53 Pave Low helicopters. His attention to detail and perseverance ensured all combat flight crews had the appropriate equipment and working, secure radios and were trained to use them enabling 100% on-time launch of alert aircraft. His dedication to the morale, welfare, and safety of his extended family of 180 unit personnel supported a solid mission focus and recognized by the Army, Navy, and Air Force personnel he served and protected. The distinctive accomplishments of Airman Little reflect credit upon himself, his unit, and the United States Air Force.

Citation to accompany the award of the Air Force Commendation Medal:

Master Sergeant David M. Smith distinguished himself by meritorious service as Noncommissioned Officer in Charge, Satellite Systems, 6th Communications Squadron, 6th Fighter Wing, MacDill Air Force Base, Florida. During this period, Sergeant Smith's decisive leadership proved invaluable to Team MacDill's satellite terminal operations. He skillfully constructed a comprehensive communications package for the Joint Staff Director of Communications and the United States European Command. This critical reach-back capability in support of Task Force Anvil was instrumental in the insertion of ground forces into Kosovo and the ultimate success of the mission. Sergeant Smith provided vital oversight in the development of the United States European Command Communications Annex, which supported deployed ground mobile forces with reach-back communications during Operation ANVIL TREE WEST. The distinctive accomplishments of Sergeant Smith reflect credit upon himself and the United States Air Force.

Citation to accompany the award of the Air Force Commendation Medal:

Staff Sergeant John A. Smith distinguished himself by meritorious service as Supply NCOIC, Dental Clinic #1, 35th Medical Squadron, 35th Medical Wing, Yokota Air Base Japan. During this period, the professional skill, leadership, and ceaseless efforts of Sergeant Smith contributed to the effectiveness and success of Dental Clinic #1. He provided critical technical support to the organization by timely management of expenditures in excess of $800,000. Sergeant Smith's contributions serve as a sterling example of the effective and judicious use of organizational funds and was characterized by continuous proactive solutions ensuring the availability of critical supplies and equipment. His actions produced a zero balance of all funds prior to the Air Force mandated fiscal year closeout and ensured the continued success of the mission. The distinctive accomplishments of Sergeant Smith reflect credit upon himself and the United States Air Force.

The Meritorious Service Medal

The Meritorious Service Medal (MSM) may be awarded to any member of the United States or foreign Armed Forces, on active duty or inactive reserve, who distinguishes himself or herself by heroism, meritorious achievement or meritorious service.

The Meritorious Service Medal is awarded for outstanding noncombat meritorious achievement or service to the US when the level of achievement or service is less than that required for the Legion of Merit. Ref: AFI 36-2803 Air Force Awards and Decorations Program

How to Write the Meritorious Service Medal Citation

The citation is the text that will be read during the presentation of the award. The text is limited to 15 lines.

Below is guidance for writing the Meritorious Service Medal citation. See the general guidelines under the awards section.

Opening Sentence:

Use one of the two Opening Sentence formats shown below. An award for a period of service (PCS, etc) should use format 1. An award for a specific achievement should use format 2.

(1) Master Sergeant Joe B. Smith distinguished himself in the performance of outstanding service to the United States as (duty title) **OR** (while assigned to the (office or unit) from _____ to _____).

OR

(2) Master Sergeant Joe B. Smith distinguished himself by outstanding achievement as (duty title) **OR** (while assigned to the (office or unit), (on _____) **OR** (from _____to_____).

Narrative Description:

Use one of the two Narrative formats shown below. An award for a period of service (PCS, etc) should use format 1. An award for a specific achievement should use format 2.

(1) During this period, the outstanding professional skill, leadership, and ceaseless efforts of Sergeant Smith resulted in major contributions to the effectiveness and success of Air Force (programs). *Add two or three sentences here that describe the problems resolved or calamity prevented.*

OR

(2) In this important assignment, Sergeant Smith's outstanding leadership and devotion to duty were instrumental factors in the resolution of many problems of major importance to the Air Force. *Add two or three sentences here that describe the problems resolved or calamity prevented.*

Closing Sentence:

Use the first/standard Closing Sentence format shown below for all purposes except for Retirement, Separation, or Posthumous award. In those cases, use the labeled formats shown below the standard closing sentence.

(*Standard*) The singularly distinctive accomplishments of Sergeant Smith reflect great credit upon himself and the United States Air Force.

OR

Retirement Award. The singularly distinctive accomplishments of Sergeant Smith culminate a (long and) distinguished career in the service of his country and reflect great credit upon himself and the United States Air Force.

OR

Separation Award. The singularly distinctive accomplishments of Sergeant Smith while serving his country reflect great credit upon himself and the United States Air Force.

OR

Posthumous Award. The singularly distinctive accomplishments of Sergeant Smith in the dedication of his service to his country reflect great credit upon himself and the United States Air Force.

Meritorious Service Medal Citation Examples

Citation to accompany the award of the Meritorious Service Medal:

Master Sergeant Joseph T. Kirk distinguished himself in the performance of outstanding service to the United States as Chief of the C-141 Maintenance Section, Air Mobility Squadron, 437th Airlift Wing, Charleston Air Force Base, South Carolina, from 2 April 2002 to 31 August 2004. During this period, the outstanding professional skill, leadership, and tireless efforts of Sergeant Kirk resulted in superior aircraft maintenance and operations in support of the personnel and activities of the wing during a period of time when the operations tempo was at its highest level in 20 years. His unflagging efforts were directly responsible for a 30 percent increase in on-time launch rates during the most critical manning shortages experienced in recent memory. The singularly distinctive accomplishments of Sergeant Kirk reflect great credit upon himself, his unit, and the United States Air Force.

Citation to accompany the award of the Meritorious Service Medal:

Master Sergeant Joel S. Fitzpatrick distinguished himself in the performance of outstanding service to the United States as Frequency Manager while assigned to the United States Special Operations Command European Field Office from 19 March 2004 to 30 April 2007. During this period, the outstanding professional skill, leadership, and ceaseless efforts of Sergeant Fitzpatrick resulted in an increase of radio communications support for operations across the European Command theater. Sergeant Fitzpatrick's talent and dedication to duty and earnest research into all aspects of inter-agency communications support led to the discovery of several unused UHF satellite channels that were subsequently assigned to special operations missions. His consistent support ensured the success of all US European Command operations and exercises during his tenure as Frequency manager. The singularly distinctive accomplishments of Sergeant Fitzpatrick reflect great credit upon himself and the United States Air Force.

Miscellaneous Citations

Certificate of Appreciation

For your outstanding support in recognition of Asian Pacific American Heritage Month 2009 observance, "Unity in Freedom", held 12 May 2009, 6th Area Support Group, Stuttgart, Germany. Your logistical and operational skills significantly enhanced the execution of this event and gave the audience a better perspective into the Asian Pacific culture. I want to thank you for a job well done and look forward to your continued success in the future.

Certificate of Achievement

For support of the 437th Airlift Wing Desert Star Exercise 2006. As a contributing member of the 437th Special Operations Division, Seventh Air Force, you provided critical staff analysis and communications support to deployed warfighters and were critical to the success of the exercise. Your contributions serve as a sterling example for all and are in keeping with the finest military traditions. Your distinctive accomplishments reflect great credit upon yourself, the 437th Special Operations Division, and the Seventh Air Force.

Certificate of Appreciation

For outstanding service and support to the United States Pacific Command as the Supervisor of Food Preparation, United States Pacific Command, Hickam Air Force Base, Hawaii. Your exceptional customer service skills, courteous smile, attention to detail, and extreme patience have combined to produce the best service this unit has ever enjoyed and are at once commendable and noteworthy. Your distinctive accomplishments reflect credit upon yourself, your organization, the United States Pacific Command, and the Department of Defense.

Generic Citations

Have to write an award on someone you don't know or have no knowledge of their accomplishments? I know --it shouldn't happen that way but sometimes it does. These generic citations will fit any situation anywhere. Just add name, dates, unit, and location.

Generic Citation

Staff Sergeant Campbell M. Soup distinguished himself by meritorious service as Team Chief, Satellite Systems, 35th Communications Squadron, 35th Fighter Wing, Misawa Air Force Base, Japan from 1 January 2009 to 31 December 2009 . Throughout his 24 years of service, Sergeant Soup has distinguished himself by exceptional duty performance in positions of importance and responsibility. During his career, Sergeant Soup exhibited extraordinary leadership, technical, and training skills thereby enhancing the readiness of numerous Air Force units. His career has been marked by true professionalism and dedication and reflects great credit upon himself, the 35th Communications Squadron, and the United States Air Force.

Generic Citation

Staff Sergeant Campbell M. Soup distinguished himself by meritorious service as Chief Cook and Bottle Washer, 214th Operations Squadron, while deployed to Kuwait in support of Operation Enduring Freedom. Sergeant Soup's dedication to the mission and outstanding performance were significant in the communications success of the mission. His professionalism and commitment to duty were an example to his peers and provided inspiration under the most austere of conditions. The distinctive accomplishments of Sergeant Soup reflect credit upon himself and the United States Air Force.

Generic Citation

Staff Sergeant Campbell M. Soup distinguished himself by meritorious service as NCOIC while assigned to JSC-A, Afghanistan from 3 January 2009 to 29 Dec 2009. Sergeant Soup's dedication and commitment to success make him an outstanding leader. Sergeant Soup, through his actions, has gained the respect of Airmen and Non-Commissioned Officers at all levels. His determination toward self-development and the improvement of the organization set the example for all enlisted Airmen and Non-Commissioned Officers. The distinctive accomplishments of Sergeant Soup reflect credit upon himself and the United States Air Force.

Generic Citation

Staff Sergeant Campbell M. Soup distinguished himself by meritorious service while assigned as a Team Leader and Vehicle Commander in support of military operations against terrorist aggression in the Republic of Afghanistan. During this period, Sergeant Soup surmounted extremely adverse conditions to consistently obtain superior results. Through diligence and determination, and despite a lack of personnel and equipment, he accomplished all assigned tasks quickly and efficiently. His unrelenting loyalty, initiative, and perseverance brought him wide recognition and inspired his peers and subordinates to strive for maximum achievement. Selflessly working long hours, he has contributed greatly to the success of the multinational effort. The distinctive accomplishments of Sergeant Soup are in keeping with the finest traditions of military service and reflect great credit upon himself and the United States Air Force.

Generic Citation

Staff Sergeant Campbell M. Soup distinguished himself by meritorious service while assigned to the 1837th Electronic Installation Squadron, Yokota Air Base, Japan, from 2 January 2007 to 21 March 2009. During this period, he consistently displayed exemplary professionalism and initiative in obtaining outstanding results. His rapid assessment and solution to numerous problems greatly enhanced the Squadron's capability and effectiveness. Despite significant and continuing changes to the Squadron's organizational structure and severe time-constraints, he consistently performed his duties in a resolute and efficient manner. His loyalty, diligence, and devotion to duty contributed significantly to the successful accomplishment of the Air Force mission during this rotation of Operation Iraqi Freedom and were in keeping with the highest traditions of military service. The distinctive accomplishments of Sergeant Soup reflect credit upon himself and the United States Air Force.

Generic Citation

Staff Sergeant Campbell M. Soup distinguished himself by meritorious service as Operational Planner, 1st Special Operations Detachment, 22nd Air Operations Group, Republic of Afghanistan. Sergeant Soup made a tremendous impact on the proficiency and increased state of readiness of troops entering the theater. Sergeant Soup's organizational abilities dramatically enhanced the planning, coordination, and execution of the multi-national force deployment during a very operationally demanding period. Sergeant Soup was instrumental in the development of a cohesive staff capable of rapid and effective military decision-making. His organization and leadership was one of the most significant contributing factors to the success of Task Force Anvil Tree resulting in over 250 Airmen being trained and in-processed in less than a week. The distinctive accomplishments of Sergeant Soup reflect credit upon himself and the United States Air Force.

How to Submit Quarterly or Annual Awards

The AF Form 1206

Quarterly awards, although they have no promotion points, are just as valuable as decorations. If you can claim an EPR bullet stating that you earned NCO of the Quarter, it's that much easier to justify an overall 5. And the points difference between a 5 EPR and a 4 is huge --easily enough to make the difference in whether you get promoted or not.

A lot of people don't realize how easy it is to win a quarterly or annual award, especially at Squadron level or below. Many people don't know it but very often, quarterly awards are not awarded just because no one submitted a package. And very often, the winner of a quarterly award was the only package submitted. So do yourself a favor and submit a "package" on yourself or your troops every time the opportunity presents itself. If you want to be an outstanding supervisor, don't let a single opportunity go by without submitting an award. I once knew a Master Sergeant who submitted one of his crew for a squadron quarterly award every single quarter without missing a single one. And he also made sure he submitted the workcenter for every quarterly and annual award. The packages he submitted won 3 out of 4 quarters for at least two years. I strongly suspect that many of the awards were due to being unchallenged --meaning no other workcenter submitted a package. His workcenter and his troops won so many awards that the Squadron eventually quietly discontinued the program.

I don't mean to say that it's so easy that all you have to do is submit some paperwork and you win an award. The reason that Master Sergeant and his troops were so successful is that he prepared to win. He demanded, every week, a list of that week's accomplishments, from every member of the shop. Because of the constant focus, it made everyone aware of how many accomplishments they had and encouraged them to participate in one or more of the many volunteer and educational opportunities the Air Force offers. That simple habit made it simple to compile thorough and competitive awards packages. And those densely packed quarterly awards made writing the annual awards and EPRs easy.

The Air Force requires that all nominations for awards be submitted on AF Form 1206, Nomination for Award, IAW AFPD 36-28, Awards and Decorations Program. They are limited to two pages using 12 pitch, Times New Roman font, unless otherwise indicated.

AF Form 1206 Format

The format required on the AF Form 1206 depends on the award being applied for. The most common award is the Squadron-level quarterly award. For Squadron quarterly awards, in the SPECIFIC ACCOMPLISHMENTS block, additional categories must be added to the form:

- PERFORMANCE IN PRIMARY DUTY

- LEADERSHIP

- SIGNIFICANT SELF-IMPROVEMENT

- OTHER ACCOMPLISHMENTS

The above categories should be roughly evenly spaced in the Specific Accomplishments block.

The categories shown above are common but not universal. The categories required for awards in your Squadron depend on what your Squadron has established as a standard. The following are other commonly required categories for quarterly and annual awards:

- LEADERSHIP AND JOB PERFORMANCE IN PRIMARY DUTY

- LEADERSHIP QUALITIES (SOCIAL, CULTURAL, RELIGIOUS ACTIVITIES)

- SIGNIFICANT SELF-IMPROVEMENT

- OTHER ACCOMPLISHMENTS

- POSITIVE AND ARTICULATE REPRESENTATIVE OF THE AIR FORCE

OR

- LEADERSHIP AND JOB PERFORMANCE IN PRIMARY DUTY

- SIGNIFICANT SELF-IMPROVEMENT

- BASE OR COMMUNITY INVOLVEMENT

There is not a specified number of lines required for each category but each category of service must be addressed and to be competitive and present the image of a well-balanced Airman, the number of entries per category should be roughly equal if possible. You should be aware that a board of NCOs scores the completed forms, assigning a value for each category of accomplishment. If, for example, no Base or Community Involvement bullets are listed, you will receive a zero for that category, lowering your overall score. So make sure every category is addressed.

The squadron determines how much justification is required but usually, for quarterly awards, the entire front of the form should be filled. For annual awards, both front and back should be completed.

Note that, because of the available space, two or three-line bullet statements are permissible. And the requirement to end each bullet with an impact isn't as strict as with an EPR.

The AF Form 1206 submitted for a quarterly award must only contain descriptions of events that occurred during the time frame of the award (3 months). Bullet statements or achievements previously used in EPRs may be used as justification if they occurred during the time period of the award. But, if you use an achievement as support for one quarter, it can't be used again for the next quarter's package unless it actually spans both quarters. In case you're wondering, normally no one checks your dates to see if all your entries actually occurred between the cut-off dates. It's an honor system

If the award being submitted for is a MAJCOM or Air Force level award, refer to that award's instruction. High-level MAJCOM or Air Force Awards have Air Force Instructions written that contain guidance on format and submission requirements. Examples are:

- AFI 36-2822 The USAF Installations and Logistics Award Program

- AFI 36-2848 Air Force Security Forces Awards Program

- AFI 36-2852 ANG SUP Air Force Services Awards Program

The above are examples. There are many others, too numerous to list here. Google the award you're submitting for to find the appropriate AFI.

Award Bullet Statement Examples

Performance in Primary Duty

- Agile Combat Support! -Reviewed, prepared over 3K troops in less than a week for deployment--100% met requirements

- Arranged loan of scarce resources for 11D pre-deployment tactical training--increased deployment readiness

- Arranged week-long operations planning class for USEUCOM planners--trained 9 component planners

- Conducted daily heat stress evaluations; protected over 12,000 workers and children in three day care centers

- Configured software for substitute satellite radio while ship under repair--insured continued 7th Fleet C2

- Coordinated ground operations for Silver Shield mission supporting Gen. Flintstone--textbook operation

- Developed new research methodology--improved the accuracy and timeliness of reports by 25%

- Disseminated daily image reports and indexes via SIPRNET--100% accurate, correctly formatted and ahead of schedule!

- Documented procedures for resource tracking software, distributed--increased equipment fielding efficiency

- Emergency deployed to Vicenza, Italy, trained 171st Airborne Brigade on high frequency radio operation

- Expertly processed and delivered 50K+ lbs of UK destined mail--boosted morale for 100K UK postal patrons

- Helped 129th Signal Bn troubleshoot high data rate comm links in Iraq--quickly restored links critical for C2

- Instructed 88MI personnel on secure tactical radio operation--added new tool to MI communication inventory

- Maintained shift schedule, training, equipment and ADPE (Automated Data Processing Equipment) inventories--100% effective!

- Monitored theater communications during activation of new data switch--coordination with V Corps soldiers

- Moved 12,000 passengers and 500 short tons of baggage with zero aircraft delays--extremely proficient!

- Participated in numerous teleconferences planning the transition to new standard communications network

- Performed end-of-runway, through flight, and phase inspections--attention to detail resulted in zero mishaps

- Provided support for US Army Europe tactical radio operational training--increased unit comm capability

- Quick-witted; when communications failed with Nellis controller, assumed control of camera suite--prevented loss of critical feed

- Quickly replaced a defective RC-135 engine feed manifold valve--installed new component in 5 hours--ahead of schedule!

- Re-engineered inadequate 2.5-ton air conditioning system at busy 22nd Comm Squadron snack bar

- Recommended use of user-friendly thermostats and filter replacement media--modernized without expense

- Scheduled both recurring and emergency maintenance on work center equipment--ensured data on target at 99% rate!

- Stellar up-keep of $2.5M vehicle fleet--achieved 99% in-commission rate--mission readiness enhanced

- Superb manager; programmed/executed recurring work program with impressive 100% completion rate

- Superior performer! Certified over 60 items of TMDE, key to laboratory's 5 day backlog--lowest backlog in years

- Updated Cargo Movement Operating System (CMOS) for all deploying pax with 100% accuracy

- Visited USAFE/6ASOS and USAREUR HQ to increase operational knowledge--reduced obstacles to success

- Trained 8 troops, configured interoperable network--responsible for successful Joint Operations in Liberia

Leadership

- A respected leader and recognized expert, sets and expects stringent, yet achievable, performance standards for subordinates

- A self-starter, completes many tasks before others realize that they need to be done

- Actively leads deployed team members in daily physical development and trains to excel in semi-annual fitness evaluations

- Adhered to standards; professional competence generated immediate confidence/improved subordinate morale

- Attended AF Operational Network Implementation conference--advanced interests of tactical planners

- Coached work center members to win both Squadron and Group Airman of the Quarter Boards; 2 out of 2 this year!

- Edited, contributed to Logistics and Deployment Standards Handbook, and Future Ops Planning and OTP Execution Plan, DR prioritization--responsible member of military profession

- Enrolled every member in his workcenter in the CLEP Program to earn college credit; two members gained 12 credits this quarter

- Excellent Mentor. His inclusive leadership style was directly responsible for work center attaining 100% retention

- Expertly prepared his flight for Middle East deployment. Ensured flt always in excellent material condition, ready for sustained performance

- Led by example while executing over 10 challenging training operations; conducted thorough readiness drills to ensure his Airmen were always prepared for any eventuality

- Member of pet welfare organization, cares for deployed members' pets--relieves stress, facilitates mission

- Organized visit by 14AF Commander & staff, arranged base tour--fostered growth of mission awareness

- Oversaw On-the-job training program, resulted in nine Airmen receiving their upgraded status ahead of schedule

- Performed exceptionally well while leading subordinates in difficult, constantly changing combat operations

- Six of eight flt members attended seventh member's ALS graduation--excellent unity and positive example

- Stepped up to the plate in absence of NCOIC--assumed, performed leadership duties in a decisive and positive manner with exceptional results

- Trained 3 shift supervisor successors in half the usual time required; increased qual shift coverage 75%

- United a diverse team of active duty and reserve Airmen into a cohesive and effective flight--focused efforts

- Volunteered for, planned and participated in annual POW/MIA ceremony--powerful display of integrity

- Volunteered to head CFC charity drive for the work center--positive role model, bettered conditions for all

- Volunteered to oversee unit participation in annual base fund raiser--increased unit morale, benefited charity

- Worked 30 hours during AF Sergeants Association fund raiser--raised over $400 for local charities

Significant Self-Improvement

- Arranged contractor tutoring of new member on advanced security procedures--100% qualified on major task

- Attended base sponsorship training, passed on info to workcenter--increased in-processing efficiency satisfaction

- Awarded Bachelors Degree for Technical Management from Embry Riddle Aeronautical University; 3.6 GPA

- Best in command! HQ AFSPC's Financial Management Specialist of the Year for 2008

- Completed math requirements in pursuit of AA degree--positive example to subordinates

- Consistently strives for improvement, working diligently towards career progression--recommend promotion

- Dedicated to healthy lifestyle; competed in Okinawa open wrestling tournament--won second place trophy

- Dedicated to self-improvement through increased education; completed BS in Information Management

- Deployed, attended training on new deployment planning software at Scott AFB--braced for transition

- Earned 19 credit hours toward Bachelors Degree in Information Systems--maintained impressive 3.2 GPA

- Exceeds all training requirements; evident by a 98 percent on his 7-Level, End-of-Course examination

- Exchanged language lessons; learned basic Japanese/ taught English--improved important US/Japan relations

- Hazardous Material Awareness certified--enhanced skills needed to quickly identify threats to mission

- Improvement-oriented; enrolled in Wing Action Officer course from Air University; 12 of 21 courses completed, 95% average

- Instituted new quality control inspection procedures; adjusted algorithm, raised customer satisfaction 25%

- Involved in local Head Start Program; read books to over 35 children--gained experience, bettered community

- Maintained a 3.0 GPA in term 1, 2 with the University of Maryland College while excelling at primary duty

- New member, on site only two months, already 70% qualified--great contribution to growth of cell skills

- Pursued off-duty education--completed nine credit hours towards CCAF Transportation Management degree

- Reviews regulations constantly; sharpens knowledge while providing an honest service to all AMC travelers

- Superior performance in all phases of professional military education garnered his selection out of 26

- Tutored high school students--raised students grade from an "F" to an "A" in a mere four weeks--inspiring!

- Utilized process improvement techniques; reduced military performance reporting delays by 75%

Base or Community Involvement

- Active in community--Prepared family style barbeque for 35th FW at Hirosaki's Cherry Blossom festival

- Community minded; volunteered & represented Hickam AFB in Waipahu May Day parade

-- Raised over $12K for local community center supporting the Boy and Girl Scouts, Womens' Club and YMCA

- Dedicated to improving team building--put together, hosted weekly evening meals for the MSHS football team

- Donated items to RAF Croughton British American Committee Toys for Tots drive--selfless, sterling character!

- Dynamic! Created the 2007 MSHS football team highlight film--showcased achievements at Fall Awards ceremony

- Exchanged language lessons; learned basic Japanese/taught English--improved important US/Japan relations

- Head coach of Patch high school wrestling team; taught safe/proper techniques--zero mishaps/injuries

- Intense competitor and model ambassador within the Croughton intramural basketball league--valued teammate

- Involved in local Head Start Program; patiently read books to over 22 children ages 5 years to 7 years

- Joined Japanese Air Force/civilian authorities bus accident response; fostered strong partnership

- Orchestrated timely food/clothing donations for Hurricane Katrina disaster victims--a timely godsend for charity

- Organized a team for the March of Dimes "Walk America" 20K march--raised over $500 to combat birth defects

- Presented the MSHS football team over $600 of safety equipment for students unable to purchase personal gear

- Provided administrative support to 100K visitors to 2007 Charleston AFB Air Show; ensured 100% support

- Regularly participates in and oversees the weekly Meals-on-Wheels program--aided local community

- Security minded! Collaborated with North Charleston community leaders on Neighborhood Watch programs

-- Programs have made contributions of considerable and lasting value--3K active residents & 50% less crime

- Showed a positive, cooperative spirit during the San Antonio area Hospital blood drive--contributions saved lives

- Spent 100 hours mentoring high school students; imparted importance of academics and right decisions

-- Tutored students traveling and missing school during sports season--kept students on track to graduate!

- Stimulates harmony and high spirits! Personally invited by Base Chaplain to help infuse holiday community cheer

-- Santa's helper! Decorated Christmas tree, passed out Xmas carol sheets, served hot chocolate--rekindled spirits

- Strong community leader--chaperones school functions--regularly mentors elementary school children

- Tutored high school student--raised students grade from an "F" to an "A" in a mere four weeks--inspiring!

- United communities during the Misawa Air Base Open House--over 2,000 local nationals attended celebration

-- Put best foot forward, no job too large or small--help clean and deliver food to six different 24-hour work centers

- Visited 2 Philippine orphanages; donated over 40 hours labor on new building--solidified community support

- Volunteer phone bank supervisor at Easter Seal telethon; surpassed its goal--raised $30,000

- Volunteered 10 hours supervising and cleaning up for the Ramstein AFB Youth Halloween Harvest Party

-- Developed, orchestrated games for 70 children--provided a safe haven--a huge Halloween night success!

- Volunteered 20 hours off duty time assisting Lowry Open Window Foundation Nov 08' Thanksgiving holiday

-- Prepared dinner for 60 combat wounded soldiers; support greatly increased morale for OEF war fighters

- Volunteered 3 hours for Adopt-a-Pet at Vandenberg Team car wash; helped raise over $500--promote soonest

- Volunteered as youth group leader at chapel--enhanced the lives of local teens through positive guidance

- Volunteered to assist local Red Cross in distributing food and clothing to flood victims in the Gulfport area

- Volunteered to lead Punt, Pass, & Kick fundraiser--raised over $3,000 for football team uniform items

Other Accomplishments

- Aided in facility excellence program; 100+ hours of base beautification--enhanced installation appearance/QoL

- Attended annual Air Force Ball--positive conservator of Air Force culture in a joint environment

- Briefed weekly in-processing group on space available travel benefits--positive military spokesman

- Consummate law enforcer; professionally handled any of a variety of situations thrown in his direction

- Created Personnel Support Center CD for distribution during site visits--streamlined personnel support

- Despite increased workload, maintained qualification for Force Protection duties--ensured mission protection

- First to take charge! Assumed responsibility of Det's AF Assistance Fund Campaign--100% contact in 24 hrs

- Involved in local Head Start Program; read books to over 35 children--bettered community

- Member selected, flown to AMC Headquarters to accept AMC C& I Professional of the Year award

- Participated in Airman Leadership School renovation; improved quality of life for over 2,600 students

- Participated in annual base charity fund raiser, the 24 hour marathon--increased military stature

- Participated in squadron intramural basketball--American league champions--earned 20 points toward CC cup!

- Reorganized and upgraded Pass & ID facility on off-duty time--saved over $5,000 in labor costs

- Served as Secretary, Kaiserslaughtern German-American Association--good community ambassador

- Strong community leader--chaperones school functions-- regularly mentors elementary school children

- Taught Sunday School--positive spokesman for military values, responsible citizenship

- Volunteered to set up tents for annual volksmarch--support integral to success of yearly event

Sustained Job Performance

- Assisted in the installation of the next generation network planning software and UNIX workstation

-- Extensively evaluated new tool, identified and reported several deficiencies in hardware and software

-- Identification and detailed reports insured the operational success of new system by users worldwide

- Assisted JMAST personnel with joint operations with C6F flagship; configured, produced terminal image for SCAMP

- Assisted Naval terminal operators at Bahrain with repeated UHF and SHF comm problems

-- Intensive analysis of telemetry data pointed to widespread use of unauthorized user IDs and satellite time

-- Instructed operators on frequency requests procedures— skilled troubleshooting crucial to Naval ops and theater support

- Coached Sigonella Air Station sailors on tactical satellite terminal operation and network planning

-- Enabled unit to deploy and train Sixth Fleet radiomen-- increased NAVEUR comm flexibility, efficiency

- Designed radio terminal database for 693rd Airborne Brigade deployment to Liberia for peace-keeping ops

-- Skilled inter-operable design insured communications between Army ashore and Navy support at sea

- Identified error in scheduled sequence of events for transfer of critical circuits from existing Tech Control Facility to new facility

-- unsolicited input to ops center prevented loss of critical communications

- SSgt Smith has been the most consistently energetic, talented, and motivated airman I have ever worked with

-- Often works late when focused on a project, often comes in on his day off to check ops tempo

-- Always dissects problems in more detail than ever before; never failed to identify cause of ops failures

- Supported 693rd Airborne Brigade war plans; tackled training and planning problems threatening mission

-- Ensured 100% reliable comm during 1,100 paratrooper night drop into Iraq--secured defensive positions

-- Identified incorrect net configuration, coached operator by phone in reconfiguring his equipment

-- Unique skills directly responsible for activation of links, successful mobile operations in Iraq

- When new software and link was installed, immediately became the most proficient in using its capabilities

-- Documented procedures for operating terminal software and analyzing findings, distributed, increased ability of others

Letters of Recommendation

Because of their nature and purpose, letters of recommendation almost always follow the same format. They normally consist of three paragraphs. The first paragraph states the purpose of the letter --that you're writing a letter of recommendation and identifies the person being recommended. It should establish credibility and explain how you know the individual, in what capacity, and for how long. Be very clear about the working relationship. That is, explain whether he or she was your subordinate, co-worker, friend, etc. The relationship is the greatest factor in establishing credibility. If the writer is a co-worker, the reader may think this recommendation is merely a buddy doing another buddy a favor. If the author is a supervisor or a Senior NCO, the letter will have somewhat more influence. In general, the higher the rank, the more weight the recommendation will carry. Not just because of the rank but because the less personal and more distant the relationship, the less reason a person has to embellish on the subject's record.

The second paragraph, the body of the letter, should address whatever details are relevant to the recommendation. For example, if the position being sought requires supervisory skills, list examples of the subject's leadership in his or her current position. Use this paragraph to describe the character of the individual in general terms. List personal attributes that you feel are appropriate and for which you have direct knowledge.

Use the last paragraph for closing comments. Express your level of confidence in the individual. Explain the extent to which you believe he or she is suited to the job or program sought.

These letters are used as a basis for choosing leaders and filling key positions. Integrity demands that we always tell the truth in letters of recommendation. You should not write a letter of recommendation if you don't truly believe the person deserves to be recommended. It's your responsibility as a member of the Air Force to make sure the system is not abused. If someone asks you to write a letter of recommendation for them and you have any doubt as to whether they deserve it, find a way to avoid doing it or, if you have to, write a very vague and unenthusiastic recommendation. Below are examples of successful letters of recommendation.

Letter of Recommendation Example

21 Jul 2009

MEMO FOR United States Air Force Academy Admissions Office

SUBJECT: Letter of Recommendation for SSgt Anthony Sims

To whom it may concern,

Staff Sergeant Anthony Sims has my sincere recommendation for acceptance into the United States Air Force Academy. As a Master Sergeant with over 22 years in the United States Air Force and an understanding of the importance and gravity of this assignment, I take this recommendation very seriously.

As Sergeant Sims' immediate supervisor, I have spent a great deal of time with him and can state without reservation that he is positive, sincere, and professional at all times. He is an NCO with good character and a level of integrity that makes him my most dependable shift manager. He takes his responsibilities very seriously and consistently evaluates and improves his performance. Sergeant Sims is the type of Airman that needs little or no supervision to get the job done.

Not satisfied with merely doing his job, on his own initiative, he has continued to advance his education. He

319

continuously seeks self-improvement and accepts greater responsibility with humility. He is a model Air Force NCO and would make a great leader as an Air Force Officer. He has self-discipline and maintains a rigorous physical training program that keeps him in top condition.

Sergeant Sims is not only a disciplined professional. He is a team player and gets along well with his team mates. His cheerfulness and consideration for others have made him an indispensable part of our unit. His fellow Airmen are drawn to him by his personality and sincere concern for others. I hope you will give this natural leader the opportunity to continue to excel by accepting his request for admission into the Air Force Academy.

Sincerely,
MSgt Wayne P. Pinckney, USAF
NCOIC, Civil Engineering, AC DIV

Letter of Recommendation Example

21 Jul 2009

MEMO FOR Keesler Air Force Base Training & Evaluation Office

SUBJECT: Letter of recommendation for TSgt Felicity Kendal

To whom it may concern,

It is my privilege to recommend TSgt Felicity Kendal for the position of NCOIC of Training and Instruction. I have known TSgt Kendal in a professional capacity for more than ten years. In that time, working both as a coworker and as a supervisor, I have always observed TSgt Kendal to be very knowledgeable in all aspects of our jobs as staff members supporting the communications division of the U.S. European Command. She has always been consistently helpful in any requirements whether planned or short-notice. She has a keen ability to anticipate requirements, not only for communications support but for operational concerns as well.

TSgt Kendal was recently reassigned to the Future Plans office in the EUCOM J6 Division. In a surprisingly short period of time, she has turned around a fledgling operation and made it a highly professional and responsive unit. Her leadership style and personality have created an atmosphere where subordinates want to work as a team and perform to the highest expectations. The diverse work is performed with outstanding success and TSgt Kendal has earned a tremendous reputation not only from her immediate supervisor, subordinates, and peers, but also from the large joint community of communications specialists.

I am confident that, if selected, TSgt Kendal would perform beyond expectations as NCOIC of Training and Instruction just as she has here, in the Future Plans Office. Even though TSgt Kendal has only been on the J6 staff for six months, she has already proven to me that she is capable of assuming the additional responsibilities required as head of Training and Instruction. If you have any questions or would like to discuss anything with me, please feel free to contact me at DSN 314-430-3456.

Sincerely,
SMSgt Wanda C. Waverly, USAF
NCOIC, TCCC

Letter of Recommendation Example

21 Jul 2009

To whom it may concern,

My name is MSgt Derek Westerfield and I am the NCOIC of the 1922nd Communications Squadron Plans and Programs office. I am recommending TSgt Wesley Johnson for the position of Element Leader. Sergeant Johnson's current assignment as Operations NCO requires a high degree of leadership, skill, judgment, and responsibility, all of which he possesses in abundance. As Operations NCO, he provides direct leadership and guidance to almost 20 personnel in several career fields.

Even though Sergeant Johnson is always busy with the administrative support tasks necessary to support a large workcenter, he manages to find time to become personally involved in resolving major process issues. I could probably count on one hand, the number of weekends that have passed without him being called into work to solve some crisis. His ability to analyze inter-agency problems, understand their cause, and establish workable and acceptable solutions is evidence of a great amount of disciplined self-study and natural management ability. He is dedicated to providing the best possible service and sets an impeccable example for his subordinates to follow.

TSgt Johnson's leadership, initiative, and abilities exceed those of his peers and I believe that he is the best qualified candidate for the Element Leader position. I strongly recommend TSgt Johnson and feel confident that his performance will exceed your expectations.

Very Respectfully,
MSgt Derek Westerfield, USAF
NCOIC, Plans and Programs

Letter of Recommendation Example

25 Sep 2009

To whom it may concern,

1. I work in the Land Mobile Radio office at Luke Air Force Base and am the government's representative for managing base radio operations and repair. In that capacity, I have worked with Mr Smith, who is employed by Sun City Transmissions, for over two years. During that time he has maintained the Land Mobile Radios supporting Luke Air Force Base under the annual maintenance contract.

2. During the time I have known and worked with him, Mr Smith has provided excellent and reliable service and met or exceeded all our contract requirements. He has repaired many of our hand-held radios that could not be included in the base maintenance contract because of their non-standard make at no charge. He has also analyzed base communications networks and made several recommendations that improved communications coverage at minimal cost.

3. Mr Smith's encyclopedic knowledge of radio maintenance and propagation has made him an indispensable member of Team Luke and something of a superstar among the Disaster Preparedness folks. His thoughtful and diligent efforts have ensured the safe and effective operations of the Flying

Training Wing.   I highly recommend him to anyone requiring 100% effective communications management.

Lynne Gilkey, YA-02
Land Mobile Radio Manager

Letter of Recommendation Example

SUBJECT: Letter of Recommendation for Instructor Duty

1. I strongly recommend that TSgt Smith be selected as an instructor for the courses taught in preparation for duty as a 2E technician and communications planner. I have worked with and observed TSgt Smith over the past two years and during that time he has consistently impressed me with both his technical and leadership skills.

2. TSgt Smith is currently working as a SATCOM Communications Planner in the Regional SATCOM Support Center, Europe, where he plans, engineers, and coordinates satellite communications network accesses for four unified combatant commanders. In this function he interacts effectively with DOD civilians, joint service representatives, and even foreign nationals. He has represented the Regional SATCOM Support Center well during dozens of missions and while deployed to many training exercises. He consistently displayed competence and instructional abilities that would serve an instructor well.

3. I believe that TSgt Smith will benefit the Air Force and this career field by serving as a course instructor for many reasons. He has all the necessary oral and staff skills and proven experience in tough, high-tempo joint operations but what really makes him appropriate for work as an instructor

is his determination to succeed. During Operation ENDURING FREEDOM, despite a lack of security escorts, TSgt Smith led an eight-man team into a hostile area and installed a communications repeater in two hours versus the four hour average. I have seen him engage in several technical discussions during planning conferences and doggedly but diplomatically argue his point to the ultimate benefit of all concerned. Additionally, during his stay at the NCO Academy, he earned the title of Honor Graduate. I am fully confident that he will represent the Ft Gordon Signal community well and exceed expectations.

4. I am available for further discussion of this matter at DSN (314) 123-4567.

MICHEL A. GALVAN
Director,
RSSC-PAC

Letters of Appreciation

Recommending someone for a medal isn't the only way to recognize someone's contributions. At the lower end of the recognition spectrum is the humble Letter of Appreciation. Although widely considered less meaningful than an Achievement Medal or other decoration because of the promotion points, a Letter of Appreciation can still pack a knockout punch! A Letter of Appreciation, received from the Commander or the Chief of Maintenance, can have a big impact on a troop's motivation. In fact, Letters of Appreciation can have just as much, or even more, impact as decorations. After all, Letters of Appreciation are awarded for genuine accomplishments which is not always the case with medals. When a person receives a Letter of Appreciation, they know they've accomplished something!

I strongly endorse the use of Letters of Appreciation as a recognition tool. It costs nothing but a few minutes of your time, they're easy to process because all the coordination is within your unit or group, and they pay big dividends in pride and loyalty. Letters of Appreciation are appropriate for just about any circumstance where a person goes above and beyond the call of duty.

There is no guidance on what you can say in a Letter of Appreciation. Below are a few examples of Letters of Appreciation you may be able to use as a starting point for writing yours. A last word of advice: award Letters of Appreciation only when they are earned. If they become too common or if everyone receives one regularly, they lose their impact.

For Personal Letter format, see AFH 33-337, Tongue and Quill.

Letter of Appreciation Example

MEMO FOR AIRMAN CARLOS GONZALEZ
SUBJECT: Letter of Appreciation - DARK ANVIL

Dear Airman Gonzalez,

Rarely in a career is a military professional called upon to respond to a vital contingency for which he or she is so confident and fully qualified. In every respect, the tiger team from the Headquarters section was ready for the challenge presented by the requirements of Operation DARK ANVIL. You and the other members of your extremely capable group of warriors did an absolutely outstanding job of securing the advanced position, setting up and establishing a Forward Operating Base, and coordinating the movement of follow-on forces. Without your dedication to duty and tenacity under extremely adverse conditions, this operation would not have been the success that it was.

General Villanueva, the JTF Commander, was extremely pleased with the results of your actions and spoke very highly of you and your unit. I know that successes like this are not automatic and are the result of planning, practice, hard work, and sacrifice on the part of you and every member of your flight. Thank you for your earnest support of our squadron and of the United States Air Force.

Letter of Appreciation Example

Example of letter to Commander recommending someone for a Letter of Appreciation. The Commander will use this information to write his own letter of appreciation.

MEMORANDUM FOR 13th AF CF/CC

FROM: 13th CF/SCM

SUBJECT: Letter of Appreciation - TSgt Baker

1.   I would like to thank TSgt Benny Baker for his outstanding work as Security Manager from April 07 to February 08.

2.   When he heard about the requirement, SSgt Baker volunteered to take on the additional duty of Primary Security Manager. Everyone knows this is one of the most thankless additional duties an Airman can have. In addition, in order to accept this duty, he elected to take his mid-tour leave early so that he would have time to attend available classes, learn the job, and work on this program.

3.   Within the last 30 days, TSgt Baker accomplished the following and more:

- Prepared six security packages, submitted five

- Loaded EPSQ security software on two workstations and three laptops
- Installed Sentinel Key and Security Clearance Tracking software on one PC
- Updated security-related forms, manuals, and instructions
- Updated the Security Manager Handbook
- Improved Security Clearance Notification letters for our members
- Brought us into compliance with established standards
- Helped us receive a satisfactory rating for the first time in 3 years

4. I appreciate TSgt Baker taking on this additional responsibility as I am heavily tasked elsewhere, preventing me from giving this program the attention and effort it requires. After seeing TSgt Baker in action, I am confident that I am leaving this program in good hands.

FIRST M. LAST, SMSgt, USAF
Chief, Maintenance and Operations
(Signature blocks are 5 spaces below the last line of text.)

Letter of Appreciation Example

MEMORANDUM FOR SSgt Yolanda Ruiz

FROM: 13AF/CC

SUBJECT: Letter of Appreciation

1. I would like to express my sincere thanks for the excellent work of SSgt Yolanda Ruiz. As a member of the Munitions Storage team, SSgt Ruiz displayed great professionalism and technical expertise in transitioning from the storage, transfer, and implementation of conventional aircraft munitions to the state-of-the-art, classified aircraft munitions complement. Working under stressful conditions, her diligent efforts overcame numerous unforeseen obstacles and ensured a minimum amount of downtime.

2. SSgt Ruiz assisted in developing procedures and policies for storage and use that corrected problems with compatibility issues and guaranteed the efficient integration into the base's arsenal. The local instructions written by SSgt Ruiz and her crew have been evaluated by several flying squadrons and adopted as standard procedure throughout PACAF.

3. I want to express my sincere appreciation for SSgt Ruiz's hard work and dedication in engineering this transition and ensuring the successful upgrade of our F-15 capability. I also

want to encourage her to continue to provide guidance and support to other squadrons in PACAF making the transition to advanced munitions. Our mission depends on the F-15s' abilities and that of capable young Airmen like SSgt Ruiz. Again, thanks for a job well done.

Signed
FRANK BURNS Jr., Colonel, USAF
Commander, 13th Air Force

Letter of Appreciation Example

Tongue and Quill Example

Colonel Jacob R. Bradley
Director of Plans and Programs
550 McDonald Street
Maxwell AFB-Gunter Annex AL 36118-5643

Colonel William J. Nash
Program Director
75 South Butler Avenue
Patrick AFB FL 85469-6357

Dear Colonel Nash,

Thank you for your outstanding presentation to the Air Command and Staff College Class of 2003. Your briefing was right on target and expertly integrated many aspects of our curriculum into a focused leadership perspective. Our students face increasingly complex challenges, and your keen insights were invaluable in preparing them for the future.

We appreciate your support and look forward to future visits.

Sincerely
Signature
JACOB R. BRADLEY, Colonel, USAF

Letter of Appreciation Example

Subj: Letter of Appreciation

Dear TSgt Young,

It is my pleasure and privilege to express my appreciation for your contribution to the success of the Team Charleston Family Service Center's Military Spouse Information School.

During 2007, over 100 spouses attended the school, bringing the total number of attendees to well over 1,000. This program would not have received the positive accolades it has, as expressed by the attendees, without the invaluable support of people like yourself. Your enthusiasm and knowledge have contributed directly to the success of the school and ultimately to the success of our mission. Your earnest participation benefits not only the attendees, but also our service members and their families. The better prepared and more informed our spouses are, the better they are able to cope with the challenges of military life and contribute to their spouse's success. Your efforts are sincerely appreciated.

Congratulations on a job well done.

Colonel William LaForgia

Letter of Appreciation Example

TSgt Juan Lujan
677th Maintenance Squadron
609 Hap Arnold Boulevard
Kunsan AFB, Republic of Korea

Dear Juan,

Your efforts directly contributed to making the squadron's 2008 Christmas Party the best I've ever seen in my 15 year career. Your contributions guaranteed our celebration was a resounding success in every way. More than 250 members and family attended and enjoyed the festivities. In addition, our distinguished guests unanimously agreed it was the best party they had ever had the pleasure of attending. Your earnest and thoughtful work increased morale among our members and their families and ensured that the holiday season had a memorable and appropriate beginning. You are truly a valued member of the 677th Maintenance Squadron family and the United States Air Force.

Sincerely,

JOHN P. QUBLIC, Lt Col, USAF
Commander

Letter of Appreciation Example

SUBJECT: Letter of Appreciation

TO: SCXXPM (SSgt Daniels)

1. The recent Misawa Air Base Open House was a grand success. All activities were well conceived, planned, and executed. All who attended and participated enjoyed themselves tremendously, as did I. Our Squadron's involvement with this activity was highly visible and I can say that our reputation as a unit that makes things happen has made us the envy of the Wing.

2. Please accept my heartfelt appreciation for all your hard work and sacrifice. Your personal involvement and dedication to the welfare of our community has contributed greatly to base morale and improved the relationship between the base and the local population.

3. As a token of my sincere appreciation, I am awarding you a one-day pass, to be taken at the discretion of your supervisor. Again, thanks for all your efforts and keep up the good work!

JOHN WAYNE, Colonel, USAF
Commander

Letter of Appreciation Example

MEMORANDUM FOR COMMANDER
1837th E&I
113 Bong Hwy
Clark AB, RP

FROM: JTF-SWA/CC

SUBJECT: Letter of Appreciation

Colonel Potter,

1. When the decision was made to move an operational headquarters within 30 days with no loss of communication or command, there were many people who were skeptical it could be done successfully and many others who predicted certain failure. The plan to move the Command Post became known as the Impossible Dream because no one believed it could be done without days or even weeks of service interruption. It was a very ambitious undertaking which required the coordinated and dedicated efforts of many people from several agencies. But despite the obstacles and the shortage of time, the members of the 1837th Electronics Installation Squadron, led by MSgt Porter, did the impossible. They hit the ground running and ran new circuits via alternate paths to our new facility, effectively building a duplicate and completely functional command post before they even attempted to cut over the existing

trunks. The end result was a brand new facility with better communications than our old one and not one minute of downtime. Your members accomplished the impossible and I'd like to single them out to express my sincere appreciation.

MSgt Bob Porter
TSgt John Little
TSgt Raymond Collins
SSgt Lamar Troop
SSgt Dan Brown
SSgt Ed Little
SSgt Owen Zumwalt
SrA Steve Kapp
Sra Rob Sweetland

2. Your team, and I mean team in the truest sense of the word, worked tirelessly, often late into the night, to keep this complicated project on schedule. It is impossible to estimate what might have been lost in terms of men and equipment if this project had not been successful. The success of our mission in Southwest Asia is a direct result of your unit's support. I can't adequately express my admiration of your unit's professionalism and pride or my gratitude for their selfless efforts. On behalf of the JTF SWA staff, please accept my thanks for a job well done.

CURTIS P. COLTRAIN
Brigadier General, USAF
Commander

Letter of Appreciation Example

Date

Dear James,

Thank you for assisting with the recent retirement ceremonies. Your thoughtful efforts helped create a world-class event and lasting memories for retiring Air Force members and their families. In addition, your selfless contributions increased the morale and esprit de corps of our squadron which is an even larger and ultimately, more important accomplishment. You truly are a valued member of the 601st Maintenance Squadron and an example of leadership that I'm certain will be emulated by your peers and subordinates for years to come.

As always, it is a pleasure serving with you. Thanks again for all your hard work.

Sincerely,

JOHN W. WAYNE, Colonel, USAF
Commander

The Trip Report

The trip report is the common name for the report submitted by Air Force members when they return from a TDY. The purpose of the trip report is to inform the supervisor or NCOIC on events encountered while TDY.

A trip report is not always required. A trip report would not normally be required for a TDY for a class or attendance of Leadership School. But they are almost always required when returning from exercises, conferences or planning meetings where plans or projects are discussed and responsibilities are distributed. Trip reports are required when the home unit does not know what transpired during a TDY.

Whether a trip report is required or not ultimately depends on your supervisor. Normally the trip report is a relatively informal communication between you and your supervisor or NCOIC and it doesn't leave the workcenter.

Occasionally, if the topic involves the squadron or interaction with other organizations, the trip report will be forwarded to the Commander or his staff for their information or action.

It should be noted that, being selected to go TDY to represent the workcenter or unit is an honor but with that trust comes responsibility. Every effort should be made to record all significant information disseminated. Your unit is depending on you to bring back accurate and complete information. Responsibilities may have been assigned to your unit but if you don't relay that information, no one will know and the mission will fail.

One of the keys to success when writing a trip report is preparation. When you're TDY, take notes while events are occurring especially at meetings. The more detailed, the better. At conferences, get a copy of the sign-in sheet to use as a reference when listing attendees on the trip report and for contact information.

Format

The format for a trip report is the same as for other official Air Force written communications, the Official Memorandum. You may notice that in AFMAN 33-326, Preparing Official Communications, Chap 3, there are very detailed instructions on preparing an official memorandum. If you can follow them, good for you, but if not, the important thing to remember is that you should include the standard headings required on an official memorandum: MEMORANDUM FOR, FROM, and SUBJECT. Paragraphs should be numbered, the report should be dated at the top right, and your signature block entered at the bottom right.

The format, while important, is not as important as the information contained in the trip report. If you don't have time or access to a word processor, your supervisor may accept a handwritten trip report. The overall goal is timely communication between the person who represented the workcenter or squadron during the TDY and his or her supervisor or NCOIC.

Note that the AFH 33-337, The Tongue and Quill, lists an example format for the Trip Report. This format may be used as a basic template. It's the same as the official memorandum with a few additions. Although the Tongue and Quill example shown doesn't list it, if meetings are attended, the first paragraph should list all attendees and the organizations they represent. If any of the sections in the example shown aren't appropriate, don't include them. This example is intended to be a basic template and variations are acceptable.

References

AFMAN 33-326, Preparing Official Communications, Chap 3, The Official Memorandum

AFH 33-337, The Tongue and Quill

Trip Report Example

MEMORANDUM FOR SCMM

FROM: TSgt Rawlins

SUBJECT: ABC Planning Conference 12 Oct 09

1. I left Charleston by air and arrived at Pope AFB on the afternoon of 11 Oct 09. The next morning I attended the ABC planning meeting held at the office of Northrop Grumman on South Bend Road, Fayetteville. The following people were in attendance:

SSgt Johnson, Dover AFB	Maj Phoenix, Dover AFB
TSgt Smith, McGuire AFB	Capt Mary, Char AFB
Mr Hammond, North Grum	Mr Smalls, North Grum
Mrs Sterling, CECOM	SSG Rock, 1ID

2. After brief introductions, the meeting was conducted by the government representative, Mrs. Sterling, and discussion focused on two main topics. First, the introduction and use of the new equipment during the planned exercises, and second, the scheduling and logistics necessary for successful operations.

3. After addressing our general concerns, we broke into two groups with Northrop Grumman and Mrs. Sterling focusing on the parameters under which the new equipment could be used and the responsibility for maintenance and operation. The rest of us hammered out the details necessary for refueling scheduling, maintenance, and operations during the three phases of Exercise Anvil Tree.

4. The end result of the Northrop Grumman/Government discussion was that the new equipment would not be introduced until phase III of the exercise and at that time, the Air Force would assume responsibility for storing and maintaining it. They were not specific as to which unit would be responsible. Northrop Grumman will provide on-site training during phase III and when needed after acceptance.

5. The operations planning was completed, with all assigned units providing the equipment and personnel as usual. We are supposed to provide 6 chalks and FLIR capability. The Rangers want access to UHF on all chalks. Capt Mary is the POC for the planning and schedule for our people.

6. The meeting was concluded Monday afternoon and we broke up and returned home.

Robert Rawlins, TSgt, USAF
Operations Planner

Requests for Exception to Policy and Waivers

Occasionally we have to write official requests for special consideration. Maybe it's a request to participate in an Air Force program like a Designated Location Move or a request for an exception to established policy. The results of a request for exception to policy can have far-reaching, even life-changing effects. There's a lot riding on this type of written communication so it pays to make sure your request is well written. Hopefully the instructions and examples below can help you produce a clear, concise description of your situation and why special consideration is justified in view of your unique circumstances.

For the best chance of success, a letter requesting exception to policy must fully describe the circumstances that justify the request for exception. It should include as much detail as possible such as:

- the requirement you're trying to circumvent
- why this exception to the rule is justified
- the Who, What, When, Why, and Where of the situation
- the impact if the request is not granted

The request for exception to policy is normally sent to the Commander for approval. For the best chance of approval, explain how making the requested exception will benefit the Air Force or, at the very least, not negatively affect it.

Commanders would rather approve your request for exception to policy than disapprove it. They want their squadron members to be happy, successful, and productive. But, at the same time, they are charged with guarding the well-being of the Air Force. Do your homework and give your Commander the reasoning they need to approve your request.

Exception to Policy Format

The format for a request for exception to policy or similar communication is the same format used for all official written Air Force correspondence, the official memorandum. To save space and avoid repetition, the official memorandum format is described in its own section.

EXAMPLE

MEMORANDUM FOR 1961st CG/CC

FROM: 1961st CG/SCMJ

SUBJECT: Request for Designated Location Move

1. I am requesting permission to participate in the Designated Location Move program in order to ensure the well being of my wife.

2. I recently received an assignment to a remote location. I am concerned for the welfare of my wife during my absence. As you know, she is a Korean citizen and has only been in the U.S. for a little over two years. She can speak and understand enough English to be able to communicate with me and the children but she has trouble communicating with most other people. She depends on me to interact with phone callers and solicitors and to perform many common, daily tasks. In addition, although

she has a driver's license, she is not comfortable driving off-base. I realize that taking care of my wife is my responsibility and I will prepare Sun to take care of herself here at Randolph AFB if necessary. As the Designated Location Move program requires, in exchange for moving my family to my wife's home country, my remote assignment will be changed from one year to two years. This program, if approved, will not only benefit me and my family but also save the Air Force the cost of moving another Airman to the remote location for a year.

3. I understand that if she and my children are allowed to move to and reside in Korea during my remote tour, they will not be entitled to the rations that Command-sponsored members are entitled to and will only be allowed to attend base schools on a space-available basis.

FIRST M. LAST, SSgt, USAF
Clerk, Maintenance and Operations
(*Signature blocks are 5 spaces below last line of text.*)

1st Endorsement, (OFFICIAL TITLE), (UNIT)

MEMORANDUM FOR (ORG/UNIT)
    (ORG ADDRESS BLOCK)

Concur/ Non-concur

Commander's Signature
Commander's Signature Block

Exception to Policy Example

MEMORANDUM FOR: HQ AFPC/DPSOAR

FROM: SSgt Steven Hastings

SUBJECT: Exception to Policy for Retraining Requirement

1. I request an exception to policy concerning my application for retraining outside the required timeframe. I was notified after resubmitting my application on 11 April 06 that I was outside of my retraining window which was September 2005 to March 2006. But when I started the process, I was well within the required timeframe. I started the process in January 2006 and then PCS'd to Yokota AB, Japan, where I continued the process. Because of the change in reporting chain, my application was delayed until it was outside the required timeframe (15th and 9th month before my DEROS).

2. On 12 January 2006 I originally requested permission to retrain and was approved. I submitted an official application on 15 March 2006. The name of the commander on the application was that of my previous commander before I PCS'd. I submitted a request to AFPC on 29 November to update my application with the name and organization of my current commander. On 14 March I was notified by AFPC that my application window would expire in 30 days. Apparently my application package was lost and I had to resubmit my application. When I received that e-mail, it was my understanding that I had thirty days

from the date of the email to resubmit my retraining application. I submitted my application on 11 April 2006, which was within thirty days of my notification. Immediately following the submission of my application I was told via email from AFPC that I was outside my window and ineligible for retraining.

4. I am requesting that I be granted an exception to policy for the requirement to submit the retraining package before the ninth month before my DEROS. My overseas assignment began Jan 2006. It was my understanding that my window began when I got to my overseas location because I was not able to apply for retraining until I reported for duty here. I am also requesting the exception based on AFPC's e-mail stating I had 30 days to submit. I believe that it is evident from my repeated efforts to retrain that I intended to retrain, was eligible, did submit a retraining package, and that the delays I encountered were out of my control and caused my submission to be outside my required window. Thank you for your consideration.

Steven Hastings, SSgt, USAF
Supply Technician

Attachment:
Email notification

1st Ind, OSS/CC

I concur/ do not concur with Exception to Policy.

Brian E. Ohanisain, Lt Col, USAF

EXAMPLE

MEMORANDUM FOR: HQ AFPC/DPSOAR

FROM: TSgt Jane D. Doe

SUBJECT: Exception to Policy for Retraining into Chronic Critical AFSC

1. I request an exception to policy concerning my application for retraining from the balanced AFSC 2A676 into the Chronic Critical AFSC 3S311. I have tried to retrain for several years into a career field where I would be more effective to the success of the Air Force mission. I am excited to finally have the opportunity and believe I can do just that in the Manpower career field.

2. Currently at Mountain Home AFB AFSC 2A676 is manned at 94.26% (authorized 93, assigned 88). AFSC 3S311 is currently manned at only 50% (authorized 2, assigned 1). In the next year Mountain Home AFB will be shutting down the 390th AMU which includes 19 personnel with the AFSC of 2A6X6. Five of these individuals are 7-levels and another four are in upgrade training to be 7-levels. These individuals will be dispersed to the 389th AMU, 391st AMU and the Component Maintenance Squadron bringing the manning numbers even higher than they are now. My recent PCS to Mountain Home AFB would make it easy and economical for the Air Force as I

could retrain and immediately fill a vacancy here without the cost of moving me and my family again.

3. I have served honorably since 08 March 1995. In my 14 years I've served in numerous positions including Shop Chief, Squadron Safety NCO, and Quality Assurance Inspector where I have utilized computerized databases to sort data and analyze trends. I have written policies, instructions and have authored operating agreements between units. I have also been involved in several AFSO 21 events. All of this experience would make me a valuable asset to the Manpower career field. I respectfully request that my retraining application be considered.

JANE D. DOE, TSgt, USAF
Electro/Environmental Craftsman

1st Ind, AMXS/CC

I concur/ do not concur with the Exception to Policy.

JOHN L. SMITH, Lt Col, USAF
Commander

The Sponsor Letter

One of Air Force life's pleasant surprises is the Sponsor Package. Few things are as exciting as receiving that big, fat envelope stuffed with travel pictures and information on your new assignment. The impending move is so exciting we can barely wait to PCS! But before that sponsor package can be sent, someone has to write a sponsor letter to accompany it welcoming the newly assigned troop. Writing a letter to a stranger can be somewhat hard to do but luckily, most shops have a standard letter that they use over and over. You just remove the last person's name from the bottom and add your own. If you can't find that letter, the examples below will serve as a starting point.

If you're assigned to write a sponsor letter, you should make sure it provides as much detail as possible about life and work at your duty station. The new person will be depending on you to provide accurate information. Use the personal letter format for the letter (see AFH 33-337, The Tongue and Quill).

Tailor the letter to the receiver. If the new person is married with kids, address family issues like schools and medical facilities. If there are limitations, make sure the assignee is aware of them. Ask them if they have pets or special medical requirements and adjust accordingly.

Describe local conditions so the new person can adequately prepare. If there's very little parking off-base, maybe the Hummer should be left stateside.

- Always describe the workcenter and the base in a positive way! Don't spoil the trip before they even arrive.

- Provide information about the unit and their duties.

- Tell them how long in-processing will take and what they can expect.

- Remind them to apply for base housing in advance at their current duty station

- Offer to make reservations at base lodging or off-base for them. Ask for a copy of their orders if needed.

- Offer to pick them up at the airport.

- Give them your contact information so they can ask questions.

Sponsorship Letter Example

Dear TSgt Jones,

   Congratulations on your assignment to MacDill Air Force Base! My name is TSgt Smith (call me Dan) and I've been assigned as your sponsor. I'm sure you will find this to be one of the best assignments of your career.

   We work at a 24-hour satellite communications facility in the 6th Communications Squadron. We have a GSC-39 terminal and a full DCSS with STEP site capabilities. Since you're a TSgt, you'll most likely be working regular day staff hours, Mon-Fri, with me and our other TSgt, TSgt Johnson. Our NCOIC is MSgt Smith and our Commander is Maj Hightower. There are 30 people in the workcenter and most of them are 3-levels right out of tech school so your experience will definitely be welcome.

   Housing off-base is plentiful although most people spend 30 minutes or more commuting as the base is on the edge of town. A lot of people who work on base choose to live in Brandon which is a newer community consisting of mostly military residents. The waiting list for on-base housing has been about a year so you'll probably want to look for off-base housing as soon as you arrive. Rents around Tampa range from $800-$1500 depending on what kind of apartment or house you want. Base housing is satisfactory and many of the houses have a million-dollar view of Tampa Bay. Don't forget to apply in advance for base housing here at your current duty station. It'll shave months off your wait for base housing (if you choose to move on base).

This base boasts two Major Commands: United States Special Operations Command and United States Central Command. In addition, the base hosts the 6th Air Refueling Wing. Supporting these interests provides challenges and opportunities for advancement enjoyed by relatively few. The base itself is one of the best in CONUS. It has a newly renovated gym, a bowling alley, an auto hobby shop, a theater, two chapels, a large child care center, and its own elementary school. It also has its own private beach and a marina where you can rent boats and fishing gear. Next to the beach is a trailer/camper park and a skeet range. In addition, it has one of the largest and nicest golf courses on the East coast!

The Tampa area is a large metropolitan area that merges with St Petersburg. Between these two large cities you can find anything you want. Within minutes of the base you can attend football games at the Raymond James stadium, hockey games at the Times Forum, and baseball at the St Petersburg Sun Dome! Disneyworld, Seaworld and all the other popular attractions in Orlando are just an hour away and we have our own Busch Gardens and a world-class zoo right here in Tampa!

Well, again welcome to MacDill AFB and if there's anything I can do to assist you with this move, please let me know. I can make reservations for you on base at TLF if you send me a copy of your orders. My address is

8711 Bayshore Dr
Tampa, FL, 33624

or you can fax it to our shop fax at (813) 828-XXXX or
DSN 968-XXXX. My phone number is (813) 964-XXX.
Feel free to call me anytime with questions. I look forward
to meeting you.

P.S. If you give me your arrival time, I'd be glad to pick
you up at the airport.

Sincerely,
TSgt John J. Smith, USAF
Training NCO, SATCOM/SCMJ

Sponsorship Letter Example

Greetings,

And welcome to the Land of the Rising Sun. I'm sure you're excited about your assignment here and eager to learn more about it. Misawa Air Base is located in Misawa City in the prefecture of Aomori. It's on the Northern tip of Honshu, the main island of Japan, on the coast and only 2 kilometers from the sea. The base hosts the 35th Fighter Wing and shares a runway with the Misawa City airport. You've been assigned to the 35th Services Squadron and will be working in the XXXXX section. Currently we work 4 ten-hour days and have three days off every weekend which allows plenty of time for exploring the countryside. We do have to pull standby but we take turns. Since we're fully manned (we have 20 people in the shop), that only comes around about once every two months.

The base has most modern amenities that you would expect from an Air Force base. It has a first-rate commissary and BX. The Mokuteki recreation center is a favorite hangout for kids while the library and bowling alley provide a welcome respite for many adults. One thing that should be noted is that medical care here is limited. Although our base hospital is new and provides excellent care, it is not staffed to care for special-needs patients. If you have any doubts as to whether anyone in your family requires special medical care, you should consult with your base hospital before accepting this assignment.

There are plenty of area attractions to occupy your off-duty time. The city has many good restaurants, a shopping mall, hot baths or Onsens, and a skating rink. Just a few kilometers north of us, in Aomori, is the Big Buddha, the largest bronze statue of Buddha in Japan. Aomori also has a very nice aquarium. Nearby Lake Towada is a favorite destination for picnics and sightseeing. In addition there are many annual festivals such as the Shimoda Salmon Festival, the Cherry Blossom festival here and in Hirosaki, and many others.

It gets very cold here in Misawa during the Winter. The winters are long and the Summers are short. It's common around here to measure snowfall in feet not inches and we might get a couple of feet in a single day! So pack plenty of warm clothes. You'll definitely need them.

One of the hardest things to get used to here is the driving. The Japanese drive on the left side of the road. It takes some getting used to but once you get the hang of it, it becomes second nature. As part of your in-processing, you and any driving members of your family will take a short course on local driving conditions and be issued a Japanese driving permit. Another unusual aspect of living here in Japan is the earthquakes. Earthquakes are relatively frequent here but they're usually not very severe.

Most people choose to live on base here because the housing off-base is on the small side and usually not very well insulated. If you have large furniture, you might consider putting it in storage because you may not be able to fit it in your off-base house. The waiting list for on-base housing is anywhere from a few days to a year or more depending on your preference. The on-base housing that may be available immediately is the tower units. These are 9 story apartment buildings which are very livable but many people prefer to wait for single-family homes or the duplexes. The wait for the latter is longer. It would definitely be wise to apply for base housing while you're still at your current base.

If you have any questions or would like me to make lodging reservations for you, please give me a call at home at 0176-225-XXXX or at work at commercial 011-81-3117-66-XXXX or DSN 315-226-XXXX. I'm sure this assignment will be the highlight of your career.

Sincerely,
SrA Scott Johnson, USAF
Services Squadron

The Official Memorandum

All the chapters in this book are about communication. It may stray into other topics but, at the core, this entire book is about communication: communicating judgment, ideas, performance, etc. And most of those communications require a specific format.

The Air Force Official Memorandum is the most common format used for written communications in the Air Force. It's used for a variety of purposes from documenting internal squadron policies to conducting official business with DoD agencies including the Joint Chiefs of Staff, unified and specified commands, and other Federal agencies.

The Official Memorandum format can be used with printed letterhead, computer-generated letterhead, or plain bond paper. The writer decides which stationery is appropriate. Type or print on both sides of the paper using black or blue-black ink. Use 10 to 12 point fonts for text.

For more information, see AFM 33-326, Preparing Official Communications, Chap 3.

References:
AFM 33-326 Preparing Official Communications
AFH 33-337, The Tongue and Quill

The Official Memorandum in Detail

Margins. Use 1-inch margins on the left, right, and bottom for most memorandums.

Date Element. Type or stamp the date 1 inch from the right margin, 1.75 inches or 10 line spaces from the top of the page. Use the format of day, month, and year, for example, 14 October 2006, for documents signed out of a military organization. Use the format of month, day, and year, for example, October 14, 2006, for documents signed out of a civilian organization. Unless the date of signature has legal significance, date the original and all copies of the correspondence at the time of dispatch.

MEMORANDUM FOR Heading. The heading, MEMORANDUM FOR allows for the entry of who the letter or memorandum is addressed to. If preprinted stationary is used, this and the other headings are usually already part of the document.

If using bond paper, type "MEMORANDUM FOR" in uppercase, flush with the left margin, 2.5 inches or 14 line spaces from the top of the page. After the MEMORANDUM FOR element, type two spaces and then add the recipient's organizational office symbol.

EXAMPLE:
MEMORANDUM FOR 1922nd CS/SCM

When addressing one office, type in uppercase the organization name or the organization abbreviation and office symbol separated by a virgule (/) as shown above.

There is an optional ATTENTION element that may be used to identify exactly who the communication is meant for. If the ATTENTION element is used, type "ATTENTION:" or "ATTN:" or "THROUGH:", followed by the name, in uppercase, one line below the MEMORANDUM FOR heading. Align under the address.

EXAMPLE:
MEMORANDUM FOR SAF/AAX
                        ATTN: MSGT SMITH

If desired, instead of using the ATTENTION heading, the recipient's name can be added in parentheses after the organizational office symbol:

EXAMPLE:

MEMORANDUM FOR 1922nd CS/SCM (MSgt Smith)

When sending the same memorandum to several different offices, list their office symbols below the first one as shown below. Align subsequent addresses with the first address. Circle, underline, or highlight each recipient's organizational office symbol on the copy sent to them.

EXAMPLE:

MEMORANDUM FOR 1922nd CS/SCM
                              1922nd CS/SCMJ
                              35th CS/SCM

Use the official office symbol of the addressee. For more information on Air Force office symbols, see AFMAN 33-326, Preparing Official Communications, Chapter 9.

FROM Heading

The FROM heading is used to list the sender's office symbol and address.

Type "FROM:" in uppercase, flush with the left margin, two line spaces below the last line of the MEMORANDUM FOR element (and the ATTENTION element, if used).

After the FROM element, type two spaces followed by the organization abbreviation and office symbol of the originator. The FROM element contains the full mailing address of the originator so that recipients may easily prepare and address return correspondence. However, if the complete mailing address is printed on the letterhead or if all recipients for the memorandum are located on the same installation as the originator, omit the second and third lines of the FROM element.

- The first line of the FROM element includes the organization abbreviation and office symbol separated by a virgule and typed in uppercase.

- The second line of the FROM element is the delivery address of the originator in upper and lower case.

- The third line of the FROM element includes the city, state, and ZIP+4 code.

EXAMPLE:
FROM: 1961st CS/SCMJ
          214 Blackbird Circle
          Las Vegas, Nevada 99810-1450

SUBJECT Heading

Type "SUBJECT:" in uppercase, flush with the left margin, two line spaces below the last line of the FROM element. After the SUBJECT element, type two spaces followed by the subject title. Capitalize the first letter of each word except articles, prepositions, and conjunctions. Be brief and clear. If you need a second line, align it under the first word of the title.

When writing about an individual/employee who is not the addressee, include rank/grade and full name in the subject line. If you refer to the person again in the text of the memorandum, use only the rank/grade and surname. Do not include names in the subject line when writing about two or more individuals. When writing about several people, state their full names with rank/grade in the text of the memorandum the first time the names appear.

Cite a single reference to a communication or a directive in parentheses immediately after the subject title.

EXAMPLE:
SUBJECT: PACAF Work Center Standard (Our Memo, 6 September 2005)

Emphasize a suspense date in the subject element by typing "SUSPENSE:" or "SUSP:" with the date in parentheses after the subject title.

EXAMPLE:
SUBJECT: AETC Letterhead Stationery (SUSPENSE: 13 September 2005)

When the communication supersedes a previous communication, type "S/S" with a reference to the previous communication in parentheses after the subject title.

EXAMPLE:
SUBJECT: Appointment of OJT Monitor (S/S Our Memo, 21 July 2005)

References Element. To cite two or more references, use the References element. Type "References:" two line spaces below the last line of the SUBJECT element. Capitalize the first letter of every word except articles, prepositions, and conjunctions.

Identify each reference by organization of origin, type of communication, date, and subject. When referencing a commercial publication, state the author's name, publisher, publication title and date, and the paragraph or page number.

EXAMPLE:

SUBJECT: Preparation of Memorandums

References: (a) HQ USAFE/IM Memo, 30 August 1994, Message Addresses.
        (b) AFMAN 33-326, 1 November 1999, Preparing Official Communications.
        (c) Strunk and White, The Elements of Style (NY: MacMillan Publishing Co, 1989), 70.

If the recipient is unfamiliar with the publication or form cited, write out the title the first time you reference it. See AFM 33-326, Chap 3 for more information.

MEMORANDUM TEXT

Spacing. The first line of the text begins flush left, two line spaces below the last line of the SUBJECT element (or the References element, if used). Single-space the text, but double-space between paragraphs and subparagraphs. You may double-space the text of a one-paragraph memorandum less than eight lines.

Paragraphs. Number and letter each paragraph and subparagraph. A single paragraph is not numbered. Indent subparagraphs 0.5 inches or five spaces and number or letter them in sequence. Use the following format to subparagraph short sentences or phrases of a half line or less:

EXAMPLE:

This format has several advantages: (a) It's compact, (b) it highlights ideas, and (c) it saves space.

Place contact names, E-mail addresses, fax numbers, and telephone numbers in the last paragraph of the memorandum text.

Punctuation. Use conventional rules of English grammar. See AFH 33-337, *The Tongue and Quill*, for specific applications.

Word Division. When dividing a word, separate between syllables (see AFH 33-337).

Quotations. When quoting numbered paragraphs from another document, cite the source and paragraph numbers in your text. See AFH 33-337 for specific applications.

Suspense Dates. If you include a suspense date in the text of the memorandum, emphasize it by placing it in a separate paragraph.

Identifying Points of Contact. Indicate contact names, telephone numbers, and E-mail addresses in the text of the correspondence, normally in the last paragraph.

Continuation Pages. Use plain bond paper. Begin typing the text of the continuation page four lines below the page number. Type at least two lines of the text on each page. Avoid dividing a paragraph of less than four lines between two pages.

Page Numbering. The first page of a memorandum is never numbered. You may omit page numbers on a one- or two-page memorandum; however, memorandums longer than two pages must have page numbers. Number the succeeding pages starting with page 2. Place page numbers 0.5 inches or four line spaces from the top of the page, flush with the right margin. Number the continuation pages of each attachment as a separate sequence.

Closing Format.

Authority Line Element. The authority line informs readers that the person who signed the document acted for the commander, the command section, or the headquarters. If it is used, type in uppercase, two line-spaces below the last line of the text and 4.5 inches from the left edge of the page or three spaces to the right of the page center. Use the words "FOR THE COMMANDER" unless the head of the organization has another title like commander in chief, superintendent, or commandant.

Use the authority line when:

- A commander's designated representative signs for a specific action.

- A document represents the commander's position or the coordinated position of the headquarters staff.

- Staff members sign documents that direct action or announce policy within their areas of responsibility.

Do not use the authority line when:

- The commander (or head of the organization) signs.

- The deputy or vice commander signs when the commander is temporarily away from the place of duty unless command action is directed by law and requires an indication of delegation.

- The correspondence expresses opinions of units, directorates, divisions, offices, or branches.

- The correspondence is addressed outside the DoD.

Signature Element. Type or stamp the signature element five lines below the last line of text and 4.5 inches from the left edge of the page or three spaces to the right of page center. If the authority line is used, type the signature element five lines below the authority line.

If dual signatures are required, type the junior ranking official's signature block at the left margin; type the senior ranking official's signature block 4.5 inches from the left edge of the page or three spaces to the right of page center.

The signature element may be added after you are sure who will sign the correspondence. Do not place the signature element on a continuation page by itself. Consider correspondence received via E-mail, copied, or stamped //SIGNED// as authoritative as long as the signed copy is kept on file at the originating office.

First Line. Type the name in uppercase the way the person signs it. Include grade and service if military; civilians may include their grade. Avoid using legal, educational, or ecclesiastical degrees or titles.

Second Line. Type the duty title as identified in the "From" element. Use the term "Acting" before the duty title of a *staff* position if the incumbent is absent or the position is vacant. Do not sign "for" or "in the absence of." Do not use the term "Acting" for any command capacity or where prohibited by law or statute (see AFI 33-321, *Authentication of Air Force Records*; and AFI 51-604, *Appointment to and Assumption of Command*).

Third Line. Type the name of the office or organization level if it is not printed on the letterhead or included in the heading. Limit the signature element to three lines if possible; however, if a line of the signature element is too long, indent two spaces on the next line.

EXAMPLES:

For an officer:

BRIAN EDWARD LEWIS, 2d Lt, USAF
Chief of Personnel

DUANE V. MOORE, Maj, USAF
Chief, Visual Information and Publishing Branch
Directorate of Communications

S. W. MATTHEWS, Lt Col, USAF
Chief, Staff Communications
   and Analysis Division
Directorate of Curriculum

For a noncommissioned officer:

RAYMOND L. KENNEDY, CMSgt, USAF
Chief, Publishing Branch
3400th Training Group

GEORGE S. SILVIO, MSgt, USAF
NCOIC, Radio Maintenance

JOHN KLINE, TSgt, USAF
Maintenance NCO

For a civilian:

ELLEN C. CAMPANA, GS-15, DAF
Chief, Quality Assurance Branch
Air Staff Systems Directorate

SUSAN L. BASS, GS-12, DAF
Chief, Information Communications Policy
Directorate of Communications

NOTE: Medical service officers should use their medical designations in their signature blocks (MC, DC, BSC, or NC).

Signature. Sign correspondence with permanent black or dark blue ink. Use black typewriter ribbons, black printer toner, or black ink for rubber stamps or signature facsimile equipment.
Refer to AFI 33-321, for authentication of Air Force documents and how to use seals instead of signatures.

Attachment Element. Type "Attachment:" or "# Attachments:" at the left margin, three line spaces below the signature element. Do not number a single attachment; when there are two or more attachments, list each by number and in the order mentioned in the memorandum.

Describe each attachment briefly, but do not use general terms or abbreviations such as "as stated," "as described above," or "a/s." Cite the office of origin, the type of communication, the date, and the number of copies (in parentheses) if more than one. Include the subject of the attachment if the receiver will not get copies of attachments or if the subject is not already referenced in text. For classified attachments, show the assigned classification symbol (in parentheses).

EXAMPLE:
3 Attachments:
1. SAF/XCI Memo, 30 Jun 05 (U)(2)
2. 380 FMS/CC Msg, 232300Z May 98 (NOTAL)
3. SAF/XCI Memo, 3 Aug 05 (S)

Type "(sep cover)" when sending an attachment separately. Send a copy of the memorandum when you send the attachment.

EXAMPLE:
2 Attachments:
1. AFI XX-XX, 26 May 94
2. AFI XX-XX, 24 May 94 (sep cover)

Do not divide attachment listings between two pages. If the listing is too long, type "Attachments: (listed on next page)," and list the attachments on a separate page.

Courtesy Copy Element. When sending courtesy copies to offices other than the MEMORANDUM FOR addressee, type "cc:" flush with the left margin, two line spaces below the attachment element. If the attachment element is not used, begin typing three line spaces below the signature element. List names or organization abbreviation and office symbol of the offices to receive copies. If a courtesy copy is sent without including the attachments, type "wo/Atch" after the office. Circle, underline, or highlight the office to indicate the recipient.

EXAMPLE:
cc:
HQ AETC/A1 wo/Atch
HQ USAFE/A1 Atch 2 only
HQ PACAF/A1 (Atch under sep cover)

If courtesy copies of a memorandum are not signed, write or stamp "signed" with black or dark blue ink above the signature block.

Do not show internal distribution of courtesy copies on the original (or courtesy copy) for correspondence addressed outside your activity. However, you may show the distribution if one addressee needs to know who received a courtesy copy, or if correspondence is multiple-addressed and reproduced.

DISTRIBUTION Element. When DISTRIBUTION is used for the MEMORANDUM FOR element, type "DISTRIBUTION:" flush with the left margin, two line spaces below the attachment element or the courtesy copy element, if used. If both the attachment element and the courtesy copy element are not used, begin typing three line spaces below the signature element.

Do not divide distribution lists between two pages. If the listing is too long, type "DISTRIBUTION: (listed on next page)," and list the organizations on a separate page.

Optional Automated File Designator (AFD) Element. The AFD element documents the storage location for data stored on disks or other magnetic media. Type the AFD two line spaces below the courtesy copy distribution element. You may include the AFD in the identification line of talking, position, and bullet background papers.

Contents of the AFD are based on the user's needs and the system being used; e.g., the element may include items such as the file name, typist's initials, and number or title of the disk.

Refer to World Wide Web (WWW) pages by typing the uniform resource locator (URL) as the AFD.

Memorandum for Record (MFR)

The memorandum for record (commonly referred to as Memo for Record, MR, or MFR) is used as an informal, in-house document. People working together generally pass information back and forth verbally but sometimes it needs to be recorded and filed for future reference. A Memo for Record is perfect for this purpose. It records information that is normally not important enough to document formally (i.e., phone messages or meeting notes) to be passed on to others. The lack of formal format requirement encourages documentation and makes it the appropriate method for documenting day-to-day work center actions.

The Memo For Record can be typed or hand-written on plain bond paper or squadron letterhead. Use 1-inch margins all around and number the paragraphs if there are more than one. If there's only one paragraph, as is often the case, don't number the paragraph. A full signature block is not necessary but the MFR should be signed. See the example on the next page.

Reference: AFH33-337, the Tongue and Quill

Memroandum for Record Example

MEMO FOR RECORD   9 MAR 2010

SUBJECT: Memorandum for Record (MFR) format

1. Use a MFR to record and pass on informal work center information.

2. Type or hand-write the MFR on a sheet of plain bond paper or squadron letterhead. Use 1 inch margins on all sides and number the paragraphs if there is more than one. A full signature block is not required but the MFR should be signed and dated.

Calvin Klein, SSgt, USAF
1961CS/SCM

; Should come after action

-- before impact

Mentored Tech School classmates; Scored highest class average
in 10 years

Made in the USA
Lexington, KY
06 September 2010